DEATH BY POISON

GARY W. EVANS

AUTHORSOURCE

Published by AuthorSource
www.authorsourcemedia.com

Library of Congress Control Number: 2018904896
ISBN: 978-1-947939-17-2 (Hardcover)
ISBN: 978-1-947939-04-2 (Paperback)
ISBN: 978-1-947939-05-9 (Ebook)

1

The early rays poured into the comfortable cabin buried in the forest of northern Alabama. The old lady puttering around the kitchen gave the wooden rocker a push, sending dust motes scurrying and waking the still-slumbering cat.

"Time for us to be up, Julie," she said to the cat, who stretched and gazed back at her with disinterest.

"There's work to do, you lazy feline. You're no help at all."

The cat stretched, then sleepily closed its eyes and rested its chin on its paws. The rocker settled to a stop.

As the woman moved to the refrigerator to find breakfast for her and Julie, she saw the card on the table, a birthday greeting from the minister of the church where she'd taught Sunday School since settling near Hayden a couple of years before.

She picked it up, glanced at the neat handwriting inside and snorted. "Happy eighty-first! Ridiculous; there's nothing happy about being eighty-one—except maybe all the experience and wisdom I've picked up along the way. Still, Julie, I don't feel a day over thirty. No idea where the last fifty years went, but they were fun."

She tossed the card into the rubbish container under the sink and closed the lid with a derisive clang.

"Now where was I? Oh, yes, breakfast. Fish for you. Flakes for me. Sound good?"

She set the bowl full of cat food on the floor, reached for the cereal box on the counter, and grabbed the milk from the fridge. The cat jumped from the rocker, stretched languidly, its eyes closed, then approached the bowl and began to eat.

"You're a lazy good-for-nothing, you know that, Julie? But I love you just the same."

The cereal and cat food gone, Rosalie Burton, the name she had taken after fleeing from Wisconsin, set the bowls in the sink, rubbed the cat's head and said, "Let's get at it; potions to prepare."

With Julie at her heels, Rosalie went into the pantry, flipped the switch hidden beneath the counter, and walked into the state-of-the art laboratory buried in the side of the mountain that guarded the comfortable cabin.

"We've got a boatload of orders to fill, Julie, and they need to be in the mail tomorrow, so you best pay attention."

The cat stretched out on the floor, closed its eyes, and slept.

The woman laughed as she busied herself at the cupboards, taking out the needed bottles and cans, reaching into the expansive fridge for several more containers, and beginning to mix things together. Although she worked swiftly, her mind was fixed on the task, her hands purposeful as they measured and mixed. She hummed as she worked, every so often speaking to the slumbering cat. "I think this'll be just what Angelo wants, don't you?"

The cat didn't respond, but she kept talking. "This is the same stuff that killed that young guy in Atlanta, remember? He died without a whimper. Swift and easy; that's how we like it, right?"

Rosalie had, since settling in Alabama, struck up working relationships with a number of influential people. Some she had met in person, some were only names in her inbox. All of them were making her niece a wealthy woman.

"Your namesake is going to be shocked one day. Every one of these orders is going to contribute to the future of her and that boy of hers."

Shadows had lengthened across the room before the orders were finally completed, packages wrapped and ready for mailing.

She nudged the cat with the toe of her slipper. "Wake up, you lazy thing. It's time to eat. That's all you do; sleep and eat."

Julie fed and given fresh water, Rosalie made a sandwich for herself before settling on the rocking chair in her living room. Her clients knew her only as the Black Widow of the Woods, a nickname bestowed by a customer in New York. She lived a good life, if not the one she would have chosen.

She had few friends, most of them members of the Baptist Church in Hayden, eight miles from her cabin. She attended services there each Sunday before returning to her cabin and her cat.

Now sitting in the rocking chair, she touched the again sleeping cat with the side of her foot.

"You know, you're not very good company. Every time I want to talk, you're asleep."

The cat stirred, purring in its sleep.

"Tomorrow I have to go to Birmingham, Julie. Lots of packages to mail. Have to pick up orders, too."

The cat slept on as the darkness closed in on the cabin. *I'm about like that cat.* Rosalie pushed off the floor with her slipper to set the chair rocking. *Eating and sleeping make up most of my life. And working, of course.*

Her new lifestyle was a far cry from the active social swath she cut in Illinois. Known there by her real name, Genevieve, she and her husband, Henry Wangen, were part of the elite social structure in Arlington Heights. Rarely was there a week without a party or some other sort of soirée. Now she lived like a hermit, something necessitated by her flight from the Midwest.

"You know, Julie, maybe I should plan a trip to Atlanta. I believe some company of the male kind would be good for me. That last young man was a good one. Too bad I had to put him down. But that's what I do." She reached down and patted the cat on the head. "That's what the Black Widow does."

2

The sun dawned grudgingly the next morning in La Crosse, Wisconsin. November was one of the bleak months, and this day was bleaker than most. Sleet cascaded from the skies as Al Rouse drove his unmarked Ford to work at police headquarters downtown.

Al wasn't a big man. He stood five foot ten, weighed 180 pounds, and had the appearance of a nerd in a handsome sort of way. He wasn't actually a nerd, but giving that impression provided him with the edge he often needed. Although slight, he was tough, as any number of criminals could attest. Al had the reputation of being one of the best detectives in the state. He could have worked for any number of metropolitan departments, but La Crosse was his home, always had been. He liked it that way—or at least he had.

Three years ago, the biggest case he'd ever worked had changed his life and career forever.

He arrived and ran from his car to the building, brushing off his coat and hat as he reached the office that had been his home for nearly twenty-five years. It wasn't ritzy. The desk was scarred, a hand-me-down from some long-forgotten detective. The carpet was threadbare, the paneling old and peeling in places. But he loved it; it was him.

Two stacks of newspapers waited for him, as they had every day for the past three years. The larger stack held newspapers from the Midwest, the smaller pile newspapers from around the country.

He glared at the piles. "What have you got for me today?" He activated the Keurig and brewed a cup. "It'd be nice if you had something. This is getting kind of frustrating."

For three years, ever since his top collar had escaped while being returned to La Crosse, Al had searched those two stacks of newspapers, seeking clues to the whereabouts of the elderly woman who had confessed to taking the lives of fourteen young men in his town.

"She had to go somewhere, you know. It'd be nice if you gave me some hint as to where, something I could really sink my teeth into."

The coffee brewed, Al sank down on his chair and wheeled himself closer to the desk. He grabbed the paper on the top of the larger stack and flipped it open. An hour later, he had pored through newspapers from around Wisconsin and Minnesota, as well as metros from Minneapolis, St. Paul, Chicago, and Detroit. Nothing. The news was as bleak as the weather.

He grabbed *The New York Times*, then *The Boston Globe*. Those two were followed by *The Cleveland Plain-Dealer*, *The Cincinnati Enquirer*, and others from the West Coast and South. He finished *The Miami Herald* and grabbed *The Atlanta Constitution*.

"Just like every other day. Not a single—"

The sentence hung there. Al tensed, totally focused on a headline in *The Constitution*: "Youth Found in Chattahoochee River."

"Goddamn!"

The article related the story of a young man whose body had been found in the Atlanta area river. The man had been missing for several weeks, the story said, noting that the death had been ruled accidental, likely caused by alcohol.

"Now isn't that familiar? Could there be a connection? Sure as heck's worth a call."

Al reached for his phone, found the number, and dialed.

"Atlanta Police, Sheryl speakin'." The voice was both sleepy and southern. "How can I help ya'll?"

Three questions and no answers later, Al realized that he wouldn't get anything from this ditz. "Could I speak to a detective?" He tried to keep the irritation out of his voice.

"Ah'll try." The message was conveyed in a manner that suggested it was unlikely she could deliver.

The phone rang, rang some more, and just as he was about to hang up, a voice said, "Detective Cunningham. How can I help?"

Al quickly explained who and where he was and then got into why he was calling.

"Detective—"

"Rusty's fine."

"Rusty. Three years ago, I was part of a group returning a confessed serial killer to La Crosse. Somehow she managed to drug me while I was watching her and she escaped. No one's seen her since."

"If there's something I can do, I'll sure try."

"It might not be anything, but I was looking at *The Constitution* this morning and saw the story about a young male who drowned down your way. I'd like to talk to someone about it."

"Sure, but that's not my case. I'd have to talk to the detective in charge of it. What's your interest in the drowning?"

"That woman I told you about, she confessed to killing fourteen young men, one every fall for fourteen years, who all died the same way. They drowned and alcohol was initially the suspected cause, until an astute doctor here found a pinprick in the ear of the last victim."

"A pinprick? You mean they'd been poisoned?"

"Looks like it. We exhumed two bodies, Rusty. We found the same mark in the ear of both of them, and realized we were looking for a serial killer. Found her in Illinois—an old woman who just turned eighty-one, can you believe it? When I saw the story of the drowning down your way, the circumstances seemed similar enough that I thought it worth a call."

"Sure sounds like it. Give me some time and I'll look into it for you."

A brush-off. Al sighed. "I'd appreciate it, Detective. I'll wait to hear from you." He slammed down the receiver. "Big city assholes. They think they're the only people who know anything."

He drove his fingers through his hair before picking up his phone again, this time dialing a number so often called that the numbers had worn off the key pads.

The response was better this time. The phone barely rang before someone picked it up and a familiar voice boomed, "You buyin'?"

"Geez, Charlie, I thought maybe a guy on his honeymoon might have eased off on the food obsession."

"Hell, I got married two weeks ago. She's wearin' me out. I need sustenance." La Crosse County Sheriff's Deputy Charlie Berzinski never minced words.

"Lucky for you, I am callin' about food. How about lunch?"

"Sure. Where?"

"La Crosse Club? Got something to tell you."

"Sure. How soon?"

"Give me fifteen minutes."

"Okay." Charlie rang off with a final message: "And you're buyin!"

Al laughed. "I'm buying—that's a good one. I always buy, you cheapskate."

Charlie was a cheapskate, but he was many other things too. First of all, he was a big, beefy man: six foot five and at least 300 pounds. Second, although he seemed to move slowly, he closed cases with great alacrity. Third, he was the best friend a guy could have, the kind who would do anything for you. And, finally, it was good to see him happy again.

When Al and Charlie had been on the trail of the serial killer, Charlie was one of the most unhappily married men in La Crosse County. His wife Charlene was, to put it in the nicest possible way, a bitch. Nothing Charlie did was good enough, nothing he offered her worth anything.

In the midst of the investigation, Charlie and Al's lives were forever changed. Charlie met and fell in love with a lovely woman, Kelly Hammermeister, a nurse at the Illinois clinic where the clues led them. Turned out the suspected killer, Genevieve Wangen, was the aunt of another nurse at the clinic, Julie Sonoma, who happened to be Kelly's roommate. Julie was something special. Al knew that, but hated to admit it. In the end, though, in spite of the fact that Al's wife JoAnne was a doll, Al had found a special relationship with Julie.

Al walked into the La Crosse Club. Charlie had not only beaten him, but was already seated at a table in the corner, enjoying a beer. He lifted the mug in Al's direction as he crossed the room to join his friend. "I know, I know, we're on duty, but what the hell, I haven't seen you since the wedding and—"

"And I'm buying." Al finished the sentence for him, a well-worn mantra.

"Yup, you're buying. Ya know, Al, you're really a nice guy, in spite of what everyone says."

Al laughed as he pulled out the chair across from Charlie and sat down. "How the hell are you?"

"Never better, and I mean it."

"That makes me happy. I hated to see you moping around like you were before meeting Kelly.

"Made me sick, too. But that's what a bad marriage will do to you. Thank God, I've got a good one now. How you doin'?"

"Pretty good; not great."

Charlie shook his head. "You know, JoAnne is a perfect woman, Al. Julie is just as perfect. Some guys have all the luck. For a while, I had none. How the hell do you live with two?"

"I feel guilty all the time. Can't look at JoAnne without feeling guilty. I can't look at Julie either without feeling guilty. I didn't want this, not at all. But I can't put it aside, either."

"Well, then, let's talk about somethin' else … like food."

The server arrived, looked at Charlie, and announced: "One and a half French dips, extra au jus, a bowl of pea soup—not a cup—and two pieces of banana cream pie, right? And oh, yeah …" she nodded at Al, "… he's buyin!"

Charlie looked hurt. "Damn, you know me well. And I'm not even a member."

Al was still laughing as he ordered a burger with a side salad and iced tea.

"You eat like a bird," Charlie told him when the server had gone.

Al shrugged. It was true. The situation with his wife ate him up inside and he hadn't had an appetite for a while. "Look, I called because I might have a lead on the serial case."

Charlie set down his mug. "Really?"

"Really." Al told him about the newspaper report, his conversation with Atlanta P.D., and his hopes, however slim, that he might hear back from them. "It's probably nothing, but at least it perked me up for a moment."

"Damn right. And it got me a great lunch. Pretty good deal."

An hour later, as they emerged into the drab, brisk day, Charlie pulled his coat up around his neck. "Thanks for lunch, Al. Let's hope this is a live lead. It'd be nice to get a handle on the old girl."

"It sure would. If ya got any relations with the man upstairs, ask for a response from Atlanta." Al buttoned up his jacket.

"Better ask yerself. Ain't had much time to do any praying lately."

3

Rosalie gripped the steering wheel in both hands as she headed toward Birmingham. Julie was with her. In fact, she went wherever Rosalie went.

"Julie, we have eight packages to mail today. We'll drop the first four in Birmingham and then scoot down to Montgomery for the last four. I've gotta meet with someone in Montgomery—a potential customer, but I have to be cagey about that. Don't want him to know too much, now do we?"

After mailing packages at Birmingham, she guided her car back to the freeway and reached for her phone.

Amber answered after one ring. "Hi, Autumn! I've been hoping I'd hear from you one of these days. How are things? Thanks to you, they're sure great here."

At first the name threw Rosalie. Then it clicked. Amber knew her as Autumn Larsen. That was the problem with aliases—sometimes she couldn't remember from one day to the next who she actually was.

"Then you're doing better than I am. Business is great, but I have no cure for the loneliness. I'm thinking I should visit Atlanta soon. Any good young men available?"

"Of course. For you, only the best. When do you plan to be here?"

"Week after next. Could you put a good one on hold Tuesday through Thursday? Prob'ly won't need all three days, but I'll pay for three; any problem with that?"

"This one's on me. After what you did for me the last time you were here, I owe you."

"Amber, that was a gift to a friend. You had a problem. I knew I could take care of it. And I did. No big deal."

"You took care of it quickly and without any fallout. That's a very big deal. I insist; this one's on me."

Rosalie thanked her and was about to end the chat when Amber said, "By the way, did you ever get a hold of Chuck Palmer … you know, the guy in Montgomery I told you about?"

"I'm gonna meet with him today. I know he's a big player, but I have to admit I hate to let a customer see my face. What did you tell him?"

"Only that I thought you might be able to help him deal with a problem he has. If he knows you're the Black Widow, he didn't hear it from me."

Rosalie's brow furrowed. "I'll need to do something to throw him off. Maybe I can listen to what he has to say and then tell him I have a connection who might be able to provide a solution. I can mail his package from another town so he can't track it to me."

"That should work. He's an Alabaman, Autumn, a good old boy, a redneck. He's got lots of money, not lots of smarts. He's done business with me for years and he's about as effective in conversation as a popgun in a war. He's not much better in bed, either. The girls here call him two-pump Chuck. The way I hear it, he made his money with muscle, not brains. He's got a big group of guys working for him, all of them dumber than spit. But they do what he tells them. Now he's got a problem that straight muscle won't solve. He needs to erase someone in a manner that leaves no fingerprints. And that means he needs you."

"I'll see him; hear what he has to say. I should be able to take care of it for him. The only problem is, it's a little too close to home."

"For god's sake, don't turn him down. He's got a worse temper than anyone I know, and believe me, I know some guys with ugly tempers."

"I'll see what I can do. If he's as dumb as you say he is, maybe …"

Rosalie tapped her fingers on the steering wheel as she considered various ways to put Palmer off her trail.

"If you can't think of anything else, tell him you're not sure if any of your friends can help. Tell him you'll think about it. Leave it open-ended. Just don't close him off. That might get you killed."

"Don't worry. I know how to take care of myself. I'll let you know how it goes." Rosalie disconnected the call without waiting for a response. A loud snoring from the passenger seat pulled her from her musings. "You know, Julie, this is a tough one. What should we do about it? Any ideas?" Julie's tail twitched, but otherwise the cat gave no indication of listening. Ten minutes later, Rosalie broke the silence. "Maybe Don Angelo could help. Whatta ya think of that idea, you lazy cat? Yes, maybe the don can help. Better see what this guy is like first. You're gonna have to wait in the car. It might not be safe."

Rosalie pulled into the parking lot at Bellini's a couple of hours later. It was six o'clock, but there weren't many cars parked there. Hmmm, maybe business isn't so good? She left the car and walked across the lot.

Walking in, she found the Italian restaurant dimly lit and smoky, and not particularly enchanting.

The hostess greeted her. "Would you, by chance, be Autumn Larsen?"

"I am."

"Right this way." The hostess led her to the back of the restaurant. She pushed aside thick velvet drapes to reveal a room shrouded in darkness. "Mr. Palmer, Ms. Larsen is here."

"C'mon in, sit your ass down, sweetheart."

The man seated at a table for two, lit by a single candle, was huge—well over three hundred pounds. At the same time, he was one of the ugliest, meanest-looking people she had met. A scar was etched on his left cheek and his right was disfigured, likely by acne as a youngster.

She entered the room, took the chair pulled back by the hostess, and offered him her hand.

"We kiss here, lady."

He half-stood to lean across the table and brush his lips across her cheek.

Rosalie gripped the edge of the table with both hands to keep from recoiling at the touch.

"So, Amber says you can erase my problem. Please tell me you got a coupla big thugs working for you who can whack this rat for me, cause a little bit of a thing like you sure ain't gonna do it." Spittle formed at the corners of his mouth and he wiped his face with a sauce-stained napkin.

Was everything about this man as crass as his welcome? The thought of her genteel husband crossed Rosalie's mind, but she pushed it aside. This was no time to get emotional. She lifted her chin. "Trust me, sir; I can take care of myself. Your problem may be another thing. But I'll listen."

Dinner was a disaster, saved only by the rib eye he insisted she have. It was cooked the way she wanted it and it might have been the most flavorful cut she'd ever eaten. The conversation failed to match the meal.

Palmer was as stupid as Amber had said, but he was also one of the most profane men it had ever been her misfortune to come across, several times commenting on her figure and what he'd both like to do and would do to her, given half a chance.

Rosalie gritted her teeth. "So, tell me about your problem, I have to get going right after we eat."

"What the hell? You ain't gonna stick around for some fun? I'd show ya what a real man feels like."

"Let's get this straight, sir. There's no way you and I are going to end up in the sack. I'll hear you out, but we're not gonna screw, got it?"

Apparently he heard what she said, because he snorted but, finally, turned to the business at hand.

She was stunned to hear it was a woman, someone he'd had an affair with who was now threatening to tell her husband unless he paid her off.

"I'd take care of it myself, but it's the goddamned mayor's wife. See? She goes public and I got a big ass problem on my hands. Years of greasing palms would go down the drain. It'd be nice if she just sorta disappeared, you know? Showed up somewhere dead, but it looked … like … natural. Her dead is the only way out of this. You'll do it, right, little lady?"

"Mr. Palmer, let's get a couple of things straight. I don't like being called 'little lady' and I don't kill people."

If possible, his dark scowl made him even less attractive. "Wait a goddamned minute. That's not what Amber said. She said you'd take care of it for me. What the hell kinda deal is this?"

"There's a difference between taking care of it, and actually doing it. I don't kill people. Understand?"

"Then how the hell you gonna help me? Ya mean this has been a goddamned waste of time?"

"Maybe. Maybe not. I do know some people who 'take care of' problems like yours, but it costs a lot of money."

"For Christ's sake, I'm loaded. Who the hell you think owns this place? Don't worry about the goddamned money, worry about getting her dead."

"If I ask a friend for a favor, it's gonna cost at least 200, maybe 250."

"That's a helluva lotta money, lady."

"Then there's nothing I can do."

She began to rise from the table.

His fist came down hard, rattling the dishes and spilling her water. "Sit yer ass down, we ain't finished yet."

"I think we are."

He jumped from his chair, placed his hands on her shoulders, and slammed her back down onto her chair. "We ain't done, understand?"

Amber hadn't been exaggerating. Unfazed, Rosalie glared at the oversized bully. "If you ever touch me again, sir, you'll regret it. Trust me."

"Well, for Christ's sake, I'm tryin' to do a deal here. Don't get so goddamned uppity."

"You have one more minute, but if you get rough with me again, I'm leaving. Is that understood?"

She was wearing the ring that a few years earlier had knocked out Allan Rouse. But this time it was loaded with a potion that would do a lot more damage. The urge to use it was strong, but she kept her hands clasped tightly in her lap. The man owed her a quarter of a million just for putting up with him this long. No sense losing out on that, not when her niece and great-nephew could use every penny.

Palmer withered a little under her unrelenting stare, seeming to shrink in his seat. "Fine. Here's the deal. She wants a million to keep quiet. All over a couple of pieces of ass. Problem is, I do a lotta business with her husband, and he'd be pissed. I don't think they sleep together, but it's the principle of the thing. Unnerstand?"

"I do; you want her dead."

"You got it."

"Amber knows I'm not a killer. But she also knows I know people who are. I'll see if one can help; that's all I can do. But if she wants a million, maybe it's worth half a million to get rid of the problem."

He glowered at her, his bushy eyebrows nearly touching.

"I ain't payin' no half million. Two fifty and we have a deal."

She pushed back her chair and stood again. This time he didn't make an attempt to stop her.

"Give me a week to see what I can do. If I can help, Amber will be in touch with you."

"No more'n a week. No more'n two-fifty. You better deliver, lady, or I'll be lookin' for you."

She turned and walked away, more disgusted than frightened by his threats.

Hayden was two hours away. Rosalie pushed the accelerator down hard; her tires scattering gravel, she spun out of the parking lot and whisked back toward the I-65 and home.

Julie was curled up in the backseat when she got into the car, but soon the cat had made his way to the front seat again. Julie was a bit of a misnomer, as the large cat was actually a "he," well, an "it" really, having been "fixed" before she found him at the pound in Birmingham.

"You know, Julie, we've gotta get that backup plan. It just might be we aren't long for Alabama."

The cat stretched, curled into a ball on the seat beside her, and slept.

But thoughts of how to get rid of Palmer kept Rosalie awake on the drive.

"I need to do it, Julie. He's the most evil, repulsive man I have ever met. Can you imagine, he wants to kill that poor woman just because she made the mistake of sleeping with him? Well, I'm sure not going to do it for him. Him, I'd be happy to take care of. Although it could be messy. He's got lots of friends, employees, really. They might not like losing their meal ticket. Of course, I bet they don't like him much, either. Frankly ..." She rested a hand on top of the cat's soft head. "I'd be doing the world a favor if I got rid of him. My guess is they'll be lining up to thank me."

4

"What the hell?"

Al shut his office door behind him and strode to his desk. It looked like a blizzard had blown through the room. Every inch of his desk was covered in paper—all kinds of paper: newspapers, reports, memos, messages. *This is a helluva way to start the day.* Knowing he'd need to fortify himself for the task at hand, he spun on his heel and headed straight to the coffee machine. When he had a steaming cup of his favorite, hazelnut, in hand, he made his way to the chair, dropped down on it, and pulled it up to the desk.

First he stacked the newspapers into two piles. Why were they so messed up? The department secretary always placed them neatly in two stacks. When he'd finished straightening those, he attacked the reports. Several were interesting, but none required immediate action. He sorted them into priority order and set them aside. Next came the messages.

"Yes! Yes!" Rusty Cunningham had come through. He wanted Al to call him, said it was urgent. Al had a hard time believing it, but the detective in Atlanta had the same name as the newspaperman in La Crosse. What were the chances of that?

Al glanced down at his watch. "8:20 a.m. in Atlanta. Give him ten and call." By the time he had sorted his messages from greatest to least importance and stacked them near the phone, the clock was inching toward 8:30 a.m.

Chief Brent Whigg stuck his head in the door. "I was in here a few minutes ago looking for the timesheets, Al. Thought I'd find 'em on your desk. No such luck. Sorry for the mess."

"No problem." Al reached into his desk and pulled out a sheaf of papers neatly paper-clipped together. "This is all of them. Meant to get them to you yesterday and forgot. Sorry."

The chief walked over and grabbed the stack of papers. "It's not like you to forget. Something going on?"

"Not really. Well, maybe. I saw this story in *The Atlanta Constitution* about a young male drowning. I called down there and spoke to a detective. His name's Rusty Cunningham, like the newspaperman here, and he said he'd look into it. I thought that was the last I'd hear of it, but I just got a message that he wants me to call him." He punctuated his statement by waving the little piece of pink paper.

The chief tapped the sheaf of papers on Al's desk. "Anything to do with our old lady perp, do ya think?"

"Possibly. It's worth checking into, anyway."

"Better get to it then. I'll get out of here." He headed for the doorway and disappeared into the hall.

Al reached for his phone.

"Atlanta P.D., Sheryl speakin'. How can I help y'all?"

Aw, shit, not this again. He took a breath. "Sheryl, put me through to Detective Cunningham."

"Which one?"

"There's more than one?"

"Three of 'em, honey."

"Oh, then I'm looking for Rusty."

The phone rang twice before the detective answered. "Cunningham. How can I help?"

"Rusty, it's—"

"Al Rouse." Cunningham's voice was full of sunshine and honey.

"You recognized my voice?"

"Hell, yah. How many Yankee callers ya think we get in a year? Hell, I thought most of you were dead—you know, after we won the Civil War and all."

"Hmmm, that cries for a retort, but since I'm calling to ask a favor, I will refrain from pointing out just who won the war and how decisively."

Cunningham chuckled. "So I looked into the death. Kinda interesting. Young guy, Brad McCoy, was workin' for a high-class escort service. He had a date with an old lady, according to the madam, and never returned. Next she knew the police were tellin' her he was dead."

"Anything suspicious?"

"You mean other than the fact that he was dead? Not at first glance. Seemed pretty cut and dried, drunk college kid falls into the river, nothing that earth-shattering. But I talked to the boys who are handling the case. Seems like this McCoy had been set up with one of the service's regular customers the night he disappeared. According to the madam, the trick's a tough old bird. Several guys have been out with her, and all of them came back dragging."

"Sex?"

"Not that I know of. Talk and more talk. Lots of gambling. Not much sleep. Usually rents 'em for three days, after which they need a week's rest. Must be quite a girl if she does all that without beddin' 'em."

"Did you get a description of the woman?"

"Older, looks about sixty-five or so. In good shape. Smart as hell. Well-heeled. At least, that's what the madam told our guys. Amber's a good gal, doesn't cause a lot of trouble so we generally look the other way. Our guys said they leaned on her pretty good, really ran her through the wringer. They were convinced she had given them all she had. Do you think the old bird might have had something to do with it?"

"If she happens to be the same one we had in custody, it's pretty much a sure thing. From what you've told me, I think it's worth digging into a little more, see if there's a connection."

"Sounds like it." Rusty went silent for a moment. Al drummed his fingers on the desk as he waited. Finally the detective spoke up. "Tell ya what, I know Amber pretty well. I think I'll amble past her place and have a little talk with her myself."

"I'd sure appreciate it if you wouldn't mind. Maybe this McCoy was just a drunk college student, but the more I hear, the more it sounds like the same old story. I'd be grateful if you checked a bit further."

"Happy to, but if I ever see you, you owe me a quart of Chivas Regal."

"I'll send one tomorrow. It'd be worth it to learn a little more."

For the next six hours, Al kept his head down. Finally his desk was clear of debris. There was nothing more of interest in the papers, the messages had all been successfully returned, and the loose ends in the reports had been firmly tied up. “That’s what I call a good day’s work.” *I wonder if Charlie and Rick’d like a beer.* Given the turn his investigation had just taken, it wouldn’t hurt to have a conversation with the coroner, let him know what was going on.

Charlie was quick to respond to his call. “Hell, yes! You buyin’?”

“Do I have a choice?”

“How’s Schmidty’s, fifteen minutes?”

Al agreed and disconnected the call so he could dial the pathology lab at Gundersen Lutheran.

“Rick Olson.”

The voice was pleasant and calming.

“Chasin’ ghosts again, doc? Thought you might talk some sense into me over a beer. Berzinski’s comin’, too.”

“Schmidty’s?”

“Absolutely.”

“See you in twenty.”

The bar clock showed 5:05 p.m. as the three friends gathered in a corner booth. Charlie, the first to arrive, had ordered a pitcher of beer. He filled everyone’s mugs and they all sampled to enthusiastic approval.

Al wiped a drop of liquid sliding down his glass with his thumb. “So I asked you here so I could fill you in on—”

The server stopped at their table, a heaping platter of appetizers in each hand. “Cheese curds, French fries, onion rings, sliders, mushrooms, pizza wedges, veggies and dips. Anything else?”

Heat flared in Al’s cheeks as he stared at Charlie. His friend dipped his head. “No, ma’am, that should do it.”

When she’d gone, he turned to Al and lifted a hand. “I was hungry, and I thought a few appetizers would be good. Plus, I knew you’d had a long day, Al. I wanted to make sure we had something to go with the beer and—”

“Shut the crap up!”

Several people at the bar swiveled on their stools to look over at them.

“Every goddamned time I say I’ll buy, you order enough food for a herd.” Al shook his head as he gazed at the ridiculous amount of food weighing down the table.

Charlie brightened. "Hell, Al, we can split the bill three ways. That'll be better." He reached for his mug of beer and took a sip, as if the matter was settled.

"Now wait just a minute." Rick, clearly delighted by Charlie's predicament, decided to fuel the fire. "Al invited me here for a beer. I presume he invited you for one, too. Nothing was said about food. If you ordered, Charlie, you get the tab."

Charlie spewed out the mouthful of beer he'd just swilled. He grabbed a napkin and wiped his mouth before swiping it across his forehead. "Yeah, sure. I'll pay. Happy to. But, umm, one of you is going to have to lend me some money. I'm broke. That honeymoon cost me a fortune."

"Yeah, we feel real sorry for you. Two weeks at a gorgeous hotel with an even more gorgeous woman. Poor thing." Al tossed his napkin to Charlie so he could clean up the table too. "Forget about it, I'll pay. This time."

"Thanks, Al."

Charlie sounded so sheepish, Al couldn't stay mad at him. He rolled his eyes at Rick, who grinned wryly. "You were about to tell us why you asked us to meet you?"

"Oh yeah." Al set his beer down on the coaster. He told the two men about seeing the story in the Atlanta paper, and that he'd contacted Detective Rusty Cunningham, who was going to look into it further.

Charlie refilled his mug of beer and set down the pitcher. "So he thinks there might be a connection between the kid who drowned down there and our missing perp?"

"We both think it's worth checking out. The circumstances are just a little too similar to brush off. They had been thinking it was just a drunk kid, which I don't blame them for, since we thought that too, at first."

Rick leaned forward in his seat. "Like Freud said, sometimes a cigar is just a cigar, but sometimes—"

"Sometimes whoever smoked that cigar is a cold-blooded killer." Al tipped his mug in Rick's direction.

"Exactly." Rick reached for an onion ring and popped it into his mouth. "So what are we going to do about it?"

"We wait." Al sighed and pulled one of the platters closer. If he was going to pay for them, might as well eat them. "But if Rusty Cunningham calls and gives me one good reason to, I'll move heaven and earth to get down to Atlanta and see if they've got anything we can use to find that old woman and stick her behind bars for the rest of her life."

5

"Let's run through it again." Rusty Cunningham kept his tone friendly but insistent. They were talking in Amber's comfortable office, but the amenities were lost on the detective, who was focused on obtaining information for his telephone acquaintance up north.

Amber Johansen sighed. "Again? I met her in the downtown post office. We got talking and went for a drink. She said she was lonely and I told her about my business. The next time—at least I think it was the next time—she came this way she called and arranged an escort. Always specifies a young man. She's probably done that four or five times."

"Isn't it funny that she doesn't want sex?"

"I suppose, but I don't press my employees for details. They know they can do as much or as little as they want. A couple of her dates told me all she wants to do is talk, gamble, and snuggle."

"Did she give you a name? How's she pay?"

"Autumn Larson. Always pays in cash. Tips generously. Everyone who has been with her likes her, although she wears 'em out."

"But no sex?"

"Not that I know of."

"Is she from the South?"

"No drawl. Midwest or West, maybe. She might have said Portland. Not sure. I've only seen her a couple of times."

Rusty pursed his lips. Twice now, she had twitched when answering, followed by looking down. It was guarded but there. Could be accidental, a habit. Could also be important.

"Does she drive a car?"

"I don't think so. I've never seen her with one. I assume she's a businesswoman and flies here. Her dates always meet her near Hartsfield. If they go out, either the guy drives or they take a cab."

The questioning went on for another half hour. By the end of the session, Rusty was fatigued and frustrated. As much as he'd love to have something to give to Al to help him find a serial killer, it looked like questioning the madam was, no pun intended, nothing more than a dead end.

A soft jangling sound broke the silence of the kitchen and Rosalie picked her cell phone up off the counter. She checked the caller ID before hitting the button to answer the call. "Amber?"

"Yes, it's me. I just had a visit from a detective friend. He asked a lot of questions about you … and Brad."

Rosalie pressed a hand to the top of the counter. "What kinds of questions?"

"The kind that made me think he's after someone and he thinks it might be you."

Her throat tightened. "Interesting. What did you tell him?"

"Just that you were a regular who went by the name of Autumn Larson, that I thought you might be from the Portland area, and you always paid cash. Nothing that would help him figure out who you were or how to find you."

"Good. That's very good, Amber. Thank you."

"Of course. I owe you a huge debt, so you don't have to worry that I'll turn on you. I am a little concerned though. The police are practically camping on my doorstep and they return again and again with the same questions. They obviously think I know something that I'm not telling them. And it's not great for business, either."

Rosalie grinned wryly. "I guess it wouldn't be. Listen, if you stick to what you've already told them, which is pretty much nothing, they'll give up soon and leave you alone. And when they do, you can consider that your debt to me has been paid off."

"I will. I promise."

"Good. Thanks for calling." Rosalie set the phone back down on the counter and nudged the cat, sleeping near her feet. "Julie, we've got to come up with a plan. We may have to move. Any ideas?"

The cat stretched, wriggled, and went back to sleep.

Rosalie tapped her fingers on the counter for a moment before straightening her shoulders and returning to her work. She was busy completing a deadly compound ordered by the Carbone family. The Carbones controlled Louisiana and they had a politician they wanted to put away, innocently, of course. She forced her thoughts back to the task at hand.

This'll do it. She hummed as she worked. She was certain she could have the package in Birmingham in time for the last Fed Ex dispatch. The Carbones had used her services before, with successful results, and the $400,000 for this job had already been deposited in a blind trust for her niece.

When the phone rang, Al forced himself to wait a few seconds so Rusty wouldn't suspect he'd been sitting there, waiting for his call. Even though he had been. Finally, after the third ring, he snatched it up. "Al Rouse."

"Al, it's Rusty Cunningham. I'm calling to let you know I talked to Amber Johansen today."

"Any luck?"

"Not really. For the most part, she seemed to be telling me everything she knew."

Al straightened up in his seat. "For the most part? What does that mean?"

Rusty sighed. "I don't know if it was just me wanting to see something that wasn't there, but a couple of times it felt as though she might be holding something back."

"What made you think that?" Al picked up a pen and twirled it in the fingers of his free hand.

"I asked her the same questions over and over. The fourth time around, she twitched and looked down at the critical point. The same thing happened the fifth time."

"How much would you bet on her hiding something?"

"Not much. I'd say it's a fifty-fifty deal. I know her pretty well. She's usually calm, collected, and in control. This seemed different. But not different enough to bet the farm."

"I know what you mean, Rusty. I want to believe she's hiding something too. I *want* to believe this is our gal. I want it so bad I can taste it."

"And I'm not helpin' much by waffling, right?"

"That's not it; you know what you saw and what it might be. But if you're not convinced, you're not convinced. I think I need to roll this around overnight. You in tomorrow?"

"Absolutely."

"Great. I'll call you in the morning."

"I'll be waitin'. By the way, you buy that Scotch?"

"Sent if off this morning. Who knows, maybe I'll be down to help you drink it."

Al replaced the receiver and leaned back in his chair. For several minutes he stared at the picture of four dogs playing poker on the wall across from him. Finally he pushed away from his desk and grabbed his coat. Before he left, he made a detour past the chief's office.

"Got a minute, Chief?"

"C'mon in, Al. Have a seat. What's up?"

"I've got the itch. Need some advice."

"The old Rouse Rash, right?" Brent Whigg laughed.

"I just talked to Cunningham in Atlanta. He talked to the owner of the escort service today, and thinks she might be withholding information."

"What makes him think that?"

"It's not really anything hard, Chief, but Rusty is suspicious. He says she looked away when he asked several important questions."

The chief glanced at his watch. "If you could have anything you want, what would it be?"

Realizing he was wearing out his welcome, Al pondered the question for a moment. "I'd go down and talk to this Amber woman myself."

"That serious, huh?"

"Yup, I have the itch, no question about it. It just feels like the real deal. I wish I could explain why."

"God knows the Rouse Rash has led to several successes. Don't ignore it, Al, don't ignore it."

"I won't." Al pushed to his feet and offered the chief a salute. "I do want to think about it, though. Probably another sleepless night ahead."

6

Al bounded into the office at 6:15 a.m. the next morning, even though, as predicted, he had not slept. He had, however, effectively sorted out his thoughts and arrived at some conclusions. One thing he did know was that he believed in his gut; it had never let him down.

He brewed himself a hazelnut coffee and settled in at his desk. What should he say to the chief when Whigg punched in?

Al had a great relationship with his boss, born out of working together for more than a decade and the fact that Al tried never to ask for more than he felt he was due. Was what he wanted now pushing too far? He thought not. He closed more cases than anyone on the force, never slacked off, was quick to volunteer for difficult assignments, and always put the integrity of the department first.

What the hell. He threw back the last swig of lukewarm coffee and set the mug on his desk with a thud. Just ask. *All he can say is no.*

The chief walked in promptly at seven and poked his head in the door of Al's office. "How was the night?"

"Sleepless, as expected."

"And?"

"Chief, I thought about this all night. I'm gonna ask a favor—a big one."

"Uh-oh, better sit for this one." Whigg removed his hat, moved into the office, and sat down. He sniffed. "That hazelnut?"

"You know it is. Want a cup?"

When the chief nodded, Al went to fetch him a mug. His hat resting on the coat he'd tossed over the arm of the chair in front of Al's desk, and a cup of coffee in his hand, the chief settled back. "Let's have it."

"I wanna dig McCoy up. Assuming, of course, that he wasn't cremated." Before the chief could respond, he rushed on. "I want to go down there myself, and I'd like to take Charlie and Rick along. I need Rick, and Charlie's been with me on this case every step of the way, he deserves to be there."

Out of thoughts and out of breath, Al clasped his hands on his desk and looked the chief in the eye.

"That's a lot of money, Al. A whole lotta money. And, as you know, Sheriff Hooper, who will have to okay Charlie going, doesn't have any more than I do."

Al clenched his hands together to keep from drumming his fingers on the desk as he waited for the chief to ponder his requests.

Whigg finally looked up. "Ya know, Al, you don't ask for much around here. But when you do, it's a whale."

"I know, but—"

The chief held up his hand. "I wasn't finished. You guys don't know it, but I've been putting money aside whenever there's a little extra to be had. We desperately need a portable evidence kit, preferably the latest and greatest."

"That would be great."

"Yes, it would. And I now have about enough money put aside to make the down-payment on the machine and the peripherals. Coincidentally, that's just about enough money to send three guys to Atlanta and pay for an exhumation and autopsy."

"I completely understand. If that's what you've been saving the money for, that's what ..." Al unclasped his hands and sat up. "Wait, what?" Had the chief just said what he thought he had?

"Al, if you have one of your famous Rouse Rashes, I think we should go with it. Get on down to Atlanta. Make us proud. This woman has been a thorn in our side for too long; let's get her behind bars where she belongs."

Al fell back in his chair, mopping his brow with his hand, his mouth open but no words forthcoming.

The chief grinned, picked up his hat and coat, and got to his feet. "Just remember, we want full reports on this little escapade."

"Yes sir! Damn right, sir! Yes sir!"

Al's mind raced as the chief crossed the room and disappeared into the hallway. *Gotta call Charlie. Gotta get a hold of Rick. Whoa, wait a minute. What if McCoy was cremated? What if . . .* Al took a deep breath. *Slow down and think this through, man.* He grabbed a pen and pad and scratched "Things to Do" at the top of the page. Number one: Call Rusty; find out if McCoy cremated. Find out if exhumation possible.

Might as well do that right away. Al twisted his wrist to look at his watch. "Nine in Atlanta; Rusty oughta be in."

He grabbed the phone and dialed the number to Rusty's cell, now committed to memory.

"Cunningham."

"Hey, Rusty, it's Al. Just wanted to see if—"

"Hold on a minute, Al. Ya caught me eatin' breakfas'. Don't y'all eat up there?"

"Not today, Rusty." He waited through the sounds of chewing and swallowing before speaking again. "Look, I need a favor. Can you find out what happened to the McCoy body? Was he cremated or buried, and if he was buried, can you find out where?"

"Sounds like you're fixin' to pay us a visit."

"If there's a body, yes I am. Can you also let me know what's needed to get an exhumation underway in Georgia?"

After a moment of silence, Rusty responded in his slow, southern drawl. "Guess you'd like answers soon, right?"

"As soon as possible."

"The process has been simplified, but let me check. I'll try to get back later this morning. Soon enough?"

"Absolutely."

"Oh, Al, better get the paperwork started, explaining why it's needed."

"I'll do that. If you check on the specifics, I'll have our coroner, Rick Olson, and his associate put something together. Get back to me ASAP, will you, please?"

"No problem. Just happens I'm havin' breakfast with a state's attorney. I'll talk to him and get back to you."

Al began working through the newspapers and messages waiting for him. Twenty minutes later the phone rang.

"Pretty simple stuff. Good news, too. First off, he went into the ground whole. If you have the papers, send 'em over and I'll take 'em to the coroner. Talked to him a few minutes ago. He'll approve the request. When that's done, it's a matter of dealing with the cemetery officials. I'm gonna call them now. See when we can do it."

Al talked with the chief, went through his mail, returned two phone calls, and chafed as he waited. He also called Rick Olson and Pat Grebin, who assured him they could have the paperwork done in an hour. Thirty-five minutes later his phone rang again. He glanced at the small display screen on the unit. 678. Bingo. That was an Atlanta exchange.

He almost dropped the receiver in his haste to take the call, and Cunningham was already talking when he pressed it to his ear.

"… from the funeral home director. The guy's been in the ground over a week. No cremation, just a simple service and burial in a cemetery on the edge of town. The funeral director needs to know who's payin' to dig 'im up."

"That'd be us—La Crosse County. I can have a P.O. to you within the hour."

The call over, Al retraced his steps to the chief's office. Whigg was waiting.

"The guy was buried whole, but before anything happens, Cunningham wants to know who's payin'."

The chief grimaced. "Of course he does. Look, don't you worry about the money part. Dwight and I will work something out. You just get a hold of Charlie and Rick and tell them what's going on, then the three of you can start packing. The sooner we wrap this thing up, the better."

"Will do, chief. Thanks." Al hurried back to his office and called Charlie and Rick to arrange for the three of them to meet at Schmidty's.

Soon the three friends were in a booth at the popular bar and grill on State Road.

Al quickly brought Rick and Charlie up to date.

Charlie smacked a palm on the table. "So we're going to Atlanta?"

"That's the plan. Before we go, though, we've got work to do with Atlanta P.D. and the authorities down there. Rick has to write up a report to justify that exhumation and autopsy. Then there's the issue of three guys from the north getting involved. They may not look on that too kindly down there."

"Why not?"

"Haven't you heard, Charlie?" Rick decided to jump into the fray. "They're still fighting the Civil War down south. They don't much like Yankees." He barely managed to deliver the message with a straight face.

"Goddamn. Really? They hate guys like us?"

Al took his turn. "Hell yes, Charlie. They still have a bounty on Yanks in some of the areas south of the Mason-Dixon line."

"Really? But I thought ..." Charlie's eyes narrowed. "Goddamn you guys! You think you can take advantage of me all the time. I'm gettin' sick of it. Maybe I'll just let you go alone. Without me to protect you, the guys down there will be collectin' those bounties pretty quick."

As Charlie stared into his beer, Rick winked at Al. "Charlie, they are tough on guys from the north down there, although we might have laid it on a little heavy. But since you brought it up, yes, we do need your protection, you big teddy bear."

Charlie looked up. "Damn straight! You need me along just to take care of your asses. Hell, left alone in Dixie, you'd be done for."

"No doubt." Al tugged the wallet from his back pocket and tossed a couple of bills on the table. "I better get home; JoAnne'll be wondering where I am." Guilt pricked his chest, but he pushed it back. He had more than enough on his plate to deal with at the moment. His relationship issues would have to wait.

They walked outside, the north wind an immediate force. Charlie buttoned his coat and turned his back to the wind. "Just think boys. Soon we'll be in the sunny south. Warm temperatures, southern fried chicken, grits, and pecan pie."

And one dead body. Al kept the thought to himself as he waved to his friends, pulled up the collar on his jacket, and headed for his car.

7

"When can we do it?" Al twiddled with his pen, trying to tamp down his excitement so Rusty wouldn't think they were any less professional up in Wisconsin than they were down south. A sip of hazelnut coffee helped.

"Relax, Al, you sound like a bobcat in heat. Now, back up. We southerners move a little slower … talk a lot slower. But we always finish the race."

"Sorry. Up north we don't just like to finish the race; we want to win it. Just like we did the war."

"Revisionist history." Rusty's voice held laughter. "So when can we do what, the exhumation?"

"And the autopsy." Al leaned back in his chair. "We're paying all costs. We'd like to get it done as soon as possible.

"If you have the document, the coroner is willing, so we should be able to get things going pretty quick."

"It'll be done this morning, but I have a question or two."

"Shoot."

Al told Rusty that Charlie Berzinski and Dr. Rick Olson would be traveling with him. "I'm hoping Rick can help with the examination." He described both men for Rusty's benefit, and told him that he and Charlie, a sheriff's deputy, had combined their efforts on several investigations. "We were together every step of the way on the serial case. We're both smarting, too."

His fingers tightened on the arm of his chair. "Charlie's a big guy with a big appetite, so if you could supply the names of a few good restaurants, we'd appreciate it. Not too pricey, though."

"If you're looking for good food, you're coming to the right place. I'll show you all the best places, don't worry. Just come hungry."

Al grinned. Charlie was going to be a happy man. "Rick is one of the best pathologists in Wisconsin; he and his partner are the ones who found the pinprick in one of the victim's ear. That gave us the best lead we've had on this case, and led us to the killer. Hopefully he can find something that will lead us to her again and help us lock her up, for good this time." He cleared his throat. "Rusty, do we have to have a doc from Atlanta there, too?"

"That's the rule, at least I think it is. But Belinda's pretty laid back. I'll talk to her, but I'm sure she'll be okay with your guy taking the lead on this. Tell you what, send me that paperwork and I'll set up a date and time as soon as possible."

"Thanks. I appreciate it." Al disconnected the call and tossed his cell onto the desk. Now what? With the finish line in sight, the last thing he wanted to do was sit around and wait to hear back from Atlanta. He glanced at his watch. Maybe he'd take Charlie out for lunch. Even paying a hefty tab was better than staring at his phone all afternoon, willing it to ring.

The phone vibrated just as Al was about to walk out the door. He tugged it from his pocket and pressed it to his ear. "Rouse."

"Al, it's Rusty. The coroner is fine with your guy handling the work. As of right now, if it works for you, we can do it next Tuesday."

"That's great, Rusty, just great. I'm sure that will work for us to. I'll let you know the details when we have the arrangements made. What's the weather like down there?"

"The weather's gorgeous, and expected to stay that way. Leave your winter stuff at home."

"Great! It's been brutal up here—cold, about four feet of snow, and more expected."

Al worked hard to get everything set. When he had checked with Rick and Charlie, he called Rusty back. "We'll be there a little after noon on

Monday, 12:40 if everything's on time. That should give us enough time to prepare, right?"

"Should work. Where are you guys staying?"

Al said that was on his to-do list. Rusty suggested booking rooms at the downtown Marriott. "It's about a half block from our offices. Tell 'em you're coming to see us and I think you'll get a great rate."

With work to do now, all thoughts of lunch vanished. He called Charlie to change the plan. His buddy, as expected, wasn't happy. "I was lookin' forward to a couple of those French dips, Al. What the hell am I gonna do now?"

"Your problem. I'll call you later to fill you in on everything." Al turned his attention to Marriott reservations. He soon had three rooms booked and got them for seventy-nine dollars each when he told the agent they were coming down on police business.

Work done for the day, Al headed home. JoAnne greeted him with a kiss, took his coat and scarf, then rewarded him with another kiss.

"You're late."

"For what?"

"Kelly Berzinski's birthday. Don't you remember? We're invited there for dinner."

"Damn! I forgot. Tough day. I was hoping those two kisses might lead to something more."

"Allan Rouse! Is that all you ever think about?"

"Well, er, I guess not, but those were two great kisses. It's been a tough day; I need to relax."

"I'm sure we'll have a good time at Charlie's, and if you're a real good boy, I just might reward you later. Deal?"

"Deal." He grinned. It had been far too long since he and his wife had spent any quality time together. Even with everything that was going on with Julie, he missed JoAnne. "What time are we supposed to be there?"

"A half hour ago. You'd better hustle."

Forty minutes later, the Rouses and the Olsens were seated in the Berzinskis' living room, drinks in hand and conversation flowing.

Al turned to the three wives. "By the way, Rick, Charlie, and I are heading to Atlanta next week."

Kelly Berzinski set down her wine glass. "Atlanta? Why are you going there, for heaven's sake?"

Charlie grinned. "We're gonna get in a few rounds of golf, maybe stay on for the Masters. Our friends in the police department down there challenged us to a three-round tournament. Each side is allowed one ringer, so we're takin' Rick. He gets so damn much time off that his handicap is down to zero."

Kelly's eyes narrowed. She clearly wasn't buying it. "Charlie Berzinski, I've never heard you talk about golf. Do you play? And if you do, I'm ticked that you haven't played with me."

"But Kelly, I play with you all the time … almost every day."

"Damn you, Charlie, I wasn't talking about that and you know it. We don't have to talk to these good friends about our bedroom life, now do we?"

"I guess not, but can we tell 'em about the living room, kitchen, and basement?"

"Charlie, you're incorrigible! If you weren't so cute, I'd probably throw you out."

The dinnertime banter went on throughout the evening. It was a wonderful get-together and Kelly was rewarded with a gift certificate for dinner at one of La Crosse's finest restaurants, and tickets for the Viterbo College fine arts series.

Charlie snatched up the gift certificate, but left the tickets on the table. "Fine arts! What's that?"

"Charlie, it's time for you to get an education in culture." Rick held up his champagne flute. "We can't let poor Kelly struggle alone to try and civilize you. This is our contribution to that effort. You'll hear The St. Paul Chamber Orchestra, a stop by the Metropolitan Opera's traveling cast doing *La Bohème*, and the off-Broadway production of *South Pacific*, in addition to two Viterbo orchestra concerts, and a play done by the Viterbo students: *The Man Who Came to Dinner*."

"What the hell? Chamber music, opera, plays … who the hell could put up with that?"

"You will." Kelly pointed a finger in his face. "And you'd better not say one disparaging word about my gifts or you will lose all privileges for a month."

"Privileges?" Charlie gulped. "You mean …?"

"Exactly. So if you aren't as happy as I am with the gifts, you're going to be one very sad boy."

Al pressed his lips together to keep from bursting out laughing at the hangdog look on his friend's face.

The rest of the evening was filled with conviviality, and by the time Rick and Peggy and Al and JoAnne departed at ten, Charlie seemed to have extricated himself from the doghouse and he and Kelly were again acting like lovebirds.

"Isn't it wonderful to see Charlie so happy?" JoAnne snuggled against Al on the drive home.

"Yes, it's great to see him that way, but how about me? Let's get home for dessert!"

When Monday arrived, Al was ready for the trip. He stopped first for Charlie, who yanked open the door as Al started up the front steps. "About goddamn time! Thought you'd never get here."

"Whadda ya mean?" Al checked the time on his phone. "I'm early."

"Not early enough. I want to get going. Southern fried chicken, grits, collard greens, pecan pie …"

"Collard greens? You know damn well you wouldn't know a collard green from an Idaho baking potato."

Charlie jumped out of the car when they got to Rick's place. He shot a glance at the pile of bags and briefcases piled on the sidewalk and lifted both hands. "What the hell, you think we're goin' for a month?"

Rick just smiled. "There's a lot involved with digging up someone's grave, Charlie. And we want those southern boys to know we're ready for anything, don't we?"

8

When the trio reached Atlanta and moved from the concourse to the outdoor waiting area, the heat was staggering. The thermometer on the concrete post hovered around niney-four, and Al tugged a handkerchief from his pocket, wiped it across his forehead, and replaced it just as Charlie clapped a hand on his shoulder.

"It sure would be nice if this turned out to be something other than a wild goose chase. Wish I'd brought some shorts."

The three friends were waiting outside the main terminal at Hartsfield-Jackson International Airport after two routine plane rides filled with speculation, hopefulness, and, of course, lots of ribbing. Now, waiting for Rusty Cunningham, Charlie was at it again.

"Yeah, shorts sure as hell would be nice. I'm gonna melt in the stuff I brought."

Al forced the mental picture of his giant friend's pasty legs aside. "It probably would be best if we didn't get too optimistic. It's a long shot at best. A trail cold for two years probably isn't going to heat up, even down here in the South. I'm betting Genevieve is abroad somewhere where there's no extradition treaty."

Rick nodded. "We know she's one bright old lady. It's doubtful someone that smart would hang around where we could catch her."

"Crepehangers, both of you. I'm hopin' this might be a live one."

The red and blue lights built into its grill flashing, a limousine pulled up to the curb. Wondering which celebrities might be on board, Al stared as a tall man in a chambray shirt and smartly pressed jeans, a shield clipped to his belt, jumped out of the back seat.

"Are you the guys from Wisconsin come to Atlanta to escape your Yankee winter?"

The voice was familiar to Al, but the person wasn't anything like the man he'd pictured. "Rusty?"

"You must be Al. Welcome." Rusty grabbed his hand and shook it vigorously. "And you gotta be Charlie. Got some first-rate eateries lined up for you. And that makes you Rick. Welcome."

Charlie scratched his head. "You dicks down here ride around in limos? How the hell does that work?"

Rusty grinned. "You're just like Al said. Not to worry, Charlie, we don't ride around in limos. This is a city limo. I convinced the chief to let me use it to pick you guys up … you know, southern hospitality and all."

"He must be a helluva chief to trust you with this thing."

"The chief's a she, Charlie, and she is a good one, a very good one."

Al was still reeling at the Cunningham persona. Rusty was a big man, bigger than Charlie, but more heavily muscled. His hair, not surprisingly, was rust-colored, but graying at the sides. He had a kindly face, and when he smiled, it made Al want to smile, too.

The detective helped his guests into the limo before folding himself into a seat facing them. "So, how was the trip?"

They described the flights as Rusty pointed out sights along the way downtown.

Charlie pressed his forehead to the glass. "What the hell do you need a dome for? It's warm down here. You must be a buncha sissies; the Packers play outside."

"I've seen some of those games on TV, Charlie. Playing football in below zero temperatures doesn't appeal to me—hell, nothing appeals to me if it's below zero. But to answer your question, it gets damn hot down here. And it rains, too. Even sleets sometimes."

"Only sissies play football indoors."

Rusty took the ribbing good-naturedly, and continued pointing out all the tourist attractions between the airport and the hotel. When they reached the Marriott Downtown, Rusty instructed the driver to stop the car and, with a friendly wave and a promise to meet them at the precinct, he left them.

A half hour later the three of them had checked into their expansive and comfortable rooms and had congregated in the bar downstairs to sing the praises of their friend at the Atlanta Police Department.

"I s'pose this is how docs travel all the time." Charlie punched Rick lightly in the arm. "It's sure as hell not how cops travel, I can tell ya that. In fact, I might just skip tomorrow morning's events so I can enjoy these digs."

"Nice try, but you'll be with the two of us all day tomorrow. If you aren't, the sheriff is going to have your ass for lunch, Charlie."

"Yeah, yeah, I know, Al. I was only dreamin' of breakfast in bed after sleeping in 'til ten or eleven."

"You couldn't afford to have breakfast in bed in this place." Rick slugged him back, a little harder than Charlie had hit him. "Even I couldn't swing that, and I think I make more than you."

"Hell, Rick, everyone makes more than me. Okay, dream dashed. I'll be ready to go, bright and early."

Police headquarters in Atlanta was less than a block from the hotel. With temperatures still near ninety toward the late afternoon, the three men slung suit coats over their shoulders and made the short walk in a few minutes.

Rusty was a great guy, and soon the four had picked up as if the limo ride had never ended. They got along famously and when Rusty had to attend a meeting, they agreed to meet for dinner to plan the next day.

Al made a reservation for four at Antebellum for 7:00 p.m. When dinnertime came, Charlie was in heaven. He ordered the 32-ounce steak for two with three sides—which he claimed were just for him—and when he had reduced the ribeye to a bone that looked as if it had been lying in the desert sand for years, he consumed two desserts: pecan pie and bread pudding. After shoving the last bite into his mouth, he slapped some money on the table and took off without saying good-bye. Rusty caught Al's eye and raised an eyebrow. Al smiled knowingly. "Charlie'll be right back. I'm betting on a gas attack and a trip outdoors to relieve the pressure."

The three were still chuckling when Charlie returned. "I had a pressing issue to attend to."

The merriment over, the four got down to business, planning out the next day. Forty-five minutes later, an empty pot of coffee was all that remained on the table. As the four got up to depart, Rusty lifted a hand. "It's been great to break bread with y'all. Get some rest now. Tomorrow should be an interesting day."

The next morning, the Wisconsin trio arrived in Rusty's office before seven. Al shifted his weight from foot to foot and looked at his watch every ten seconds, feeling as though he might burst.

"I sure hope something turns up today. We need to find something solid, something interesting. If we don't, our bosses are gonna be pissed."

"I'm plannin' on interesting!" Charlie clapped his hands together with a decisive smack as the group got ready to head for Arlington Memorial Park where the body of Brad McCoy was interred. It was a glorious day, sunny, unseasonably warm, just enough breeze to be pleasant, and a constant chorus from feathery creatures filling the air overhead.

When they arrived at the park, the mortician was there, along with the coroner. Rick and Dr. Bartholomew—Belinda—hit it off at once and soon were chatting like longtime colleagues. When the cemetery staff arrived, they made short work of digging up the grave and removing the casket. Soon, at the county morgue, the doctors and detectives robed for the examination, Rick nodded at Belinda. "This should be simple and quick. If we find no puncture wounds in the upper body, it's not likely the work of the person we are looking for. If we do find the wound, we'll see if it makes sense to go further."

The body was placed on the cadaver table. The doctors rolled it onto its right side then moved in. Belinda gave Rick the prime position. Al and Charlie pressed in behind. Charlie moved gingerly and covered his nose with his hand, obviously bothered by the putrid smell in the room. Rusty observed from a distance, sitting on a stool near the door.

Rick peered at the ear, asked for a magnifying glass, studied the ear again, and stepped back. As he handed the glass to Dr. Bartholomew, Al pressed close to the body, straining to see what the doctors were looking at. Was it possible they'd actually found something?

"Belinda, take a look and see if you come up with anything."

After studying the ear, Dr. Bartholomew straightened and handed the glass back to Rick. "I see what appears to be a pinprick. I'm sure you saw it, too. It's surrounded by a bit of a milky stain that has tan tinges at its outline."

"Exactly. And that's what we're looking for."

Rick met Al's eyes. "I think this is our gal. It's too picture-perfect to be a coincidence."

Charlie slapped Al on the back and suddenly everyone was talking. Rick held up both hands and a hush fell over the room. "I think we should remove a small tissue sample from the wound area and run a substance test on the stain. I'm betting it's Propofol mixed with either Etomidate or Midazolam. Belinda, would you be kind enough to help me with the excision and the test?"

"I'd love to. I find this intriguing, very intriguing, indeed. Maybe you can catch me up on the story as we work?"

Rusty looked at Al and inclined his head toward the door. "This will take a while. Why don't you and Charlie come back to the office with me until the results come in."

As soon as they walked into Rusty's office, Al asked if he could make a call. "We need to bring the chief and the sheriff up to date. Once that's done, maybe you and Charlie and I can figure out where we go from here?"

"Absolutely, Al. Wouldn't miss it for all the pralines in Georgia."

Al got the chief on the line, and Sheriff Dwight Hooper was soon linked in. With their La Crosse bosses listening, Al and Charlie excitedly told the story of finding what appeared to be a pin or needle prick inside the ear of McCoy.

"Chief, the needle mark was obvious," Al told them.

Charlie broke in to say, "No doubt about it, it was there, plain as day. I saw it with my own eyes. Had to jostle the docs a bit, but I saw it."

The two summed up the rest of the examination then Chief Whigg wanted to know the next steps.

"Rick and Dr. Bartholomew removed a piece of skin from around the needle mark and are having it tested for drugs." Al stood with his back to his companions, staring out the window at downtown Atlanta. He was anxious to be about the chase. "Results probably won't be back until tomorrow."

The sheriff cleared his throat. "What's next when the test results are in?"

"That's what Rusty, Charlie, and I are about to discuss. For starters, I'm hoping Rusty can put us in touch with the call-girl service owner to see what we can find out about the customer this john was with last." Al glanced over at Rusty, who was leaning back in his chair with his feet crossed on his desk. Rusty nodded, and Al turned back to the phone. "Rusty will try to set that up. We're thinking a couple days, maybe more. We're not sure if Rick will stay too, but we'll ask him. I guess it'll depend on the test results, and how conclusive they are."

The chief and sheriff agreed and they ended the call. Charlie and Al talked for a few more minutes. Charlie said he wanted to call Kelly. Al thought maybe he'd call Julie Sonoma, just to let her know they might have a clue to her aunt's whereabouts

Al tugged his cell phone from his shirt pocket and stepped into a nearby room to try and reach Julie at work. Her voice, when she answered, sent a thrill coursing through him.

"Honey, you may not want to hear what I have to say, but that Atlanta death I told you about—we're pretty sure your aunt did it. Everything about the autopsy points to her. The needle mark in the ear, and I'm certain the types of drugs used; everything bears her classic trademarks. We're going to push the investigation down here, hoping to find her."

"If you do find her, Al, please be kind. Brody and I owe her so much. I know you feel terrible about her escape, but down deep she really is a good person. I believe that."

"Julie, good people don't kill fourteen or fifteen people, and possibly one more, that we know of. We won't harm her, but we're not feeding her filet mignon, either."

"I only ask that she be treated with kindness. You do what you have to do, Al. I'd appreciate knowing if you find her, though."

"That much I can guarantee. Julie, I love you."

"I love you, too, Al. Find her. Please."

9

None of the Wisconsin group slept well that night—even after another great dinner. They were again in Rusty's office pretty much as the sun rose. While Charlie and Rick waited quietly for Rusty, Al was restless, drumming his fingers on the desk and waiting for the detective to arrive.

When Rusty walked into his office, he hung his coat on the freestanding rack, looked at his visitors, and focused on Al. "You look ready to explode, man. Something wrong with the accommodations?"

"They're great, just like you said they would be, but we are dying to hear what you have to tell us. Our bosses took a big financial risk, sending us down here, and I want to have something good to share with them."

Rusty ran a hand through his hair, smiled and said, "You're gonna like what I have to tell you."

Al was about to respond when Charlie, who'd been pacing by the door, stopped and whirled around. "Rusty, I'd appreciate it if you'd remind these bozos that normal people eat at least three good meals a day. They seem to think we can go for hours on an empty stomach. That don't work for me."

While Al chafed at the interruption, he was overruled when Rusty agreed with Charlie.

"I'm hungry as hell, too, Charlie. Tell you what, you buy breakfast and I'll bring you up to date and tell you everything you want to know."

"Anyone talking about food is a friend of mine. Hell, yes, I'll buy breakfast … well, at least Al will; he's the treasurer."

"Treasurer?" Al frowned. "That's a pretty fancy word for patsy. Why can't we just hear what Rusty has to say? Is there really any reason to go to breakfast?"

Al's comments clearly weren't heard. By the time they were out of his mouth, Rusty had retrieved his coat, grabbed Charlie by the shoulder, and all that Rick and Al could do was follow them out the door.

Al tried to start the conversation again as Rusty drove them, but his effort was stymied when they pulled up to a café, where Al had to wait while they placed their orders and talked about the pros and cons of Atlanta life until their food arrived. Three of them were eating modestly; not Charlie. In fact, the waitress looked on in wonderment when she delivered his breakfast, which required five plates.

Charlie may have forgotten Rusty's earlier comment, but Al was more than ready to get back to it. He pushed away his plate, the toast half eaten. "So, Rusty, I've been humoring you guys—especially this human garbage can. Now that he's grazing, how about you tell us the news he so rudely prevented you from sharing."

Rusty laughed. "Al, once in a while, you've gotta relax a little. Gettin' a little food in us isn't a bad thing. Now you'll be ready for the day. You'll be glad to know I've got you that appointment you wanted. Amber Johansen will see you this morning, but she told me to make sure it was at a reasonable time, 'not the crack of dawn' as she put it. I've got a few other things to share with you, too."

Al and Rick leaned forward. Charlie kept stuffing his mouth after assuring Rusty that, "I'm ambidextrous. I can eat and listen at the same time."

Rusty took a sip of coffee. "The background report's done on the woman who, as far as we know, was the last one to see Brad McCoy. Came back late yesterday." He set down his mug. "As we assumed, there is no such person—at least not where Amber said she might be from. There's no evidence of an Autumn Larson anywhere in the Portland area. It's pretty obvious that 'Autumn Larson' doesn't want us to know where she is."

Al wasn't deterred. "But you scored an appointment with Ms. Johansen. That's huge."

Rick set down his fork. "Before we go see her, I'd like to make some calls and also talk to Belinda about some of the final tests we ran yesterday.

Those results weren't in when we quit last night. If Charlie ever finishes eating, maybe I could tie those things up before we go see Ms. Johansen."

Later, at the station, Rick reported that the lab had confirmed that the stains were made by Propofol and Etomidate.

"That sort of closes the loop, doesn't it?" Rick turned to Rusty. "That combination killed at least four people in Wisconsin. There aren't many people who even know about that combination of drugs, let alone how to use them. I think we have a live one here."

Al nodded. "No question, but she's been gone for two years without a trace, so we shouldn't get our hopes up too much that we'll be able to track her down now."

Rusty tapped his chin with one finger. "Amber has tended to be really helpful on cases in the past. She wasn't that helpful on this one when I talked to her earlier, but I'm hoping if she knows anything more, that we can get her to tell us."

Al pursed his lips. He was hoping too, but somehow he doubted that Amber Johansen, whose livelihood depended on her showing the utmost discretion when it came to her high-end clients, was going to be much help at all.

An hour later, the four men were ushered into a room off the spacious foyer in an expansive home near downtown Atlanta. The sprawling ranch-style house, set amid a forest of trees and shrubs, was barely visible from the sidewalk.

While waiting, Charlie asked Rusty about the neighborhood. Standing at the window, Rusty swept an arm through the air. "This is one of the most affluent areas in the country and it's certainly the most exclusive in Georgia. The governor's mansion is right down the street."

"So I guess a home here is out of my pay range, right?"

"Unless you make a helluva lot more than I do, you're right. In fact, my guess is that even Rick would struggle on his doctor's salary. Homes here start above a million, and there aren't even many that you could get for that."

"Wow! Maybe I'd better stand. Sure as hell wouldn't want to get a bill for furniture cleaning, would I?"

"And just why would you get a bill for cleaning, young man?" asked a beautiful, middle-aged woman as she entered the room. "You're an honored guest in this home."

Charlie ducked his head, his cheeks turning crimson.

The madam smiled. "I'm Amber. Rusty, this is the group from Wisconsin?"

"It is, Amber. And we are all hoping you can help us with a series of crimes that began in Wisconsin and now has reached Atlanta."

"Why don't you boys come with me and we'll find somewhere more private to visit."

As the quartet followed their hostess down the hallway, Al couldn't help but marvel at her beauty.

Amber Johansen was, he guessed, five foot ten. She had milk-white skin and long auburn hair. Her figure was as stunning as any he'd seen, and she swayed her hips as she walked. Carnal thoughts passed through his mind before he pushed them away sharply. *Aren't two women enough for you, you old fool?*

"Is this better, gentlemen?" Amber's voice was soft and sexy as she led them into a conference room where the table was laden with pastries, juices, and other beverages. "Please help yourselves. We have a great cook here at Lorelei Lane. She's set out a few things for you."

"A few things! This, ma'am, is a feast fit for a king." Charlie had already grabbed a plate and was making his way around the table.

"You must be Charlie. You have a reputation for a prodigious appetite, Deputy Berzinski. It is, in fact, true that I had the chef prepare refreshments with you in mind. But I do hope all of you will enjoy the food."

Charlie continued to dig in, clearly pleased by the woman's use of the word prodigious.

Al shook his head. *Probably thinks it's a compliment.*

Rusty introduced Al and Rick to the madam. She shook Al's hand, her skin soft and warm against his. When she let him go, she gestured toward the table. "Does anything tempt you?"

Although he suspected she wasn't talking about the food, Al tore his gaze away and grabbed a plate. "We hope, ma'am, that you won't judge us all by the manners of our colleague here."

Amber's eyes twinkled as she smiled sweetly. "We love food in the

South, Detective Rouse. Like most of my fellow Georgians would, I find Deputy Berzinski and his appetite quite charming."

"See! I've been telling you guys about the value of a great appetite, and all you do is pick on me. Ma'am, thank you for vindicating me. All I ever hear from these bozos—and Doc Olson is the worst—is criticism about my eating habits and how I should be eating healthy. Maybe if they ate a little more, they could be *prodigium*, too."

Everyone laughed. Charlie's brow furrowed, as if wondering what it was he'd just said that was funny.

The woman came to his rescue. "You will notice, Charlie—may I call you Charlie?—that there is much on the table for those of us who eat with our health in mind."

Al set his plate down on a side table, beneath a vase of blue and white hydrangeas. "With all due respect, Ms. Johansen, we'd like to ask you some questions and we're hoping you can help us."

"If you'll call me by my first name, I'd be happy to answer any questions you might have. I have all day, but I suspect you boys have places to go, so why don't we get started?" She gestured toward a seating area over by a nearly floor to ceiling window and they all found a place to sit.

Al launched into a background report on the murders in La Crosse. When it came to the Atlanta death, he turned the explanation over to Rusty. After just a few comments about the autopsy and the findings, Amber shook her head.

"Well, that is a most disturbing report. I surely hope you don't think I had anything to do with whatever went on. Goodness, she's a customer—but not for *that kind of business*. Autumn has used my services for a while, since I met her at the post office. I have personally seen her only twice, although she's been a good customer. She calls about every three or four weeks, if she is going to be in Atlanta, and I send one of my boys over to keep her company. I assume she's some kind of salesperson. She always stays at the Omni when she visits."

Al leaned forward, pressing both elbows into his knees. "Can you give us a description? Rusty's not given us much of an idea of that, and I'd like to hear it from you."

"Her appearance is, well, let's call it sophisticated. She's not particularly tall—about five foot five—but she carries herself well, as a woman of means might. She's probably a handful of pounds over a hundred. None of that is particularly remarkable, but there is one thing that is truly exceptional, her reputation. Apparently she is one unbelievable lady."

Al's eyebrows drew together. "How so?"

"It seems that Ms. Larson is exceptional in a number of ways." Amber crossed her ankles and glanced down at the hands she had clasped in her lap, as though what she was about to say might be considered indelicate.

Rusty broke in. "Not to worry, Amber, these folks know about your business and how we work together."

"In that case, let me tell you that, whenever I send one of my men to her, he returns talking about her as though she is the most incredible woman he has ever met. Of course, they enjoy the night off—at least they claim it's a night off—but apparently Ms. Larson, Autumn, is as good with words and stories as most of my people are with actions. To be honest, there is only one of them who didn't want to be put back on her schedule."

"I'm guessin' that's our girl. She's one horny broad. Oops …" Charlie blushed, clearly recognizing his indiscretion. "Amber, I'm very sorry. That was crude. But fact is, she has a reputation for being great in the sack. You didn't say a thing about that."

"In my line of work, Charlie, that wouldn't approach crude. And you are suggesting something I don't know anything about. To the best of my knowledge none of my men has ever been asked for sex, although I'm sure they would have been happy to oblige."

Al's forehead wrinkled as he contemplated Amber's words. "Hmm, Charlie, Rick, maybe this isn't our girl?"

Charlie sat forward on his chair, as if he was about to speak.

Al propped an elbow on the arm of the couch. "How about we let Amber finish. Is there anything else you can tell us?"

Amber shook her head. "No, Al, not unless you want details of the conversations. I understand she has a wide vocabulary and many interests, some of them carnal enough to make you blush."

Al smiled. "No, I don't think we need to go into those kinds of details."

The look on Charlie's face suggested he didn't like Al's answer. Amber must have seen it too, because she rested a hand on his arm. "Charlie, we can talk later if you'd like me to fill you in."

A red flush creeping up his neck, Charlie stammered, "Well, ummm, I don't think that's gonna be necessary. It just seemed interestin', you know. And maybe there'd have been something there that might have helped us track her down."

"It's very interesting. But not helpful, I assure you. Not in that way, anyway." She pressed a finger to her full, ruby-red lower lip. "Let me think. Is there anything else? Oh yes, I assume Ms. Larson flies to Atlanta. The airport is near the Omni and there has never been mention of a car. Quite the contrary, she has always asked that my employees pick her up for dinner, after which they return to the Omni for the rest of the night. By noon the next day, she's gone. I know that because on two occasions my employees left things behind and each time she called them from another city to say that she had left the items at the front desk."

Rick cleared his throat. "We had hoped you might be able to give us a little more than that. A clue to Ms. Larson's current whereabouts, for example."

"Hell, yes, we hoped for more. A shitload more!" Charlie's face flushed an even deeper red. "Damn, ma'am, I am really sorry."

Al ignored him. "Ms. Johansen—"

She held up a hand. "Amber, please."

He swallowed. "Amber, might it be possible to talk to the guys this woman has, umm, dated?"

"Well, one is dead, as you know. Another has left my employ without a forwarding address, but two still work for me. It should be possible for you to talk to them. Do you want me to call them?"

Al's response came quickly. "No, ma'am; I think we'd like to make the calls, if you don't mind. We'll take their phone numbers, though."

"Absolutely. Right away. I'll be right back."

Right away became thirty minutes. After ten minutes, Al was pacing, Rusty was on his phone, Rick was studying something out the window, and Charlie appeared content to keep eating. When she finally returned, Amber was apologetic. "I had trouble finding the numbers then had to clarify what seemed to be discrepancies in one of the them. I am terribly sorry. But here is the information you wanted."

Thanking her, the men excused themselves. Amber escorted them to the door and waved as they went out onto the porch. Al was the last to leave, and she winked at him before closing the door behind the men.

They climbed into the car in silence. Only after Rusty had driven a block down the street lined with mansion after mansion did Al, who sat in the passenger seat, turn to him. "Do you think that absence was for real?"

"I'm not sure. Her demeanor was a bit unusual, I'll say that much."

"Unusual how, Rusty?" Charlie leaned forward, clearly in investigator mode.

Finally. Al eyed him. Charlie might come off as a big buffoon, but when he became focused, no one was better at sniffing out clues on a case.

Rusty glanced over his shoulder at the big man. "She came off as being very self-assured and in control, but she still seemed nervous to me, at least more nervous than I've seen her in the past. Little things, like staring down at her hands before speaking. She didn't make eye contact, either."

"Exactly what I was thinking." Al tapped his fingers on the door ledge. "I don't believe we saw the real Amber until the last couple of minutes. I think she's hiding something."

Charlie nodded. "Damned straight. She was goddamn nervous, if you ask me."

"You're just copying, Charlie. I'm not sure you would know nervous from ecstatic," said Rick.

"Would too. I learned a long time ago to know when people are nervous. She *seemed* nervous."

Al ran his finger under the seat belt that crossed his chest. Clearly the heat was getting to all of them. "No need to bicker. We all agree. Let's get back to the station and call these guys before Amber has a chance to warn them."

Later, the calls made, the four got back together. Al and Charlie confessed their lack of additional information. One man hadn't answered, in spite of their repeated attempts to reach him, and the other had offered next to nothing by way of information. Rusty asked if Charlie and Al felt meeting with the one man they had reached would be valuable.

Charlie looked to Al for the answer. "He was stoned, Rusty. I don't think he knew his name. Given what he could remember, I really doubt that he'd have anything valuable to share. Let me sleep on it, though. Maybe I'll change my mind in the morning."

Rusty had better news. "I talked with Amber and she has agreed to let me know the next time she hears from Autumn Larson. When she calls, we'll be all over it, hoping to make a collar. And when we do, you will be called immediately. Fair enough?"

Al nodded. "Eminently fair." As much as he hated to leave without anything more concrete to take to the chief, he couldn't justify extending their time in Atlanta, when it appeared as though they'd gotten all the information they could at this point.

The trio from Wisconsin thanked Rusty for all of his help, provided an address to which the bill could be sent, and left for their hotel and what they hoped would be a trip home the same day.

10

When the phone rang, it startled Rosalie, at work in her lab. "Who could that be?"

Only a few people had the number and the phone rang only when there was trouble, it seemed. She glanced at the screen before picking it up.

"Amber?"

The voice on the other end was barely distinguishable. "I just had a visit from an Atlanta detective and three officers from Wisconsin, Detective Al Rouse, Deputy Charlie Berzinski, and a doctor named Rick Olson. You know them, right?"

"Yes dear, I know them. I knew they'd be around one of these days."

"Did you really kill all those people up there? I know what you did for me, but fourteen is a lot of deaths."

Rosalie sighed. "It's a long and complicated story, not one I'm going to tell over the phone. But how about you tell me what those boys had to say and what they wanted to know?"

"I tried to remember everything, because I was sure you would want to know. First, they wanted a thorough description of you. I didn't think I could fudge that too much, but I tried to be vague yet reasonably honest. They wanted to know what you had told me in booking my employees. That was easy to fake. They wanted to know if I had any idea where you lived. I said you had told me Portland and I had no reason to doubt what you said. I told them I was certain you worked in sales and periodically visited Atlanta. Then they wanted to know if I knew where you stayed when you were here. I told them that I presumed it was the Omni because that's where the men met you. All in all, it was a pretty short discussion. I think they quickly concluded that we had a one-way business relationship—me supplying you with men—so the questions were directed there and there weren't many follow-ups to my answers."

"Did they ask if I had done work for you?"

"No, nothing like that. It didn't come up. They did ask if you drove a car and I told them I didn't think so because you always had people come to the Omni to meet you, and if you and your date went out to eat, either he drove or you took a cab."

"How about questions about drugs?"

"None of that. Nothing even close."

"Anything else?"

"Not really. They did ask for the names and numbers of the men you've dated. Of course, Brad McCoy is dead; they knew that. I had to give them the names and numbers of two others. I did a pretty good job of that, I think. Luke Jameson has left town and if he has a new phone number, I don't know it. Roger Britton is around, but he doesn't work for me now. Hasn't for six or eight months. Last I heard he'd started using and was one step away from living in a gutter. It's highly unlikely they'll be able to track him down, and by the time they do, chances are it'll be in the morgue."

Autumn winced. "I'm sorry to hear that." She'd liked Roger, but he had disappeared into the washroom a couple of times the night they were together and had returned a little loopy, so she wasn't too surprised to hear he'd gone downhill. Terrible waste treating a gorgeous body that way.

"It is too bad. He really did seem to enjoy his night with you. When he came in here the day after your date, he looked happy as hell, even though he was dragging. Said he didn't want a date for a week. Said you had talked his ear off. Didn't let him sleep all night. You do make a powerful impact."

"Funny, I never thought of myself as extraordinary. My Henry said I was, but I thought he was only making nice." Rosalie sat down on a bar stool at the counter. "You know, I enjoyed your young men, loved every minute, in fact. I guess we are going to have to end our relationship though, unless you can think of some way to keep it going without getting either of us in trouble."

"I'll give that some thought. I'd love to keep the business, but I'm more interested in the work you do. I might need that kind of help again sometime. Based on what you did for me and what the police told me about your past, you're the best."

"Let's both think about it. Right now, we have to cool it."

Rosalie left the lab, walked to the living room, and sat down in the rocking chair to analyze the discussion. Was the visit by the team from La Crosse so troublesome that she should move? That was the key question. Going over every angle, she felt she was secure enough in her home in the woods—at least for now. But her trips to Atlanta were probably going to have to end, at least for a while. *Damn. I'm sure gonna miss them.* She chuckled to herself at the thought of what Amber didn't know about those visits. Yes, those young men were exhausted after she had finished with them, but it wasn't just from conversation. No, it wasn't. *I'm a woman of many surprises.*

If age had left her unable to experience all the finer things in life, it was still nice to have the company of younger men and to be seen with them on her arm. And there were potions for them, too—more kindly ones than those she sold.

Up early the next morning, Rosalie got busy. After thinking much of the night about the situation, she'd talked herself into her home in the woods being a safe haven, although she wasn't quite comfortable. *It's the best choice for now.*

Her first task that day was to get encrypted messages to her customers, telling them she would no longer be picking up mail at the Atlanta address. She would replace Atlanta with Huntsville, she wrote them in a previously agreed upon code. That box would be opened in a few days, she would let them know when.

She drove to Birmingham, put the letters in the mail, purchased groceries, and returned home mid-afternoon.

She grabbed her atlas and sat down in her rocking chair to try to find places she might like to live if she did end up needing to move. Julie curled at her feet, and Rosalie talked to him from time to time.

"Julie, we could either try the Northwest or the Southwest. The Southwest is more populous. That offers some protection, but it also puts us in closer contact to the FBI and other law enforcement offices.

"The Northwest—at least the far Northwest—is populous, too, unless we move east a bit, into Montana. I just love Montana, Julie. You would too, I think. Henry and I vacationed in Glacier Park right after we were married. My, what a time we had. And the Bitterroot Mountains are among the most peaceful and beautiful I've seen. Lots of open spaces, lots of birds for you to watch. You might even be able to be outside some there."

So taken were they that Henry bought a large plot of land in the mountains. Rosalie straightened up abruptly in her chair. *That's it! That plot in the mountains of Montana would be perfect.*

"We don't have to be in a hurry, Julie." She poked at the cat with her toe, but the only reaction she got was the partial opening of one eye.

"You know, Montana would be perfect. For the time being, I'm pretty sure Amber will protect us. I think we can stay here for a while, but we need to have a long-range plan."

Feeling at ease, now that she had one piece sorted out, she went outside and fed the birds then came in to make dinner. She ate her meal and sipped on several glasses of wine as she watched the news. There was no report on the investigation in Atlanta.

When she'd turned off the TV, she considered her other big dilemma: how to effectively appease the need for company that gripped her every few weeks. Without her Atlanta fixes, what would she do?

11

T*hat's it!*

Rosalie's eyes sprang open the next morning, fueled by the thought that came to her as she emerged from her deep sleep. As she moved to get out of bed, her feet encountered an obstacle.

"Julie, you good-for-nothing cat, it's time to get up! Wait 'til you hear what I'm thinking."

Julie was groggy. His left eye opened, then closed again as if to say, *Idiot woman, it's barely dawn.* The sun's not even up. Not to be hurried, the cat stretched its front paws, resembling a jaguar ready to pounce. Then it got its front feet under it and made the little mewl that signaled hunger.

"Sure, now it's your stomach. Just once couldn't you get excited along with me?"

Rosalie had been awakened by a stroke of genius, she believed. She'd gone to bed thinking about having to give up the activity that made her life tolerable: companionship. But why should she? After all, she was in the twilight of her life, she had more than enough money to live the lifestyle she wanted, and she did not want to live without the company of her handsome young men.

It was a simple solution, really. Could she cultivate the friendship of another madam? Certainly Montgomery and Birmingham were large enough to have sex workers, but they were also small enough that someone with prying intentions could more easily discover the same sort of relationship she had with Amber. Both those cities would have to be ruled out.

Amber would likely be under surveillance—both personal and

electronic. Could Rosalie remain engaged with her Atlanta friend without endangering either of them? That was the dilemma for which a solution was needed. Now she thought she had one.

She could use one of her dons as a "carrier pigeon" to get a message to his counterpart in Atlanta for relay to Amber. Comfortable with her plan, Rosalie fed the cat. Julie, happy now, tagged along as she made her way to the laboratory and worked through some orders. She finally had fourteen packages ready to ship.

"We're gonna have to make a trip, Julie. How about we just send some from Hayden and the rest from Birmingham? That'll be easy, won't it? Then we can have a great evening. But I've got one little thing to do before we leave."

She sat at the kitchen table and picked up a pen and paper. As she wrote, she listened to the birds sing.

Dear Angelo,

Although we have not met, we have had a long-term business relationship and have gotten to know each other well through our letters. I am writing today because I have served you faithfully and I am in need of a bit of help that I believe you can supply. I am certain that you have, from our business dealings, figured out that I have a past from which I am trying to escape. To be more direct, I am being sought by police across the country because of acts I committed to help a family member.

While fleeing from the law, I found my way to the south, but I have never disclosed my address, nor do I intend to. To maintain my freedom, it is best that way. And it is because I want to maintain my freedom that I write to you today.

You see, recently the police have come much closer to my whereabouts than makes me comfortable. That was because I availed myself of the service that Amber Johansen supplies. You might remember that it was you who pointed me toward Amber when I told you of my desires. Recently it was necessary to "take care of" an employee of Amber's. Because a Wisconsin police officer saw the news report and was interested enough to talk to the Atlanta police, an informant there tells me the body was exhumed and my trademark wound area was found. Now I am afraid my whereabouts might become known. The police and medical officials from Wisconsin and Georgia have questioned Amber. While Amber remained silent on these issues, I suspect that her headquarters might already be under surveillance and her phone and Internet connections tapped.

It is my wish that these actions be verified and, if possible, halted. While it may not be possible to halt them all, at the very least I would like some early warning of accelerated threats that might lead to my discovery. At the same time, I imagine you have expertise in wiretapping. If that is the case, would you consider listening in on Amber's personal line? That would provide additional insurance against any threats. I also wonder if you would be kind enough to, from time to time, communicate messages from me to Amber. I assume you have a way to do this discreetly.

I do not make these requests lightly, nor do I request that they be done without recompense. If you are either willing to take care of these problems for me or to arrange for it to be done, I will offer, without question, an exchange of my services in the amount that you deem worthy of your work.

Should you have questions, please contact me at the Birmingham postal address using the code that we have agreed upon, and in which this letter appears, so its contents are known only to the two of us.

With grateful thanks for your consideration.

Sincerely,
Rosalie Burton
P.O. Box 5465
Birmingham, AL 35233

That task completed, Rosalie showered and dressed, then decided to drive to Birmingham to mail the letter. On the way home, she could pick up a few needed supplies, and maybe see a movie. She especially wanted to see *Gravity*, starring Sandra Bullock. Rosalie felt particularly sorry for Ms. Bullock because of the personal problems she'd experienced.

A few hours later she was on the road again and contemplating the movie she'd just seen. It had been all right, but not what she had expected. Sandra Bullock had done a wonderful job, as did George Clooney. *My, what a hunk he is.* But a movie without much dialogue was like her existence without a man in it. She tapped her palms against the steering wheel, trying to rein in her impatience. *Someday, Rosalie, someday soon.*

Two uneventful weeks later, she drove to Birmingham and, almost afraid to look, stopped at the post office. She asked the desk clerk for mail for Jane Ambrosen, the name she used for deliveries. Her excitement grew when the clerk handed her an envelope postmarked in New Orleans.

She stopped halfway home at a wayside rest. After visiting the restroom, she returned to the car and nervously tore open the envelope.

My Dear Rosalie,

Thank you for your letter. You know that these kinds of tasks are not typically of interest to me. Invading another don's area is something that is rarely done, and only after great thought. But as I did that thinking, the projects you have done for me—even though you have been well compensated—caused me to conclude that I owe you this. Of course, your offer to pay for the services rendered was also a motivating factor.

First the price. Since I will be providing round-the-clock surveillance of Amber's residence and place of business, I will charge you only what I pay for such services, $50 per hour. My employees are highly trained and do their work well. For my time, nothing is required from you, dear lady. You have served me well. This is one small way I can pay you back.

To you I make one more offer. Since you know that I control the sex industry in New Orleans, Mississippi, and *western Alabama, I offer to you the very best of my stable of young men. All have been thoroughly vetted. All are skilled conversationalists—and more, should you be interested. None will open his mouth about any assignment. All you have to do to take advantage of my offer is send me $3,000, specify the date you desire, the place for the meeting, and instructions on how to identify you.*

In closing, my dear Rosalie, let me tell you how happy I am to be able to pay back, even in such a small way, the excellent work you have done for me.

Most sincerely,
Angelo Carbone

How nice. Now that her working relationship with Amber had been challenged, she was grateful for Angelo's offer. The more she thought about it, the more she liked it. Returning to the post office, she quickly wrote a note to Angelo, telling him what she wanted and when.

She had been far too long without the company of a young man, so she specified a date ten days away. She told Angelo she would be staying at the IP Resort and Casino in Mobile, and would meet his employee at the hotel check-in desk at three. He would know her, she wrote, by the colorful purse she carried—a bag done in reds, oranges, and yellows.

12

For the next nine days, Rosalie hardly thought of anything else. A young man, a handsome young man, hers to do with as she wished, a captive audience.

It was the longest nine days Rosalie had spent in Alabama. Even the first few weeks there had passed faster.

Thursday she awoke to rain pounding on the roof. The view outside her bedroom window was frightful, with low-hanging and fast-moving clouds of deep gray and black scudding across the sky. A bad day, but she couldn't stay huddled in her cabin. She had things to do and people to see.

She packed the things she needed for Mobile, tidied the house, gave Julie extra food and water, checked the bird feeders, showered and dressed, then began the long trek to the Gulf. She planned to stop in Birmingham for breakfast and again in Montgomery for lunch. That would leave the longest part of the drive, but she had nothing else to do.

When she got to the resort, she'd visit the poker tables. She liked to play high stakes. She'd do some of that then get to bed early.

She made the turn onto I-10 east at Mobile with the clock ticking toward five, traveled down the peninsula, and pulled into the IP Resort and Casino a few minutes after six. The place was as beautiful as the ads promised. She turned the car over to the valet, tipped him generously, and checked into one of the hotel's best suites. She had a great dinner, won $2,800 playing Texas Hold-em, and was in bed by ten.

At 5:00 p.m. the next day, refreshed after a massage and pedicure, she strolled into the lobby carrying the bright Vera Bradley bag that complemented her skirt.

A couple of minutes later, a stunningly handsome man walked up to her and asked if she was Rosalie.

"I am, and your name?"

"I'm Dino."

She smiled. "And do you have a last name?"

"Carbone, ma'am. I'm Angelo's youngest son."

He'd sent his own son? Her eyes widened and warmth spread through her chest. Her work really must have pleased the don. "My goodness. If you take after your father, he must be one good-looking man."

"Yes, ma'am, he is." A smile spread across his face, exposing perfect and very white teeth.

He was about six feet tall, weighed, she guessed, in the vicinity of 200 pounds. *My, he does fill out that tuxedo.*

They chatted as they walked to the casino. Rosalie asked direct questions and Dino's answers were even more direct.

"I work out every day, ma'am. As you can see, my body is hard and well-muscled."

In answer to another question, he told her, "No ma'am, you are my first for-hire work. My father thought it would be good for me to talk with you. He said you are a wonderful supplier of special services and that I should make sure I don't leave until I have learned all I can from you. He said you were older, but he sure didn't tell me how well-preserved you are. I hope I don't insult you when I tell you that you look more like fifty than whatever age you are. If you're younger than fifty, I guess I'll be leavin'."

Rosalie laughed heartily. "No, Dino, it's a wonderful compliment. I hope later to prove your estimate was accurate. I think you will find me, shall we say, interesting."

"Dad told me you would be fit, but I sure didn't expect this."

"Was that a compliment? I hope so."

Before Dino could respond, they arrived at Tien, the resort's Asian Pacific restaurant. Rosalie slid her hand through his arm. "I thought Asian would work well. It will be substantial, but light enough to leave us alive and active, at least I hope it will."

When the host greeted them, Rosalie asked for the table she had reserved. "Yes, ma'am, please follow me. I think you will approve of the accommodation."

The host drew open the drapes sheltering a small room that held one table set with fine china. *This will do very nicely.* He waited, eyebrow raised, until she nodded. Escorting her to her seat and then moving to assist Dino, the host bowed, thanked them for their business, and told them their waiter, Daichi, would soon be with them. "If you want to impress him, his name means great and noble in Japanese." He smiled, bowed, and was gone.

Daichi was exactly as his name indicated. The biggest Japanese man Rosalie had ever seen, he was gracious, formal, and efficient.

Although Daichi was amazing, it was Dino who occupied Rosalie's attention. As they ate, she became more and more amazed by the handsome young man across from her. He seemed well-versed in everything she brought up. She covered New Orleans architecture, Bible Belt habits, politics, food. At the same time, she carefully avoided talking about her business, and he was equally careful to avoid references to his family and its affairs.

Rosalie tried pushing him in that direction, discreetly. He seemed surprised by the questioning, but he didn't appear to be upset, at least she hoped he wasn't. He was attentive, seemed anxious to please, and gave her all the answers she hoped for. She tested him on many fronts and was happy to discover that he appeared to be a well-educated gentleman with charm and good humor. To say she was impressed would have been an understatement and she hoped this would not be the only night she spent with him.

The wonderful meal ended with Tozai Blossom of Peace Plum sake made from plums in the north of Japan. As they left the table, Dino grasped Rosalie's arm firmly, as if sensing that she might be slightly tipsy.

She patted his hand as they walked. "I hope you are ready for the night?"

"I've been ready since the moment I saw you in the lobby."

Good answer. More than sake brought warmth to her cheeks.

When they reached the elevator, which was empty, Dino asked her for the floor number, pushed the button, and leaned against her gently.

"Rosalie, Father told me he didn't know what to expect. He said he thought it would be good for my education. He may just have become master of the understatement."

"You should find this quite an easy night, actually."

He tilted his head. "Now you have me intrigued. Why will this night be so easy? Father said it would be good for me to learn about wise and skilled women. Beyond that he said little."

"All I desire, no, let me rephrase that, all I can handle, is stimulating conversation. I will ask you for no more than that, but I expect you to be on your toes and to satisfy me with your words as I once was satisfied physically."

"You mean erotic conversation?"

"Among other things. Much of it will be conversation, just plain conversation. Living alone, I long for it like a garden needs sunshine and water."

And so they talked and talked and talked. As the night wore on, his questions became more probing, more suggestive.

"Dino, are you taking me to places I'd rather not go?"

"No, dear Rosalie, I sense I am taking you to exactly the place you want to go. Protest all you will, but I don't believe you are being totally honest with me. Your words say this is all you need, but everything else tells me quite a different story. Clearly you are a learned woman, wisdom abounds. And yet, you are holding something back. There is something you want; why do you not say it?"

"You are an amazing young man, Dino. Never have I met someone of your age so well-versed in topics from A to Z, and so perceptive, too. Yes, you are right, there are things I want, but before I could disclose them you had to pass the test. You have been fabulous; your father has chosen well."

"And just what is it that I can do for you Rosalie?"

"I am a woman, Dino. You are a young man, virile, it would appear. I want that, too."

"I thought so, Rosalie—hoped so, in fact. What test was necessary? Can I not demonstrate my manliness? It's not something I can tell you about and have you believe, is it?"

"You are right, of course. But I am always very careful, my young friend. I do not wish my adventures to become public in any way. I have tested you throughout the night, trying to determine if you were as circumspect as you are intelligent. I am pleased to say, you have scored marvelously well."

"And so, Rosalie, it is true that I will score some more tonight, yes?"

"Ah, yes."

"I'm grateful, for I sense my education at your hands has just begun."

"You are correct. But be advised, if word of the rest of the night should creep out—if you talk—please understand that I can be quite lethal. That's a literal statement. I would hate to have to destroy a talent like you. But if you talk, Dino, I will do it in a heartbeat."

His face broke into a smile. "You have nothing to fear. I sense you know that. So what are we waiting for?"

As she took him by the hand, he looked down at her. "Dad told me you are known as the Black Widow of the Woods, and we don't even know where you live. Rosalie, you have my word that never will I say a word. I will have fond memories, though, of the woman who provided the most interesting night of my life."

"I'm glad, Dino. Now, how about we take a little nap? I know I could use one. We can talk a bit later? Maybe play a little, too."

With that, she let him lead her to the bedroom, where they laid down on the bed. Rosalie closed her eyes. Dino stroked her arm gently then leaned in close to whisper, "If I'm a student here, you've just taught me a profound lesson. And all I know for sure at this moment is that I hope there will be many more lessons to come."

Soon his breathing indicated he was asleep. She was tired, too, but sleep didn't come as quickly. She was captivated by this young man in a way she thought could never be. *What is it about him that draws me so strongly?* It was marvelous, but she had not yet figured it out.

Dino woke just after midnight. When his eyes met hers, his face flushed. "I'm sorry—I didn't mean to fall asleep."

"We all must rest, Dino. I have been having a marvelous time watching you. Your dreams must have been interesting because the expressions on your face were fascinating, to say the least." She snuggled closer. "I couldn't wait for you to wake up, but you were sleeping so soundly I didn't want to disturb you."

"That's nice, but to be honest, you are disturbing me. In a very pleasant way. Perhaps we could take this lesson just a bit further. Are you willing?"

"Of course I am."

He helped her undress then she helped him. She turned on the shower and what seemed to be a hundred heads sprayed water everywhere. They gently soaped each other. He admired her body, and said so. "It's like from the neck down you are a teenager." A look of horror crossed his face. "Oh, I'm sorry, I didn't mean …"

Rosalie waved a hand through the air. Clearly he was terrified at the thought of offending her. *Also good.* She liked to be treated well by the men she was with. "You were about to say the body doesn't match the face. I'm fine with that. It doesn't. I work out. My body remains wrinkle free, taut. My face, not so much. I have tried many treatments to take them away. All were a waste of money."

"But …" His voice was husky. "You are beautiful. The body and face may be different, but you are beautiful. You have a sophisticated look. The gray hair complements your appearance. It fits. But your body? Well, that is stunning. It is …"

"Surprising?" She finished the statement for him before leading him to the bed.

"Please," she whispered, as they settled into the downy softness, "do not think of me as anything but a woman desiring to give and receive pleasure. If you do that, this night will be wonderful."

For almost an hour, the mild stimulation continued, until Dino became impatient. "May I pick it up?"

His comment brought a gentle squeeze, and so he did. He was like a wild man, a young stallion. When she was limp and breathless, he stopped, looking at her appealingly. "Are you okay? Did I hurt you?"

"Oh, my, no. You reminded me of how it once was. You were wonderful. Simply wonderful. You are special."

He laughed.

She blinked. "Is that funny?"

He touched her cheek. "No, it's just that I made this trip against my will. It was a favor to Father, at least that's what I considered it. And I have had the time of my life."

Rosalie retrieved her watch from the bedside table.

"It's after one, but the hotel has room service. Will you stay the night?"

He smiled and nodded. "Rosalie, you are unbelievable. I'm not an amateur. I've had many women, none as old as you, but you make them all seem like kids. When Father told me you would teach me many things, I thought him foolish. I know now he's a wise man, just as people think."

His words sent warmth coursing through her chest. While they ate, Rosalie told him about her life, confessing all of it. He was amazed, but rather than horrifying him, her exploits increased his admiration.

"I am stunned. You are amazing—even more amazing than I thought before we had this talk. I wouldn't believe you if I hadn't just spent the most incredible few hours with you. I want to know all there is to know."

"You pretty much know it all now. We can talk again, assuming we spend more time together. Right now, we should spend more time in bed. This time we will sleep."

When they awoke, it was approaching checkout time. "Should we stay another day?"

His look nearly made her laugh. "Only if it's going to be a very quiet day. I've had all the exercise I can handle; anymore and every piece of me, every inch, will rebel. But every inch is also grateful."

"I feel like the student. You can be sure I will ask your father for more time. You do want me to go through Angelo?"

"Only for the next time. When I tell him about this weekend, I'm afraid he'll want to replace me. That won't happen. Mama would kill me—and him. But let me ask him if this must continue to be a business deal or whether we can grow as friends."

"Even lovers, perhaps?"

Her question made them both laugh.

On her way back to Hayden, Rosalie ached. *I hope these aches never stop.*

Two weeks later, though, they had disappeared and she was ready for more.

She wrote to Angelo, asking for more time with his son. Her fingers trembled as she wrote. She mailed it in Hayden, hoping for a quick answer.

Very quick.

13

Al was restless. His restlessness resulted in many calls to Charlie. But there was little to talk about. Winter in La Crosse was slow, ugly too, with cold, snow, wind—everything miserable you could imagine.

This winter had been as bad as any. Even the crooks were in hiding. That was not good for the mental makeup of either of the two lawmen trying to catch a serial killer.

By the time winter turned grudgingly into spring, Al and Charlie began meeting more frequently. Having seen less of each other in the past few weeks, the serial killings were the lead topic. Though they hoped for a break, there was none, and more and more they began to believe their quarry had successfully eluded them and was comfortable in a foreign land where they were unlikely to find her.

Al wasn't giving up. Each morning he searched two dozen newspapers. He found drownings, but none seemed to bear Genevieve's trademark.

Charlie chafed, too, Al knew, but he was less action prone than Al. Al suspected that, on some level, his friend was a little bit glad to have a quiet winter, being a newlywed and all.

For both, there was one good development: the annual drownings in La Crosse had stopped. Four years now had passed since the death of Rolf Evenson. No more major crimes had hit the docket. But Al and Charlie were frustrated by their failure to bring this one to closure.

Rick Olson and his wife, Peggy, remained friendly with Al and JoAnne and Charlie and Kelly, although the Rouses' inclusion created some awkwardness because five of the six people in the group knew what was going on between Al and Julie Sonoma. Al and Julie saw each other a few times a year, most recently a few weeks before.

Al and Brody Evenson, Julie's son, had become great friends. Brody now was a full-fledged football star at the University of Wisconsin, where he would be a sophomore running back in the fall. He was being promoted for all-American status and mentioned by a few Midwest sports writers as a Heisman Trophy candidate.

Al had become the father the boy had never known. He had attended all the games the previous season, always sitting with Julie, which gave him moments of great comfort, but also pronounced sorrow. The get-togethers were too brief. Because of the three-hour drive between La Crosse and Madison, Al, Rick and Peggy, Charlie and Kelly, always traveled to the games together. JoAnne was comfortable at home. She despised "the barbaric nature of football." But she always had a late dinner waiting for the tired travelers, and professed interest in their endless discussions of the game. Peggy and Kelly loved football too, but they humored JoAnne by avoiding the subject when the three of them were together.

On the rare occasion when Wisconsin played a night game, Julie and Al would share a room, but they were always careful to exercise caution when Brody was around. Even those times presented Al with trouble, because being with Julie reminded him more and more of her aunt, and he'd be distracted, wondering where Genevieve Wangen—her real name, not one of the many aliases she used—might be.

Although JoAnne gave no evidence of knowing about Al's affair, she had met Julie and liked her. And she was very supportive of the relationship Al and Brody had. The young man called almost every night, and Al really enjoyed providing him with advice.

He was the son Al had never had. He and JoAnne had three daughters, two in college and one married, and while they were close to their dad, Brody was a special deal.

In Madison for the annual spring game, the six friends and Brody enjoyed dinner at one of the city's best restaurants, Delaney's Steaks and Seafood. They liked the place because it afforded Brody a bit of anonymity. He now was a recognized celebrity in Madison and they tried to provide him with rare times when he could just sit back and relax without having everyone in the place come up to request an autograph.

Julie left the restaurant with Brody about nine then joined Al back at the Concourse Hotel after dropping Brody at his apartment. The Concourse was the most luxurious hotel in Madison, and while it was beyond Al's pay as a La Crosse Police Department detective, Rick somehow always managed to wrangle deals that made a room affordable.

When Julie walked in and dropped onto a chair, she looked drawn and tired.

Al was watching a game, but he saw the look on her face and immediately switched it off. "What's the matter?"

"Oh, nothing important, I guess." But as she sat there, tears began to trickle.

Al's stomach twisted. This situation was difficult for him, but it killed him to see how hard it was for her. Should he end things? For her sake? He knelt in front of the chair and rested his hands on her knees. "What is it?"

She drew in a shuddering breath and swiped at a tear on her cheek. "These weekends are so wonderful. But they end too soon and I have to return to Chicago and you go back to your life in La Crosse. I love you so much, and I miss you terribly when we're apart. And I feel guilty, too. JoAnne is a wonderful woman, and the thought that I love her husband makes me feel sick sometimes. What kind of a person does that to someone else?"

Al's throat tightened. "I know it's hard, but are you telling me you want to break off our relationship? Because I don't think I could live without you in my life, Julie. Not for a second."

She shook her head. "No, it's not that. It's just that I hate the thought of you going away tomorrow and the fact that I won't see much of you until fall."

"I'm sure we'll see each other in the summer. You know Peggy and Rick and Kelly and Charlie will have you up several times. And Rick and Charlie and I will be making our annual golf swing, too. That will give us a whole weekend."

"I suppose, but in a year Brody is going to be a junior. Soon we won't have these excuses to meet."

He squeezed her knee. "Let's not make it worse than it is. Charlie, Rick, and I have had season tickets for years and I suspect we are going to continue to have them. If you can drive up to the games, we'll still see each other then. And we can figure out more ways to be together, too. I promise."

"It just seems so hopeless. I already lost one lover to death, and now a second is not available. The sneaking around is awful, and it's even worse because I love JoAnne."

Al reached for her hands. "How about we try to look on the bright side? Why don't we be grateful for each moment we are together? The strangest of circumstances brought us together, and I am so very thankful to have met you. I love you with all my heart. I can't stand to see you sad."

"I know, but . . ." She squeezed his hands and attempted a smile. "Why does everything have to be so difficult?"

Al returned her smile. "Difficult? You're a beautiful woman, with a good and talented son, a beautiful house, a terrific job, and a mostly satisfying life. What's so bad about that?"

"What's bad about it is that I never see you."

"Never isn't true. We see each other almost once a month. And if you wanted to move to La Crosse, you know Rick would have a job for you in a heartbeat."

"You always look at things so objectively. But when we're together, I'm a nervous wreck at the thought of you going away the next day. It's hard to enjoy myself when I know in a few hours you'll be gone again."

"Why don't we see if I can make you forget tomorrow for a few hours?" He kissed her gently and held her tightly, rubbing her back.

She sighed. "If you keep rubbing my back like that, I just might. Maybe you think my complaining is silly. But I am so conflicted. I love you with all my heart. But I love JoAnne, too. This is very hard for me."

Al tugged her to her feet and led her to the bed. He settled down beside her and she moved gently into his arms. Neither seemed interested in letting the moment go.

After they had made love and Julie dozed, Al again began to think about the whereabouts of Julie's aunt, Genevieve.

"Do you have any idea where she might be? Any thought at all about where she might go?"

His comment roused her. She rubbed her eyes and moved to where she could look him in the eyes. "None. I know she is my aunt. When she vanished, I didn't even know that. She made a wonderful gift to us of her house. Brody and I enjoy the place, but it's really too big for one person."

"But you have the occupants of the garage apartment."

"I do, but it's not the same as having someone to come home to every night."

Al knew that and he worried about her whenever they were apart, but he also knew that some of the worry for both of them wouldn't end until he either captured her aunt or the woman was dead. Until that happened, he vowed to himself to avoid the topic best he could.

It was almost as if she had read his mind. "Can this kind of relationship exist, Al? Won't you capture her one day and then weary of me and just walk away?"

Al pulled her closer. "I could never walk away from you, Julie. You and Brody are family to me now. I would never give that up." He shifted to face her, sliding a finger under her chin and tilting her head until she was looking at him. "You might, though. I know you're lonely when I'm not around, and you're a beautiful woman. Maybe you'll meet someone and be gone."

"That's hard to imagine, but I suppose it could happen. Brody needs a father figure in his life. You work so hard to be that, but it isn't the same as having someone here all the time. He's a bright young man."

"That he is. I would love to have him as a son. But for now …"

He left the statement hanging there. A heaviness settled in his chest and he grew silent. Julie snuggled closer and he rested his chin on her head, overwhelmed by the despair an affair created for people who were otherwise essentially decent. Neither fell asleep until dawn's light began to filter into the room. Then they slept, but only for a couple of hours before it was time to rise and meet the others for breakfast. Before they knew it, their brief time together was finished. There was little prospect of seeing each other for at least a couple of months. Al felt as terrible about the distance and the absence as Julie did, but there seemed to be no way around it.

14

Late winter blues were present in Alabama, too, and it wasn't because of the weather. Spring had sprinted into the area; flowers were abloom in the forests near Hayden and temperatures were climbing. Rosalie continued her deadly craft, safe from any challenges. Business had been good. The trust fund set aside for her niece and great-nephew grew steadily.

In spite of the weather and her booming business, the old woman wasn't happy. That morning she sat at her kitchen table and listened to and watched the birds. She was as restless as the fluttering creatures outside her window were. Her thoughts centered on Dino Carbone. He was the best lover she'd had since her husband died. His imagination outdid hers. *How long can I keep up with him? Keep him interested?* She worried about that incessantly. She had come to enjoy their dalliances that occurred regularly now. But even that wasn't enough to satisfy her. She hesitated to appeal for more, even though he might agree, because she knew they were tempting fate and more frequent get-togethers would expand the risk.

But, my oh my, he seems devoted to me. Could it be real? She hoped so, but she doubted it.

As the sun rose, she realized she had left herself in a state of unsatisfied arousal. That happened every time she thought about Dino, which was happening more and more often.

"I need to see him. I need to see him now."

Sitting down in front of her laptop, she sent an email to the address he had assured her only he knew about. Seconds later she had a response: "Ready as you are!"

The words were enough. Soon she was packed and on her way to the Palace Casino Resort in Biloxi and another day or two with Dino.

When she arrived at the Palace, her suite was ready, one of the most luxurious in the house and befitting of the woman who spent thousands on each of her visits. Interestingly enough, she never visited the casino here. The manager knew that, had encouraged her several times to give it a try, but she'd only laughed and told him not to worry about it, that she would spend enough on her stay to make up for any losses he might have if she didn't take her money to the casino.

Settled in the suite, she texted Dino the number.

Moments later he was in the room, she was on her feet, and he had wrapped her in his arms. His kiss reverberated throughout her body. She was ready for more, but her young beau let her go. He appeared nervous, anxiously pacing the room. "Not yet—not yet. We need to talk first."

Her chest tightened. *What is it?* What could have happened?

"Rosalie, my dad is in conflict with the Atlanta family. The Cabreras believe Dad had something to do with the Gambinos, and that has resulted in us falling out with the Cabreras. Dad thinks it's a serious threat—not just to our organization, but to him personally."

"What's it all about?"

"Apparently the Gambinos' main consigliere was killed in New Jersey. Poison, we're told. Whatever was used, it imitated the concoctions you make for us. Don Al Gambino believes Dad provided the drug and the method. Thus, it isn't just a Gambino-Cabrera battle. We're involved by presumed association—and you're involved, too."

Rosalie sat down on the bed, stunned. "It's not true, is it? The association to you and me, I mean."

"Not to our knowledge. But a few months back, Dad was entertaining one of the Cabreras. He told him about the poison you make, showed him a vial, and said he could get some for them if it was needed. Before you ask, they weren't interested in ordering anything at the time. He thinks that when the guy left, though, there may have been a vial missing, but he wasn't positive of the inventory. Then he forgot about it until this broke."

Damn. It was bad enough to have a couple of cops chasing her, but having a Mafia family upset with her was much worse. If they wanted to find her, they could. She knew that. They could also kidnap Dino, torture him, and find out how to catch up to her. This was not funny.

"Dino, this isn't a very good situation."

"No, it isn't. That's why Dad wanted me to alert you."

She bit down on her thumbnail. "I admit I didn't see this coming; it's a real challenge. I don't want to lose you, but keeping you might be a problem. What if you were tortured?"

His extended silence was not comforting.

"I'm going to have to think about this."

"I agree, but we're here. Seems silly to waste the opportunity." He unknotted his tie, tossed it onto the sofa, and held out his hand.

Rosalie lifted her dress over her head then took his hand. He led her into the bedroom. Their union was not satisfying—she had too much on her mind, and clearly he did too—and soon they gave it up to talk about the situation, the dilemma it presented them, and how to get out of it.

"Dino, you don't know where I live. Neither does your dad. All he knows is that I am a series of post office box numbers in various places around the country. Maybe we should just drop out."

He stared at her for a long time without blinking. "Rosalie, I'm number two in my family. A year or two and I'll be Don. Are you asking me to give that up to run off with you?"

"I am."

"That's crazy. As Don, I'd be a made man."

"If you drop out with me, we'd have it made, Dino. I'm filthy rich, with more money than we could ever spend. If we want to live abroad, we can do it. Buy a yacht and sail the world? Sure. You name it, I can afford it."

"But Rosalie, I'd be in your debt. I'd be a kept man."

"Have I ever treated you like one?"

"No, but how could I help but feel that way if I headed out with you?"

The doorbell rang. Rosalie climbed off the bed and donned a robe. Dino headed for the bathroom. Their lunch had arrived. Rosalie signed the check.

She opened the wine and called Dino. They took some time to enjoy lunch and talk. After attacking and demolishing dessert, it was time to get serious.

She told him about growing up, finding out she was not living with her birth parents, marrying and moving from eastern to western Wisconsin. She told him about Henry. And she shared with him how she'd acquired her ability to make death-dealing potions.

He responded by opening up to her completely. It was interesting to her that when he turned fourteen, his father sent him to a number of women in New Orleans active in the sex trade operated by his family. He said they told him he had earned a Ph.D. in the sexual arts. He reached across the table and ran a finger down her bare arm. "Do you think that's true?"

"Absolutely. You are the most accomplished, the most incredible, the most fantastic lover I have known."

"And you are extraordinary, the best. That's why I'm thinking of accepting your offer."

She blinked and leaned back in her chair. "Really?"

"Yes. I just have to figure out how to make it right with my father. I have to talk to him. Do you understand?"

"I do, and it's okay because I know this is a huge, life-changing decision. You shouldn't make it lightly. If you decide to come with me, I'll want you with me forever."

Another day and their time together was over. But she was happier as she headed back to Hayden. She made plans for Dino's presence in her life. Should she buy another property for them? Something bigger than her cabin? Perhaps as near as 200 miles away—in Atlanta or Augusta? St. Petersburg, maybe? As she thought, she quickly ruled out Atlanta due to the trouble with the Cabreras. Augusta might be nice. Big enough and remote enough to offer a hiding place. She discarded St. Petersburg. Too many tourists, way too many nosy tourists. *Augusta. That's the place.* A nice colonial hidden in the pines. She couldn't wait to get home, go online, and see what she could find.

She arrived too late and too tired to boot up the computer.

Dino awoke, showered, shaved, and contemplated visiting with his father to discuss his plan to join Rosalie somewhere unknown. Just how would Dad respond to that?

An hour later, he entered the back door of his parents' house and found his mother visiting with the cook. He kissed her on both cheeks then did the same to Maria, the cook with whom he had grown up.

His mother broke the welcome. "Your dad's in the den. He's alone and stewing about the trouble in Atlanta. He hasn't slept for two nights. Be gentle."

Dino backed out of the kitchen, walked through the dining room and the expansive marble-floored foyer, and knocked at his dad's office door.

"Come." The closed door muffled the message.

When he walked in, his father stood up, smiling, and came around the desk to embrace him.

"Dino, Dino. What a joy to see you on a bleak day."

Dino listened as his father talked about his problem with the Atlanta family, told his son his plan, then sat back and rubbed the furrows on his forehead. "Dino, we have to find a place to hide you. If the Cabreras want revenge, you and your mother are the two losses I couldn't endure."

Dino looked at his father and smiled. "Have I got a solution for you."

Over the next hour, he and his father talked and talked. Dino told him about his feelings for Rosalie, and that she had invited him to drop out and live with her.

As they talked, his father appeared to listen carefully. When he had heard enough, he spoke. "My son, I think you have fallen in love with this woman's talents more than you have with her. But no matter, this could be the answer to my prayer. You know how worried I am about your safety. You are the future of the Carbone family—the heart and soul of our long-term survival. And you are also a man about town. Always in view, always present. That, too, is who you are. Therein is the worry. If there was a war between families, each side would seek a bargaining chip. Nothing would be more valuable to the Cabreras than kidnapping a member of our family. You are too visible. You would be an easy target—a big one, too. You might as well have a bulls eye painted on your back."

Dino nodded. The same thought had crossed his mind. "So maybe it is a good idea for me to go away for a while?"

"Normally I would object, but it just might be a way to hide you until the heat eases. There may also be another benefit."

Dino cocked his head. "What is that?"

"Perhaps you could learn this woman's secrets. If you want to sleep with someone three times your age, so be it. But don't waste too much time on lust. Have your fun, but put the majority of the time to good use. Learn something about her killing arts. That would be a good use of time."

He turned back to his son, looked him in the eye, and said, "I think your dropping out for a while is a good idea. I worry about you and your playboy habits. Spending some time with the Black Widow may do you good. Maybe you can learn something valuable, more valuable than just feelings of love."

Dino nodded. "Father, I know you think I'm a playboy and you're concerned about me learning the things I need to know to lead the family. But I watch you carefully; I listen. I do learn, Father. I do."

"Yes, you learn, Dino, but the minute there's a skirt around and you pick up the scent, you're gone. Your compass is in your trousers and you follow it carefully. Family life is about hard work, knowledge, developing a sixth sense about the things around you. You are a good son, Dino, but you need to become more serious. Watch your older brother, Angelo Jr. He thinks he's ready to replace me, but his deformity makes that impossible. People will not follow a cripple. He is a great lieutenant, but he will never be the head. So the family will be yours to lead, but you have much to learn. Much."

His father swiveled his chair to look out the window of bullet-proof glass behind him, his back to Dino. Finally he spoke again. "So go, my son. Live with this old woman. Enjoy her skills. But learn from her. You must stay in touch with me, but you must never disclose your whereabouts. It is about trustworthiness, and most of all you must learn that. She will teach you that and many other things. Be alert, learn all there is to learn. When it is time to return here, I will let you know. I will have a phone for you before you leave. We will stay in touch via text, nothing more. And nothing we write can identify us as a member of the family. Do you understand, Dino?"

Dino nodded solemnly. He wanted to argue with his father on several points, but that would be seen as disrespectful, and no don could accept disrespect.

As he began to back from the room, his father asked, "When will you go?"

"When I hear from Rosalie and she is ready for me."

"You let me know."

Before Dino could respond, his father had already swiveled around again to stare out the window.

Rosalie got up early. She'd been too tired to power up her laptop the night before, when she got home from being with Dino. This morning she was online before five, anxious to find a secluded but comfortable hideaway in rural Georgia. She found one she really liked for $1.7 million in west Augusta. *But is it secluded enough?*

Frustrated, she kept looking. Suddenly she brought her palm down onto the desk with a loud smack. She'd found it. A home in west Augusta that seemed perfect. An old colonial, apparently meticulously restored, offered everything she wanted. Seven acres. A home buried in the trees. Formal gardens near the house that would satisfy her gardening instinct. There was a small bungalow on the property, a guest residence, that would make an ideal lab. The main house was wonderfully done. Four bedrooms, four baths, three half baths, and lavish interior decorating. It was priced at $1.5 million.

Her forehead wrinkled. Why was it that low? Other homes in the area with seemingly fewer attributes were priced higher.

She'd get answers to her questions later, including what sort of price point would be necessary to purchase the house with the furnishings in place.

The big question at least partially answered, she headed out to the lab buried into the hillside behind the house and busied herself with work. Rosalie worked for a couple of hours on orders for families in California and Albuquerque. Those completed, she slipped the bottles into small boxes and wrapped them in plain brown paper. Addressed as specified, she applied a phony return address label. She would later repackage them and send them to an address in Brooklyn from which they would be re-mailed.

She exited the lab and drove from the property, stopping an hour later at the wayside rest on the way to Birmingham to dial the Augusta realtor. Sally Demarais was a pleasant-sounding woman of, Rosalie presumed, middle age. Rosalie introduced herself as Carolyn Rawlins and soon had the information she wanted.

"The home is not occupied and is available now," the realtor said. "It is the vacation property of a Boston family. The owners haven't been in Georgia for more than a year."

"Will they sell the home furnished?" asked Rosalie.

"They might prefer that. I'm guessing they might want as much as $200,000 more, but in reality you'd be doing them a favor."

"Tell you what. Offer $1.5 million cash for the property as it is. Tell them I want a quick closing."

"Of course. Once we have a deal, I can get everything set right away. Will you be in the area anytime soon? If so, we can work quickly."

"I can be there with a couple of days' notice."

"Then let me see what I can do. Do you have a number where I can reach you?"

Rosalie gave her the number of a burner phone, after which Sally said she'd call when she had information.

"I hope it can be fast. I'm anxious to get this done."

Sally assured her she would work quickly and try to get back to her before the end of the day. The conversation concluded, Rosalie started the car and pulled back out onto the highway.

At ten minutes before noon, the phone rang.

"I have good news," Sally told her. "At $1.6 million you can own it as is."

"I'll take it. This is great work, Sally."

"I try to meet my customers' expectations. I think we can get this done quickly. Will you be ready to close within a week?"

"Absolutely. The sooner the better."

"Let's see, this is Friday. How about next Thursday? Could you be in Augusta?"

"Yes, no problem."

"Good, then all I need is a check for at least $200,000 to bind the deal."

"I'll see that it is wired to you today. A cashier's check will work, right?"

"Perfect."

"You'll have it before five."

Rosalie drove into Birmingham and stopped at the bank to arrange for the wire transfer. Her business concluded swiftly, she drove home.

She made a sandwich, accompanied by the singing of birds, and put the kettle on the stove for tea. A few minutes later, its whistle pleasantly interrupted the silence. As she poured water into the waiting cup, the phone she used for communication with Dino rang.

"How soon will you be ready for me? I talked with Dad and he thinks it's a great idea for me to move in with you for a time. The situation with the Cabreras has heated up and he's worried about me."

"My goodness, Dino, I didn't expect to hear from you this soon."

"Are you disappointed? Have you changed your mind?"

"Of course not, I just didn't expect to hear from you already. But it's great news. I shall have a new house for us in less than a week. How does that sound?"

"Do I really have to wait that long?" He was teasing her now. She recognized the playfulness in his voice.

"Hmmm, well, it's five after two. Can you be ready by five?"

She had called his bluff and silence settled in. "Well, five might be a bit of a stretch. How about tomorrow?"

She laughed and he joined in. "Dino, I'd love it, but perhaps I will need a couple more days. Maybe we should get together in Biloxi next weekend to make the final plans."

"Perfect. That should give me the time I need … and time to recover, too."

They visited for another couple of minutes, after which she told him she loved him and was anxious to be with him.

"I'll bet I'm more anxious than you."

She was stunned and delighted. The week, she guessed, wouldn't pass fast enough.

15

Four weeks later, Carolyn Rawlins, AKA Rosalie Burton, AKA Genevieve Wangen, owned a home that was being remodeled to her specifications and she was ready to make the transition with Dino.

The closing had proceeded quickly. She got her first look at the property a week later. Sally had offered to be present when she arrived, but Carolyn said no, that for reasons she couldn't disclose she needed to maintain anonymity. Sally, clearly a consummate professional, didn't press her for details, simply told her where the keys would be. Carolyn drove past the entrance to the property twice before finding it on the third attempt. *That's terrific; just how I want it.*

The house was perfect. The furniture needed to be uncovered and the entire place cleaned, but those were simple tasks she could hire someone to do. It was larger than she and Dino needed, but perhaps that was good, too, because there was plenty of space to allow either of them to "get away from it all"—including away from each other.

She loved the gardens, although they needed attention, and the bungalow was perfect. It would make an ideal lab. Could she convince the workers who had built the one at the cabin to install this one, too? She'd try, because they were perfect: taciturn mountaineers with great carpentry skills and no interest in talking.

Rosalie worked around the new house and the grounds. She found that the new place had an abundance of wild birds that tweeted and chirped at her while she weeded. Squirrels scampered all over the property, and she was startled when a fat-bodied, furry animal waddled out of the one large overgrown flower bed in the backyard. *What is that?* She resolved to see if she could find it on Google later.

As she worked, she couldn't believe how perfect it was for their needs. They would be hiding right under the nose of the Cabrera Family, but they would be invisible. Perhaps they could find a reliable, tight-lipped person to help with housework, grocery shopping, and other odds and ends.

When the sun tipped over the bungalow roof and began to slide toward the horizon, Rosalie went into the house and washed the dirt off her hands. She loved the feel and smell of the place, both inside and out. The ground was rich and reddish. The kitchen smelled of spices that overrode the mustiness, the remnants of which would be swiftly dispatched by opening a few windows.

When she drove away from the property, an old man trimming a hedge down the road from her place startled her by waving. *Southern hospitality.* She forced herself to relax and contemplate her new life. Who should she be here? Carolyn? She shook her head. Only the real estate agent knew her by that name, and she wouldn't be dealing with Sally again for the foreseeable future. Besides, she now had so many identities that keeping them straight was starting to get problematic. *I'll go back to Rosalie.*

Home and spent, she popped a frozen dinner into the oven and, while waiting for it to heat, booted up her computer and told Dino about the new property through his "hidden" email address. There was much to be done, she told him, and she planned on using the people who had done work for her in the past. He quickly approved, saying he didn't want anyone known to his family to discover his whereabouts. She replied that she hoped to have an estimated move-in date for him later in the week.

The next morning, she drove over the mountain to the home of the lead worker for the crew that had constructed her previous lab. He was in his workshop, finishing a beautiful piece of furniture. The aroma of sawdust mingled pleasantly with the smell of varnish. She brushed off a sawhorse then leaned against it while watching him work. She'd come in so quietly, and he was so absorbed in what he was doing, he didn't appear to have noticed she was there.

"That's a beautiful piece. Is the wood cherry?"

Adam Nottleman jumped, then straightened and pushed the goggles covering his eyes up to his forehead. She laughed at the generous measure of wood dust that covered his hands and arms.

"Rosalie!" He walked toward her, hand outstretched. "How are you? I haven't seen you for a coon's age."

As he spoke, the gap caused by a missing front tooth became prominent. He caught her looking. "Only wear the damn partial when I have to. It bothers me. I think the missing tooth helps business around here, though. Makes me look like everyone else."

Rosalie let go of his hand and discreetly brushed the wood dust from hers as she told him about her project. "It's a day's drive from here, Adam. Not sure if that interests you or not."

"Sure does; work's hard to come by these days. I'm worried about keeping my crew busy. You got work for them, too?"

"Absolutely. I need you to build me another lab. This one will go in an existing building, but it needs to be hidden in such a way that no one knows it's there. I'll need a couple of other things built, too."

"Like what?"

"A passageway from the house to lab, for one thing. A tunnel, preferably."

"How soon?"

"Soon as you can get at it."

"How's next week? Nothing else going on around here."

Rosalie nodded. "Next week is perfect." She gave him directions to the place. "I'll get a complete list of the projects ready this weekend. I could drive it over Monday, if that works for you."

"No need. Gotta go that way Monday. I can stop in the afternoon."

They discussed price and where to get supplies, and soon the deal was struck. Adam tugged the goggles back into place and prepared to return to his sanding.

Rosalie watched him work for a while, marveling at his skill. Realizing she was beginning to look like him, she arose, brushed herself off, waved, and left the shop. He didn't appear to see her go.

Home again, she checked the bird feeders, then the alarm and cameras, and found everything to be normal. She had loved the solitude of the forest surrounding her last property. *Hopefully this place will be the same kind of secluded, quiet home.*

Settling herself in front of the computer, Rosalie began the list she had promised Nottleman. She had taken plenty of pictures and she included them all. It took her more than three hours. By that time, the sun was tumbling down the back side of the mountain and her stomach was grumbling.

Satisfied, she sat quietly in the rocking chair, Julie at her feet, and thought about the future. Could she and Dino find long-term happiness? She sighed. If she was being completely honest with herself, a long-term arrangement was unlikely. He was young and handsome. She was old and worn. That considered, she would work hard to bind him to her as long as she could, because he was just too good to let go.

16

Nine weeks later, nerves gripped her. They were ready to move in. She had seen the house for the fourth time a week earlier; the remodeling had been done exactly as she'd ordered. Nottleman was incredible. He had purchased the supplies far from the house at a substantial savings.

After seeing everything, she just had to call Dino. He answered on the first ring, and even before he had a chance to say a word, she was running on about the house.

He laughed. "Hold on, just hold it, okay?" Once she had slowed down, he told her, "Rosalie, it is you I want to be with, not a house. Yes, yes, the house will be great, awesome, I'm sure. And I am happy if you are happy."

"I am. The house inside and out is beautiful, and the gardens are wonderful, too. Dino, are you listening to me?"

"I'm trying, Rosalie, but it's like attempting to drink from a fire hose. You want to tell me everything at once. Slow down. I have things to tell you, too. My world is not as serene and inviting as yours."

The news he shared was sobering. There now was real war between the Cabrera and Carbone families. Two members of the Carbone insider circle had been kidnapped, tortured, killed, and then delivered to Angelo's property, where they had been found propped up in chairs on the front porch. "It's a warning about how close the Cabreras can get without detection."

His voice was sober, and the words doused the excitement she'd been feeling over the house as effectively as the fire hose he'd mentioned earlier would douse a flame. "Does your father still think you should come stay with me?"

"More so than ever. With the heat intensifying, Dad is preparing his response, but before acting he wants me safely hidden. The only thing we have had trouble agreeing on is whether or not my bodyguards should come too. Dad says yes, I vote no. I told him, 'Father, if you send Sal and Sonny, it increases the chances that what we want to avoid could be the thing we allow to happen.' We've been discussing it for two weeks now. I'm not sure we would have ever reached a settlement if Mother hadn't come into his office while we were talking yesterday."

Rosalie could picture her, a tall, strong, dark-haired Italian woman. She smiled.

"Dad stood there, massaging his chin, and said, 'Dino, you are young and impetuous, and like all young people, you think you are invincible. I am growing old, my eyesight dim. You and your brothers and sister are the world for your mother and me. If anything happened to one of you, your mother would die; you know that.'"

Rosalie's chest tightened. She had no children of her own, but if anything happened to Julie or Brody, her reason for living would disappear with them.

Dino exhaled. "I do know that, but still I insisted that the chances of my survival would be better if he allowed me to disappear alone. Then my mother came in. Planting both hands on her hips, she said, 'Angelo, Angelo, it is well past your bedtime, and here you are still arguing and plotting.' As always, her scolding was mild but pointed. My mother may have aged considerably in the past few years, but she is still a beautiful and formidable woman. When she sets her jaw, it's like nothing you have ever seen."

Rosalie chuckled. "As impenetrable a fortress as my old lab set in the mountains, I'm sure."

"Exactly. And while my father mounted a great argument, he was no match for Mama. She simply asked him what we were arguing about, and when Dad told her, she said, I agree with Dino. In this day, finding someone is not so hard. Finding three people is easier yet. In this case, Dino is right. And she stamped her foot to emphasize what she had said." He chuckled. "That foot stomp takes care of it every time, Rosalie."

She laughed. "I'll have to keep that move in mind when we are arguing and I've had enough."

"But I could never argue with you, my love. Just as my father never argues with his Rosalyn. She is his most trusted advisor and he learned long ago that her judgment is impeccable. She seems content to stay far in the background, away from family affairs, but when there is trouble, she somehow knows everything." Dino voice warmed, displaying an obvious affection and respect for his mother. "It ended when Mama got up to leave and said, 'So it is settled then?' And if that weren't enough, she followed that up with *the stare*. After that, all we could do was nod." Dino said. "Mama, appearing very pleased with herself, turned to go. When she reached the door, she reminded Papa it was time for him to be in bed. Papa got up, told me we'd talk the next morning, and did as Mama said."

Rosalie chuckled, picturing the scene. Although she'd never met Dino's mother, she liked her already.

"The next morning we got everything taken care of," Dino said. "So soon I shall be on my way. Alone."

Nine days later, on a Friday, Dino left New Orleans for one of his regular trips to Biloxi. This time he and Rosalie would be staying at the Beau Rivage Resort & Casino. They had not stayed there often because it was one of the independent resorts. That meant none of the "families" in the South controlled it. More typically, they stayed at one of the Carbone family operations because of the cost, the amenities, and the protection.

It was late that afternoon when the two met in the Governor's Suite. They were excited. This was the day they would vanish. All was ready, planned to the most finite of details.

Around midnight, Dino went to the casino for poker. Rosalie made her way to the parking garage and moved luggage from their car into an escape car, a nondescript older-model Ford. By the time she had finished, Dino had left the table and casually strolled to the back of the casino, then down the stairs to the parking garage.

Together they drove north on I-110, then up to I-10. There they switched cars for something newer and faster before driving east into Florida. As they neared the Osceola Forest in Florida, the sun now up,

Dino tensed, checked the mirrors then swiveled to look. A black Chrysler town car swung in behind them and followed them all the way from Lake City into Jacksonville. When they took I-95 north, however, the Chrysler disappeared and they saw nothing suspicious in their rearview mirror for the next hundred miles. Nonetheless, it took a long time for Dino to relax and settle back in the driver's seat.

By the time they reached St. Mary's near the Florida-Georgia border, he could barely keep his eyes open. The excitement had worn off hours ago and the tension caused by their flight and the heightened vigilance had evaporated into fatigue. Dino pulled off the freeway and drove toward the ocean and to the Spencer House Inn.

They went straight to bed and fell asleep almost immediately. They didn't arise for fourteen hours, and when they did it was to the aroma of tantalizing baked goods.

After breakfast, they headed north. Dino chose Highway 25 for the last two hours of the drive. They saw nothing to make them suspicious and arrived in Augusta about four.

When they entered the city, Rosalie touched his elbow. "Why don't we stop for groceries before going to the house?"

Dino nodded and a few minutes later turned into a Food Lion parking lot. They purchased staples and enough food to allow them to eat at home for a few days.

Dino was like a hunter in Cabela's. He raced through the main house and pronounced it perfect. Then he walked quickly to the bungalow and marveled at what he found. The new laboratory sparkled with stainless steel fittings and cupboards. Inside he found row upon row of pullout shelves filled with carefully labeled bottles placed in alphabetical order. Even the smell was comforting, the odor of newly installed stainless steel mixing with a medicinal undertone.

He walked the grounds carefully and smiled approval at the cameras hidden at critically spaced intervals around the perimeter and in the interior as well. Rosalie had taken great and expensive steps to ensure that they would be safe.

There was only one problem. As far as he knew, there was just the single entrance and therefore only one way to leave the property. They would have to think about possible solutions to that situation before it was too late.

Later, after he and Rosalie had unloaded the car, he helped her put the groceries away. When they'd finished, they carried their suitcases upstairs. Their outerwear they hung carefully in their respective closets. Selecting which closet each would have became a bit of a jousting match, with Rosalie having to concede great favors to get the one she wanted. The folding clothes went into bureaus, one for each. Inspection of the bathrooms revealed fully stocked towel closets.

"We have everything!" Dino stuck out his chest and folded his arms. "I couldn't have done a better job of preparing the place myself."

Rosalie grinned, obviously happy that he approved. "I suggest we open a nice bottle of wine, have a plate of hors d'oeuvres, and just relax."

"But Rosalie, we need to celebrate the fact that we are together now. I want to make love to you, christen our new home. Would you deny me this?"

"No, Dino, but your youth brings an impetuousness that causes some of the things you experience to pass too quickly. To really enjoy love, one has to be deliberate, patient. Then when it happens it is so much better."

"If we must, then yes, let's have wine and talk—but I will only be patient for so long."

"Perhaps this will help." She massaged his shoulders, first gently, then harder and harder still until his eyelids drooped and he was almost purring.

And later, when she led him to bed, well …

The night was one that neither Dino nor Rosalie would forget. They celebrated the start of their new life together well into the wee hours of the morning. When Rosalie finally fell asleep, Dino lay on his side, watching her, for a long time. This move was the best choice for him. Rosalie was a great teacher, an extraordinary woman. He would do as his father suggested, and use this time to glean knowledge from her—in all aspects of life.

They settled into a routine. Amazing as it was, Dino never tired of the time with his older companion. Her imagination was incredible, constantly thrilling him. And, as his father had hoped, he was learning her business.

He was completely happy with Rosalie. He worked hard at being a student who learned quickly and forgot nothing, to please her. And he doted on her. When they went out, he kept his focus on her entirely, not once letting his eyes stray to any of the beautiful women who may or may not have walked by them.

Over the next days and weeks, Rosalie taught him the art of compounding and the use of various chemicals to achieve a desired result. Over time he grew proficient, to the point that she now allowed him to fill orders under her supervision. "You have a knack for the subtleties of this work," she commented, peering over his shoulder as he mixed.

"I've had the best teacher." He stopped what he was doing long enough to kiss her on the cheek. When he turned back, he reached for a bottle. "I did wonder, though, about substituting this for Propofol in this potion. I think that might work even better, quicker. What do you think?"

She squeezed his shoulder. "I think the day I met you was a fortunate day for me indeed."

Rosalie seemed as happy as he was with the relationship, but as weeks turned into months and as spring turned to summer and then summer to fall, a bit more freedom was desired, not individual freedom, but freedom from the hideout that now seemed more and more like a prison.

On one windy October day, as leaves pelted the windows, Rosalie took Dino by the hand, led him to the sofa, and sat with him. "Dino, I just love our life, but don't you ever long for different company? I mean, we have only each other to talk to. Do you not miss other people?"

He reached for her hand, massaging one gently as he looked into her eyes. "You have again read my mind. Most moments are fine, but once in a while I wish there were others we could talk to. So the answer is yes. But what do we do about it?"

"Because of who I am and what I have done, I have very few friends. And only one that I can really talk to. There is a woman in Atlanta, Amber Johansen. She runs a business there. We have done favors for each other, and I would love to see her."

"Can we? I mean, can we take the risk? If she is a friend of yours, surely I will like her, so if you think it's okay, let's contact her and arrange a meeting."

"Oh, Dino, thank you. Thank you. That would be wonderful. And, yes, I believe this is a risk we can afford to take."

The day proceeded lightheartedly. Dino looked forward to the outing that would break the bonds of their home in the woods, and Rosalie hummed as she went about her work, clearly happier now that they'd made plans to go out for an evening.

Later, as he read a book by the fire, she clapped her hands and looked up from her laptop to meet his eyes. Dino closed the book, holding his page with one finger. "Can she meet us?"

"Yes. She says she be happy to get together; she's anxious to meet the man who, as she put it, finally tied me down." Her cheeks tinged pink. "We're to meet her at what she claims is the best steakhouse in Augusta a week from Wednesday."

"Excellent. Did you tell her she would need to be very careful not to be followed?"

"Of course. She assured me she would stay alert to any threat of detection. In her line of work, she has learned how to be completely discreet, and I trust her completely."

"And what line of work is that?"

Rosalie offered him a mischievous smile. "I think I'll let you ask her that yourself."

Risking the loss of his place, Dino set down his book and went to try every method at his disposal to persuade her to talk.

When they met, Dino liked Amber immediately and soon the three were visiting as if they had been friends for years.

The food was delicious, but he barely noticed as the three talked and talked.

Dino had not been successful in his attempts to get Rosalie to share personal information about her friend, so he wrapped his fingers around his snifter of brandy and sat back in his seat. "So Amber, Rosalie has told me very little about you. What business is it that you are in?"

Their visitor laughed, glanced at Rosalie, and then told him, "I am in the business of bringing men and women together for pleasure."

Ah. No wonder Rosalie had been coy. He shot her a look but she didn't meet his gaze. "Now it makes sense that you are friends. You have kept Rosalie in young men. Is this so?"

"Well, it was. But I haven't heard from her in months. Now I know why. I must say, I also understand."

Dino's cheeks warmed. Amber chuckled. "She has always had terrific taste in men, and you, Mr. Carbone, are no exception. Now I know why my business has slumped."

The thought of Rosalie with other men bothered him a little, but Dino brushed the feeling aside. He didn't own her. It wasn't his business what she had done in the past, particularly before they had met. Letting another sip of the brandy chase away the slight coldness, he relaxed his shoulders. When Rosalie finally met his eyes, he was able to offer her a genuine smile.

Far too soon it was time to leave. Rosalie and Dino were tired and a bit tipsy. He was glad they didn't have to drive two hours to Atlanta. Although he watched carefully as Amber left the parking lot, he saw nothing that would suggest that she had been followed.

The next two weeks passed quickly. Except for two trips to mail drug orders to customers, they stayed home. Dino could see that Rosalie was more comfortable. She was less anxious, more relaxed. Encouraged by Dino, her days were spent gardening. The garden was lush now and the trees beautiful too. Dino enjoyed the smell of her roses that mingled with the woodsy odors, creating a truly remarkable sensory experience for both of them. While Rosalie worked outdoors, Dino worked on small projects around the house, or sat nearby and read. It was a relaxed time, one they both enjoyed.

But the quiet wouldn't last.

17

Four weeks after their dinner with Amber, on a Friday night, Rosalie was cuddled with Dino on the couch, watching television and thinking about bed. Suddenly an incessant beeping interrupted her thoughts. Rosalie's head jerked. *What's going on?*

Dino was immediately on his feet, striding toward the panel that showed views of all cameras mounted on the property.

"Must be an animal." Visits from nocturnal animals, raccoons, opossums, and the occasional deer, were not uncommon.

Dino was back in a flash, crossing the room to silence the television set and extinguish the light. He turned to her, his finger to his lips. "We have visitors and I don't think they're friendly. They are not four-legged, and they are heading toward the house."

Rosalie stood up. Dino grabbed her by the arm and pulled her to the monitor bank. Just as Dino had said, two people could plainly be seen sneaking toward the house. The camera set on the drive captured two others crouching by the hedge. And on the other side of the backyard, two more people had been picked up by another camera.

All of the intruders were dressed in black and it looked as if all but the two heading for the house were waiting for something. Was there another, the leader, who would signal them when it was time to invade the house? Or were they waiting for the lights to go out, so they could move in?

Rosalie stared at the screen. She'd known this was a possibility when she invited the son of a don to live with her, but she'd hoped they had covered their tracks well enough. She sighed. "It would probably be a good idea to turn on lights in some of the other rooms so they can't pinpoint where we are." Rosalie moved into the kitchen and pressed the switch inside the door.

Dino turned the lights on in the living room. The monitors were visible from where they sat. As they watched, none of the visitors moved. Dino checked the monitors again, and retrieved a gun from the safe near the front door. "But one little gun is not enough."

"Let's go upstairs so they'll think we are retiring for the night." He followed her up the stairs and they separated to turn on lights in two different rooms. When they met in the hallway, she reached for his hand. "Dino, I told you I prepared for this."

Rosalie explained that she'd had carpenters build an escape into the place for just such a moment. "We need to go through the furnace room in the basement to a room hidden behind the back wall. From there, there's a passageway to the back of the property. The passageway opens into the gardener's shed. There's something there that might help us. Wait until we get there and you'll see."

"Rosalie, you have to tell me. If you don't, I can't be well prepared."

"It's a motorcycle. A big one."

He frowned. "I've never been on a cycle."

"Not a problem. My stepfather had an EMW motorcycle. I was fascinated. It was one of only a few from East Germany. He taught me to drive it."

"What the hell is an EMW?"

"We don't have time." She took his hand, pulling him along. "EMW was the name given to what had been a copycat BMW, which had to change its name after the real BMW sued them."

Dino nodded and waved a hand through the air. "So lead me out of trouble."

"And into temptation?"

"We'll see about temptation later. Now let's get the hell out of here, if we can."

They fled down the back stairs to the first floor and then down another flight to the basement.

Dino held her hand tightly as they made their way to the furnace room. She crossed the room, flipped a switch on the back of the furnace, and led him to the back wall. The concrete walls were thick with cobwebs. Then she pushed a button and suddenly there was neither a wall nor cobwebs there. She pulled him past where the wall should have been, flipped another switch, waited a moment and then turned on a light. As he looked around, he saw a plain concrete block room, no windows, no sign of a door, or any way either in or out.

"What the—?"

"Trust me." Rosalie went to the back wall, where she felt around, apparently found what she was searching for, and pressed a spot. A section of wall swiveled noiselessly, exposing a passageway.

Dino gaped. *She's thought of everything.* His heart, which had been thudding against his ribs, slowed its rapid rate a little.

Rosalie flipped a switch on the wall and the passageway lit up. They moved quietly down the walkway. When they came to a set of stairs, she motioned for him to follow. When they had walked up to near the floor above them, she pushed another switch. Following a click, a section of the floor lowered slowly on well-oiled hinges.

Dino shook his head. "I don't know what you paid that carpenter," he whispered, "but it wasn't nearly enough."

She managed a tight smile before sticking her head into the opening. Together they stepped up into the gardener's cottage. A large motorcycle stood in the middle of the room. It gleamed in the moonlight filtering through the windows.

Dino's eyes widened. "It's huge. Can you really drive this thing?"

"I just had it serviced and it's electric start. Let me get the floor switch then you help me move the cycle near the front door. I'll get the automatic door, and grab the keys on the nail beside it. I'll start the cycle when the door's open, and you fire a few shots with that gun as we take off."

Together they coaxed the bike toward the door, stopping a couple of feet in front of it. Rosalie gripped the handles and checked to make sure Dino was settled on the seat behind her before hitting the garage door opener. As the door rose noiselessly, she inserted and turned the key and the bike roared to life. The two sped through the opening, down the driveway, and into the street. As they escaped, Dino fired several wild shots at one of the figures who had hunkered down near the house, but who leapt to his feet as they approached. Dino thought he might have hit him, and when he glanced back the man was slumped over. As Rosalie steered the bike into the street, a volley of shots whizzed overhead.

The motorcycle sped toward I-20 and soon crossed into South Carolina. Rosalie kept the bike headed east at a steady seventy miles an hour. They exited onto 178 after a half hour and traveled south. They caught I-26 southeast of Orangeburg, South Carolina, and then I-95 as they began to move back to the west. Using back roads, they drove for another two hours, until they deemed it safe enough to stop and take a break.

It wasn't until they sat in the restaurant of a truck stop north of Savannah, Georgia, that the fear hit Dino. Rosalie could have been hurt. Or even killed. He lifted his mug of coffee to his lips with trembling fingers. *I never should have put her in that kind of danger.*

As if sensing his thoughts, Rosalie reached across the table and gripped his hand. "I have a hideaway in Alabama. We can keep moving until we get to Montgomery, overnight there, then drive to Hayden tomorrow. I don't want to be on the back roads on a motorcycle in the dark. Too dangerous."

"Too dangerous? What the hell do you call what we just went through?"

She laughed at him. "Child's play, Dino, my dear. Mere child's play."

He just shook his head as she slipped on her coat, clearly ready to be on the road again.

Before they left the truck stop, Dino insisted on calling his father on the burner phone Angelo has supplied him with. He hit the speaker button so Rosalie could hear their conversation. The old man listened carefully then said, "You know this means war, right? Dino, you and your woman have to get somewhere secure. When you are safe, the real fight begins."

"We have a place to go. I'll let you know when we arrive."

"Very good." Angelo sounded concerned. *Was he that worried about them?* Dino gripped the phone tighter at his father's parting words. "Son, if anything happens to you, your mother will have my head. But things could get ugly from here. Whatever you do, you and Rosalie keep your heads down."

18

In New Orleans and Atlanta, the families were meeting. Angelo was furious at the attempt made on his son. Don Juan Cabrera was furious, too, but his anger was with his son.

As Alejandro Cabrera lamented the escape of Don Carbone's son and his girlfriend, first via a tunnel and then by motorcycle, his father's face grew redder and redder. "The motorcycle was gone in a flash, Father. I called in every favor I could think of, but no one reported seeing a cycle carrying two people and driven by a woman."

No matter what he said, it did not quiet his father's anger. In fact, when Alejandro told him about Alonzo Ramirez, who had been shot, his father paced the room, flinging his arms through the air. His temper clearly at a peak, he told his son, "A good man is lying in a hospital bed right now with a shoulder injury because of you and he may lose the use of his arm permanently."

Alejandro flinched, but he couldn't argue with his father. He had failed the family. But what could he do? He had asked his father for help and the don had put out a call for information, but no answers arrived. He hung his head in shame. "I'm sorry, Papa."

"Sorry? What good is sorry?" His father stopped pacing and whirled to face him. "Estupido baboso! Tu eres mas feo que el culo de un mono!"

Heat crept up Alejandro's neck. He felt badly enough already; he really didn't need his father calling him a stupid idiot and uglier than the butt of a monkey.

His father hammered the table with his fist. "I want to know two things: how could you have lost them, and how do you plan to find them?"

"Papa, how was I to know of the tunnel ... and the motorcycle? And how am I to find them? I have not a clue where they are." Alejandro spoke the words in Spanish in an effort to appease his father.

"You donkey," his father thundered, also in Spanish. "Must I tell you everything? Get on the phone. Figure it out. Don't return until you have them!"

"Sí, Papa." Alejandro bowed and backed from the room.

In backing from the room, he bumped into his stepmother, Ainsley, who had arrived with his father's breakfast.

"How is he?"

"Pissed off as hell!"

She smiled at him, set the tray on a table outside the door to the office, and drew him into her arms. Only six years separated them in age. She was beautiful, everything a Spanish matriarch often was not. She was blonde, of fair complexion, tall, and shapely. Alejandro had loved her ever since his father had brought her home two years ago, but not once had he touched her, beyond shaking her hand or an expected and formally delivered hug during the holidays.

As she drew him close, her curves were evident as they pushed into his chest. She kissed him on both cheeks, and smiled. "Your father is used to getting his way, Alejandro. I have learned in these years that if an assignment is troublesome it is better to ask for assistance from him than to return after having failed to achieve whatever he asked. Remember that, my friend."

With that, she kissed him on the lips, pushing into him even more firmly before picking up the tray, knocking on the door and entering when his father yelled, "Vienen."

Alejandro was shocked by the kiss and moved away from his father's study, his fingers on his lips, still burning pleasantly from the touch of Ainsley's lips.

He went into the kitchen, sat down, propped his elbows on the table, and lowered his head onto his hands. No matter how much he thought, though, no reasonable path forward came to him.

A half hour later, his stepmother returned. Her cheeks were flushed, her clothing in a bit of disarray. She carried the tray filled with empty dishes.

She looked at him, sensing his dejection. "Alejandro, let's go into the family room and talk. Perhaps I can quiet your concern just as I have quieted your father's anger."

He stared at her. She smiled even more widely, as if reading his mind. "No, Alejandro, not in the same way!"

"I w-w-was n-not ..."

"Sure you were, and I would have been disappointed if you had not figured out my special way of calming him down. But that is not for us. A solution, however, is."

She led him to the family room off the kitchen. Sunlight warmed the room as it reflected off the pale yellow of the walls, but Alejandro was too chilled by his father's anger to feel the warmth as he dropped into an armchair in front of a wall-to-wall case filled with books, most first editions.

Ainsley sat down gracefully in the chair across from him. "Alejandro, I met your father as the result of an introduction arranged by a woman from Atlanta named Amber Johansen. And before you ask, it was a business meeting. Your father was lonely and hungry. I was for sale. I think we found each other charming. He returned week after week. We grew closer and closer. One day, he stunned me by asking me to marry him. When I protested, saying I had made a commitment to Amber, he silenced me, saying, 'That is all behind you. I think you will find Amber quite willing to give you up. And if it is your wish to accept my offer, I will be a happy man.'

"It was as he had said. Amber was quite happy to let me go. I suspect your father made it well worth her while. He is wealthy, personable, controls almost everything in Atlanta. How could she refuse, especially when he offered her, I suspect, big money?

"Amber and I have remained friends since. When I told him I wanted to continue our friendship, he accepted that as long as I promised to never again work for her. I have not broken that promise. I tell you this because Amber knows everyone and everything about the goings on in Atlanta. I bet she has heard all about this and may have useful information for you. Start there, and see if she can help."

"Is Amber's business one of ours?"

"It receives protection from us, but it is not one of your father's businesses. He and Amber are longtime friends, but I will ask her to help you without telling your father."

"You are wonderful. Thank you, Ainsley, thank you!"

As she stood, he kissed her on the mouth. She offered no opposition, quite the contrary. Her lips opened slightly and her tongue lightly traced his lips. He was smitten, and might have taken it further if not for the fact that the cook and housekeeper, Estelle Vazquez, opened the door from the backyard into the foyer off the kitchen. She came on duty each day at 10:00 a.m.

Hearing her approach, he broke off the kiss, whispered his thanks again, and headed toward his bedroom. About fifteen minutes later he had a text from Ainsley, telling him that Amber was expecting his call. He immediately called the number his stepmother provided.

A pleasant voice with a heavy southern accent answered. "You must be Alejandro. When Ainsley told me you would call, I asked her to give you my very private number."

"Yes, ma'am."

"And how may I help you, Mr. Cabrera?"

"Well, ma'am, I want to talk to you about someone I'm looking for. Ainsley thought you might have—or could get—information."

"And just who are you seeking?"

"A woman by the name of Rosalie. I don't know her last name."

"Can you describe her?"

Alejandro provided her with a description the best he could: average height, gray hair, maybe in her sixties, well-built, in shape.

"Mr. Cabrera, that description fits hundreds of women in the Atlanta area, but let me see what I can do. How about you come in about eight tonight? We'll have dinner and talk."

Alejandro thanked her. The call concluded, he stretched out on his bed and slept. But dreams of his enraged father haunted his thoughts.

19

Alejandro awoke to the tone of his cell phone alarm at 7:00 p.m., rushed through a shower and a shave, and at a few moments before 8:00 p.m. arrived at the address Amber had given him.

He walked to the door, saw the *Welcome, Enter, Please* sign on the door and let himself into a spacious foyer. An attractive redhead with a spectacular body—what he could see of it—sat at a desk to the side. She smiled. "Can I help you?"

"Umm, yes, thank you." Alejandro consciously kept his eyes on the more benign parts of her body. "I, um, have an appointment with Ms. Johansen?"

The woman pointed to a chair at the rear of the foyer. "Please have a seat. I'll let her know you are here."

He waited just a few moments until the door across from him opened and one of the most attractive women he had ever seen swept into the room. Alejandro leapt to his feet.

She was about his height—five foot ten, give or take an inch—and much better built than any brick commode he had seen. Her dark brown hair glistened, as did her lips. A hint of jasmine drifted from her. He was mesmerized.

"Mr. Cabrera?"

He shook his head. How many times had she said his name? "Oh, yes, ma'am, I'm sorry. I am Alejandro Cabrera. Thank you for seeing me."

"You are quite welcome. Your father and mother are good friends of mine. I am happy to help if I can."

"Stepmother."

"Oh, yes, stepmother. Why don't you come with me and we will have dinner and talk."

She turned and Alejandro followed her through the door. She led him to a door at the end of a long corridor, opened it, and ushered him in.

"Welcome. This is my apartment. I think we will be comfortable here. The staff prepares excellent meals. Deanna will be in shortly to take drink orders. She will also bring us some canapés. After we've had a chance to talk and have a couple of drinks, we'll eat here, if that's all right with you."

"Great." Alejandro was used to the opulence of his family home, but that was nothing compared to the handsomely furnished room that was connected to what appeared to be a spacious dining area.

As he examined the space, Amber seemed to pick up on his interest. "After Deanna takes our order, I'll show you around."

Another very attractive young woman entered through a door at the end of the dining room, took their drink orders, and exited as noiselessly as she had come in.

"Want to have a look?"

"That'd be great."

"Okay, come with me." Their first stop was in a bedroom, the likes of which Alejandro had never seen. It was anchored by a huge heart-shaped bed, covered in pink and red. Every type of erotic device imaginable was displayed on the walls.

"This is my room. Or perhaps I should call it my playpen. In my business, I must be careful to select only the most beautiful and most skilled young men and women to work here. I feel compelled to audition each prospect and it's helpful to have a room where they can find anything they need to convince me to employ them."

"Wow!" The single word was all he could muster.

"I have entertained members of your family here. Perhaps one day I will have the pleasure of your company."

"Umm, well ... yes ... of course, that would be great." Heat flooded his face at the thought.

She walked him through the rest of the apartment, which he found just as spectacular as the bedroom, then led him back to the living room. Deanna had already placed their drinks on tables near where they had been sitting in chairs that faced a fireplace, unneeded this night because of the heat. Amber lifted her wine glass and proposed a toast. "To the beginning of a great friendship."

After he had sampled the best brandy old-fashioned he'd ever had, Alejandro set down his glass.

Amber wrapped slender fingers around the stem of the wine glass. "So, Alejandro, what brings you here? And how can I help?"

Prompted by her questions, Alejandro gave her a complete explanation of his dilemma. "My father is furious. I set out to find this old lady and kill her companion, but they escaped."

"And how did they escape?"

"Secret tunnel and motorcycle, ma'am. The woman drove the bike like an expert. Her companion wounded one of my men as they fled."

"That's quite a story. I might have an idea or two, but let's have dinner first. Then we can talk more."

Soon Deanna had returned, this time pushing a cart that held two silver domes. The smells coming from the plates under the domes made his mouth water. When Deanna lifted the covers, Alejandro saw the most sumptuous filet. The other held seafood.

"Perhaps, if you'd allow me to sample your steak, I could share some lobster and a shrimp or two with you?" Amber spoke in a tantalizing manner that began to seduce him. He hoped he wasn't wrong about where that might be headed. Dinner was excellent. When they had finished, Amber moved to the sofa and patted a spot next to her. When Alejandro was seated and comfortable, Deanna returned with glasses and a bottle of cognac.

As they sipped, Amber ran a finger around the rim of her glass. "I have an idea who you might be seeking. I am familiar with a Rosalie Burton who just might be the woman you saw. I have always felt there was something about her that was a bit out of place. She's a customer; a good one. She likes her boys young, hung, and skilled of tongue. But she's kind of dropped off the face of the earth. Your description of the woman and her young companion may have answered my question about what happened to her."

Alejandro moved to the edge of his seat. "Really?"

"I met her a couple of years ago when she called about a date. She's nearly seventy, I think, but once she has been out with one of my employees, they always ask about her. Apparently she is extremely skilled and nearly insatiable. I have met her on a few occasions, but not recently. I haven't provided her with a date for months now. I thought maybe she had retired. I always thought she was in sales, but after meeting her and then hearing "Black Widow of the Woods" stories, I realized she did far more than that. I employed her to take care of a problem worker. She did it quickly, smoothly, and, if killing someone can be humane, she did it humanely. But now she has vanished. In fact, the last I heard of her was a couple of weeks ago when some cops from Wisconsin came by with a friend of mine, a detective. She's apparently wanted for a number of murders up there."

"That sounds like her. Any idea how I might find her? Father is enormously upset with me for letting her escape a trap in Augusta."

"I don't have any information right now, but I can snoop around a bit and see what I can come up with. Would you like that?"

"Absolutely; the sooner the better."

"I'll get right on it. Now, would you like to meet some of my employees? You may have one for the evening on the house, if you desire."

"Amber, after meeting you, I'm sorry to say that I don't think any of them would measure up. I'm happy to meet them, but if I selected one, I would simply be thinking about you."

"What a nice compliment. Perhaps we should move to my playroom?"

"Now that would be a real treat."

Afterwards, they relaxed in her living room, sipping more fine cognac and talking. Amber rested a slim hand on his arm. "I can't tell you how much I have enjoyed your visit, Alejandro. Will you return again soon?"

He liked the way she said his name. "That would be wonderful, but I don't want to make a pest of myself."

"Don't worry, I will let you know when you become a pest."

When he returned home, Alejandro found his stepmother and told her about his visit to Amber.

"And was she helpful?"

"She was unbelievable." His face warmed again.

"And just what made her unbelievable?"

"Well … ummm, she was nice, friendly. And her business seems like a first-class enterprise frequented by the rich."

"And that caused your cheeks to grow red?"

"Well, ummm, no, but we talked a lot and she told me she might be able to help me. That was pretty much it."

"Do you mean to tell me she did not show you her playroom?"

When his face grew hotter, she laughed.

"I see that you did visit that special place. Wonderful! Amber is a terrific teacher. She makes certain that her staff is also wonderfully skilled. I'm pleased it was a good night for you. Perhaps now you can forget your father's scolding."

She rose, kissed him chastely, and left the room.

Alejandro headed upstairs, puzzled by all that had happened to him. But he was also grateful. It appeared as though his experiences were about to be broadened considerably. Even remembering all his father had said to him didn't stop the fantasies that danced through Alejandro's head all night long.

20

Rosalie and Dino pulled down the long, winding, tree-shrouded lane to Rosalie's cottage in Alabama, after creeping along the last twenty-five miles, watching for wildlife that might dart across the road in front of them. The roads they had taken to get there were so tangled in his mind that Dino knew he could never duplicate them. Was that why she had chosen that route? He shook his head. She was probably only being careful. After what had happened in Augusta, they would both have to be. They couldn't let their guards down again.

Dino looked around the property, fascinated. After telling him about the functional comfort of the place, Rosalie gave him a tour of the laboratory. Once again, Dino was extremely impressed.

They ate a simple dinner taken from the freezer and heated in the microwave. Afterwards, Rosalie poured them each a glass of a fine Syrah.

They moved across the open space to a sitting area, Dino choosing a comfortable Ethan Allen couch for them. After they'd made themselves comfortable, Dino shifted on the couch to face her, leaning a shoulder against a cushion. "This place is incredible." He lifted his glass. "To a brand new start."

Rosalie clinked her glass to his. "Obviously this place was built for me so I could stay out of sight. I think we are safe here for the moment. This is not a good place for us to stay very long, though. People in Hayden are going to wonder about the younger guy who is living with me. It's a typical small town and people are nosy. That kind of speculation could be a problem for us."

Dino nodded. "I'm sorry I brought you into all of this."

Rosalie rested a hand on his knee. "Any danger you may be causing me is more than offset by the pleasure you bring me by being with me. Besides, a little danger and excitement keeps a person young, as far as I'm concerned."

He grinned. "You must have had a lot of danger and excitement in your life then."

"See?" Rosalie smiled. "Those kinds of comments are why I'm so happy to have you around." She leaned forward and kissed him. "Still, my intent is to stay only long enough to find a new place to hide. We could go to Montana, I suppose, where my late husband and I owned a cabin, but that's a very long trip. I don't think flying is an option, too easy to track us. Train? Too long, too problematic. Driving is a major risk. We need something nearby for now. Maybe we can start looking as early as tomorrow. With the motorcycle in the garage, it's possible no one will know we're here. Even if someone sees the lights on, it won't raise questions, since I have the lights on a timer whenever I'm gone."

He sighed. "I hope you're right, but we'll have to stay vigilant. The Cabreras are vicious. My father has tried to keep peace between the families, but there has always been an uneasy calm between us and the Cabrera Family. If by chance my shots as we left hit anyone, and I'm pretty sure they did, it could touch off a war."

"You're right. Probably no place will be completely safe for long. Why don't we see if we can find another place that would work for us for now?"

She walked to the computer, turned it on, and waited while it booted up. She brought up Zillow, and they looked for places that were relatively nearby, comfortable, and secluded. They finally found one that looked interesting in Modoc, South Carolina, just across the Georgia border.

The log cabin appeared to be secluded, but upon further inspection, it wasn't secluded enough for their purposes, and the more they thought about it the less they thought of it.

"Rosalie, look at this one." Dino grabbed her hand and pulled her to the computer. "This one's in Evans, Georgia, close enough to drive to. It sounds like what we want."

Rosalie perused the description. "$1.9 million, large lawn that fronts on a lake, an enormous screen porch, part of which is covered, two marvelously equipped kitchens, *and* an apartment above the garage, which would work for a laboratory." She looked up from the screen. "It does sound perfect," she agreed. "Let's check it out first thing in the morning."

Excited by their find, but worn out from their flight from trouble, Dino grabbed her hand. "Time for rest; I'm dead and you look exhausted, too."

Rosalie agreed with him and guided him to the bedrooms. He was surprised, but too tired to argue, when she pointed him toward a guest room and wished him a good night. She came in, briefly, to shoo the cat off the bed, then laughed lightly. "I sure hope you're not allergic."

Dino kissed her on the forehead. "Only to being away from you, my darling. I hope it will not be for long."

Her cheeks pink, she pressed her hands to his chest and gently pushed him away. "It won't be, I promise." When she had gone, he shed his clothes and climbed between the covers. In spite of his fatigue, sleep wouldn't come. He replayed their flight from Augusta over and over in his head. Although they were far away, and hadn't seen anyone following them, he couldn't shake the fear that they likely weren't safe here after all.

The sun was streaming through the windows when Rosalie awoke and she was startled to see on the digital clock on the bedside table that it was 8:30. Dino was still asleep as she tiptoed past his room and into the kitchen. She started the coffee maker and pulled open the fridge door. "Hmm." She glanced over at Julie, curled up on the windowsill in the sunshine. Asleep, of course. "Nothing here to eat, you lazy cat. We'll have to get groceries soon." She closed the door. Thankfully, she kept the freezer well-stocked because she never knew when those meals would come in handy.

She made eggs and sausages for herself, ate it with two cups of coffee and then shook Dino gently. "I'm going to town to check the mail. It's been more than five weeks since I've been here. There might be orders that haven't been forwarded. Maybe I can intercept them. I have to remove the order to forward mail, too, I suppose."

The only response she got was a soft snore. Rosalie almost laughed. Dino and the cat. They were quite a pair this morning.

She made the trip quickly and stopped at the post office.

"Wondered what happened to you," said the postmaster, smiling. "Are you back for a while now? You've got lots of mail." He handed the pile to her before removing the order to forward. That done, she visited the Piggly Wiggly on Main Street in Hayden and purchased sufficient groceries for a stay of several days.

When she got back home, Dino had showered and dressed. He was sipping coffee as he watched the noon news. The report was void of any item on gang war, so they both relaxed. Rosalie opened the mail. She found seven orders for her potions, the largest from the Cabrera Family.

"What do I do about this?" She handed the letter to him.

"Let's start with the others. I want to think about this one."

They concentrated on the other orders. Dino had become proficient as a lab assistant and set out most of the items she needed before she even had to ask.

After a couple of hours, the other orders were filled. The only one left was from the Cabreras. "I've been thinking about it, and I think you have to fill it. To do anything else might give away who you are. What do you think?"

"I was hoping you would say that. It's the best solution, but I wanted to hear it from you."

"I considered several alternatives such as mixing a harmless potion, but that would blow your cover. Still, I hate to hand them something deadly that could be used against us at some point."

Rosalie tapped her fingers on the counter. "What if we mix what they want, then let your family know? There's a simple antidote, which I have on hand. We can send it to New Orleans as protection. What do you think?"

"Sounds perfect; let's do that."

They made the desired drug and packaged it. Then Rosalie took the antidote from the refrigerator, measured a liberal portion of it into a bottle, and handed it to Dino for packaging.

"This will do the trick."

She was pleased when he smiled and nodded.

As evening settled over the woods, she and Dino took the nondescript Taurus that had remained in the garage while she was gone and drove toward Birmingham. They stopped in Homewood on their way and used the UPS store to send off the packages they had prepared earlier.

With that done, they drove to Bellini's Ristorante & Bar. Rosalie had always liked the place, and thought Dino would especially appreciate it, given his Italian heritage. The food was excellent as usual. Then disaster struck.

As they were eating, owner Dominic Bellini came through the dining room. His eyes widened when he saw Dino, and he headed straight for their table. "My goodness, what brings you here?"

Rosalie hadn't even considered the possibility that someone here might recognize Dino. *What have I done?* She forced herself to speak casually. "Mr. Carbone is a business associate. He was in the area and I convinced him to come here. He protested, but here we are."

Dino lifted a hand. "Please, the protest was simply because I had not called in advance. I was headed north and needed to meet with Ms. Burton to discuss several business matters. One thing led to another, it got later than I intended, and we decided to have dinner. It was only when she suggested Bellini's that I realized the mistake of not calling you as courtesy would demand."

"Not to worry, not to worry. Dinner is, of course, on me. It is a great pleasure to see you Dino, and a great honor to have you dine here. And the next time you come this way, you will be sure to let me know, yes?"

"Yes, absolutely. But, please, I meant no harm. It was a late decision to have dinner."

"No offense taken. I'll have my staff bring you a special dessert immediately." Bellini bowed and departed.

The dessert, an Italian delicacy that Rosalie could not put a name to, was delicious, but Dino was obviously unsettled. He fidgeted and seemed lost in thought, several times failing to hear what she said to him.

Dessert over, he tossed his napkin down on the table. "We must go—now."

When they reached the car, he took her elbow to guide her inside. "Bellini is very close to Cabrera. My presence will soon be known in Atlanta. We must get ready to move."

Rosalie apologized profusely, but the damage had been done. Unfortunately, there was nothing she could do about it now.

Dino sighed. "It's not your fault. This is something I should have realized when you said the name, but my mind was elsewhere. It should not have been. Now we must move, and quickly. I fear the Cabreras will soon be here."

Rosalie nodded and climbed into the car. "Should we leave tonight?"

Dino closed the door after her and went around to the driver's side. After getting in, he sat for a moment, gripping the steering wheel. Finally he nodded his head curtly. "I think we'll be okay to wait until tomorrow. It will take time for word to get to the Cabreras and for them to assemble a group to come after us. If we leave first thing, we should be ahead of them."

They reached home about 11 p.m., showered, and headed upstairs.

As Rosalie left the bathroom dressed in a sheer nightie and toweling her hair, Dino grabbed her and kissed her. "I've missed you, girl. Maybe we should sleep together. What do you say?"

"I think it's a marvelous idea, if we can get Julie to cooperate."

"That cat is the laziest thing I have ever seen. He's on the bed I slept in last night, snoring up a storm. So …" He pulled her closer. "Might I invade your space, Ms. Burton?"

"Why Mr. Carbone, I do believe you are propositioning me." She stood there trying hard to affect an aloof persona and failing abysmally.

"Hell, Rosalie, I'm starved for you. I can't wait another minute."

He picked her up, carried her to the bed, deposited her there, removed his shorts and straddled her.

Tonight there was plenty of stamina, fueled by good food. They participated equally and enthusiastically and had just settled into a steady rhythm when one of the trip wires that surrounded the property in the woods was activated, creating an insistent buzz in the cabin.

In an instant, the mood was shattered. They wasted no time in moving swiftly from the bed. Dino stopped at the gun cabinet and grabbed a Glock for Rosalie and an AK-47 for himself, plus silencers for each. Rosalie activated the door to the lab and, when both were safely inside, closed the swivel door. They waited.

"I hope this is just a false alarm," whispered Dino.

That hope was erased by the sound of glass shattering and crashing onto the tiled kitchen floor. The intruders weren't even trying to be quiet.

Were they that confident that whoever was in the house wouldn't be able to escape if they heard them coming?

"They must have the place surrounded," said Dino. "We need to find somewhere to hide." He moved to the area opposite the door and behind a cabinet. Rosalie squeezed into a spot beside the door.

As they waited silently, footsteps echoed in the hallway, growing louder as whoever was in the house burst into the living room. Suddenly there was nothing, no sounds at all. The intruders must be surveying the room. Seconds later, a voice broke the silence. "They have to be here. We saw them come up the drive and the Taurus is still in the garage. We need to tear the place apart and find them or Juan's gonna be furious!"

She winced at the sound of heavy furniture scraping across her oak floors. Doors opened and slammed shut.

"Look under all the rugs; there could be an escape hatch or tunnel, like the last place," a man called out. Her eyes narrowed. *What was that banging sound?* Were they tapping the walls? Her breaths were coming in short bursts that sounded deafening in the small space. The Cabrera family was known for its ruthlessness. What would they do if they found them? Torture them? A horrible thought struck her; would they use her own potions against them?

In the dark, Dino crept close to her. When he whispered in her ear, his breath was warm against her cheek. "If the wall sounds hollow, they'll know we're here. Get ready."

While Dino retreated to his former hiding place, Rosalie positioned herself to the right of the hidden door, behind a wall of boxes. Dino disappeared behind the cabinet. They waited, hardly daring to breath.

The tapping came closer, then closer still. Suddenly they heard, "There's a hollow spot behind this wall. It seems pretty big, too. Let's hack it open."

Several seconds more of silence led to the sound of heavy hammering on the wall. Although the wall into the room was of sturdy construction, Rosalie knew it would not withstand the blows of a sledgehammer.

As the hammering continued, light began to filter into the lab. The assailants were ready to break through. Rosalie and Dino prepared for battle.

The sledge came through the wall and was followed by tearing sounds as the visitors broke down the drywall. When the hole was large enough to admit a person, one of the attackers cautiously stepped into the room, gun drawn. Rosalie waited in silence.

"You gotta see this!" exclaimed the man who had entered the room, turning back and gesturing to his pals to come inside. "It's amazing."

Soon he was joined by three others. They gaped as they stared at the laboratory and its gleaming equipment. Then one of them found a light switch. As the lights came on, Rosalie and Dino acted. The AK-47 made quick work of three of the intruders and Rosalie downed the one nearest her with a shot to the back.

The three people Dino had hit were dead, but the victim of the Glock lay on the ground, gasping for breath. Rosalie reached his side and knelt. "We'll see that you get help, but we need to know how many of you there are."

Wincing in pain, the man whispered, "Six."

"Where are the other two?"

"End of driveway," came the gasping reply.

Dino dropped down at his other side. "How many cars?"

Faintly, with labored breath, the man whispered, "Two." He made a rasping sound. Dino placed his hand on the man's neck, then turned to Rosalie and shook his head. The man was dead.

Rosalie glanced at Dino. "Good thing we used the silencers." She scrambled to her feet. "We'll need to neutralize the other two before we can leave."

"Let's try to get into the woods before we head for the cars," Dino suggested. Rosalie nodded and they started for the front entrance, picking their way over and around broken furniture and glass as they went. Dino stopped at the door and scrutinized the yard before gesturing with his gun for Rosalie to follow him. They crept across the dark property, entered the woods, and moved silently toward the place where the driveway met the road. As they drew close enough to see, the moon broke through the clouds. Two cars were pulled across the driveway, just out of sight of the main road. The two remaining intruders sat together in one of the vehicles.

Dino's shots shattered the windshield and both men immediately slumped down.

"Not very smart, sitting together that way," said Dino. He crept to the car, opened the door and carefully checked the pulse of each man.

"They're dead." He slammed the door. "We have to get out of here. How about we pull the cars up to the house and take off in the one that isn't damaged? Their bosses will know about the Taurus by now. The men may have even tampered with it to keep us from getting away."

Rosalie nodded. "Good idea." She inclined her head toward the men in the car. "Maybe we should get these two inside the house and then set fire to the lab. The chemicals should trigger a hot fire. It won't eliminate evidence of the bodies, but it will burn them beyond recognition."

"Sounds good. We'd better get at it. We have about four hours of darkness left."

Moving the two bodies was a chore, but with Dino grasping under their arms and Rosalie taking the legs, they got the two men into the cabin and placed them with the other four in the lab. As Rosalie gathered up the things they would need and loaded them into the back of the black Mazda 3, Dino made sure placement of the flammable chemicals was right to create a hot, extended fire.

Rosalie grasped his arm. "Why don't you call your father, let him know what's going on?" He nodded and pulled out his phone. She moved away to give him some privacy, but occasionally Dino's voice would rise and she'd catch snatches of his side of the conversation. His father was clearly not happy, but whether that was with Dino, her, or the Cabrera family, she couldn't tell. When he finished, Dino shoved the phone back in his pocket. He walked over to her, face grim.

"Dad's pissed. The Cabreras are going to pay—heavily. The fact that they have continued to come after us means war, he says. He wants us on the road right away. He told me where to go."

They got into the car and headed west toward the address Dino had gotten from his father. As they turned onto the main road, the sound of an explosion reached them. Rosalie looked back. Flames shot above the treetops.

She was sad to see the cabin go, but she understood the necessity of getting away from Hayden, Alabama, and her cabin in the woods. "Where are we going?"

"Our family owns 832 acres in a place called the Dewey W. Wills

Wildlife Management Area Wills Park in the Catahoula National Wildlife Refuge in Louisiana. We'll be safe there. I doubt anyone will find us, but we need to watch for anyone tailing us as we go."

As they drove, Rosalie pressed him for details while carefully watching behind them.

"There is a comfortable house in the middle of the property. It is almost impossible to get to the place except by the one road. And Dad has it heavily guarded. He thinks we'll be safe there until the heat is off."

"How far is it?"

"About 200 miles. We should be there in four hours or so. Dad wants us to take the back roads rather than the freeway. That will add an hour but it will be much safer. How about I take the first two hours while you sleep? You can drive the last two hours, okay?"

"Sounds good." Rosalie rested her head against the window, staring out the front windshield at the impenetrable darkness ahead.

21

Two days later, as he was making his normal morning newspaper search, Al came across a report in *The Birmingham News*. His chair snapped into place as he straightened up abruptly. Six bodies, burned beyond recognition, had been found in the remains of a cabin north of Birmingham. According to the report, the fire began in what appeared to be a secret space that held a laboratory.

Immediately he came to attention. First he called Charlie at the La Crosse County Sheriff's Department, told him about his discovery, and suggested Charlie take a look at the article. Then he dialed his friend in Atlanta.

"Cunningham."

"Rusty, I was reading the Birmingham newspaper and came across the story of an explosion in a cabin in the woods and the discovery of bodies in the ashes. Did you see it?'

"Nope, rarely see the papers from Birmingham."

Al read him the key points from the story. When he finished, Rusty cleared his throat. "Sounds like it could be mob related."

"Exactly."

"Tell you what, I know the sheriff over there. Met him at a conference. Let me call him and see what I can find out. If I get him, I should be back to you shortly."

Al had just hung up when his phone rang. It was Charlie suggesting lunch.

"Sure. Four Sisters sound good?"

"Hell, no!" exclaimed Charlie. "I want a real lunch, Al, not one of them goddamn small-plate specials they have at the Sisters. I have a hunger for some barbecue. Let's go to Piggy's."

"Okay, but we're going Dutch treat, understand?"

"If that's what you want."

They agreed they'd meet at the restaurant in twenty minutes.

When Al got there, Charlie was already seated and looking at a menu.

"Hi, buddy." Al slapped his friend on the back.

"Have a seat. Take a look at the menu. I'm damn hungry. Wanna order in a minute or two."

"Charlie, you're always starving. But okay, I'll order when you're ready."

After they had given the server their orders—a pulled pork sandwich for Al and a full rack of ribs for Charlie—Al pulled a copy of the news story out of his pocket.

"Here's the report. What do you think?"

Charlie studied the document, his face growing more animated as he read. He finished and set the paper down. "This could be it! Have you talked to Rusty?"

"Right after I called you. He promised to look into it and call me back. Not sure when that will be, but probably not today."

"Did he think there might be something to it?"

Al shrugged and picked up his water glass. "It's in the right area. He did wonder if it might have something to do with some crime family war, which wouldn't likely involve our girl." He set the glass down with a thud. "Unless, of course, she's working for one or both of them, which is quite possible." He rubbed his chin. "It'll be interesting to see if Rusty comes up with anything."

The two chowed down their food. When they finished, Charlie astounded Al by picking up the check.

"What's this? A new Charlie?"

"Yeah, yeah, I know. Kelly says I gotta get more generous. But it ain't becomin' a habit. I got too many bills. Goddamn divorce. It's costin' me thousands. Charlene needs somethin' every other day and the kids are little hoarders. They always need the latest and greatest. They're driving me into bankruptcy."

"But look at how much better you feel. You're in love, Charlie, and it shows. Kelly has been great for you."

"You can say that again. She's dynamite. She's a great cook, makes and manages money, takes care of whatever I need. I couldn't be happier. As soon as the ex-wife and kids get off my payroll, things will be terrific. Just two more years and Charlene can kiss my ass!"

Al shook his head and chuckled. Charlie shot him a funny look and Al held up a hand. "Sorry, I was just thinking about what you are going to be like when you have nothing to complain about. Will you still be the Charlie I know and love, I wonder?"

"Shut the shit up. You rarely hear me complain. Admit it."

"Whatever you say, Charlie. You're right, you're always sweetness and light. How could I forget?"

He tried to hide the grin that tugged at the corners of his mouth, but Charlie obviously caught it. "Stick it, Al. You're just jealous that I have my life together and you're struggling."

"You're right, Charlie. I have two great women in my life, and I love them both. It's really tough. JoAnne is wonderful and always has been. Julie is a dream I can't forget. I am constantly walking on thin ice around JoAnne, thinking I'm going to slip. So far, so good, but it's a challenge."

"Don't know how to help you, buddy. You're gonna have to come to grips with this yourself. One more year and Brody's gonna graduate. Then what'll ya do?"

"Right now I'm trying not to think about that. I know the time is coming when trying to have them both is going to end. The thought of it is driving me nuts. Guess I'll call Julie when I get back to work and see how she's doing. I'll let her know about Alabama. Maybe she'll have some thoughts." Al wiped his mouth with a napkin before tossing it onto his plate and pushing back his chair. "Say hi to Kelly, Charlie."

"Sure will, pal. The four of us gotta get together one of these days, have dinner and a few beers."

"That'd be great."

Back at work, Al found a message to call Rusty on his desk. He dialed the number and his friend answered on the first ring.

"What's up, Rusty?"

"This one might be linked to your escapee, Al. Not sure why I'm saying that, but it just feels good. Know what I mean?"

"Yeah, I do. It's a feeling you get when things seem aligned and ready to pop, right?"

"Yeah, like that. Here's what I know. Looks like this fire involved some type of disagreement between the Atlanta and New Orleans crime families."

"The Carbones and the Cabreras?"

"Yeah, rumor has it they got into it over something the Carbone Family gave the Gambinos in New York. Apparently the Cabreras were on the short end of the deal and have decided to take it out on the Carbones."

"That doesn't sound too unusual."

"On its own, maybe not, but there was another event in Augusta a few days ago that was rumored to be between Angelo Carbone's son and the Cabreras. Another Cabrera man injured there. The two events have to be linked. And the interesting part, for you, is that the Carbone boy was escaping from the Cabreras when he shot one of their men. Flew by them on a motorcycle, apparently, only he wasn't the one driving."

Al's eyes narrowed. *Could it be?* "Who was?"

"An older woman, according to our informant working undercover with the Cabreras."

"Really." Al slouched against the back of his chair. Had he been correct? Genevieve was working for the mafia and had gotten herself tangled up with Don Carbone's son?

"That's what he said. In any event, I'm going to head over to Birmingham tomorrow to nose around with the Blount County sheriff's boys. I'll let you know what I find."

"Please do." Al thanked his Georgian friend and the conversation ended.

Al tried to concentrate on the pile of paper work on his desk, but he couldn't focus. Finally the clock showed five-thirty. He cleaned off his desk and decided to call Julie before heading home.

"How are you? I miss you, Julie."

"I know, I'm missing you, too."

They talked for fifteen minutes, a tender discussion that gave each time to tell the other how much they cared, missed each other, and longed for the time when they could be together. Al also told Julie about the apparent gunfight in Alabama.

"Do you think it's Genevieve?"

"Not sure. But both Rusty Cunningham in Atlanta and I have the feeling, so we think it could be your aunt."

"The feeling?"

"Yeah. It's hard to explain, but it's something veteran officers get when something starts to bubble in a case, kind of like an itch way down deep inside."

"You mean like the itch that I get sometimes when I want to see you?" she teased.

Al chuckled. "I think your itch and my feeling are different, because I get itches, too, that involve you, and they're pretty different than this feeling."

"Would you do one thing for me? Promise me you'll let me know if you discover information that suggests Genevieve was involved with the incident in Alabama? I know she's done some horrible things, but she is still family to me."

Al sighed. "I will, but not out of any consideration for that woman, only because I love you so much."

"I love you too, Al."

When the phone went dead, he sat and stared at it for a moment until setting it down with a heavy exhalation of breath.

It was mid-afternoon the next day before he got a call from Rusty.

"We think maybe we found your girl. If you have her fingerprints or DNA, we might be able to prove it."

Al's heart rate picked up. "Based on what?"

"The cabin was the home of a woman, that much we know. Her prints are all over the place, and we have plenty of DNA evidence, too, we think. There are toothbrushes and other things left behind that weren't burned that we can test. I know we're supposed to have the stuff on file, but our guys can't find it."

Al gave him the key to the Wisconsin database on which Genevieve's tests and DNA information were stored.

"I'll get this right over to the lab, and the minute we have something, I'll call."

Not an hour later, Al got the call he was waiting for. He had called Charlie after hanging up earlier and his pal came right over. The two of them were waiting in Al's office when Rusty called.

"It's her, no question. She must have been living there for a long time. The rear of the house is a mess, but the firemen got there in time to save much of the living space. We think the fire started in the lab. Near as we can tell, the room was built into the mountain behind the place and hidden from the house. We've got a full CSI crew on the way up there. Do you guys want to come down?"

Al glanced at Charlie, who gave him a thumbs up. "I'd love to, and so would Charlie. We'll talk to our bosses, and as soon as we have an answer, I'll be in touch."

While Al went to see the chief, Charlie headed over to the Sheriff's Department to find Dwight Hooper.

The chief was pleased by the news and readily agreed that Al should take another trip south.

"Let's hope," Al told the chief, "that this trip produces something. Wouldn't it be nice to get the old girl back into custody?"

The chief nodded. "It sure would."

Soon, Al backed out of the chief's office to give Charlie a call and see how he had made out.

"It's a go for me, too," Charlie said. "When I called Kelly to ask her to get some clothes out for me, she suggested I invite you and JoAnne over for dinner. How about it?"

"Sounds great, but before I commit, I'd better call JoAnne to make sure she doesn't have something planned." When he hung up after talking to Charlie, Al lifted the receiver again and dialed his home number. The sound of his wife's voice sent both happiness and guilt coursing through him. "Hey, hon. Charlie and Kelly have invited us for dinner. Are you free?"

"Oh Al, I'm sorry. I've made plans to go to a movie with some friends. You go though. I'll feel better if I know you're having a good dinner, especially since I had nothing planned for you."

"JoAnne, you're still the best. You look out for me like I'm one of the kids. You've kept me going this long and I'm grateful. I'm sure I'll enjoy dinner, but maybe I could have dessert when I get home?"

"Dessert?" For a moment she sounded confused then she laughed. "Oh, that kind of dessert. My guess is that by the time I get home you'll be sound asleep. Dessert will only be a dream."

"Well, what the hell time do you plan to be home? Are you staying out all night?"

"All night? You're usually in bed by nine and snoring by the time I come to bed after getting my work done. The movie ends at nine-fifteen, then we'll probably have a sandwich and a drink on our way home, so it might be ten-thirty. I'm not getting my hopes up that you'll be up to dessert."

"C'mon. Given the proper incentive, you know I'll manage to stay awake."

"Promises, promises. If I come home ready for a tussle and you stand me up, you're gonna be in deep trouble."

Al laughed. "I promise I'll be up, and more than ready for you when you get home."

"I'll look forward to it. Have fun with Kelly and Charlie."

"I will. You have a good time too." Al hung up the phone and sat staring at the wall in front of him for several minutes before pushing to his feet. Throwing on his jacket, he headed out of the office.

Dinner was a lighthearted affair, with good conversation and a great dinner. With JoAnne absent, the three friends could talk openly about Julie. After dinner, they called her and brought her up to date on the upcoming trip that Al and Charlie would make to Alabama.

"All the signs point to it being your aunt, Julie," Al told her. "According to the officials down there, they have her fingerprints and DNA on samples they took from the wreckage."

"I know you're determined to catch her, Al, and I'm sure you will. But promise me you'll be gentle. She's an old lady. She's not a bad person. She made some very bad decisions for some very good reasons. She knew that I was totally distraught over the death of Shawn and that I wanted revenge. She had the means and the talent to get revenge for me, so she did."

"And that," noted Al, "turned her into a serial killer, one who embarrassed me badly."

"I know that, and I want you to capture her. I just want you to treat her gently."

The call over, Al left the Berzinski house about nine-fifteen. When he got home, the house was quiet. He showered, shaved, put on clean pajamas, and stretched out on the bed to wait for JoAnne. His eyelids heavy, he turned on the TV and began watching *Limitless*.

He was almost asleep when JoAnne got home, but as she removed her coat and hung it in the closet, he rubbed his eyes and struggled to a sitting position. She laughed.

"What's so funny?"

"I was thinking about dessert and realized it was nothing more than a fleeting notion," she teased. "Go back to sleep. I'll pack your bag."

"No damn way," he told her. "I'm awake now and I want that dessert, so there will be no copping out."

Pushing thoughts of Julie out of his head, Al took his wife's hand and tugged her gently down onto the bed. Their time together was sweet, and reminded him of why he had fallen in love with her in the first place. Could the two of them get back to where they had been when they first got married? So deeply in love they could barely think about anything else but being together?

And if they did, what would happen to him and Julie?

When Al and Charlie met at the La Crosse Municipal Airport the next morning at 6:30 to catch a 6:55 a.m. flight to Minneapolis and then one to Atlanta, Al was grouchy.

"What's the matter?" Charlie nudged him in the arm. "Didn't we feed you good enough last night?"

"Dinner was great, but I'm thinking about JoAnne. We had a really good time together after she got home. And before that I had a great talk with Julie. I love them both, Charlie, so now I'm more confused than ever."

Charlie pursed his lips. "There's no question JoAnne is great. And she never gets upset with you, even when she should. I'm not sure she'd even be upset if she found out about Julie."

Al's chest clenched. "She's a terrific woman, and I couldn't bear the thought of hurting her. That's why I'm so damn conflicted."

At that moment, their flight was called and Al and Charlie were off on another adventure.

22

Friday dawned bright and sunny. Al stared out the window of Rusty's car, trying to enjoy the scenery, but he had too much on his mind. The law enforcement trio of him, Charlie, and Rusty—who had picked them up at the airport the day before and filled them in on what they had so far—had already been on the road for nearly an hour. As they passed through Birmingham, they stopped at McDonald's for Egg McMuffins, hash browns, and coffee. Charlie added two orders of pancakes, a large orange juice, and a second McMuffin.

Rusty shook his head. "Charlie, you never cease to amaze me. You eat like an elephant, but you still remain in shape. How do you do it, man?"

"Clean livin'," answered Charlie, grinning. "Clean livin'."

"A couple of years ago, I'd have disputed that," Al responded. "But Charlie has a new wife and she's brought him around to someone we can all live with now."

"Here we go again, goddammit," swore Charlie. "I get passels of crap that I don't deserve."

"I think you love it," said Al, smiling at the deputy in the rearview mirror. "Because I think you know that only people who love you tease you."

"Crap, then I must be the most loved person in the history of the world."

After a good laugh, the men concentrated on their breakfast. Rusty turned the unmarked vehicle onto I-65 for the short ride to Hayden. A few miles east of Hayden, they saw a collection of police vehicles parked on the shoulder. As they rolled up, Rusty flashed his credentials and the trooper guarding the driveway waved them forward.

A minute later, they drew up on the east side of what was left of the log cabin. The back half of the place was a jumble of smoking ruins. The front looked a bit worse for wear, but not damaged severely.

They were greeted by a big man in uniform; Rusty introduced him as Blount County Sheriff Bo Vinton.

"Welcome, gentlemen," greeted the sheriff. "The scene is all yours. We'll be stickin' aroun' to ward off any curiosity seekers, but we're finished with our investigation. Explosion was set in what we presume to be a lab built into the hill so it couldn't be seen from the outside. Anything you need, you just let my boy over there know. Wave, will you, Roy?"

A tall, tanned man with the look of someone who lived outdoors and loved it, waved at them, wiped his hands on his well-worn jeans and ambled over. "Ahm Roy," he said, his voice dripping with southern honey. "Happy to help you boys any way I can."

The visiting lawmen thanked the sheriff and Roy and began poking around the ruins. From the things left in the bathroom and the drawers in the bedrooms, it was obvious that the occupants had left in a hurry. A woman and a man had been staying there, judging from the clothes in the main and guest room closets. Under the mattress they found an album of photos that featured people Al and Charlie knew. There were lots of photos of Julie and Brody, in addition to a few of Peggy and Kelly.

"I'd say it's her," said Charlie.

"No question," replied Al. "Do you really think it's Don Carbone's son that she's with?"

"We've been leaning on the Cabrera Family members, trying to get more information, but it appears so." said Rusty, leading the way back to the decimated lab. "We sometimes have run-ins with the Cabreras, but for the most part they conduct their business quietly and outside of our view. We think they might have been involved in a scuffle at a home near Augusta the other night.

"We had a tip from one of our informants that they may have been after one of Angelo Carbone's sons. The squeak said the son was sent to live with an older woman for safekeeping. I imagine that could be Rosalie or Genevieve or whoever she is."

"Seems likely." Al picked his way carefully through the bits of broken glass scattered across the floor. "Any reports of deaths within the underworld due to poison?"

"Not around here," replied Rusty. "But there was a report out of New York that one of the high-ranking members of the Gambino family in New York died recently of a mysterious illness. The family made sure no one could get close enough to tell for sure; it could have been poison."

"The fact that she had a lab in her home suggests to me that Genevieve is continuing her deadly work." Al stopped in the middle of the room and looked around, hoping to spot anything that might lead them to the old woman. "But other than the death of that kid in Atlanta, nothing has turned up in the news. And I check many papers every day."

Rusty propped a shoulder against the door frame and studied Al. "Maybe she's workin' for someone?"

Al shrugged. "That's what I'm thinking."

"I say, let's see what we can find in what's left in here." Charlie inclined his head in the direction of the counter in the center of the blackened space.

"Look at it." Al waved a hand around the room. "It's a mess, nothing left."

Charlie pointed at a charred cabinet that had tipped onto its side. "Have we looked in those drawers?" He waded into the debris and made his way to the chest. The first two drawers were reasonably intact and filled with melted plastic jars that could possibly have contained drugs. The third drawer was filled with papers. They were neither charred nor wet.

"See, smart ass?" Charlie reached into the drawer and pulled out a handful. "Maybe these will tell us something."

Al pulled out the entire drawer and they carried it to the kitchen table to go through them. Most of the papers were orders for concoctions. The addresses on where to send them were all over the country. Two were to be sent to Jamaica and one to Mexico City.

"I'm guessin' if we search these we'll find some interesting characters," offered Charlie. "Any chance your guys can run 'em, Rusty?"

"Absolutely." Rusty pulled out his phone, placed a call, and provided several addresses in different parts of the country. That done, he disconnected, looked at Charlie, and reported, "We'll know something in a half hour or so."

The detective was as good as his word. In less than thirty minutes, reports had come back on three of the addresses. In each case the address was linked to organized crime.

Al tapped his fingers on the table. "Definitely sounds like Genevieve has started providing poisons to crime networks. If so, that's a dangerous game she's playing."

"Maybe we oughta go over and pay a visit to this Carbone Family, ask them if she's supplying them with poison and see if they can help us find her," suggested Charlie.

"Sure, Charlie, we can just drive over to New Orleans, knock on the door, and ask them if they could please tell us where Genevieve is. What kind of reaction do you think we'd get?" asked Al.

Charlie scowled. "Well, why can't we knock on the door and ask them some questions? Do we know what the kid's name is?"

Rusty nodded. "It's Dino, or so we've been told. I think if we're going to go over there and pay the family a visit, we need more information than we have. I've got a friend who's a detective in their area. How about I ask him?"

"Goddamn great idea," agreed Charlie.

"Sure sounds better than a cold call." Al watched as Rusty punched a number into his phone. It seemed to ring for a while before he left a message for someone he addressed as Aaron.

When he hung up, Rusty met Al's questioning gaze. "Aaron Wingate." He held up his phone. "Good man. I'm sure he'll be happy to help us out when we fill him in on what we're doing here."

Their inspection as complete as it was going to be, the three lawmen returned to their vehicle for the drive back to Atlanta. They had been on the road for about half an hour when Rusty's phone rang. He answered on the car's Bluetooth system so everyone could hear.

It was Wingate. Rusty talked to him for several minutes about the prospect of gaining access to any of the higher-ups in the Carbone Family if they visited New Orleans.

Wingate told them the don, Angelo Carbone, was on decent terms with the police. "He's a pretty good guy. The family has gone at least partly straight under Angelo's leadership. That's one reason why the Carbones and Cabreras don't like each other. The Cabreras feel the Carbones have gone a little too straight and cooperate with the police a little too much.

In addition, when the Carbones loosened the reins on their illegal booze business, the Cabreras decided they could take over the Carbone's territory. There was a bloody battle. The Carbones prevailed, but the two families have been sparring ever since."

Rusty eased onto I-65. "What do you know about Dino Carbone?"

Wingate snorted. "He's a young buck sewing lots of wild oats. He's Angelo's youngest and the apple of the don's eye. Angelo has been pretty distressed at Dino's willingness to walk with one leg on either side of the line. The don's tried everything to bring him around. The story around town is that the latest effort centers on an older lady who apparently lit Dino's fire in a night out a few months ago. Dino's been missing—or at least staying out of sight—for the past several weeks. We think Angelo worked a deal with the woman to try and break Dino of some of his bad habits."

As the talk swung to where Dino might be hiding, Wingate told him the Carbones maintained a place up in the Catahoula National Wildlife Refuge in Louisiana. "The place is huge and secluded and it's rumored to be the place family members go to when the heat is on. Unfortunately, we've never been able to pinpoint its exact location."

"Thanks Aaron. We'll be in touch." Rusty disconnected the call and shot a look at Al in the passenger seat. "What do you think?"

"Sounds to me like the heat is on." Al shifted to look over the seat at Charlie. "I think we should get ourselves to New Orleans, find the Carbones, and have ourselves a chat."

23

Thursday afternoon, Al climbed into the passenger seat next to Rusty, who had offered to drive to the airport in his unmarked car and leave it there as the three of them flew to New Orleans. They weren't sure what they would find, if anything, but Al agreed with Charlie that the best plan, since they didn't know the exact whereabouts of Dino, was to pay a surprise visit to Angelo Carbone the next day. Depending upon how that went, they could rent a car and head to Louisiana, drive through the Catahoula National Wildlife Refuge on the off chance they might happen upon the Carbone family hiding place, where Dino, and possibly Genevieve, might be. Before heading to the don's house, they would meet up with Aaron Wingate.

They decided to eat breakfast at Coulis the next morning, a restaurant near the Carbone house where the don was said to breakfast often. Since he normally appeared about seven o'clock, Wingate said he would pick them up at 6:45 a.m. The breakfast date set, they decided to find a hotel nearby.

Ultimately they settled on Chimes, on Constantinople Street. Charlie had lobbied hard for Maison Perrier on a street of the same name, but he was overruled for two reasons: first, the rooms there were the most expensive of all those they had looked at, and second, it seemed Charlie's reason for wanting to stay there was that at one point in its history it had been known as a gentleman's club.

"Charlie." Al sent him a withering glance. "I told Kelly I'd keep you out of trouble, and I'm not taking any chances. Knowing you, you'd find the last ghost of a prostitute left in the place and I'd be in hot water with Kelly."

Charlie dropped his head. "C'mon, Al, you know me better'n that. I just thought it would be fun to experience a little local color during my first visit to New Orleans."

"Color, fine. Trouble? Definitely not. And your middle name is trouble. If you don't find it, it finds you."

Charlie leaned forward. "Rusty, don't listen to him. I ain't like that at all. I just like to learn somethin' if I'm in a new place."

Rusty glanced back at him in the rearview mirror. "So you're saying you find whorehouses educational, is that it?"

"It ain't a whorehouse now." Charlie's face reddened. "It's a B&B that gets good reviews. Al left that part out purposely."

Al watched houses and businesses stream by outside the car window as they drove toward the airport. "I'm just trying to save your ass. Without me, you'd be in big trouble with your wife. Not to mention that Dwight wouldn't likely be all that happy with a $149-a-night bill for a room."

"I thought maybe we could bunk together?"

Rusty smacked a palm against the steering wheel. "Now that's a non-starter. Sleeping three to a bed is not my idea of fun, unless …"

"Unless, nothing." Al cut him off before the conversation could head into dangerous territory. "You're right, we've got to take care of Charlie, Rusty, 'cause he's clearly incapable of caring for himself. That means we're going to find a nice but inexpensive place where we each can have our own room. And I'm going to booby trap Charlie's room to make sure that if he tries to leave in the middle of the night, I know it."

"Goddamn, Al, when have I ever done that sort of thing?" Not only was the large lawman's face bright red, now sweat stained his shirt under his armpits.

As they arrived at Hartsfield International for their Southwest flight to New Orleans, Al suppressed a grin at his friend's discomfort. "Don't get me started, pal; don't get me started."

The weather in New Orleans was miserable. Rain pelted the jetway as they deplaned and Al was grateful that Aaron Wingate had pulled his car up to the curb so the group could enter without getting drenched.

Once in town, they drove down Canal Street. Water splashed beneath their wheels. Al glanced out the window. The streets in the French Quarter were flooded. "There's no one around. Is that unusual?"

"It's a common phenomenon," explained Wingate. "When it rains, water in the Quarter rises because the area is below the water table. The pumps will catch up pretty soon and the place will be alive again."

As they passed St. Peter Street, or *rue Saint-Pierre*, as Al had heard the locals call it, he was immediately attracted to the St. Louis Basilica-Cathedral. Charlie was gazing out the back window. "Hey, you guys, there was one of those bengay shops back there. I hear they're great. Can we get some?"

Aaron, laughing heartily, said to Rusty and Al, "Now I understand what you mean about your friend. Charlie, it's pronounced *ben-yay*."

Looking hurt, Charlie responded, "You know what I meant. Can we get some of those bend-yay things as soon as we see another shop?"

By now everyone was laughing and Charlie was looking even more mystified, hurt, too.

"We'll soon be at Coulis," promised Wingate, "and you'll love the cuisine. Their buckwheat pancakes are tremendous and the Eggs Benicio will be the best eggs you have ever eaten, I promise."

"Oh, man, buckwheat pancakes, it's been ages since I had buckwheat pancakes." Charlie's face brightened. "Okay, I'll wait. Let's get there soon; I'm starved."

"Starved?" chorused Rusty and Al, "you're always starved!"

"C'mon you guys, lighten up. A growin' boy needs his food."

Aaron turned into an alley, eased the car up next to a light brick building, and stopped.

"We're here," he announced.

Charlie quickly exited the car, rounded the corner then stopped to look at the sign that featured a dripping egg.

"That's the biggest damn egg I have ever seen." He pointed at the sign. "I want one of those!"

The four of them entered the restaurant, were greeted by an attractive, dark-haired, dark-skinned hostess, and soon were seated at a table roughly in the middle of the room.

Charlie ordered a large glass of freshly squeezed orange juice and studied the menu intently as Al and Aaron talked strategy.

The pleasant waitress returned and looked at Al questioningly. Before he could order, Charlie broke in. "I want one of those eggs benicio, but I also gotta have the grillades and grits. And then, on the side, how about some of them buckwheat pancakes? Can I have four of 'em? Oh, yeah, and I want blueberries, strawberries, and bananas on them, and lots of powdered sugar. Please."

The waitress, who had been scribbling feverishly, paused, looked at Charlie and said, "Mister, either you have a bigger appetite than anyone who has ever eaten here, or you're gonna waste a heckuva lot of money."

"I'm just a growin' boy," said Charlie as the waitress turned to Rusty, Al, and Aaron for far more normal orders.

When she had gone, Aaron announced, "Here's our boy. He just walked in. Don't ogle, but catch a glimpse."

Al shot a furtive glance toward the front of the restaurant. He saw a fireplug of a man. The man wore a black coat and black hat, which cast a sinister aura over him, but his pleasant, smiling face erased the specter.

"Hell, he don't look so tough," scoffed Charlie.

Aaron shook his head. "Don't be fooled. He looks pleasant, but you don't want to be on his bad side, that's for sure. You can afford to look nice when you've got an army of tough guys to do your dirty work."

The don seated himself two tables away. He greeted the waitress by name as three large, tough-looking guys filled the remaining chairs at the table.

"Hi, Angelo," said the waitress with a big smile. "Will it be the usual?"

"Absolutely, Rosie." The don waved a hand around the table. "Pancakes for all of us. I'm having coffee made my way with extra chicory. How about you guys?"

The three toughs all ordered coffee, too, but the largest said, "Rosie, we want the regular brew. Not sure how the don handles that stuff. You gotta eat it, it's so damn strong. You stir it, the wake stays in place."

As his goons laughed, the don scanned the half-filled eatery. His eyes settled on the table of lawmen. He smiled and said, "Yo, Aaron. What the heck are you doing slumming around here?"

Aaron nodded in his direction. "Morning, Angelo. To be honest, we hope to have a word with you, if you have time?"

Al blinked. The two of them sounded on pretty friendly terms. Just how tight were they?

"Sure," said the don, a grin spreading across his face, "but we've gotta have some food first. Can you wait?"

"We don't have our food yet, either, so no rush," answered Aaron.

Don Angelo spread his napkin across his lap. "This business or pleasure?"

"Bit of business, Angelo. Only take a minute," said Aaron.

"Okay, let's go back to my house. Easier to talk business there."

"Sounds good." Aaron leaned back in his seat.

"How well do you know this guy?" Al picked up his fork and twirled it between his fingers. "It seems like you're old buds."

"That's an appropriate description," said Wingate. "We've known each other for years. Since Angelo's family has gone straight, for the most part, we've become better and better friends."

When their food arrived, the don glanced over at their table. Al guessed he'd caught sight of all the plates in front of Charlie when his eyes widened. "That all yours, my man?"

"Yup," said Aaron, "he's just a growin' boy, he says."

"Well, that'll put meat on your bones, for sure," said Angelo. "Now that is a breakfast! I take it back, Aaron, you're not likely to have to wait for us; in fact, I'm sure we'll be finished first."

Knowing Charlie as well as he did, Al doubted it. As the food disappeared into Charlie faster than a garbage disposal digests the remains of a meal, the don and his tablemates looked on. More than one of them watched, slack-jawed.

"Pardon me," said the don, laughing, "but how do you move after all that?"

"I can run as good as you." Charlie wiped his face with the cloth napkin.

"I bet you can." The don pushed back his plate. "But we're not going to find out. Better that way for both of our hearts."

Half an hour later, after they'd paid and driven to the don's stately manor, they were seated in comfortable chairs in his spacious office. A coffee pot and a plate of pastries sat on the coffee table in front of them.

"I heard you wanted some beignets," said the don. "Help yourself."

"Don't mind if I do." Charlie slid to the front of his chair, poured himself a cup of coffee and heaped four beignets onto a small plate.

The don laughed heartily and said, "You've gotta be Charlie. I've heard about you, and how you can eat!"

Charlie looked startled. Al's head jerked. *How in the world had the don heard about Charlie?* His stomach tightened. Being known by a don was rarely a good thing.

"Don't look so surprised. Do you think it was an accident that we bumped into each other at Coulis? Detective Wingate called me yesterday to say that a couple of northern law boys were interested in talking to me. He told me what he knew. And, Charlie, what he knew about you was that you love to eat. That was good enough for me," said the don. "I love to eat, too, and watching you put down breakfast was a treat. Now then, what can I do for you boys?"

"Well, Mr. Don," Charlie set a half-eaten beignet down on his plate, "we're hopin' you might be able to direct us toward a little old lady we've been huntin' for three years. Down here, I guess, she's called the Black Widow of the Woods."

"Hmmm." The don tapped a finger against his chin, "I've heard of her. She's quite a woman, as I understand it. She's the one who makes death-dealing potions, am I right?"

"Yes sir." Al straightened up abruptly in his armchair. "That's the one."

The don nodded. "I heard she helped out friends of mine in New York. And she's also helped enemies in Atlanta, I think, which is probably why you're here."

"She embarrassed me terribly three years ago," admitted Al, "and I'm not going to rest until I have her in custody again."

"I heard about that," said the don. "Something about fourteen or fifteen drownings in Wisconsin that she is believed to have assisted in? And then she escaped, right, and came south?"

"We believe she had a hideout in Alabama, sir," said Al. "The place was burned a few nights ago. There's some evidence that she and the man with her darn near burned to death, too."

"Now, now," the don placed the cup of coffee he'd been drinking down on the coffee table in front of him, "let's not beat around the bush. I don't do business that way. I know the rumors say she was with my son, Dino.

She wasn't. I don't know who it was, but it wasn't Dino. He's on vacation in the Virgin Islands."

He laughed. "Of course, if there were any virgins on those islands, there likely aren't anymore, not with Dino around. He's a virile young man, but he's not with your gal. Tell you what, let me do a little poking around. Maybe something will turn up."

"Much obliged, Mr. Don," said Charlie.

The men talked for a while longer then Charlie asked about a good place for lunch.

"Lunch?" The don raised both eyebrows. "Charlie, that breakfast you just ate was big enough for five men. And you're hungry already?"

"No, no, Mr. Don," said Charlie. "I just think that while we're here, we should sample some Creole or Cajun food, you know?"

"I agree." The don turned to Aaron. "Take them to Antoine's for lunch. I'm going to call Tony Alciatore. I'll tell them to take good care of you."

The don paused, mopped his brow and mouth with the napkin then turned to the big man. "Charlie, you can call me Angelo. It was a pleasure watching you eat. Lunch is on me!"

Al bit back a grin at the sight of Charlie's swelled chest. His pal could turn anything into a genuine compliment. He stood up. "Thank you for your time, Mr. Carbone." He stuck out his hand. "We'd really appreciate it if you could let us know if anything turns up."

The don shook his hand firmly as the other men rose to take their leave. "I'm happy to help out any way I can."

He saw them to the door personally, and closed it behind them when they had gone out onto the expansive, wraparound porch.

"See, you guys?" Charlie grinned as he started down the stairs. "Where would ya be without me? He liked me; liked how I eat. And he's gonna help us, too. And that's all because of me."

"Don't break your arm pattin' yourself on the back, Charlie." Rusty shook his head. "I think if he helps it's gonna be because of Aaron. He likely wants to pay off a debt, or maybe get Aaron into one, right Aaron?"

"Well, we occasionally cooperate with each other," admitted Aaron. "I'm sure he'll assist us if he's so inclined. And you're right, Charlie, your presence helped a lot."

24

Out of the don's house and back downtown, Al lagged behind as they returned to Wingate's office.

Aaron slowed down and nudged him in the ribs with his elbow. "Why the long face?"

"All of this puzzles me," Al admitted. "I like my cases to be organized; I like to know what's next. And in this case, I have no idea what the next move should be. And I'm worried, too, because Charlie and I can't stay much longer, and short of a solid lead, our stay is going to be extremely brief."

"I'm not sure what to tell you," answered Aaron. "Usually Angelo responds to our requests quickly, but in this case, if he's being coy about Dino, I'm not sure what to expect."

"I'd hate for us to go home without finding out something," said Al. "I just wish we had gotten a hint of a suggestion from the don."

Aaron shrugged. "That's the way he is, cards close to the vest, agreeable but quiet. I'm guessing we might hear something by morning. Can you at least stay that long?"

"That'll work, won't it?" Charlie looked back over his shoulder at Al.

What have we got to lose? He really detested the thought of going back to the chief empty-handed. "Yeah, I guess we could give it one more night."

"Great!" Charlie clapped his hands together. "They got some great eateries here, Al. I'd say Antoine's for lunch, just like the don said. How about Brennan's for supper? Is that a good one, Aaron?"

Aaron laughed. "Brennan's is very good, Charlie ... and *very* expensive."

"Whadda ya say, Al? You only go around once." Charlie offered him the sad puppy-dog look Al was sure must have gotten him his first date with Kelly. "Antoine's for lunch and Brennan's for supper?"

"Okay." Al could rarely resist Charlie's patented look either. "Rusty and Aaron, join us; our treat."

Aaron grimaced. "Do you know how expensive Brennan's is? Not many cops eat there."

"We'll work it out; Al always does." Charlie slapped Al across the back so hard he nearly stumbled forward a couple of steps. "Tell me something, Aaron. I read that Brennan's serves Creole food. Is that different than Cajun?"

"They are different," replied Aaron, "but only subtly. Creole cuisine uses tomatoes, and proper Cajun food does not."

"No tomatoes?" Charlie's expression was incredulous. "How the hell do you cook without tomatoes?"

"Trust me, they do it," said Aaron, "and very well."

"Okay." Charlie, always agreeable when it came to food, lifted his massive shoulders. "How about heading to Antoine's?"

"Charlie, for god's sake," admonished Al. "You finished a humongous breakfast an hour and a half ago and now you want lunch?"

"Well, Al …"

"I know, I know, a growing boy's gotta eat," said Al, smiling at their companions. "Guys, you are now being treated to one of Wisconsin's natural wonders. If eating is involved, Charlie's all over it."

"I think that's a compliment," suggested Charlie.

Rusty nodded. "I suspect it is, too, but how about we work for a while before heading to lunch?"

For the next two hours, the four lawmen explored the case from all angles. As they prepared to finish up, Aaron powered down his laptop and closed the lid. "Ordinarily I'd say the don will come through. But since Dino could very well be involved, and he clearly doesn't want us to know that, I'm not sure if we can count on that."

"We'll just have to wait and see." Rusty stood first and the others followed suit.

When they got outside, the temperature was high and the humidity was staggering. Aaron looked up at the cloudless sky. "We can walk. It's only about eight blocks."

"Eight blocks!" Charlie looked as if Aaron had just told them they were going to make a quick trip to the moon and back. *And to Charlie, walking eight blocks is not much more feasible than a trip to the moon.* Al's lips twitched as Charlie pressed a palm to his forehead. "Eight blocks? I ain't walkin' eight blocks."

"If you wanna go to Antoine's, you're walkin', Charlie." Aaron sounded firm. "We wouldn't find any place to park that's closer than here."

"You gotta be kiddin'." Charlie, clearly reluctant, fell into step behind them. "Well, I'll just have to eat a little more to replace the energy lost."

As the four walked into the French Quarter, Charlie elbowed Al in the ribs, his eyes wide. "Did you see that? She practically had her coconuts hanging out."

"Aaw, Charlie ma man, you ain't seen nothin' yet," drawled Aaron. "Just remember, you're a cop. You gotta behave yourself."

For the rest of the walk, Charlie didn't complain once, his head swiveling as if on a turntable. *He's so intent on the "scenery" I'm guessing he wishes the walk was even longer.* Al bit back a laugh. His friend made an easy target, but at the same time Charlie's heart was as big as the rest of him, and surprisingly sensitive. It hurt his feelings when other people made fun of him, something Al tried to keep in mind at times like this.

"Shit." Charlie took a last look around the neighborhood as he pulled open the door of Antoine's. "How do you guys get anything done down here? Women hardly wear any clothes."

Al punched him lightly in the arm. "Charlie, I'll be sure to tell Kelly how much you appreciated the local sights."

"Awww, Al, there's no harm in lookin'."

"We'll see if Kelly agrees." Al smiled broadly.

No sooner had the four been seated, than a beaming man with dark, slicked-back hair and a Roman nose materialized in front of them. "Gentlemen," he waved an arm expansively around the table. "I'm Tony Alciatore. We're delighted to have you at Antoine's. Please be comfortable. Lunch is on Angelo Carbone, as you know. Which one of you is Charlie?"

Charlie held up his hand. Tony beckoned to him. "Come with me, young man. We're going to take a little tour."

Al watched as Charlie got up and accompanied Tony out of the dining room. What, exactly, had the don told Tony Alciatore about his friend? A waiter served Virgin Marys all around and the men studied the menu and talked, settling on their entrees, all of them light.

Thirty minutes later Charlie was back. He had the biggest grin on his face Al had ever seen there, which was saying something. He'd barely reached the table before he launched into a story about meeting Chef Michael Regua and getting a full tour of the kitchen, including tasting all the delicacies being prepared there.

"Man, you ain't seen anything like it, it's goddamn amazin'. And the food? I ain't ever had anything like it, never, nowhere."

The look on the big man's face was one of pure joy, and he emphasized his wonder by gently rubbing his stomach as he sat.

"Considering you've eaten just about everything there is to eat everywhere you've ever been, that's high praise indeed." Al lifted his drink in Charlie's direction.

"Goddamnit, Al, you wait. It's ain't just food; I mean it!"

And he was right. The food, though rich and likely calorie-laden, melted in Al's mouth as if it were a sliver of ice on a hot day. Charlie was in his glory. While a lovely young waitress tied a napkin around his neck, waiters and waitresses lined up with trays of food that would genuinely have been fit for a king.

Everything from Les Amuse-bouches of fresh grilled figs brushed with honey and stacked with fresh mint, Parma ham, and halloumi, to the entrée comprised of Cajun shrimp, olive oil, tomato dressing, and parsley, the main course of boeuf bourguignon, a rich stew that cast off unbelievable aromas, a prickly pear sorbet that apparently served as a palate cleanser, a platter of delicate French cheeses served with champagne for the table—although Charlie ate most of it—to the dessert, an indescribably light custard swimming on a butterscotch sea that Chef Regua called Crème au Caramel, was perfect.

"Wow." Charlie gasped as he leaned back in his chair and pressed a hand to his stomach. "If I had known that 'amused douche' was that good, I would have had it long ago."

That sent his tablemates into gales of laughter. Even Chef Regua, who had come out to personally check that everything had suited them, quaked with laughter. Only Charlie failed to see the humor as he looked around the table, a bewildered look on his face. "Wha'd I say?"

"Nothing, my Sharlee, it was just a good time for a hearty laugh to exercise the body," offered the chef in a heavy French accent, winking at Al.

"Well, it didn't seem that funny." Charlie glared at his companions. "I ain't that funny."

Sensing his friend's indignation, Al bit back another laugh. "Charlie, when you're on, you're one of the funniest men I know. You're definitely on today, that's for sure."

As they were preparing to leave, and thanking the chef and Alciatore, who had appeared to remind them that lunch was on Angelo Carbone, Al removed a twenty from his billfold and handed it to their waitress, thanking her for her excellent service.

"Oh, no, monsieur, it is I who should be tipping you. Never have I seen anyone eat like that one." She pointed at Charlie, smiling.

"There likely is no one in Charlie's category. And because of that and Mr. Carbone's generosity, you had to work very hard." Al pressed the money into her hand.

As they walked from the restaurant, Aaron's phone rang. The rest of them waited while he talked quietly for several minutes then ended the call. "Let's get to the office; there are things to talk about."

They hurried back to the precinct headquarters, Charlie struggling and panting to keep up. Once there, Aaron waited for them to be seated. "We have a report that your old lady is north of here near Little Lake in the Catahoula National Wildlife Refuge. It's a pretty wild area, and the place I told you about where the Carbone family has a secluded getaway. We still don't have the exact coordinates, but hopefully we'll soon know more. We're going up to the boss' office."

Blood pounded in Al's ears. *Could they really be this close to their quarry?* He shoved back his frustration. He'd give anything to be able to drive straight to the Refuge to check out this latest report, but going in alone and unprepared, with no real idea of where the hideout was, would be foolhardy. This woman had already proved herself to be extremely slippery; when they went after her this time, they needed to be fully prepared. And fully armed.

Fifteen minutes later, they were seated around a large square table in a conference room at police headquarters on Broad Street. With them were two members of the New Orleans bilingual task force, Dante Alvarez and Jamie Mahooda.

Mahooda cleared his throat. "Last night, as we were monitoring circuits across the city, we picked up a conversation in Italian. After we figured out the language, which was trickier than it sounds because it was tainted with touches of Cajun, we confirmed the communication to be between Angelo Carbone and his son Dino. Dino was looking for advice on where to disappear to for a few days. Apparently he was running from a group presumed to be from the Cabrera family in Atlanta.

"We believe Dino, who is traveling with a female companion, is now headed for a remote safe house maintained by the family somewhere in the Catahoula National Wildlife Refuge. That's a pretty swampy, desolate area. The conversation was not specific on a particular location. It sounded as if they would be there by tomorrow morning."

"Interesting." Al pursed his lips. "With that information in mind, we ought to have a serious talk about next steps. Aaron, Jamie, Dante, I suspect you folks will want to bow out at this point, right?"

"Much as I hate to do that, I think we've reached the limit of where we ought to go, Al." Aaron held up both hands. "We have a great relationship with the Carbone family and have pretty much adopted a hands-off posture, as long as things don't get glaringly bad."

The comment rankled Al, but he too made concessions to those who helped him. It was the way of the world. "We understand. I thought that would be the case. Charlie, Rusty, we probably should get back to the motel and decide what we are going to do next. Aaron, we'll see you tonight, right?"

"If you're sure you want to have dinner, I'll be there. Might as well swing by the precinct to pick me up."

Back at the motel, Al and Charlie decided a first step was to call the chief and sheriff in La Crosse for advice. A short chat later, they had the go-ahead to extend their stay and to make a trip north to the wildlife refuge.

Rusty then called his boss, and was also cleared to make the trip. Soon thereafter, the morning flight was canceled and a car was rented to take them north to what they hoped would be an encounter with the woman, the elusive Genevieve Wangen.

25

When the weekend arrived, Rosalie and Dino were tucked away in a complex on stilts in the backwoods area of Dewey W. Wills Wildlife Management Area, a state-owned portion of the Catahoula National Wildlife Refuge. The cabin in which they were housed was beyond comfortable. It was bright, filled with technology and the latest in appliances. There were two bedrooms, an office, kitchen, great room, and bathroom. As Dino slept late, Rosalie padded around the cottage in bare feet, exploring every nook and cranny. *It's perfect.*

They had arrived in the wee hours of the morning, after pushing through Mississippi on I-20. They crossed the Mississippi River into Louisiana just south of Vicksburg, stopping only once, in Tallulah, for gas, a bathroom break, and snacks to munch on. The small town of 7,000 residents had seen better days. It was the perfect place to stop, Dino had said, because no one seemed to care one way or the other about visitors.

As far as Rosalie was concerned, that was a very good thing, because the town looked as if the world had left it behind about sixty years earlier. It had all the personality of a hat discarded by Minnie Pearl in 1940.

Back on the road, they picked up 425 and drove south on the two-lane road for a couple hours. At the intersection with Highway 8, they were met by two Lincoln Town Cars, each carrying four people. Dino pulled over and climbed out of their vehicle, greeted the folks in the other two cars, and spent several minutes talking to them. He returned to the car and slipped in behind one of the Town Cars. The other followed closely behind.

The night now black as ink, they drove for another hour and a half, then turned onto an even narrower blacktop road for a short time, then turned again, this time onto a road that was little better than a dirt trail. After a half hour of bumping along the path, the cars came to a stop. The headlights revealed a body of water and a long wooden dock. An airboat floated next to the dock. They greeted the pilot, who introduced himself as Hank Thomas and said he would take them the rest of the way. Two occupants—Joe and Sammy—of one of the cars that had accompanied them for the last part of their flight got into the boat with them.

Rosalie had never been in an airboat, but she found the ride smooth and the engine so muffled that it barely made a sound. As they glided over the water, the wush of birds taking flight, seemingly by the hundreds, filled the air, and every now and then there was a loud splash.

"Gators," grumped Hank. "There's tons of 'em around here."

With the exception of that brief statement, the ride was accomplished without anyone talking and by the light of the moon.

After an hour, Hank cut the power and the boat glided to a stop with a gentle bump. He lowered a device at the bow of the boat that acted as a ramp and Rosalie and Dino followed their two burly companions onto a path cut through shoulder-high grass.

Joe led the way, with Sammy falling in behind them, for a walk of about ten minutes. "Here we are," said Joe softly. Moving aside, he revealed steps that led to a deck. "Gimme just a minute and I'll have power for you."

Momentarily, they heard the snort of an engine that lapsed into the soft, not unpleasant burbling of a generator. Joe returned, climbed the steps, and soon a soft glow lit the porch. "Welcome home," said Sammy, looking at Dino. "You recall this place, right? We've had a helluva lot of fun here. Remember the time we brought those girls out here from Harrisonburg and—"

"I remember," snapped Dino, cutting him off, "but I believe we agreed not to talk about that."

"Sorry, Dino," mumbled Sammy. "Well, hope you find the place to your liking. Me and Joe have been out here for two days cleaning and filling it with provisions. We'll be in the cabin just behind you. Don't be walkin' around outside without lettin' us know. Joe set the perimeter alarm when he started the generator. You want anything, use the walkie-talkie, okay?"

"Got it." Dino clapped him on the shoulder. "Thanks, guys. We appreciate your presence and your help." He climbed the stairs and reached back to help Rosalie. She took his hand and, with his help, scrambled swiftly and effortlessly up the four steps.

Joe unlocked the cabin and handed the key to Dino. "Shut the porch light off right away, okay? Never know when there might be poachers out here and I'd just as soon not have to wrangle with any of 'em tonight." He offered Dino a salute. "See you tomorrow." In seconds, he and Hank had disappeared silently into the darkness at the bottom of the stairs.

When they got inside, Dino drew Rosalie to him and kissed her tenderly. "Sorry, baby, but we might have to hang out here for awhile, until the heat eases. Those were some bad, bad guys chasing us. We'll be supremely careful and on the lookout, but I don't think they'll bother us here. This place is damn well hidden."

"What is there to do here?" A coy smile crossed her face. "Maybe I'll get all my ashes hauled before we leave."

"I wouldn't be a bit surprised," said Dino, smiling, "but it probably won't be tonight. I'm totally bushed. How about a shower and bed?"

"Sounds good to me," replied Rosalie, and twenty minutes later they were scrubbed and in bed. For the first time in weeks, she had closed her eyes, feeling completely safe as she slipped into a deep sleep.

Rosalie had been up since dawn. She tried to look out the windows, but they were carefully sheltered, offering only a view of bare, moist ground. As much as she would have liked to go outside and look around, she dared not upset Joe and Sammy, as they were counting on the two men to keep them safe here. She found a collection of books and magazines in a rack next to a recliner and was pleasantly surprised that they were current. With nothing else to do, she sat down in the chair and opened a copy of *People* and paged through it to the story on Leonardo DiCaprio, who had won a best actor Oscar for *The Revenant.*

What a nice young man. Apparently he had emerged from humble beginnings and stumbled around low-budget television and movie offerings until blowing onto the big stage as Jack Dawson, who fell in love with Kate

Winslet's character, Rose DeWitt Bukater, on the maiden and ill-fated voyage of the huge liner, Titanic.

It was nice to see people of humble origins make it big. Rosalie closed the magazine and absently tapped her fingers on top of it. Suddenly Julie leapt into her lap. The cat had been on edge since the attack. From the moment they'd arrived at the cabin, the cat had been exploring and it had been a while since Rosalie had seen him. She scratched her pet behind the ears. "Will the fortune being amassed for Julie help that dear girl make it to the top?" She sighed and returned the magazine to the rack. "I sincerely hope so, Julie," she murmured to her niece's namesake. "Otherwise, what has all of this been for?" Looking up, she prayed, "Dear God, please give me a few more good years. I still have work to do."

There was no thought of the macabre nature of the "work" she did; none at all.

As she rocked and dreamed, the squawk of birds became a dissonant background chorus. In its own way, the cacophony enveloping her was pleasant, as if the birds acted as a guard force of thousands. She lapsed into a conscious coma, closing her eyes and shutting out all the worldly thoughts that invaded her head. She stayed that way for more than an hour, until the sound of running water broke into her reverie. Dino was up and in the shower.

In ten minutes, his footsteps sounded behind her. Hair still damp, the scent of soap drifted from his as he crouched in front of her and reached for her hands. "Are you hungry? I could cook us breakfast."

"I'm hungrier for you, my dear," said Rosalie softly. "I let you off the hook last night, but you look rested enough now for a roll in the hay."

He smiled at her and shook his head. "My darling Rosalie, you have an insatiable appetite for sex. I would never have believed that someone like you existed, if someone had tried to tell me before I met you. And I love it, although you challenge my stamina. But yes, a pre-breakfast roll in the hay would make a delightful appetizer to a new day."

And so they played, Rosalie exercising a number of talents Dino had not yet experienced. An hour later, he was spent, lying on the bed, arms outstretched and gasping for breath.

"Wore you out, did I?" she teased. "I'm guessing your promise to make breakfast has been withdrawn. Well, you were a good boy—a very good boy—so I shall do the honors. What will it be? Your wish is my command."

It took him a while before he answered, and the response was more squeak than voice. "Something sweet, I think. Maybe waffles or pancakes?"

"Now just where do you expect me to find a waffle iron?"

"I'm quite sure that you will find every modern-day cooking convenience in the pantry off the kitchen." Propping himself up on his elbow, he smiled.

Moving from the bed into the kitchen, she found three doors. When she opened the first, she discovered it led to the deck surrounding the cabin. She opened the second and blinked to see that it only led to another door. When she attempted to turn the handle of that one, she realized it was locked. The third led to the pantry, a room nearly as large as the kitchen. Dino had not exaggerated. One side of the room was lined with shelves that held cooking gear—pots, pans, a deep fryer, food processor, three blenders, a griddle, and, yes, a waffle iron that was no doubt as expensive as it looked.

The other three walls of the room were also lined with shelves, those laden with cans, bottles, and packages of nearly every kind of canned and packaged food imaginable. There was waffle mix, beignet mix, packages of batter, flour, sugar, and lots of things she could not pronounce nor knew how to use.

Beside the door to the kitchen was one of the largest refrigerators she had ever seen. It too was fully stocked, including the generous compartment for frozen foods and another for fresh vegetables and fruits.

As she moved back into the kitchen carrying the waffle iron, she again heard the sound of the shower. She smiled at the thought of having caused Dino to perspire enough to need a second shower. It certainly wasn't the temperature of the cabin, because what must be a great climate-control system kept the place comfortable.

Soon the smell of bacon frying permeated the living space, and when Dino came into the kitchen she had a waffle ready for his plate.

Dino kissed her cheek. "You know, Rosalie, I just may have to marry you to keep you from leaving."

She studied him. *Was he teasing?* She couldn't imagine anything enticing her to leave, but she wasn't naïve. Sooner or later he would grow tired of a woman three times his age. Rosalie pushed back the thought. Better not to dwell on such things, but just enjoy each moment they had together now.

Breakfast finished and the dishes done, Rosalie tidied up the bedroom. She examined the two walk-in closets and found them as well stocked as the pantry. And when she checked the sizes of the women's garments, they were all in her size. The drawers held lingerie, socks, slacks, and shorts, also perfect for her.

Dino entered the room and she turned and kissed him. "My goodness, your family is filled with wonderful surprises."

"Nothing too good for the woman who fills my every sexual fantasy. In fact, we may never leave this place."

Rosalie's eyes met his. "You know, I haven't thought about the outside world once since we got here last night."

"I know, it's magical isn't it? Who would believe a deep woods swamp could be so compelling?" He reached for her hand. "How about we have a look around?"

He grabbed the walkie-talkie, talked briefly with Joe, then opened the door and led Rosalie outside. The pristine beauty of their surroundings was breathtaking. At the bottom of a small hill was a spacious swamp with hundreds of birds—colorful ducks, white swans, several species of geese—paddling on the water. On the other three sides, the cabin was guarded by towering hardwoods, maple, and oaks, reminding her of her girlhood home in Wisconsin.

He took her hand as they walked around the wide deck to the back of the cabin. Rosalie found a walkway that led to another cabin in the woods, nearly hidden by the shadows. As they made their way towards it, she could make out two other cabins through the trees.

"This is a complex."

"It is. There are lots of things to do here, actually. That's good, too, because we are likely to be here for a number of weeks."

"I suppose you're right. The Cabreras have proven to be extremely difficult to escape from, and ruthless in tracking us down, haven't they? I can't imagine anywhere safer than here until the danger has passed." Rosalie slid a hand through the crook of his elbow. "I guess that makes me your captive, so I'll just have to lie back and enjoy myself."

"And you do that well." He winked at her. "Actually, dad has plans for you. He thinks you could, with a little help from him, continue your work here."

"You're kidding. Where would I work?"

"Come with me." he answered, leading her toward a structure in the woods. When they got there, Dino opened the door and swept his arm in an invitation for her to enter. When she did, her eyes widened. It was a laboratory, equipped with what appeared to be every type of herb and powder she could possibly need. The more she explored, the more astounded she became. "This is perfect! It's much more modern and well-equipped than anything I have worked with."

"I thought you'd be impressed. I think Dad was worried about my survival if there wasn't anything other than sex for you to do here. I hope you'll have fun. God knows, we have lots for you to do."

They meandered back up the pathway to the deck. After they'd settled on chairs on the porch, he told her of his family's enemies, and how the gangs in various parts of the country were working together in an effort to exterminate the Carbones.

"They want to break our hold on the south," admitted Dino. "We must counter in kind. And that means there will be lots of uses for your concoctions."

"You know I'll be happy to help in any way I can. After all, I have become more and more attached to you as the weeks have passed. I don't think it will be a hardship for us to be here. Work during the day, play at night, what could be better than that?"

"Just not every night. I can't keep up with you. I'm not sure how you do it, but we all want to know if you've found the fountain of youth, or what your secret is."

"It's good, clean living." Rosalie reached over and patted his hand. "Just good clean living."

26

Al repressed a surge of irritation as Rusty drove him and Charlie down the interstate, heading for the Catahoula National Wildlife Refuge north of them.

Charlie had been complaining for the last half hour. "Goddamnit, you guys, this is intolerable! I gotta have something to eat, and I gotta get outta this heat!"

Al gritted his teeth. This was worse than taking a toddler on a road trip. "Charlie, it's damn near freezing in here and you're sweating. It's only eleven in the morning and we just ate a couple of hours ago. We'll stop at the next town if it's okay with Rusty. And when we get back in the car, you sit up here in the front. I'm sick of freezing my ass off."

Soon the outskirts of Alexandria, Louisiana, came into view and shortly after that, Rusty pulled the car into a Kwikway Exxon station. While Rusty filled the tank, Charlie sought advice from the clerk as to the best places to eat in the area. When they pulled back onto the road, Charlie settled in the front seat and, professing great temperature relief, directed Rusty to Darrell's Restaurant in Pineville. An hour later, Charlie rubbed his stomach, burped repeatedly, and talked constantly about how good the food was.

Hopefully that will hold him for a while. Al sincerely hoped so. He'd hate to have to explain to the sheriff why they'd dumped Charlie in the ditch and left him in the wilds of Louisiana. The three of them pushed toward Catahoula Lake and the wildlife areas that surrounded it. Optimism swung toward high and all three were on alert as they drove along narrow Highway 28.

Three hours later, they had talked to every person they'd seen outside as they drove—all fourteen of them—in stops in Holloway, Buckeye, and Deville. They also stopped at Honey Brake Lodge on the southeastern side of the wildlife management area. When they asked about visitors, everyone looked at them like they were crazy. No one had seen anything. No one had heard anything. No one had caught any gossip about visitors. Their spirits waned.

"Not 'ceptin you," offered one old-timer, seated on a bench outside Honey Brake Lodge. "Who'n the hell would come here now? There's nothin' to do. Huntin' season's closed, fishin's lousy. It's hotter'n hell. This is the worst time o' the year for a visit. Nothin' to do, not a damn thin'."

Frowning, Charlie kicked at one of their tires. "Let's get the hell out of here. Nobody knows anything. I think we're the first visitors seen here in months. Must've had some bad intel."

"Aaron seemed pretty certain that the intel they received was solid." Rusty appeared determined to defend the choice they had made to come this far. "I, for one, want to poke around a bit more before we head south again."

"That's crazy! There's no place left to look."

Al, too, was dejected and about ready to give up on this part of the chase. To think they were this close to their quarry and have to turn back though … He blew out a long breath and drove his fingers through his hair. "I was so certain we would find something. But Charlie is right. Where else can we look? There isn't much around here except birds, and probably snakes and gators we've been lucky to avoid so far. I hate to say it, but maybe we should head back, although I wouldn't mind making a call to Aaron first, see if he has any advice for us."

Charlie pulled out his cell phone, powered it up, and scanned the screen. "Crap, there's no damn service here. Head south, Rusty; we'll try again when we get to the outskirts of New Orleans."

Rusty dropped his own phone back into his shirt pocket. "Let's not give up that quickly. We'll go a bit farther and keep checking for cell service. As soon as we find it, we'll make the call. And if Aaron has any suggestions for other places to go, we're gonna do it."

Al was tired and demoralized, but he too wasn't so sure abandoning the chase was the right idea, not when they'd come this far. *And she is this close.* He clenched his fists as he tried to force himself to relax in the back seat.

In the front, Charlie grumbled under his breath, no doubt about the unfairness of it all, but he uncharacteristically kept his thoughts to himself as they pulled back onto the road.

Two hours later, the sun, now a burning orange ball, was sinking toward the earth. They'd gotten a hold of Aaron and had stopped at more places he'd suggested, but had found nothing.

"Goddammit, the next time I suggest we get the hell home, let's get the hell home."

"C'mon, Charlie, what else did you have to do today? And think of the fine company you got to spend it with."

Al suppressed a grin. Rusty had clearly learned just what it took to push Charlie's buttons.

Charlie slumped down in his seat. "Yer okay Rusty, but I can see Al any damn time, and it's no big thrill. Get us back to New Orleans so we can eat and get to bed. I wanna go home."

Al didn't have the energy to argue with him, and apparently Rusty didn't either. The detective turned the car around and the three of them headed back to New Orleans in silence.

27

With Dino making up things for them to do, little contests that took advantage of Rosalie's love of reading chief among them, they settled into a routine that for many might have been boring. Rosalie, though initially concerned early on, grew content and willing to stay out of harm's way in the depths of the Dewey Wills area swamp. They were well taken care of. Their five companions—four bodyguards and a cook-housekeeper, Miranda Perez—provided for their needs and Rosalie decided she could be happy living a life of leisure.

For the next couple of weeks, they slept past sun-up, lounged around the cabin, played with each other on a daily basis and enjoyed being cared for and pampered. Rosalie also spent a few hours each day in her lab, but not having too much to do was a new experience for her. For a couple of weeks it was fine. Then she got antsy again. While there was no cable TV, there were movies to watch, magazines and books to read, and puzzles to assemble, but for someone used to being active all the time, those quickly lost their appeal.

When she raised the issue one evening when the seven of them were enjoying a great catfish dinner prepared by Miranda, their five watchdogs seemed surprised.

Joe set down his fork. "Why didn't you say so? How about some fishing? There's great fishing in the area, and I think Hank and I know all the good—and hidden—spots."

"That sounds like fun. I haven't been fishing since my stepdad and I used to go out for salmon on Lake Michigan. I love to fish, and I'm pretty darn good at it, too."

Dino smiled at the comment. "Rosalie, you've been plenty busy in the lab. I didn't know that wasn't enough for you. But now that fishing has come up, is there anything you can't do, or haven't done?"

"Not a lot. But I really do love to fish."

Joe smacked a palm down on the oak table. "We'll go out in the morning. You going, too, Dino?"

"Nah, fishing moves too slow for me. I'll just stay here and catch some sleep then get Miranda to make me one of her famous breakfasts."

Joe turned to Miranda. "Speaking of food, would you pack us something for our outing?"

Miranda set a bowl of potatoes down on the table. "Of course."

"I'll come too." Sammy grabbed the bowl and helped himself to a spoonful.

"Great." Judging by the enthusiasm in his voice, Joe was as eager to do something as Rosalie was. "Clarendon, you stay back with Dino and Miranda, keep an eye on the place."

Clarendon, another of the bodyguards that Angelo had sent to help guard Dino and Rosalie, and a man of few words, nodded curtly. Those bases covered, Dino and Rosalie retired to their cabin. While Rosalie was excited, it was about the morning's adventure. There were no lessons for her younger companion that night.

The next morning, Rosalie was up well before dawn, and when Joe rapped at the door at about 4:45 a.m., she was ready and out the door noiselessly so as to not wake up Dino. Sammy poled the boat for the first ten minutes before Joe started the motor. They spent the next fifteen minutes cruising the bayou until Rosalie was thoroughly lost. Thankfully, Joe seemed to know exactly where he was going. Before the expedition was over, they had landed a few sizeable trout and several redfish, too.

"We'll eat well tonight," noted Sammy, as he lifted the heavy stringer out of the water and the group prepared to head back. When they reached the cabins, Miranda was waiting. She took the stringer from Joe as though it were a feather. "I'll have these cleaned and filleted in a flash. Broiled or batter-fried, Rosalie?"

"Let's go batter-fried. Could we have some French fries, too?"

"Absolutely. How about some onion rings for appetizers? And maybe a salad as well. How about I surprise you?"

It was one of the best dinners Rosalie had eaten. The batter almost floated from the fish, which had the most delicate taste she had ever experienced. The French fries were also delightful, as were the onion rings.

"Creole batter is light, not so many calories. Better for you and easier on the stomach." Miranda's tone left no room for argument.

Rosalie slept well that night, and from then on, a fishing trip was on the agenda every two or three days as she and Dino adjusted to their time away from lights and noise. The stars in the evening seemed as if they could be picked, they were so bright and near. And she came to embrace the sound of silence as a welcome change from the bustle of the outside world.

Then one day, after about four weeks, Joe and Sammy returned to the hideout with two boats filled with boxes and packages. In the afternoon, the assembly began. After a couple of hours, Rosalie realized they were adding some equipment to the lab. She had indicated to Dino there were a few pieces of equipment, neither expensive nor large, that would aid her in putting together special killing concoctions. Obviously he had found a way to get them for her.

Coming up behind her, Dino wrapped his arms around her. "What do you think?"

"Everything is great. It's just what I wanted. I am so grateful to you for passing the requests along to your father."

"Pop thought you might be able to turn out even more effective concoctions if you had the equipment you indicated. Now he hopes you'll be able to get a lot of work done with all your new playthings."

"You're about the only plaything I need. But I'm anxious to try these out too."

The new equipment was assembled and installed quickly, and whenever there were things missing or needed, two of the guards would leave to get the items.

When the equipment had all been installed, Rosalie told Dino that everything now was perfect. "I doubt there is anything I can't make in this environment. It's just perfect, Dino. Perfect in every way."

Soon thereafter, he and Rosalie walked to their cabin. "I am so excited." Rosalie bestowed a deep, loving kiss on her beau. "Dino, I need some attention."

"Come, my love, let me see what mischief we can find."

As always, his skills as a lover left her breathless and content. "That was wonderful. For someone your age, you are an unbelievable lover. Although you haven't yet topped my Henry, you are coming closer and closer. Our time here must be doing you good."

"It is. I think I'm following Father's wishes. I am trying to learn. I pay attention to everything you say and do. Then I try to put it into practice and make you proud. When you compliment me, it makes me feel wonderful."

"You are wonderful." She kissed him again, then laid back and invited him to embrace her once more. He took advantage of the opportunity, easing her back to desire then taking care of the need.

"Dino, you are a most wonderful student. I believe your father would be pleased at all you have learned in this department."

"That is high praise. I appreciate it. Now if you can help me erase Pop's image of me as a playboy, it would be even better. I think he believes me the best-suited to lead the family when he steps down, but unless I get rid of the man-about-town image, he'll work longer than he should. Mama worries about him terribly. She knows he works too hard and she thinks it's killing him. Now these problems with another family have added to the stress. He's not young, Rosalie, and he's showing his age. I worry, too."

"Dino, you are young, but you are not a child, you're a man. If your father has aspirations for you, we must convince him you are ready for them. We have had a marvelous time here. We've done exactly as we pleased. It's been good for both of us. But now it is time for us to focus on what your family needs. I think we can demonstrate to your father that you are exactly what he is looking for."

"If you can do that, I will be forever grateful." He yawned and settled deeper under the covers. In moments, his breathing had deepened and slowed.

When she was sure he was asleep, Rosalie crept from beneath him, removed his pants from around his ankles, covered him with a blanket and retired to her room.

Rosalie puttered away, testing the new equipment to make sure it was installed correctly and worked as it should. The three new mixers increased the amount of a material she could produce, and the new filtration products allowed for much purer poisons than the previous equipment had.

After a few days, she walked into their cabin, kissed Dino, and told him that the things his father had sent were perfect … absolutely state of the art. "I can now produce poisons that are totally pure and amazingly lethal. Please tell your father how happy I am."

Dino shook his head. "You tell him, he's joining us for dinner. You've been so excited about the new equipment that I let him know. He decided he wanted to come and meet you and see the new and improved lab in operation."

Her eyes widened. "Oh my, I've never met a don. All my work for them has been done via mail order. But it will be fun to have some new faces at the table, I'll admit that."

It was a festive meal to be sure. Angelo and Rosalie hit it off at once and dinner was filled with conversation about their pasts. It was both entertaining and sobering. Rosalie forthrightly told him about the fourteen drowning deaths she had facilitated in Wisconsin. Angelo countered with stories about moving to the top of the mob scene in New Orleans. "It was a bloody fight all the way." He shared tales of massacres and beheadings that left no doubt in her mind of the truth of that statement. When he had finally driven the Cabrera family out, they had moved to Atlanta. Angelo dabbed his mouth with the cloth napkin. "The competition between the families has heated up again recently, to the point where the Cabreras have put a hit out on Dino." He sighed.

"They won't quit until they have accomplished their goal, so I'm afraid the only avenue for me is extermination—total annihilation. And I am too old for an assignment of that magnitude." Angelo drew a long black cigar from the vest pocket of his suit. He lit it, sucked it into life, then sat back, puffing contentedly.

"There was a time when Juan Cabrera and I were close. Then he sought to get rid of us so he could have New Orleans to himself. He found out that we weren't as weak as he must have thought. Through the years, the war has intensified, flaring up every few years over a variety of reasons. But when he ordered the hit on Dino, the feud ratcheted up dramatically. Now it's gonna be a fight-to-the-death battle, I'm afraid. So when you think about the laboratory, just think about it as an investment in survival. It is my hope, dear Rosalie, that you will help us rid the world of our enemies."

"You have my word, Angelo." She took his hand and held it gently. "Whatever you need that I can supply, you shall have."

"I hoped you would say that. Do you think it would be possible to develop a deadly spray that at a range of, say, three to four feet could kill a target?"

Rosalie pondered the question. "I've never thought of that. Seems funny that I haven't, but I always wanted the certainty that an injection could deliver. I can definitely try. I'm thinking something based in Rosary Pear or Monkshood. Those are pretty lethal plants. I'll have to work on it. Just the thing for my new lab equipment, right?"

He smiled. "I admit that was one of my thoughts in securing it for you. It is my hope that you will work quickly. The Cabreras are getting bolder, and they are getting some help from other families, too. I would love to have a deadly spray in my possession."

"I will see what I can do. At the very least, I should be able to develop a spray that would allow you to paralyze your victim long enough to give them the lethal injection. I'll let you know as soon as I come up with something, okay?"

They talked on for a while. When darkness had firmly enveloped the swamp, the don checked his watch then rose. "My ride is on the way. I must not keep them waiting. After all, we want to make certain this place stays hidden." When she stood too, he kissed Rosalie on both cheeks.

"Good-bye, my dear Rosalie. And, Dino, please be patient a few more weeks, maybe a month or two, until we have the tools to neutralize the Cabreras. Only then will it be safe for you to re-emerge."

The door opened. Hank was there to spirit the don to some predetermined spot for pickup by one of his aides. Rosalie was sad to see him go. *He's a nice man, and dynamic in every way.* She couldn't wait to get into her new lab and come up with something that would provide him with the tools he needed to take care of anyone who threatened him or—she shot a look at Dino—any member of his family.

28

Back in La Crosse, Al and Charlie were bored. Winter continued to cling to the region. Even criminals seemed to sense it was hibernation time. The number of incidents for the two lawmen to investigate declined.

The football season was long over. Brody had starred as a University of Wisconsin running back, and Al and his friends had made it to most of the games. Since then, Al's meetings with Julie had diminished to none. In some ways he was almost glad, because he felt extremely guilty about cheating on JoAnne, but in others it was maddening. He loved the dark-haired beauty. Much as he wanted to be with her, however, he couldn't bring himself to think of a life without his wife.

Kelly and Charlie were so in love, it made Al laugh whenever he thought about the two of them. Charlie was even more entrenched in domestic chores. He loved to cook almost as much as he loved to eat, and he had taken up baking with a vengeance. He quickly found he was good at it, and soon dinners with the Rouses and the Olsons at the Berzinski house, a rustic four-bedroom home hidden in the woods beneath a bluff in south La Crosse, were events to look forward to. The house had a lovely kitchen, and Charlie and Kelly made the most of their new appliances. Rare was the week when the three couples were not together. And whenever they were, the whereabouts of Genevieve Wangen was the topic of discussion. How anyone could vanish so swiftly and completely was beyond them. Al sometimes suspected that Julie might know something, but he didn't press her on it. She had assured him that there had been no contact—not a card, letter, or email message in the years since Genevieve had confessed in the guest house on North Kennicott in Arlington Heights and then escaped from custody near Sun Prairie on the trip back to La Crosse, and he desperately wanted to believe that she was telling him the truth.

Al's continued his ritual of studying the four online subscriptions to southern newspapers—*The Advocate* in Baton Rouge, Louisiana, and the *Clarion-Ledger* in Jackson, Mississippi, in addition to New Orleans and Atlanta publications—but the news on murders that bore signs of Genevieve since they had returned from their latest trip south was nonexistent.

Life in La Crosse returned to normal and, other than Al, Charlie, and Rick, few were the discussions of the serial killer or the killings she had carried out. From time to time, the *La Crosse Tribune* would run a mostly newsless update, but that was the extent of it.

Al didn't believe, however, that he had heard the last of Genevieve. He was certain that news of her would surface again, if not by name, at least by trademark killings. He knew her talents were of interest to those who dealt in criminal activities, and so he searched faithfully day in and day out.

He was also glad that JoAnne either did not suspect his extramarital affair, or was saying nothing about it. And when he was not in Julie's presence, it was easy for him to be the dutiful husband. He did catch himself sometimes, about to talk to JoAnne about Julie. *It's sad that I can't, because they are such great friends. I wonder what JoAnne would say if she knew?*

It was the greatest of life's ironies, Allan Rouse in love with two women. Straight-arrow Allan Rouse. The guy who never got in trouble, never crossed the line, never did anything to cause people to look askance; the guy who attended church faithfully every Sunday, came straight home from work every night or at least made sure JoAnne knew his whereabouts, the guy who worshipped his wife, something everyone quickly knew by his loving, protective actions.

He and Joanne had met in high school; she was the beautiful cheerleader, the all-American girl. A blonde with freckles got to Al every time, and JoAnne had glistening blonde hair and her freckles were subdued, but present.

She was about his height, and as Al was starring as a running back for the La Crosse Central Red Raiders, he stumbled over a cheerleader chasing a wind-driven pompon. As he helped her up and apologized, young love was born.

That was their sophomore year. He asked her out a week later and they had been together ever since. They were married Al's junior year in college. He was a criminal justice student at Winona State University, thirty miles upriver from La Crosse, and JoAnne was, conveniently, at the University of Wisconsin-La Crosse.

They had two daughters, Ginger and Natalie. The kids were in college now and just as Al and JoAnne were looking forward to a life of economic freedom, along came Julie Sonoma. JoAnne knew that Julie and Al were good friends, but Al was sure she had never feared her husband could be cheating on her. They had been devoted to each other for too long.

Julie was another UWL graduate, emerging from the nursing program with a bachelor's degree and then years later returning for a master's as a physician's assistant. She had begun working for the Kahn Clinic in Arlington Heights right out of college and had been there ever since.

Julie, like JoAnne, was one of the sweetest, kindest women Al had met, and he just couldn't bring himself to terminate either relationship. He was still happily married, but he also met someone who thrilled him to no end. And her tender personality, dusky beauty, and vulnerability had reeled him in soon after they met. He didn't expect it, really hadn't wanted it, but one kiss was all it took for him to begin to worship her, too.

The fact that Julie was related to the woman he'd been hunting for years haunted Al almost as much as the affair did.

The other participants in the capture and escape were invested, too, but not as invested as Al.

Julie Sonoma now lived alone in the large home on North Kennicott in Arlington Heights. She had been promoted to a new position with much more responsibility at the Kahn Clinic, and while her job was fulfilling, she wasn't happy.

She loved Al with all her heart and it was heartbreaking to her that she had lost one soulmate to drowning and now another was unreachable because neither she nor Al was willing to take the step to happiness that would destroy two families. Brody and Al had bonded, though. Without a father all his life, Brody looked up to Al and took many male-type problems to him. Julie knew they had each other on speed dial and talked several times each week. She enjoyed the fact that they were good friends.

After meeting Al, there was no one else for her. No matter how many friends tried to set her up with dates, she turned them all down, just as she had when she was studying at the University of Wisconsin-La Crosse before she met Brody's father. And while that love affair was torrid, it was also very short, three blissful weeks that ended when he drowned, triggering what ultimately became fourteen additional deaths.

For a while she had believed she was the direct cause of the deaths, but weekly visits with her psychiatrist had brought her to the point of agreeing that those thoughts were caused by the trauma surrounding Shawn Sorensen's death.

And so she rattled around the large house in the northern Chicago suburb. The coach house apartment was rented to a married couple, two co-workers. Julie and the couple were good friends and spent much time together, but the couple now was thinking about starting a family and Julie knew that someday soon she would again be looking for tenants when they moved away.

She saw Al whenever she could. Their meetings were filled with tenderness and love. They were also too short. Without a reasonable scenario to carry her forward, she feared a life filled with loneliness.

29

The situation some 900 miles south, as the crow flies, was not so passive. Rosalie's new lab was stocked with the root cause materials of every known airborne poison. She now was also studying something on which the United States government was spending billions: aerosolized oil and associated gases coming from the Gulf of Mexico, a phenomenon called Gulf Toxicity Syndrome.

The emissions were coming from the 25,000 square mile area affected by the explosion and resultant oil spill in 2010. Following the 18 billion dollar settlement, the government began pouring money into the study of how to prevent the gases created by the spill and the methods used to prevent it from harming human and wildlife in the area. Rosalie, however, was interested in the gasses for a different reason—as a paralytic or killing agent. Angelo sent a number of his employees to collect samples from the affected area. While she hadn't yet cracked the code, her latest efforts appeared promising.

She hoped to combine the poisonous agents separated from the samples found in the Gulf with one of the most deadly gases known to man: sarin. In her research, Rosalie wasn't seeking to amplify the power of sarin, she was trying to throttle back the distance at which the gas was effective. To do that, she was delivering the odorless, colorless gas within a spray of Gulf toxin.

Angelo was pressing her for the solution, as the Cabreras were becoming ever more combative. To date, the Carbones had kept them from New Orleans, but the situation was volatile and Angelo wanted the certainty of a deadly agent to force them back or perhaps even out of the underworld of profits.

Rosalie desperately wanted to assist her benefactor, but she wanted to do it with a hammer rather than a sledge. She had perfected her solution. The next round of tests might show that the ultimate weapon she sought to make had become a reality. She wanted a solution that could be delivered by a small plastic container with a pump disbursal mechanism. Anything else was too risky.

There were several challenges to using the gas, the most critical of which was handling sarin. The substance had been banned since 1997. Rosalie had no way of knowing how Angelo had gotten his hands on it, but the fact that he had was no surprise. Angelo seemed able to do and get anything he wanted.

When he brought her the gas, she told him she was afraid to handle it. He insisted, but agreed to supply her with a self-contained robotic chamber to use as she put together her concoctions. The chamber helped her use the sarin in the tests she was carrying out. The big issue was delivering the poison without blowback to the person with the dispenser. She also needed to make sure the dose was miniscule, because the tiniest amount of the gas could have widespread lethal impact. There was also the matter of the agent in which to deliver the poison.

Angelo, in many ways, was wonderful to work with. If she had need of anything, it was quickly supplied. She tried to be judicious in her requests, not just because of cost, but also because of space in which to keep it. Her lab was equipped with the latest and greatest equipment and chemicals, but it was also, out of necessity, compact.

Tonight she would see if her decision to use kerosene mixed with Gulf water as the agent in which to deliver the gas was a good one. The kerosene was ideal for several reasons. First, it was dense enough to limit the range of the spray; second, it was oily and remained on the target; third, it neutralized to some degree the gulf toxin; and, fourth, it evaporated after being delivered in such a way that its killing capacity was limited to the primary target.

Tonight would be the key. She, Hank, and Joe would head for the depths of the swamp in the Dewey Mills Wildlife Area. There they would seek out gators and deer to see if the spray would deliver the lethal knockout punch Angelo sought.

The deer and alligator were chosen for specific reasons. The deer was roughly the weight of a human and would approximate the potion's killing impact. It would also allow them to know how quickly the desired result—death—could be achieved. The alligator was chosen because it lived on both land and water. They would spray an alligator on land. They expected that it would quickly seek water, thus enabling them to see if the chemical was effective when submerged.

Rosalie was nervous and could hardly sit still as daylight began to fade and the moment approached when she and her two bodyguards would head into the swamp. Dinner was a somber affair. Although the white perch they'd caught that morning had been prepared in an excellent manner, the three who would invade the swamp were quiet. Their mission was dangerous, and Rosalie couldn't help but wonder whether they would be at this meal the following night. She offered up several prayers that her calculations would prove accurate, enabling the spray to kill quickly and without harm to the person who dispensed it and with a quick death to the animal. Still, she was apprehensive.

Angelo had managed to find heavy masks for them to wear, but whether they would be helpful or not remained to be seen. Dino, too, was unusually quiet. He sat next to Rosalie, touching her from time to time. Was he trying to assure her that he believed in her? He had also been uncommonly loving the past few days, something she appreciated, but didn't welcome. She had been thinking a lot about her relationship with Dino over the past number of days, and more and more she realized that, although she loved him dearly, he needed someone much younger as he assumed his father's role. In addition, she was locked in on her task. There was no time for dalliance, even if she might desire it. If things went well, later tonight they would celebrate the end of her temporary celibacy.

After the lemon meringue angel cake, the group dispersed. Rosalie headed to the cabin she and Dino shared. Although he was especially attentive, she largely ignored him, quickly getting into her swamp gear, much of it canvas. It was uncomfortable to move around in, exacerbated by the high temperatures outside. She would be ready for a cool shower later, one she hoped she would get to enjoy.

Darkness settled quickly over the swamp and the cacophony of nighttime sounds filled the air. Hank and Joe helped Rosalie, who carried the canister, aboard the airboat, then boarded themselves. Joe started the engine that had been effectively silenced to a whisper, the whoosh of the propeller making more noise than the motor.

Each was lost in thought as the boat left the compound and moved downwind, then turned left and threaded its way into the heart of the swamp under Hank's expert navigation. He whispered directions to Joe and soon they were into a pond of deep darkness, surrounded by huge trees strung with Spanish moss.

When they went ashore, Hank led the way, carrying both a rifle and a handgun in case any curious critters, two-legged or four-legged, impeded their progress. They walked the quarter mile to a meadow area and settled down to wait. It didn't take long. Although Rosalie neither heard nor saw the target, Hank took her gently by the hand and led her into taller grass. Hank directed each of them to their positions. Rosalie uncapped the canister and removed the pump-spray dispenser. When the three were ready, Joe pointed and turned on a heavy-duty flashlight. The meadow lit up, freezing four deer in their tracks not eight feet away. Rosalie aimed the sprayer over the head of the nearest deer, a large doe, and depressed the pump twice.

As the kerosene-based solution found its target, the deer jumped as if to turn then fell into the tall grass. As previously agreed, Joe turned the light toward Rosalie, but avoided hitting her in the eyes. She carefully inspected the pump container and found no trace of the liquid that had been dispensed. She nodded at Joe before placing the container carefully into the metal cylinder and tightening the screw-top cap. Noiselessly, aided by the grass that covered the meadow, Hank led them back to the boat. Once they were safely aboard and the canister was carefully stored in its lead container, Rosalie took off her helmet. Hank and Joe did the same. "So, what did you observe?"

Hank propped an elbow on the motor. "I walked up to the deer, very carefully, as you can imagine. I stopped several feet away, wondering if that was too close. I watched the deer carefully; there was no sign of movement. If you're sure the gas will be gone by tomorrow, maybe Joe will come back with me to look for the carcass."

"I'll go if Rosalie says it's okay. I'm not ready to die and that stuff seems potent." Joe had kept his distance, she had observed, so his comment didn't surprise her.

"I think it'll be okay, Joe." While she intended the comment to be reassuring, he didn't look entirely convinced. Still, he nodded. Angelo picked out his employees well.

Joe shoved the boat from the shore into the water and Hank steered toward what was a popular overnight area for Louisiana's largest amphibians. As they turned into a narrow slough, Hank throttled back and whispered to Rosalie to get the dispenser ready. When she had done that, Joe removed a pike pole from the side of the boat and began to push them farther into the slough, which was so narrow he could have touched either bank with the pole. A couple of minutes later, he gave a strong but silent push, removed the pole from the water, waited a moment then told Joe to direct the light to the starboard bank. As the swamp lit up, Rosalie scanned the shore intently, but there was nothing there. Joe extinguished the light and they sat there for about fifteen minutes, suffering in the heat.

Eventually, Hank took the pole and pushed them farther up the slough. Three times they stopped and lit up the swamp, seeing nothing but empty banks. The fourth time was the charm. When Rosalie had the dispenser ready, Hank activated the light. On the bank, snout facing the water, was the largest alligator Rosalie had ever seen. It was so close she could have nearly reached out and touched it. She depressed the pump three times. After the first spray reached it, the gator heaved itself into the water. Hank quickly poled to move them away from the area, but there were no more sounds. It was if the gator had slipped silently into the deep and vanished. Rosalie put the canister in its container and they settled in to wait.

Finally, having seeing nothing for fifteen minutes, Hank suggested it was time to go. "Nothing to see here and I'm hot as hell and hungry as a bear. Joe and I'll come back tomorrow and take a look. If the gator's dead, it should bloat enough to surface. We'll see what we find then."

Hank used the pole to maneuver them back out of the slough. When they reached the lake, Joe started the engine and whisked them back across the placid waters to the compound. While he tied up the boat, Hank helped Rosalie ashore and walked with her back to the cabin. She went straight to her laboratory, placed the lead canister in its storage space, then stripped off her canvas outerwear.

Soaked in sweat and badly in need of a shower, she was nonetheless more in need of food. Inside the kitchen cabin, she washed her hands thoroughly multiple times and encouraged Joe and Hank to do the same. Miranda had laid out a lavish spread of meats and cheeses, breads and crackers. Dino mixed drinks for everyone, and the three swamp-goers ate heartily without speaking.

The heavy snack consumed, Hank praised Rosalie for the spray she had put together. "You should have seen the doe; it went down the first time Rosalie released the gas. When I went back a few seconds later, it was deader'n a doornail."

Joe nodded. "The gator was the same damn way. Biggest gator I ever saw, too."

"You sure you didn't get some of that spray in your nose, Joe?"

"I'm absolutely sure, Dino, you shoulda seen it. Gator was lying on the bank, snout toward the water. When Rosalie hit the spray, it made one huge flop into the water and it was gone, no sighting, no sound."

"Now, now," Rosalie held up a hand. "It was a good night, I'll give you that. But I'm not going to celebrate just yet. If we go back tomorrow and the carcasses have been chewed on and there is no other carrion at the site, then we'll know that the kill was instant and the gas wore off completely enough not to kill the predators who came along to feast on the carcasses. As soon as we know that, we can declare victory."

She looked toward Dino for support. She didn't get it.

"I disagree. You heard what Hank and Joe had to say. They think you nailed it. And you were able to activate the spray with no harm to any of you. That's worth celebrating."

"If we celebrate, we will do it after Hank and Joe make their run tomorrow. Until then, we're going to wait."

"Oh, all right, Rosalie, but there are certain things that are not going to wait. I have been too long without some attention. That is going to end tonight."

Rosalie smiled, and soon she and Dino departed for their cabin. Once there, she stripped off her clothes, and although Dino wanted to shower with her, Rosalie pushed him away.

"I don't want you in the shower with me until I am certain there are no leftover traces of poison." So emphatic were her words that he didn't argue with her.

When she came out of the shower, Dino told her he wanted to shower before coming to bed with her. That she permitted, telling him she had been thorough in washing down the shower.

Afterwards, they had their reunion, and it was one to be remembered.

"Ah, my sweet Rosalie, you beg me to stop. Never did I think I would hear you say those words."

She was too tired to argue, but she was grateful when he rolled into position beside her and pulled her close. She continued to think about how he needed someone younger until the light of morning was streaking the bedroom.

They didn't awaken until nearly two in the afternoon. After they showered and returned to the kitchen cabin, Miranda was waiting for them.

"Joe and Hank left about two hours ago. They didn't want to disturb you and were careful to be quiet as they made their way from the complex. What can I get you for lunch?"

Rosalie waved a hand through the air. "Whatever you have on hand is fine." Dino poured mango juice and coffee for them as Miranda busied herself at the stove.

She served them baby shrimp and scallops in a delicate white sauce and wrapped in crepes so light they threatened to fly from the plate. The food was delicious, and Dino and Rosalie gorged themselves on the crepes, served with a light rye toast and jam.

As they were finishing, Joe and Hank walked in, smiling.

Hank clasped his hands together and raised them over his head in a victory salute. "I think we have a winner. Both animals were dead. The deer was still lying where it fell. The gator was floating belly up. Both of them had been gnawed on, but there was no sign of any predators anywhere near the carcasses, alive or dead. Dino, I think you can tell your dad that Rosalie has produced what he wants."

Rosalie shook her head. "Not so fast. I think another test should be completed before we declare victory. Right now, Dino, all I want you to tell your father is that the first test has been conducted with positive results."

As Dino began to protest, Rosalie held up her hand and silenced him. "No arguments. None. I want to make sure we have tested the spray in inclement conditions. When that's done successfully, we can celebrate."

And so, for two days they waited, until the weather changed and a summer storm moved over the bayou. With rain pelting the area, Rosalie, Hank, and Joe again made their way into the swamp. This time they had to walk farther into the woods to find the deer, but Hank led them to a small herd and managed to isolate a buck from the others. Rosalie maintained a distance farther than the first kill and twice depressed the sprayer. The buck fell where it stood. Rosalie was close enough to see that it made no move of any kind after it was down.

They returned to the slough Hank had taken them to the last time. They found gators in the same place as before, but this time Rosalie insisted that Hank make enough noise to get them moving. When that was done, they waited until they spotted the eyes in the glow of the light Joe held. When the gator swam toward the light and Rosalie could see its nostrils, she depressed the sprayer once. The gator immediately submerged.

The next day Hank and Joe confirmed what she had hoped for: both the buck and the gator were dead, signs of predator scavenging were prevalent, but no dead animals were anywhere near either carcass.

Dino alerted his father; Angelo flew up and the group partied heartily that night. It would be, Angelo said, the great differentiator in helping him secure the South for his family.

"My son, it is your future that I intend to secure with this magical potion from Rosalie. And you, my dear," he nodded at her, "shall have a privileged position for life in the Carbone Family. Anything you want that I can supply, you shall have."

Rosalie pressed a hand to her chest. "Don Angelo, if there is one thing for which I long, it is to be mainstreamed back into society. I would love to live a life of service to others, but obviously I want to avoid prison."

"Tell me, my dear, can I count on you to continue to bless me and my family with your scientific work?"

It took Rosalie only a second to answer. "You shall have the best work that I can produce."

"And you shall have the best of everything, including a new face and a new identity—a new life that will put you back into society. And not just in it, but atop it!" The don was ebullient.

For the next two hours they ate heartily and drank much, amid the merriment of success. As the celebration wound down and the don made ready to leave, he arose from his chair, smiled at Rosalie, and said, "Tomorrow I shall begin work on your new life, my dear." Turning to Dino, he asked, "Am I to assume, my son, that you wish to remain with Rosalie?"

Before Dino could respond, Rosalie spoke up, startling Dino but failing to surprise the don, since they'd had several quiet conversations about the future over the last two days.

"Don Angelo, I have enjoyed the attention of your son. He is a wonderful man and a great lover. But he needs someone much younger than I am as he seeks to learn your business so that one day he may be Don. Dino, I shall miss you terribly and I hope that you will return from time to time, but I feel it best if we break off our relationship and go our separate ways. Please don't argue. This is the toughest decision I have had to make in a long while, but I think it is for the best, especially for you."

Angelo, who had looked on contemplatively, nodded. "I cannot argue with the logic. I think, my son, you have been blessed to have met this wise lady. I shall leave you alone to say your good-byes and then, Dino, let us leave together."

It was an order, not an invitation.

As the door closed behind the don, Dino came to her. "Please, my darling, please tell me this is but a nightmare and that I shall awake to find you in bed beside me."

She gazed at him, sad, yes, but committed to do what was needed.

"Dino, I love you with all of my heart. But unfortunately my heart is way too old for a man of your age. You need someone young, vibrant, someone who can help you with the work you will have as don. I am an old lady, almost three times your age. When you ascend to power, I shall be dying, I fear."

The look on Dino's face hurt badly.

"Please, Dino, this is the hardest thing I've ever done. But it is right. Believe me, I would love to be younger, not just made to look younger, but that isn't possible. And as much as I want to be with you, it would be enormously unfair to you."

A knock sounded on the door. It was time for him to go. Dino rose, embraced her tenderly, kissed her deeply, and said, "I understand what you are saying, and the reasons for it. But I must also tell you, this is not yet decided."

Then he turned and walked from the room, closing the door quietly behind him.

As the airboat carrying the don and Dino back to civilization left the complex, the tears she'd held back as she talked to him slid down her cheeks. In fact, Rosalie cried much of the night, finally falling asleep toward dawn and slumbering until noon.

When she awoke, a heavy mood gripped her. *Did I make the right decision?* Even though her heart was broken, she was sure the answer was yes.

30

Over the next two weeks, Rosalie was too busy to be sad. She missed Dino, of course, but there was much work to do. She spent at least twelve hours a day in her laboratory, perfecting the spray she had developed. Twice more she and Joe and Hank made midnight forays into the swamp. Each time, her spray performed as it was supposed to until she was certain that it was ready.

She told Joe and Hank they could inform Angelo that the spray appeared to be as good as it was going to get. At breakfast the next day, Joe told her that he had heard back from Don Carbone. He was thrilled with her work. Now it was time for them to leave the swamp. He and Hank would accompany her on her journey. Miranda would stay behind with her husband Jorge and Clarendon. They would keep the place ready for its next use.

For two days, Rosalie worked to break down the lab and pack her things into the boxes in which they had arrived.

On the third day, Joe walked in and surveyed the work. "You have done well. The don asked that things be made ready for shipping, and it appears that you have done exactly that."

"What happens now?"

"All I know is that the boxes are going to New Orleans. Don Angelo has told me that he is working to find you a house there, so my suspicion is that is where the boxes are going. But that's only a guess."

On the morning of the fourth day, Joe returned to tell her that she would depart that night with him and Hank.

"We'll take the airboat in to the landing and link up with a helicopter for a ride to Honey Brake Lodge. Not sure what happens then, but I know the don will have planned everything in great detail. No reason to worry."

"How much should I bring with me?"

"Nothing at all; that's how the don wants it."

That night was clear but dark, the moon no more than a toothpick on the horizon. Joe, Hank, and Jorge accompanied her back to the landing. It was as if even the creatures knew she was leaving. The swamp was silent as they glided over its surface, the airboat's engine burbling quietly. A short hop later in the helicopter and they were at the lodge. There, waiting for them, was another helicopter, this one bigger than the other. Black in color, it appeared sleek and powerful. As Rosalie, Joe, and Hank entered the copter, Jorge waved from the dock, cast off, turned the airboat, and vanished into the inky fog.

The pilot was ready to go. The flight back to New Orleans took little more than an hour, and when they landed at Lakefront Airport after skimming in over Lake Pontchartrain, so low Rosalie was sure the skids were touching the tops of the waves, they were met by a Lincoln Town Car, black, of course, and Rosalie was hustled from the terminal while Joe and Hank remained.

Her driver, Cajun and kindly, told her to make herself comfortable, because they were going to be driving for a while. "We'll be on the road for more than hour. Road's bad, very bad, but distance is short."

They drove along narrow roads lost in darkness before breaking out into the first lights she had seen since departing the city. Another ten minutes and the Town Car pulled up at a modern building bearing the sign *Plaquemines Medical Center.*

Before she could open the door, it was opened for her and a nurse with a pleasant face leaned into the car, smiling. "Ms. Burton, we have been awaiting your arrival. Your room is ready and the doctors are waiting."

Standing in front of the modern concrete and glass three-story structure, her knees grew weak. Suddenly a pall of fear shrouded her as she stepped out of the car. Almost ready to turn and run, her mood shifted abruptly when Dino stepped into her view, helped her from the car, and embraced her tenderly.

"My darling, I have missed you so. It seemed this day would never come; I was afraid that it would not and then I would not see you. Please, I will explain everything."

The fear lifted. He guided her inside the gleaming structure where she was greeted by a sparkling interior. Pastel colors brightened her mood and the furniture blended smoothly with the walls. As he took her arm and began to walk her down the hall, she glimpsed what she thought must be the reservation desk and a wide, curving marble staircase led upstairs.

Although her stomach continued to do flips, Dino's words reassured her as they walked down the hallway. He told her that he and his father were indebted to her, and that they both felt she would be the salvation of the Carbone family. "Rosalie, we're heading to the third floor, a room of private suites. You will be quite comfortable there, I'm sure. Please know that my father and I will do whatever you ask, no matter how difficult or how costly. And to make sure that we protect you from people searching for you, we will keep our promise to you and begin by making sure you have a new face. Are these surroundings not exquisite?"

"Oh, yes, they are, but Dino, suddenly the thought of getting that new face frightens me. How dangerous will it be? What if it's not successful? I'm scared, Dino, scared to death."

"Many times I have talked with my father, and he assures me that you will be as safe as you are standing here. And the future is bright. After the operation, you will be even more beautiful than you are today. And, dear Rosalie, although you have said you want to send me away, I will love you as much or more when I see you then."

Dino went on to tell her that his father was serious about meeting her request.

"It's been years since I've seen him this energized," he told her. "His whole being suddenly is centered on installing you in a new life with society stature."

"But Dino, can it happen? Can I really become a new person?"

"All has been planned. The best surgeons, the best nurses have been assembled. Tonight, you will get a new face, one that your friends from the north will not recognize. You will be transformed into a woman of late middle-age who is beautiful beyond compare, just as you are now. And when you return to New Orleans, my father will introduce you as his newly found relative Savannah Harlowe. You will then have status equal to that of my father and our family, and you will live in a beautiful mansion that he has purchased for you. A mansion that I will visit often."

Overwhelmed by what she just heard, Rosalie burst into tears. "But Dino, how can I ever repay such kindness? I don't think I'm worthy."

"Of course you are worthy. You have already proven your worth, my darling. The potions that you have developed for us are more valuable than you will ever know. Nothing that is done to you now will begin to repay what you already have done for us."

Dino appeared sincere in his comments, and convincing, too. Her sniffles stopped and she took a tissue from her purse and dried her eyes. But she was no less overwhelmed.

"The fact that anyone would do this for me is more than I can comprehend. How… how can I ever repay you and your family?"

Dino kissed her tenderly on the lips. "Rosalie, how many times must I tell you that you are doing more for us than we can ever repay. We want you to have a wonderful new identity, whatever you want our doctors will achieve. You are not to worry about any request in this regard; we are committed to you being happy."

"Can I really look younger?"

"You can look however you want, my dear, just as I have said. But please know that I love you the way you are. Still, the doctors will do as you ask, and they are the very best. Shall we go in and meet them?"

They reached a set of elevators and Dino pushed the button. He slid an arm around her to guide her inside then pressed the number three. As the elevator ascended, he reached for her hand. "Are you worried?"

"Maybe, but more than that I am excited. I wanted a new life, and you and your father are giving me a far greater one than I could have ever imagined."

31

When the elevator door opened, a tall man with a kind face, crowned by curly salt-and-pepper hair, smiled widely and reached for her hand. "You must be Rosalie. Dr. Rhett Wilcox at your service. Come, I want you to meet the rest of the team."

As they walked down the corridor, Rosalie couldn't help thinking that if there ever was anyone who looked like a doctor, it was Rhett Wilcox. He was handsome, exuded confidence, had a winning smile, a soft gentle touch, and a manner that put you at ease, made you know things were going to be all right. And when she met the other eight members of the team she was blown away by the kindness, the professionalism, the confidence, and the courtesy. Each member of the team made her think that he or she was there only for her. Her comfort and satisfaction seemed to be all they thought about. And from her vantage point, she was sure they had everything under control.

Introductions over, Rosalie sat down with the doctors to plan her new look.

"I want to look younger. How much younger can you make me look?"

"We can make you look almost as young as you want," Dr. Wilcox told her. "But I think you want your look to be reasonable. I would suggest we think about taking twenty to thirty years off your facial features."

"You mean you can make me look fifty-five again?"

"Absolutely. And with your posture and walk, you can handle that kind of new look."

"So the wrinkles will be gone."

The doctor laughed. "I wouldn't be much of a surgeon if I left the wrinkles in place, would I? If I leave the wrinkles, do you think you will look fifty-five?"

She thought about it for a while. "I guess not." She pursed her lips. "What about my cheek bones? I've never liked them. They're too prominent."

"We can soften them. Good. What else?"

"My nose is long and pointed, like Helen Mirren's. I'd like something more youthful. Like Cary Mulligan's, with a subtle upturn at its end."

Dr. Wilcox reached for a book on a shelf above his desk, thumbed through a few pages, then held up the open page. "Like this?"

The page held a collection of nose shapes. "Well, kind of, but not quite."

He turned another page and pointed. "This one?"

"Yes, exactly like that one. I love the curve, don't you?"

He nodded. "Anything else?"

They went through each detail, from eyebrows to chin, agreeing on the look she wanted.

When discussions about her face had ended, Dr. Wilcox replaced the book on the shelf and sat back down. "My dear, your body is exquisite. It is many times younger than your age; that's wonderful. The only change I might advocate is a tightening of the tissue above your breasts to perk them up just a bit. What do you think?"

"That would be a wonderful and welcome change. They seem to sag a bit more each year. Having them lifted would be wonderful."

"We can do that. Beyond that, though, I think your body is perfect. There is little we can do to improve that, unless you want the mole to the right of your navel removed?"

Rosalie chuckled. "Doctor, that mole has been with me all my life. I am quite attached to it, to be honest. I'd rather leave it the way it is. But, ummm, you know, if you could tighten a few things a bit lower, that would be terrific."

She said it jokingly, but Dr. Wilcox responded immediately. "Yes, we can do that. Dr. Heston is one of the foremost vaginoplasty and labiaplasty surgeons in the world. I'll let her talk to you about that."

"You can even do that?"

"Oh, my yes. We can do just about anything, even make you up to two inches taller, although that gets into a whole new level of improvement."

"I am quite all right with my height, but I would like to talk to Dr. Heston. Pelvic adjustments would be welcome, both for my pleasure and for my lover's."

"You are a marvel, Rosalie. You are a beautiful 'canvas,' and I can promise you a masterpiece that will enhance your natural beauty, but will also leave you unrecognizable to close relatives."

"Really? Just how unrecognizable will I be?"

"I can change you so completely that your sister could stand next to you and not know who you are, at least until you speak. Although there are even some things we can do about your voice if you'd like."

"Really? Tell me more."

"Over the past few years, we have learned much about what we call the 'voice-lift.' We can use both surgery and injections, or a combination of the two, to make your voice sound younger. We can't give you a totally new voice, but we can give it the 'Benjamin Button' treatment."

Dr. Wilcox touched a finger to her throat. "The procedure involves inserting small implants to narrow the space between vocal chords, which will improve the pitch and remove the hint of hoarseness that I hear when you speak. We can also use injections to add a youthful lilt, if you'd like."

"I would very much like that. Is it terribly dangerous or painful?"

"The risk is very low. There's no real pain, just a minor inconvenience. Dr. Sutherland is the expert. I'll have him talk to you about the risks and rewards."

"That would be perfect. When do we begin?"

"We will use today to gather all the information you want to give us. We'll use that along with a number of photos of you to make the adjustments graphically. That way you can decide what you like and what you don't, and we can agree on any tweaks you'd like to make. Depending on how all of that goes, we should be ready to begin the conversion either the day after tomorrow or Friday. How does that sound?"

"Just perfect. Will Dino remain here with me?"

"He'll stay tonight and tomorrow, but then he'll return to New Orleans. You will see him again, certainly, but we would ask that you keep a realistic distance to make certain your reintroduction into society does not set off warning bells for anyone."

"So what you are saying, doctor, is that whatever intimate time I am going to experience with Dino should occur here?"

"You've got it. I think you will find your suite very comfortable."

It was both exclusive and comfortable, Rosalie soon found. And for forty-eight hours, she gladly gave up her vow to stay away from Dino. It was a sensual and tender time for each. They made love, but it was much more than that. They found in each other the teacher they had always longed for. Each was naturally skilled, but never before had they called upon their inner beings in such a demanding way. It was a perfect two days, and when the sun was setting on Thursday, they ate dinner and talked about their wonderful time together.

Dino lifted his glass of wine. "Tomorrow you will begin your new life. And dismayed as I am, I understand that our time together must end. It is best for you, darling. I want to do nothing to disturb your wish of again being mainstreamed. You have earned that."

"Oh, Dino, I have found in you something incredible—something totally different from others with whom I have made love and have loved. In the story of my life, you are a chapter in yourself, better by far than anyone else in my life."

His gaze was understanding, his words morose. "As are you. I shall never forget our times together. You will always be, I know, the very best. I am grateful to know you."

"And I you, but from now on we shall be cousins. Perhaps it is best for both of us if we are not 'kissing cousins.' Do you agree?"

"My heart disagrees, but my head understands the realities of our worlds and so, yes, cousins we shall be … good friends, but friends only."

He took her in his arms, kissed her deeply, hugged her tightly to his body while whispering good-byes in her ear. Then he kissed her again. As he turned, she thought she saw a tear begin its trembling journey down his cheek. But she couldn't be sure, because tears dripped from her own eyes as she held his hand tightly, until he at last loosened her fingers, touched a finger to her lips, and walked out the door.

It was another tear-filled night for Rosalie. Finally, two nurses came in to begin preparing her for her transformation. She had spent her last day as

Rosalie Burton. When she arrived in New Orleans she would be Savannah Carbone Harlowe, the daughter of Angelo's brother Rayford Carbone and Mrs. Honey Harlowe of France.

Was she ready for a new life? She thought so. She hoped so. Fervently.

32

Seven hours later, according to the large white clock with black hands on the wall of the recovery room, Rosalie began to emerge from her drug-induced surgical sleep. She fought a bit against the elephant that seemed to be sitting on her chest, and when she coughed, a nurse immediately held her tightly to make sure the stitches didn't tear.

Slowly, ghostly figures came into focus, although at first they seemed to be swimming in air. Then the images steadied. The first person she recognized was her nurse, Darlene, whom she had met earlier. Rosalie felt no pain, but when she lifted her hands to her face, she realized it was swathed in bandages. She tried to talk, but Darlene placed a finger to her lips.

"Just relax now, and close your eyes." The nurse tugged her blanket up to her neck. "Take a nap and let us tend to your needs. We'll make sure you're comfortable, and tomorrow you will be able to have a little food. When you awake, we'll have you take a few swallows of liquid. Now sleep."

Rosalie closed her eyes and soon was back into a dreamless sleep. She didn't awaken for six hours, but when she did, Darlene was still there and they allowed her a few sips of a sweet-tasting liquid that she sucked through a straw. Almost immediately her eyes grew heavy. *Must have been something in that drink.* She shifted a little to get comfortable, and allowed sleep to overtake her again.

This time when she awoke, sunlight streamed into her suite and both Dr. Wilcox and Darlene were there with her.

The doctor rested his hands on the side rail of her bed. "How do you feel?"

Rosalie thought about the question for a few seconds then shook her head. The room spun around her. "Wow! Dizzy. Very diz … zy."

"That's normal."

Darlene nodded.

Her stomach rumbled and Rosalie pressed a hand to it. "Hun … gry." Swollen lips and heavy bandages helped to create a voice she didn't remember.

"I don't doubt it, but we're going to have to restrict you to liquids; maybe a milkshake tonight?" The voice of her doctor was soothing but firm as he pushed her gown aside and listened to her heart through his stethoscope. He straightened. "Things sound good. We want to keep them that way, so for now it's water, soda, or juice." He shook his finger at her gently and smiled. "And don't you be begging Darlene for anything else. We need to be careful today and monitor how you are doing. Tomorrow, if all goes well, the first of the bandages can come off."

"Can't wait." Once again the voice that emerged from the bandages was muffled and strange.

As the doctor left the room, Darleen cranked down the bed. When Rosalie protested that she didn't feel tired, Darlene said, "But you're going to have to get some sleep. It's what your body needs. We want this to be a perfect work of art, don't we?"

"I guess. But I'm hungry enough to eat a steer …"

"Well, that appetite is going to have to wait. If there is anything else you need, though, just let me know. All any of us wants is for you to get better soon, and successfully. And that means lots of rest. And there is one other thing. From now on, we will be calling you Savannah Harlowe. You need to get used to that, because your new name goes with your new look."

"Mmm hmm." Rosalie tried to agree, but she didn't have the energy to form the words. She closed her eyes. It was dark when she awoke, but still Darlene materialized at her bedside as if from nowhere.

"Welcome back. Ready for that milkshake?"

This time the nod came quickly … and assertively. But with the nod came dizziness, and suddenly she wasn't certain she was hungry.

"And what flavor do you want?"

"Can I have strawberry?"

"I think we can handle that, but don't expect it to be filled with berries.

We're still doing liquids, you know. That means no food tidbits, at least not yet."

By the time the fruity treat arrived, the cold, thick liquid not only appeased her hunger, but felt good on her lips and throat. To Rosalie, it was the best milkshake ever.

When she had emptied the glass and washed the taste away with water, Darlene handed her two pills. "These will help you sleep, and sleep is the best healer you can have. I'm going to get some sleep myself, but I'll be on the couch right over there. If you wake up, just push this button and I'll be here."

Savannah—she was trying to think of herself as Savannah now—thanked her and when her eyelids grew heavy she didn't resist the temptation to sleep. Again it was a deep, dreamless sleep and when she awoke she felt rested, alive, and anxious to be out of bed. Darlene was bustling around the room, straightening up. When she turned and saw Savannah, a smile lit her face. "Well, look who's up. For a few hours there, I thought you were going to sleep forever. At least you looked comfortable."

"I was very comfortable. Or at least I must have been, because I didn't feel a thing; I didn't have even one little dream."

"Those little Estazolam pills are dynamite, but don't get too used to them, because they are habit-forming, and that we don't want."

"I expect with you around there is no chance of me becoming addicted, is there?"

"None." Darlene's tone was firm. The door opened behind her and she turned. "Well, look who's here? Dr. Rembrandt, are you ready to unveil your work?"

"I think the time has come." The doctor was smiling as he approached her bed. Savannah wondered if he smiled even when he slept. "Now Rosalie, or should I say Savannah, as I unbandage you, just remember you are still recovering from surgery. The incisions are going to be visible, but they are also going to disappear. And that won't take long. But let's have a look and see what you think."

He gently unwrapped the bandages, then used surgical scissors to snip away the final wraps. Made of a material designed not to stick to the skin, they came away easily. When he had finished, he increased the angle of her back to a more upright position, then held up a mirror so she could see her face.

She gasped, slumping back against the pillows.

The doctor looked horrified. "Oh, Savannah. I ..."

Savannah lifted her hand. "No, no, doctor; I just couldn't believe what I saw. That's a young, beautiful woman in the mirror. I can't believe the transition. Thank you, thank you, thank you!"

Dr. Wilcox's smile returned. "You are one incredible patient, Savannah. I call you that, because that is who you are after your transformation. But my happiness is because there are very few people who can look past the cuts, the scabs, and the redness and see the real beauty that has been created. Bless you, my dear!"

"Oh, doctor, you have made me the person I've always wanted to be." Savannah gave the words a southern accent. She had it down pat, even though her lips were swollen. She sounded more New Orleans than a longtime resident. "I am younger and I am beautiful. How can I ever thank you for that?"

"The thanks are due to the members of my team and Don Carbone. But your approval thrills me. I should tell you that you are the perfect patient. Your facial bone structure is magnificent. It allowed us to do exactly what we wanted. I am pleased that you like the results."

33

A week later, pampered and with the healing progressing and the scars fading, Savannah was transported by helicopter to Padre Island off the shore of Texas. Nestled in the north of the island, south of Corpus Christi, was another lavish compound owned by the Carbone Family, the ideal place for rest and recuperation. The staff was comprised of cooks, housekeepers, groundskeepers, and guards. The compound was surrounded by stone walls that were ten feet high and topped by four strands of razor wire to discourage people from trying to enter.

Although imposing, the structures, Rosalie was told, had now been there for so long that few people paid even passing attention to them, except for the occasional tourist seeking information on the fortress-like area set back from the Gulf.

For three weeks, Savannah rested and relaxed. As the third week turned into the fourth, however, she began to grow restless. She loved the staff of the compound, but now she longed to be out and about. Her cuts had healed and, as promised by Dr. Wilcox, there was no evidence of the work that had been done to her face. Her voice had changed, too. It was more youthful, less raspy. All in all, she appeared to be a woman in her early fifties. Her breasts had been lifted and any flab around her middle had been removed. She could not keep the bounce out of her step as she walked; she had been completely transformed.

On the third day of the fourth week of her stay in Texas, the mail brought a formally engraved invitation. Don Angelo was throwing a soirée to introduce New Orleans society to Savannah Harlowe, the daughter of the don's late brother, Rayford. Savannah, the card read, had lived abroad all of her life, just as her mother Honey had after her first husband, Hiram Harlowe, a wealthy Georgia plantation owner, died in the mid-1950s.

Honey had met Rayford Carbone on one of his frequent European trips. They were immediately taken by each other, and the product of their romance, Savannah, was born in the 1960s. Honey survived what was a near-fatal birth, but lingered in ill health and spent most of her time on the farm in France purchased using part of the fortune left her by her late husband. The farm was both a thoroughbred horse breeding operation and a popular French vineyard.

Savannah was thrilled to read the details of the invitation. Cocktails would be served at the Carbone compound in the heart of New Orleans at six o'clock on July 28, with dinner and dancing to follow. As a second highlight of the evening, Don Angelo promised an announcement that he hoped would be pleasing to the socially elite people of New Orleans.

No one knew what to expect, least of all Savannah, but the don supported many charities, and she assumed he would be making a significant gift to another worthy cause.

Am I ready to appear in public? Savannah walked to a full-length mirror and examined herself from all angles. *For now, all my efforts must go into making a grand appearance at the soirée.*

The next day a team of five people arrived in a large truck. Every inch of space in the truck they didn't occupy was packed with apparel—lingerie, shoes, gowns, hats and tiaras—fit for a princess. A tall, elegant woman in a fashionable skirt and blazer stepped down from the truck and extended her hand to Savannah. "Ms. Harlowe, I presume. My name is Idonna Arnette. My team and I will be with you for the next three days." When they were finished, Idonna promised, Savannah would be completely outfitted and prepared for her introduction to New Orleans society.

Overwhelmed, Savannah stood with her fingers pressed to her lips as load after load of clothing and accessories was carried into the building. When the last load had disappeared through the doors, she squared her shoulders and followed the team inside.

Although interesting, the next days were also arduous. She was coached, softly scolded, cajoled, prompted, reminded, and reprimanded until Idonna and her teammates were certain she was completely ready.

When the fourth day arrived, a black Lincoln Town Car with heavily tinted windows called for her for the eight-hour drive back to Crescent City. Idonna rode with her and challenged her continually to talk as she would if she were moving to New Orleans from France, which involved combining a bit of a southern accent with a French flare. Savannah was a good student, and they had just entered the outskirts of Houston when Idonna pronounced her student totally ready. Punching the button on the intercom system, she suggested to the driver that they find a place to stop for lunch. She rested a hand on Savannah's knee. "When we get there, you will be responsible for initiating all discussion."

Savannah nodded, her body tense. *I can do this.* After they had made their way into Houston and turned from I-45 onto the 610 beltway, the driver pulled into the Flying J Travel Plaza. While he filled the tank with gasoline, Idonna and Savannah went into the restaurant and were led to a table near the window. As the hostess turned to leave, Savannah touched her arm. "Ma'am, that's our driver out there filling the car. He is going to join us for lunch. Would you be kind enough to show him to our table when he comes in?"

"Of course."

Savannah nodded. "Merci, madame."

When the hostess had gone, Idonna clapped her hands. "That was wonderful, Savannah. "You sensed what was needed and you did it—and perfectly, too. That's the kind of behavior we need from you."

After the woman had shown the driver to the table, Savannah conferred with him and Idonna, and when the waitress came by, she provided the woman with the orders for all three of them. Idonna especially praised the fact that Savannah ordered tea for herself and coffee for Idonna and the driver.

Finished with lunch and back in the car, they turned to what the agenda would be when they arrived in New Orleans.

"Savannah, Don Angelo has purchased a home for you at 28 Audubon Place. It's a wonderful house. The 8,500-square-foot residence features six bedrooms and as many baths. It's near many points of interest, including Tulane University. The campus is marvelous and always very alive."

"Oh my, that's even larger than my home in Illinois."

Recognizing what she had just said, Savannah's eyes widened. "Oops! That wasn't good. I'm very sorry, Idonna."

"No, it wasn't good," agreed her mentor, "but it clearly points out how we must constantly be on our toes. We cannot afford the slightest slip-up."

"I promise to do better, Idonna. Now tell me more about the house. Have you seen it?"

"I have. In fact, I made sure it had everything needed for us to be comfortable. I think you'll love it."

"What is it like?"

"It's a sprawling, single-story brick dwelling built in 1915. The home has been completely renovated. The half-acre lot offers seclusion and the property is located in a gated community."

"Tell me about the rooms." Savannah bounced a little on the seat, feeling like a little girl waiting for her bedtime story.

Idonna chuckled and reported, "Besides the master bedroom and five others, there's a living room, dining room, library and solarium, a gourmet eat-in kitchen and a den. You walk out the backdoor to a large swimming pool, and just beyond the pool there's a guest house with two more bedrooms and two baths."

"Goodness." Savannah pressed her hands to both cheeks. "What will we do with all that room?"

"I think the don intends for the rest of the staff—a mother, father, daughter and son-in-law—to live in the guest house."

Savannah blinked. "The rest of the staff?"

"Yes. I will serve as your personal secretary. The mother and daughter will care for the house and do the cooking. The father will serve as groundskeeper and the son-in-law, a big man, will be your driver and bodyguard."

"Is there a laboratory?"

"Oh, my, I almost forgot. The coach house has been renovated to reduce it from a four-car to a three-car garage. An addition was built onto the fourth stall—the one nearest the house—to convert the space into a full laboratory. I am told it is a marvel of modern technology."

Although her head was spinning, Savannah yawned. "Idonna, I am suddenly quite tired. Do you think I might take a nap?"

"I think that's a wonderful idea. You go ahead and sleep. I will read and keep the driver company during the rest of the ride. I believe when we reach New Orleans, we are to go to Don Angelo's home for dinner, after which he wants to personally show you around your new house and introduce you to your staff."

Oh, my. *Staff. How nice. I must show the don how grateful I am by making sure he gets from me all that he wants.*

Her eyelids fluttered and soon she was asleep, snuggled into the rider's side corner of the backseat while the Town Car clicked off the miles toward New Orleans.

Idonna woke her as the car turned from I-10 onto the exit ramp at 234 or Poydras Street.

Savannah rubbed her eyes and looked around, surprised to see that they were in a city. "Are we here?"

"We are. It might be a good idea to freshen your makeup. We soon will be at Don Angelo's."

A few minutes later, they turned into the guarded driveway at the home of Don Angelo Carbone. After the car had passed through, the ornate black metal gates closed behind them. The driver parked behind the house, and Idonna ushered Savannah from the car into the spacious Southern plantation-style home, an oasis in the midst of the New Orleans bustle.

The don, beaming, met her at the door. "My dear Savannah, come, come. It is so good to have you with us."

Savannah hugged him. Then, in perfect voice—a French accent tinged with a hint of the South—she said, "Oh, Don Angelo, how can I ever thank you for this new me? I am incredibly grateful!"

"I am so happy that you are satisfied with the artwork of Dr. Wilcox. I see you as his greatest masterpiece. You, my dear, are even more beautiful than the last time we met over dinner. You are younger, from top to bottom, it would appear. And I can hear that the lessons Idonna taught you have been listened to faithfully as well. You are now the stereotypical southern lady. But come, let's meet the rest of the family."

The don ushered Idonna and Savannah deeper into the house, where his wife and sons and daughter awaited them. Savannah's eyes met Dino's briefly. The look of appreciation in them brought warmth to her cheeks. Don Angelo held out his arm toward his family. "Savannah, this is my wife, Roslyn. She is old-school South, a descendent of one of the founders of New Orleans, Jean-Baptiste Le Moyne de Bienville, who established the community in 1718. Her roots go deep and she allows me my place in New Orleans society."

Rosalyn was a spectacular beauty, whose face and figure were exceeded only by her graciousness. She greeted her visitors warmly, kissing Savannah on both cheeks and leading her to a seat at her side.

With Savannah seated in a place of power and prominence, the don then introduced his four older children, sons Benton, Chandler, and Elliott, and daughter Vonell. All were very good looking and likable, and Savannah immediately fell in love with the family.

As they were introduced, the don said, "Dino, of course, needs no introduction; you know him well." He nodded at his daughter. "Vonell is the family's business manager and she rules her brothers with hands of iron."

The don's statement was followed by a knowing chuckle from the men. Vonell was pure charm on the surface and seemed to Savannah to possess an effectiveness that was reminiscent of her father. Best of all, she greeted Savannah as a sister would, taking her hand and meeting her gaze directly. "Savannah, we can never thank you enough for the work you have done for the family." Her smile was earnest and Savannah liked her at once.

As the Don proceeded with the introductions, things Dino had told her earlier now came into sharper focus.

He had told her that Benton ran the family's sex businesses. Chandler was in charge of drug trafficking, and Elliott controlled the liquor trade in New Orleans. Dino had also told her that he spent much of his time working closely with Vonell. That the two of them were fast friends was quickly apparent.

Apparently the Carbone family served only as a transport mechanism for drugs pouring into the country from south of the border. It was the drug trafficking, however, that had created the tension with the Cabreras. The Atlanta family, Dino had told her, had sought to develop its own drug connections in the islands and South America, only to be rebuffed by the drug lords, who had long and profitably worked with the Carbones and admired Don Angelo for his fairness and willingness to work effectively with his suppliers. The Cabreras hadn't liked that, triggering a war with the Carbones.

The drug lords had quickly joined the Carbones, tightening a supply noose on the Cabreras that had strained relations between the Atlanta Family and other families across the country.

None of that tension seemed evident on this night, as Savannah was treated to a wonderful dinner and warm discussion. Following dessert and a final glass of wine, the don walked her to the bottom of the stairs. Reaching for her hand, he held it in his. "Tomorrow we will tour the home we have selected for you. I trust it will be to your liking."

Savannah nodded. "I'm certain it will be."

He squeezed her hand and let her go. Rosalyn and Vonell showed Savannah to her room and made sure she was comfortable.

All in all, it was one of the most enjoyable nights that Savannah had ever experienced. While she hoped that Dino might pay her a visit, even though they had agreed to treat each other as cousins, that did not happen, and she slept soundly, not awakening until the clock was pushing toward ten.

Breakfast was again a family affair, after which Angelo and Dino accompanied Rosalie to the home at 28 Audubon Place, less than a mile from the Carbone residence. Although the distance would have been an easy walk, Savannah, Dino, and Angelo occupied the middle car in a three-car caravan. As they reached the house, the gates opened and guards were clearly visible.

She loved the house, and when the don and Dino showed her the carriage house and the new laboratory, Savannah gasped in delight and hugged them both. The house was simply beautiful in every way. Savannah wasn't certain what she would do with all of the room, but the don assured her she'd find a use for it. The tour concluded, Savannah was left with Idonna, who had been at the house when she arrived. The two women began to talk about things they needed, and when a list had been assembled, Idonna left with two of the guards to make the purchases.

When Idonna returned, she and Savannah worked to put things in place before traveling back to the don's for a dinner that was far more casual and relaxing than the event the previous night. The barbecue was held in the backyard beside the pool, but not before Angelo and Rosalyn had encouraged their children and Savannah to enjoy a swim. Savannah was impressed when she entered the cubicle assigned her in the cabana to find four different swim suits, all of which fit her perfectly.

Returning to the group, she said to Rosalyn, "You taste is wonderful, but why four swimsuits?"

"Angelo and I—when I can get him into the water—despise sitting in wet suits. We don't think our family and guests should have to, either."

"What a wonderful accommodation," praised Savannah. "Thank you so much."

The evening passed quickly and pleasantly, and it was just after nine when Savannah returned to the cabana for the last time to change into her clothing. She was overjoyed to find Dino waiting for her. He kissed her sweetly then said, "I have a hard time staying away from you, or acting like a cousin. I just couldn't resist trying to steal a kiss."

But Dino went no further than that one kiss, leaving her so she could get changed. When she rejoined the family, the don ordered his driver to take her and Idonna to the new house. When Savannah walked into her room, the bed had been turned down and looked incredibly inviting.

As tired as she was after the long day, Savannah lay in bed for a long time, gazing up at the ceiling and wondering how she would ever be able to repay the don for the favors bestowed upon her.

34

Savannah was up early the next morning. Angelo was coming over to discuss business, and she was anxious to make certain everything was perfect for the don's visit. She decided that she would meet with him in the breakfast nook in the kitchen. She especially liked the kitchen. It was painted yellow, a perfect morning color. The sun streamed through the windows, making the place seem alive.

She asked her staff to make certain everything was straightened up, and requested that the cook make some delicate breakfast pastries, and to be on call for anything else her guest may desire.

At precisely 10:00 a.m., the don's limo pulled into the drive. Savannah activated the gate then went into the back pool area to await her guest.

A moment later, Angelo came out the sliding glass doors. "My goodness, you have this place looking great, and you've only been here a day." He closed the door behind him. "Tell me, how do you like the house?"

"Oh, my dear Angelo, it is wonderful, everything I could have asked for and more. I feel like a little girl in a fairytale. In fact, I was afraid to open my eyes when I woke up this morning for fear that all of this is a dream."

Don Angelo grinned and slid his arm around her to lead her along the walk beside the pool.

"Have you used the pool yet?"

"Not yet. As you have pointed out, I have been here only a couple of days, but I plan to have my first swim this afternoon."

"Good, good." His smile didn't leave his face as he stopped near the door to the house and looked around. "The gardens look perfect."

His gaze swept the lawn around the perimeter of the pool, seeming to drink in every tiny detail. The way the sun caught him and the set of his jaw moved her. This pose, she thought, she would never forget.

After studying the property for several moments, the don turned to her, smiled again and said, "It is exactly as I ordered it. To the tiniest detail, it is as I wanted. If you do not like it, you have only me to blame."

"Angelo, how could I not like it? It is perfect in every way."

"Then it is good. Come, let us go in and talk. I want to see the house, too."

Once again, as she led him through the house, room by room, he seemed to miss nothing. *He appears to be committing every detail to memory.*

"So you like it," he said finally as she brought him to her suite and showed him how comfortable it was.

"No, I don't like it—I love it!"

She led him back downstairs and took him to the kitchen. "I adore this room. I thought we would be comfortable here."

"It is a delightful room." He settled on a chair at the glass-topped table. "Now, my dear, I am concerned about the safety features."

"For the most part you have seen them already. There are TV screens in every room that allow me to see every room in the house as well as all areas outside. There's a hidden room in the basement, which ties to a tunnel that runs under the pool and into the carriage house. And of course there's Hugo." She gestured out the window where Alma and Nicando's little dog lay sleeping in the sun and the don smiled. "Everything seems to have been thought of."

"What about the laboratory?"

"I haven't spent much time there yet, but I've seen enough to know that it appears to have every modern piece of equipment imaginable."

"It must be better than any other lab anywhere," he insisted. "You—and it—are my family's future. If there is anything missing, you must tell me at once."

"I will, Angelo. You seem especially concerned about the lab. Or am I wrong about that?"

The don leapt to his feet and paced around the kitchen. "You are amazingly perceptive—just like Dino. You hear what others do not hear and you see what others do not see. Your work is what is needed to head off this most recent threat, a threat that is more severe than any in the past."

"Angelo, I am willing to try and produce whatever is needed for the family to fight off these challenges. You must just let me know what you need."

"The Cabrera Family has become uncommonly aggressive. Always before, they have kept their distance, confining their business to Atlanta and Georgia. Now, they are moving into Mississippi and some of my trusted customers have told me their *soldati* have been talking to liquor wholesalers here in New Orleans."

Angelo stopped pacing and turned to face her. "My greatest fear is open war, and I see it on the horizon. The only way to head this off is to be ready with the weapons that send a swift signal to them to back off and get out."

"Will the new spray do it? Or is there something else, something more, that you need?"

The worry lines on the don's face eased. "I am pleased with your work," he told her. "I think the spray will be incredibly helpful. It is sure to tip the balance in our favor. You have done a wonderful job on that, and I am grateful. When we deploy the spray, I expect one of two things to happen. Either the Cabreras will get the message at first use of the spray and back off, or there will be open and outright warfare. Of course, we are hoping for the former. Juan Cabrera is a good fellow; I like him. But he has the Latin blood, eh? So he is feisty, flies off the handle quickly, is impetuous. I worry about that, but for the sake of you and my family, I must protect my territory, so, yes, I will use the spray."

Savannah bit her lip. "The spray is quite lethal, as you know. Whatever living thing breathes it in will die. Therefore, you must be cautious when you deploy it. Use it as a spear, not a machine gun, if you know what I mean."

"Ah, yes, my dear. I see your point perfectly. My warriors are equipped with pocket-sized spray containers and have been cautioned to use them as a last resort, and then only on specific targets."

"That part is very important. Because if a pet breathes in the spray—even one as large as a horse—I fear it will cause death. It must be used sparingly."

"I have been careful in the training, but my fighters have revenge in their blood. I know the spray will be used. I just hope it will be used in the way that they have been instructed. In the hope of cooling things off before they heat up more, I have sent word to the Cabreras that we have a powerful weapon that we hope never to use. But I have told them we will use it if pressured."

"And that, I suppose, is the purpose for which I developed it. I want it to be a winning weapon; I just don't want it to be a weapon of mass destruction, as the soldiers say."

"I want that, too. I continue to preach the message every chance I get, but still I have fears about the young men who carry out my orders. If they are threatened, they will resort to the weapons they have, no matter the target."

"Then let's hope that the targets are few and the aim of your soldiers good."

"Yes, yes, that is the hope."

Sensing the sadness in his voice, Savannah took his hand, hugged him, and kissed him chastely on the cheek. She met his gaze. His eyes were so filled with sorrow that her heart went out to him. She embraced him. "I share your pain. I have gotten to know many of your people, and I would hate for any of them to be lost to such needless conflict."

"The Cabreras have the idea that we invaded their territory when you and Dino went to live in Georgia. In Juan Cabrera's world, that must be paid for in kind."

"Yes, we lived there, but we meant them no harm. We didn't fight them until they attacked."

"In Juan's view, it was an invasion. When you and Dino fled Georgia, the don lost several of his men. And though they may have been thugs, they immediately became irreplaceable assets. Were the situation reversed, I, too, would have to pay with death. It's a world, Savannah, that you will come to understand, but only over time."

She considered his words before shaking her head. "But such a harsh judgment. You are an intelligent man. Is that not true of Juan Cabrera?"

"Yes, he is a good man; a very smart man."

"Then why can two intelligent men not work out a situation to the problem without warfare?"

"Because, in our world, such problems can only be settled with force.

To do anything less would show weakness in the face of an enemy and invite more trouble."

"Then I must see to it that you have the weapons you need to swiftly settle this dispute."

The don exhaled and got to his feet. "I have had a good visit. I am satisfied that you are happy. That is good. And now for the party. It will be a festive affair. Rosalyn is having a great time making certain everything is as she wants it. Me, I fear there may be spies at the event. There could even be violence. But do not fear, we will be vigilant and well prepared."

"Oh, but Angelo, how can I not worry? What if something happened to you or Dino? I could never forgive myself."

"You must promise me that if anything happens to me that you will make certain Dino has whatever he needs to survive this challenge." He grasped her shoulders. "Promise me!"

"Of course, I will do whatever is needed. But, Angelo, you must promise me that you will be cautious and take no chances. Now that I am getting to know you better, I would hate to lose you. I am becoming quite attached."

"And I to you, my dear Savannah. But as much as I admire you, for now you are Dino's. I respect that. You will respect that, too."

"Of course. My remarks were not intended to be flirtatious. They were designed simply to tell you how I feel."

"I am quite attracted to you, but this attraction of mine must be moved to a place reserved for relatives. You shall be my niece, as we have told everyone. My feelings for you will be kept there."

He kissed her gently on each cheek. "Please look carefully at your new home. If anything is missing, if anything needs to be changed, you are to tell Idonna at once and it shall be taken care of. Anything."

"Angelo, the house is perfect. I have told you that over and over. There will be no further requests." She took his hand and squeezed it.

The don left, accompanied by his guards.

After they were gone, Savannah showered, changed into work clothes, and headed for the lab. She spent four hours working, and when she was done she had another twenty sprayers loaded and carefully packed into protective cases. She stepped back to admire her work. Julie hopped up onto the counter and Savannah rested a hand on her back. "Well, Julie, we've done all we can. Now we just have to hope that if there is war, it will be quickly settled."

35

The rest of the week sped past, and Saturday dawned clear and horribly humid. When Savannah headed for her third shower of the day at 5:00 p.m., she thought she might wilt. Although the air conditioning system in her new house kept up beautifully, given the heat waves wafting from her patio, she was sure she would resemble a wet spaghetti noodle by dinner.

The auto that carried her to the elder Carbone's home was actually chilly inside, and when she was helped from the car, it was only a couple of steps into another heavily cooled area. When she entered the ballroom, a crowd of manicured, coiffed, and expensively dressed people waited for her.

The doors opened and she was announced. Don Angelo immediately took the microphone, waved to the orchestra to stop playing, and introduced her as "the newest member of my family, one it gives me great pleasure to introduce to you. My youngest brother's only child, Savannah. Savannah's existence was unknown to me until recently, when a member of the French press corps visiting New Orleans told me he had met a relative of mine."

Don Angelo gestured for Savannah to join him on the stage. "That remark stunned me, and when I met Savannah a week later in Paris, she stunned me, too. My family and I are happy to welcome her into our family and into New Orleans society. We hope that you will introduce yourselves to her tonight, but also follow up in the days to come. You will find her bright, articulate, well-mannered, sophisticated, and delightful. Please make her welcome to New Orleans."

As the room filled with a thunderous round of applause, Savannah climbed the stairs to the stage. Angelo handed her the microphone and she greeted the guests in perfectly articulated French. Then, translating her words into English, she said that she adored New Orleans and hoped the guests assembled would help her learn even more about their beautiful city. "The Carbones have been marvelous. They have warmly welcomed me into their family, found me a new home near Tulane University, and are now hosting this stunning party. I thank you sincerely for being here tonight and I look forward to meeting each of you. Please do seek me out.

"I adore parties, and so I welcome this one. It is, in fact, a true coming-out party in debutante style, since I missed such a party when I was growing up in Paris. Paris society is very rigid, not at all like the fun I see taking place here tonight. I want to enjoy all of it."

A movement to her right caught her eye. "But right now I see Angelo waving at me to tell you that dinner is about to be served. Please check the number on the corner of your nametag. That is your table number. If you could find your seats now, I would be grateful. And during dinner, in a manner that I hope will not distract from your enjoying this wonderful meal, I will visit each table to meet all of you. Mais, s'il vous plaît, pas de tests! Merci."

Noticing that some guests had puzzled looks on their faces, Savannah laughed. "Which means, but please, no tests. Thank you."

Once again the room erupted into a thunderous round of welcome as the don took her hand and helped her from the stage and to her table, which was at the center of the room.

As Savannah took her place, she leaned over to the don, kissed him on the cheek, and thanked him again for being so good to her.

"My dear, you are so welcome."

At that moment the amuse-bouche was served. Savannah studied it. Rosalyn Carbone rested a hand on her arm. "It's confit of duck with spicy cauliflower and yogurt sauce, delicious."

The don gazed fondly at Savannah. "Rosalyn just loves this sort of thing. And I must say, she entertains with style, grace, and charm. I'm sure the meal will be lovely, and *very* expensive. But then, nothing is too good for you, my dear."

A course of duck pate with baby pears, fruit compote, and mango coulis followed. The servers were plentiful and excellent. Dishes were cleared and new dishes delivered almost noiselessly and with great precision and flare. The soup course featured lobster bisque with salmon pate and tiger prawns. A palate cleanser came next, a delicate margarita granite sorbet. The seafood course consisted of something Rosalyn called "butter fish" that was served with sweet potato mash, kumquat salad, and lemon butter.

The main course was reindeer filet with dates puree, sugar beans, and almond snow. The meat was delicious, far better than anything Savannah had eaten.

When the servers carried large trays out of the kitchen, Rosalyn smiled. "Here is my contribution to the meal. I made this pre-dessert dessert myself, blue cheese and chocolate truffles served with maple syrup."

Savannah took a small bite. The concoction melted in her mouth and she nearly groaned with pleasure. Even after that incredible meal, she could not resist dessert when it came—something called Lady Angel—poached orange in Cointreau served with couscous biscuit and Cointreau sauce.

Each course was served with a phenomenal wine selection. When the guests had finished their dessert and sipped the last of the more than $1,000-a-bottle champagne that accompanied it, they were invited to the patio for a brief program before returning to the dining room for dancing.

During the fifteen-minute interlude on the patio, the don told the story of how he had discovered the existence of Savannah.

"Those of you who have met Rayford know that he was the wild member of the family." The don's comment brought a wave of laughter. "He sewed many wild oats, one round of which resulted in Savannah. Rayford met Honey Harlowe, the widow of a wealthy Georgia plantation owner, on a trip to Atlanta. Rumor has it that Mrs. Harlowe is quite a lovely woman. Shortly after discovering she was pregnant with Savannah, she moved to her farm in the east of France, where she now lives and where she raises thoroughbred horses and has a successful vineyard that produces some of the world's finest burgundy. I tried to attract her to this celebration, but she declined, saying she is now too old to travel comfortably.

"It is my hope that I will meet her this May when one of her three-year-olds, Grand Garçon Doux, will, if all goes well, be running in the Kentucky Derby. You should be able to follow him under the English name of Big Gentle Boy. Dame Harlow is apparently quite excited by the accomplishments of this horse, which Savannah has told me is appropriately named. In fact, if you discuss the topic with Savannah, she may tell you that her mother chose the name because the horse, in mannerism, reminds her of Rayford. I shall go no further than that, letting you attach your own meaning. But I would add this, the Carbones are known for their manly prowess."

That drew another round of generous laughter. As the don prepared to finish his comments, the sounds of The Olney Big Band of Olney, Maryland, wafted from the dining room and enveloped the patio.

Angelo raised his voice a little to make a final announcement. "In honor of Savannah, the Carbone family this evening pledges the financial support and labor to repair every one of the early cemeteries of New Orleans. As you know, these burial grounds were decimated by Katrina, leading to the creation of the charity 'Save Our Cemeteries'. Today I told Ms. Amanda Walker, the organization's executive director, that our gift will provide funding to complete all of the work her charity has undertaken. Ms. Walker is with us tonight. Would you stand, please, my dear?"

The attractive brunette stood to the group's applause. When the clapping died down, Angelo said, "Tonight Ms. Walker will be taking pledges of time and talent from anyone interested in contributing to her work. Before the evening ends, we will have a tally of hours pledged to share with you. But now, let's dance."

As the guests drifted back inside, they found the room transformed into a fairyland of clouds and twinkling stars. The music was straight out of the forties, and soon everyone was on the dance floor.

Savannah was the most popular dance partner, and before fifteen minutes were up, her card was filled with names. Dino came up to stand beside her and perused her card. He let out a low whistle. "You'll be dancing with every wealthy member of New Orleans elite society." Before anyone had arrived, he'd penciled his name in for the first and last dances, which Savannah thought was terribly romantic. But as she left him for the arms of a tall, handsome man, she vowed to enjoy every dance until she rejoined him for the last number of the night, "Goodnight Sweetheart, Goodnight."

The dance over, Angelo and Rosalyn walked to the dais to extend a formal good night to their guests. Dino joined them for the big announcement. "You will be happy to know that guests tonight have pledged 254,643 hours to help Save Our Cemeteries complete the work we will fund." The applause was tremendous. As it ended, Dino and Savannah joined Angelo and Rosalyn at the door to say goodnight to their guests. All in all, it had been a perfect evening, with wonderful food, superb music, and great company.

At last the guests were gone. Savannah kicked her shoes off and she and Dino joined Angelo and Rosalyn in the don's study, where he poured generous glasses of cognac. They sipped as they talked. The don plied Savannah with questions and she answered without hesitation, whatever the topic. Rosalyn, who had been listening quietly, smiled. "My dear, you are an amazing woman. I am so pleased that you have taken Dino under your wing. He needs some of what you can teach him. It's wonderful to have you as a member of the family."

It was nearly three o'clock before Savannah and Dino were again at her home. Too tired to do more than partake in a good night kiss, they fell asleep in each other's arms.

When Savannah awoke, the sun was far overhead and beginning to slip down into the west. She pulled on a robe and went to the kitchen, where she found breakfast laid out and *The Times Picayune* prominently displayed on the table in the sunroom.

Her likeness looked up at her from the front page. A four-column by 10-inch photo occupied the top left corner of page one. The caption noted that Savannah Harlowe had been introduced to the New Orleans elite Saturday evening at a spectacular party at the home of Angelo and Rosalyn Carbone. She was described in lavish prose that noted that she and her date, Dino Carbone, made a dashing couple. The story directed readers to more photos on page 11A. There she found a full page of pictures, many of them in full color. And on page 12A there was a flowery story that described who Savannah was and how the Carbones had found out about her.

There was also a full guest list, the who's who of New Orleans society, according to the *Times* reporter.

She returned to the bedroom with the newspaper and she and Dino looked at the photos and read the stories together. Too drawn to him to resist, she gave in to her desires and they spent an hour making up for time lost the night before. Afterwards, they showered together, donned casual clothes, and went to the kitchen for breakfast.

They relaxed over their meal. Savannah questioned him at length about the people at the party and especially those with whom she had visited.

"There was one man, Dino, who seemed uncommonly nice. He was tall, about six foot two, give or take an inch, I suppose. Toned, too, as if he works out a lot. He also seemed a bit out of place. Oh, yes, the thing that really stood out about him was his blond hair. There weren't many blondes in the room last night, other than a few bottle-blonde women. He was also an incredible dancer, almost as good as you."

Dino gave her a look, tipping her off to the fact that something she had said displeased him.

"Dino, I'm sorry. You're a great dancer …"

He held up his hand. "I noticed you dancing with him. What was it, three or four times?"

"Oh, I don't think it was that many. Maybe twice."

"It was more than that." His words were clipped. "There are things you must learn about, Savannah. He is one of them. His name is Rauel Quinones. He's a spy."

Her stomach tightened. *A spy?*

Dino's eyes smoldered. "He's said to be the Cabreras' chief contact here in New Orleans. You need to stay away from him, far away."

Savannah thought back to her time on the dance floor with Quinones. When they had finished their waltz, she had excused herself, saying, "I need a rest. You are a great dancer, but that is more exercise than I am used to."

His response was disturbing, but also exciting. "I know many other forms of exercise that you would enjoy, I am sure, exercises that would leave you even more breathless than you are now."

This is not the time to tell Dino that. Would there ever be a right time? She doubted it.

Nor would she tell him that the man intrigued her.

Dino's voice interrupted her reverie. "He was here because my father has the philosophy that you keep your friends close and your enemies closer. Personally, I can't stand the guy. I suppose there is a little jealousy in my feelings, but mostly it's the arrogance he displays when around any of us. I noticed him seeking you out. You need to beware of him, Ros … uh, Savannah."

While she knew that Mr. Quinones as a topic of discussion was better dropped, Savannah couldn't resist a wayward thought. *Rauel might be an interesting person to get to know, quite off the record, of course.*

The rest of the day was spent in leisure. Savannah and Dino lounged around the house, read the paper thoroughly, and took a nap.

They awakened about 5:00 p.m. to delicious smells from the kitchen.

Rada Muñoz and Alma Guzman, mother and daughter, were wonderful cooks and it was apparent they were creating one of their masterpieces for the evening meal. Guillermo Muñoz and Nicandro Guzman, Rada's husband and son-in-law, were also great people. Savannah had become quite attached to them in the week they had been together. It was obvious that they had been longtime friends as well as employees of the don.

Nicandro was a giant Spaniard. He stood six foot five and weighed nearly 300 pounds, and there was not an ounce of fat on him. When Savannah was with him, she worried not a bit about her safety. Guillermo was a short man. He probably did not top five foot five, but his weight made him look like a ball. As he was constantly smiling, it seemed as if Guillermo pasted the happy look on his face each morning and didn't remove it until retiring.

The staff members and Savannah were quickly becoming a family of friends, and they bent over backwards to please her.

Never before had Savannah been accustomed to such pampered luxury. *If only I were as young as I look.* No doubt this lifestyle could be quite habit-forming. In addition to the special work they did, Alma and Nicandro had taken to helping Savannah in the laboratory, and she was grateful for their company and for their assistance. Both were quick learners, and the day was quickly coming when they would be able to do almost all of the work she performed.

Dino left after dinner, saying he would be staying the night at his parents' house because his father wished to talk with him. Savannah watched a movie and then, as 10:00 p.m. approached, she bathed and got ready for bed. She settled into bed with a novel by Sandra Brown, *Mean Streak*. She had read but a few pages when the phone rang. It was Angelo. "Good evening, my dear. Have you recovered from your party?"

"Oh, Angelo, it was the best party I have ever been to."

"It was my pleasure. This phone call, however, gives me no pleasure. Apparently the Cabreras have determined that the time has come to end the Carbone influence in New Orleans. They are preparing to undertake action that Juan Cabrera says will make the Mafia-Camorra war of the early 1900s in New York City look like child's play. We must be ready to repel them, Savannah. I fear we are going to need as much of the newest weapon you have developed as you can make. Will you help?"

"Of course. I'll begin first thing in the morning. Alma and Nicandro have become great assistants, and I will use them to help me with the production, if that's all right."

"Wonderful. Three sets of hands will be useful. I fear we shall need all the help we can get before this is over."

"I will have a report for you tomorrow night on how quickly we can increase the supply and in what volume."

"Bless you, Savannah. Now rest. The days ahead will be unpleasant, I fear. All of your talents will be needed."

36

Al Rouse sat at his desk in the space reserved for detectives in the La Crosse Police Department. His coffee cup, filled with strong, black sludge, sat at his right hand, a doughnut rested on a napkin beside the cup, and he was busy reviewing the accumulation of online weekend newspapers from around the country. He was worried that the saga of Genevieve was over, that she had successfully vanished. Nonetheless, he continued his habit of paging through each of twelve newspapers daily, concentrating especially on four from the south.

As he came to the Sunday *Times Picayune* of New Orleans, he was drawn to a full-color picture that covered the top left quarter of the front page. An attractive brunette woman was pictured between Don Angelo Carbone and another spectacularly beautiful woman. The photo caption was: "New family member welcomed!" Something about the woman seemed familiar. *It can't be* … Intrigued, he studied the additional photos on page 11A and the news reports of the society event that covered much of page 12A.

Al lifted the paper closer to his face and leaned back in chair. Apparently Angelo Carbone, whom he had met, and his wife Rosalyn had hosted a party in honor of a newly discovered family member, Savannah Harlowe. The story reported that Savannah was the daughter of the don's late brother, Rayford Carbone, and a wealthy heiress who lived in France. Angelo, the story said, had heard about this family member from a Paris reporter who was in New Orleans. He went to find out for himself if the report was true, and met Savannah.

They had formed a fast friendship, and Angelo convinced Savannah to live at least part-time in New Orleans to be near her paternal family. According to the paper, the Carbone family had purchased Savannah a "lovely home at the edge of the Tulane University campus." Savannah would now divide her time between France and New Orleans. She was quoted as saying that she hoped to spend the next several months in New Orleans to learn more about her new-found family members. It seemed she was particularly attracted to Dino Carbone, but when Savannah was asked about the relationship by a reporter covering the event, she flippantly responded, "Just call it cousinly love … but without any playing doctor privileges!"

Al pursed his lips. *Hmmm, that sounds like something Genevieve would say.* He straightened up in his chair. *I wonder if there is any connection to the "newly found" relative and our missing killer.* It was highly unlikely, but as he had no other leads to follow …

Consulting his Rolodex, he dialed Aaron Wingate in New Orleans. Aaron answered his phone on the second ring. "I thought I might hear from you this morning. I imagine you're wondering about this new Carbone relative?"

"I most definitely am. Anything you can tell me?"

"I don't know much more than I read in the papers, so you probably know as much as I do. From the photos, it would appear that she is much younger than the woman you are seeking. It is very strange, though, how this has come up now, just as you are searching, and have been wondering if the woman you are hunting has been working for the mob. I haven't had any time to do more than file this on my list of things to follow up on. It's quite likely, though, that Angelo would have had special police on the detail at the party. He uses his own muscle, but he generally likes to supplement his boys with some of ours to give the impression of being close to us.

"I know the shift sergeant who handles special policing requests and assignments. Let me give him a ring. If he's on duty, I'll get back to you this morning."

The conversation over, Al busied himself with paperwork. He thought about calling Charlie, but decided to wait until he knew more.

For two hours he worked at reports, but his mind kept drifting back to the *Times Picayune* report, and twice he left what he was doing to read it again. He drummed his fingers on the desk. The woman pictured with Angelo was about the right height and weight, but she definitely bore no resemblance to the woman they had arrested in Arlington Heights. Still, he couldn't shake the feeling that something about her, the way she held herself, maybe, or the look in her eyes, reminded him of the woman he'd been chasing for years. He needed to know more.

As the clock moved near eleven-thirty, his phone rang. Al looked at the number and snatched up the receiver. "Hey, Aaron. Find out anything?"

"I have some additional details, although there's a lot I still don't know. It seems this new relative just burst upon the scene as the *Times* suggests. We know that Rayford Carbone, Angelo's youngest brother, was a playboy of the first magnitude. He died about eleven years ago of an alcohol-ravaged liver, but not before leaving a trail of illegitimate children across the South. Near as we can tell, Rayford met Honey Harlowe in Atlanta when she was grieving the death of her super-wealthy husband, one of the Georgian aristocracy, whose blood lines flow back to the earliest white settlers in the South.

"Not much else is known, really. Apparently after Honey's tryst with Rayford back in the fifties, she sold her plantation in Georgia and moved to France. She purchased a number of farms in Burgundy and the nearby Jura. Her wines are known to be among the best in the world, and her thoroughbred racehorses are frequent winners at tracks in France, England, Italy, Germany, and the United Arab Emirates. I guess you know that one of her horses will be running in the Derby here in May and is likely to be a favorite."

"I read that in the paper," Al told him. "So nothing more on Savannah?"

"She isn't really mentioned in any of our files. We only found out about her a week ago. Her mother lives on a spacious farmstead in the Jura. It's known as *Raisins Célestes, Chevaux avec les pieds d'ailes.* The translation, I'm told, is: Heavenly Grapes, Wing-Footed Horses. The estate is actually the remodeled former royal salt works, known as Saline Royale at Arc en Senans. If you Google it, you'll find it's quite a place. The old lady, she's nearly nintey now, lives there with some thirty servants. She's quite reclusive, I'm told."

"How do we learn more about Savannah?" A tingling sensation deep in his gut startled him. The Rouse Rash? Could this woman, who on the surface appeared completely unrelated to his quarry, really be activating that strong a reaction?

"I think you might have a better chance than I do. The don gets very touchy when we start poking around in his business. Maybe Interpol could provide you with information?"

"That's a great idea. I'll get on that right away. Thanks, Aaron."

"Okay, Al. And if a chance presents itself, I'll see what I can find out, too."

Al set the receiver down in its cradle then printed a selection of the newspaper photos and reports before heading for Chief Brent Whigg's office.

The chief was alone, and when he saw Al walking toward his door, he waved him in and gestured to a chair. "What's up?" His deep, booming voice echoed in the spacious office.

"Some new developments in the drownings case, sir. I've just finished talking to Aaron Wingate down in New Orleans. There was an interesting party there Saturday night."

Whigg's face broke into a smile. "That's news? C'mon, Al. There's an interesting party in New Orleans every night."

"I know, I know, but not like this one. This one featured Don Angelo Carbone and a newly discovered female relative, Savannah Harlowe. She doesn't look anything like Genevieve Wangen, and she's way too young, but there's something about her that is giving me the old itch. You remember the trip Charlie and I made a few months ago?"

"Of course, but that trip led to nothing, right?"

"Well, not then, but now things could be different. I want you to take a look at these and I'll tell you what I know."

He handed the clippings to the chief and settled back as Whigg looked them over.

"Hmm, you think this Savannah Harlowe might know something about Genevieve?"

"No." Al cleared his throat and shifted on the hard plastic chair. *He's going to laugh me out of his office.* "I'm actually wondering if this Savannah Harlowe is Genevieve."

The chief's forehead wrinkled. Al fidgeted while the chief thought.

Finally the chief asked, "Why would you think that? Isn't this woman a lot younger?"

"She appears to be, but of course her looks could have been altered."

"Really? By that much? Seems a bit far-fetched."

"I know, but hear me out. We followed Genevieve and a man we think is her boyfriend, Don Angelo Carbone's son, from Georgia to Louisiana, as you know. We tried to get something concrete on her then, but nothing panned out. But suddenly this Savannah is on the scene when no one has heard about her before? When I read about it, it made the hair on the back of my neck stiffen."

The chief drummed his fingers on his desk, contemplating him. "I suppose it could be, but I don't know enough about the circumstances to form an opinion, one way or the other. Before we go running off on another wild goose chase, I'd like some hard evidence, that's for sure."

"I agree. I wasn't asking for permission to go anywhere. But I am curious and I asked our friend at New Orleans P.D. to try and get some proof. He said he'd try, but suggested we check with Interpol, see if they can give us any information. Are you okay with that?"

"Sure. Of course. As long as it doesn't make trouble for any of our friends."

"I talked to Aaron, the detective who helped us out when we were down there, about that. He's been on the force there a long time. In fact, he's a friend of the Carbones, including the don. We met the don, too."

"I remember that. You told me he's a nice guy."

"Sure seemed so. The don set up a reservation for us at a great New Orleans restaurant, and when we finished, he paid the bill."

"Just so it wasn't a down payment on future favors."

"C'mon, boss, you know us better than that. Check that, you know me better'n that. Charlie was pretty impressed by the restaurant."

That brought a laugh from the chief. "That Charlie. All roads with him lead to and from his stomach."

"You got that right. But this is an interesting development that I wanted to make you aware of. You're okay with me following up, right?"

"Absolutely. You know that. You've got great instincts, Al. I'd never get in the way."

"I know, Chief, and I appreciate it."

Al was up early the next morning, refreshed in spite of his night out of the house. He arrived at work at seven and studied newspapers until Chief Whigg walked in. He visited with the chief for a while then went back to his newspapers.

The phone rang shortly after eight. Aaron Wingate skipped the small talk and told Al they had hit a stone wall with the don. "We asked Angelo about Savannah during an accidentally-on-purpose encounter. The don politely but curtly told us to stay away from her. He said she's trying to start a new life and he doesn't want anything to get in the way of that. He assured us she is exactly who she is purported to be. It was as cold a brush-off as we could have gotten from the don. He wants us to stay away; that much was obvious."

Al repressed a sigh. "No need to impair your relationship with him. But maybe you could quietly let your co-workers know that if we could get a fingerprint, that would be great."

"Not sure how we'll do that. But let me give it some thought and see what I can puzzle out."

He leaned back in his chair and propped his feet on the desk. Fingers entwined behind his head, he allowed his nagging thoughts to surface.

Something told him there was more to the New Orleans story involving Savannah Harlowe. And whether the don liked it or not, Al was going to figure out what it was.

37

Savannah was up early, working to amass an expanded supply of the killing spray that Angelo believed he needed to fight off the Cabreras. She had just taken a break for a cup of coffee and a beignet, a new delicacy that she loved, when the phone rang.

"Hello, my dear."

"Hello, Angelo. Something bothering you? You sound on edge."

"Ah, you already know me well. Yes, there is something that has me a bit on edge. I wasn't sure I wanted to bother you with it, but I thought you should know. I bumped into a detective friend of mine today; I'm not sure entirely by accident, although I'm certain he hoped I would think that's what it was. He casually mentioned he'd read about you in the paper and asked quite a few questions.

"I told him you were trying to start your new life and not to bother you, but I'm not convinced that will work. Please stay near the house. Let Dino or your staff do the outside work for now, okay?"

"Should I be worried? Maybe I ought to disappear again."

"No, I don't think that's necessary. I don't want either of us to act hastily. For now, let's just be cautious."

"I can do that. But if you hear more, please let me know right away."

"Absolutely."

He turned the topic of conversation to business and her progress on amassing additional supplies of the spray.

Savannah gripped the receiver tightly. "What sort of war are you expecting?"

"That's hard to tell. It is my hope that we can make a few well-placed retaliations if they press us. I'm hoping they don't want open warfare any more than we do."

"Angelo, I'm new to all of this. When you speak of open warfare, what does that mean?"

"It could mean many things. It could mean a killing here or there of someone close to me, a family member, even. It could be even more blatant, like an attack at my house. I'm going to increase security at both your house and mine, just in case."

"Do you really think it could come to that?"

"Well, it would be unusual for this day, but in the past, yes, very much so. There were many times that this kind of attack happened. Think about Chicago and Al Capone, among others; yes, it was very much like that. I'd like to think we've come a long way since then, but I can't be sure."

"That's frightening. Are you sure I shouldn't disappear?"

"There is always time for that, Savannah, but I'm hoping the warnings I have sent to the Cabreras are heard and responded to. In the meantime, production of the spray must be increased."

For the next five days Savannah worked from sun up to sun down to stockpile sprayers. Each day the don sent someone to pick up that day's work.

On the sixth day, Savannah awoke before dawn and made her way to the kitchen, where Alma was already at work.

"Breakfast, ma'am?"

"Maybe just some toast. And some of that wonderful jam your mother makes. Oh yes, coffee. Very strong, please."

A steaming cup of coffee and the papers in front of her, she began to feel human again. Looking out the window, she saw the first streams of light reflecting off the water in the pool. Everything seemed normal and she took her first full breath since the conversation she'd had with the don a few days earlier. Then the phone rang.

It was Dino and he was all business. "It's started. They killed two of dad's bodyguards last night. Enrico and Dominic were at the front gate when a car came past, slowed, and the two men were shot with silenced weapons, according to Alessandro. You'll notice some new people outside your gate. Dad sent them. They are armed. Until you hear otherwise, stay inside."

Dino hung up and Savannah was left worrying, mostly about her younger lover. She hadn't even had a chance to tell him to be careful. She texted him then forced herself to go back to reading the paper. As there was little of interest there, she hurried through breakfast, returned to her suite and showered, pulled on her work clothes, and headed for the lab, careful to make her way there through the tunnel rather than walking outside.

The next morning, the message was worse, much worse. Dino's brother, Benton, and his wife Ivy had been dining in downtown New Orleans when a shot fired through the window hit Benton in the chest. He was in critical condition at Tulane Medical Center following surgery to remove the bullet.

Dino called to give her the news. His voice held a tremor, and he spoke so fast she had trouble keeping up with his train of thought. "Thankfully, the bullet remained intact and passed cleanly through his upper right chest. He will survive. Still, Dad is enraged. Nothing good will come of this. I will be by shortly to pick you up. Bring clothes for a few days. Also, if you've been able to get more spray containers ready this morning, ask Nicandro and Guillermo to pack them up and I'll have someone stop by for them shortly."

With that, the line went dead. Savannah stared at the phone for a moment before setting it on the table with a trembling hand. Is disappearing the prudent thing to do? She shook her head. She was in no position to do that. Getting away required resources—people, money, a plan, documents—none of which she had, at least, not in the name of Savannah Harlowe. But it's time I do. She would figure that out soon. For now, she needed to get ready to leave.

Dino arrived in a group of three cars. As they left her home for what Savannah presumed would be a short ride, they rode in the center of a three-car caravan as they drove out her gate. Soon they were at Angelo's. He met them, kissed her on the cheek, then asked her to sit with him.

"Rosalyn is at the hospital. The news is good. Benton will be fine. The question for me is whether the bullet was intended to wound or to kill. This must be carefully considered, as the answer will determine the next move I make. Come, both of you, join me in the study. Chandler, Elliott, and Vonell are already there. We must talk."

Dino and Savannah joined the group in the study. Dino's siblings were already arguing heatedly. Elliott and Chandler were determined to retaliate, swiftly and with deadly intent, with, in their words, "all the force we have."

Vonell held up a hand. "We need to know more," she argued. "Let dad call Juan Cabrera. If that doesn't go well, we can decide the best way to strike back."

Angelo nodded. "Only foolish people run off half-cocked before knowing what they are up against. I will call Cabrera. Then we will meet again and plan."

Angelo left to make the call. The siblings, now a bit more subdued, continued to discuss the situation. Dino sided with Vonell, and he and his sister worked to persuade their older brothers to calm down and think.

Angelo returned a half hour later to say he had spoken to Juan Cabrera, a discussion that could have gone better.

"He told me we are a disgrace to the organizations in this country, that we have sided with the police and withdrawn our authority in New Orleans. He suggested that we give up this territory to the Cabreras."

"I hope you told him to stick it!" Elliott's face was red and he was almost screaming. "Who the hell do those guys think they are? I say we go after them; this means war, you know."

Angelo frowned. "But, Elliott, the pledges we have made call for non-cooperation with authorities. We can hardly claim compliance, can we?"

Savannah nudged Dino with her elbow and whispered, "Pledges?"

He leaned close to speak into her ear. "Father is referring to a code the families live by. It involves silence and non-involvement in other family's activities, as well as not working with authorities."

Savannah nodded.

"Dad, we aren't cooperating with the cops!" said Chandler. "We're just not fighting with them. We still run sex, drugs, and liquor. The Cabreras damn well know that. I say an eye-for-an-eye. They have attacked our family directly. We cannot let that go unchallenged."

Savannah listened for the next hour as the family members debated what, if anything, should be done. The suggestion that nothing should be done was quickly dismissed, with all four children voting in favor of retaliation.

Dino slapped a fist against his open hand. "It's time to act. Let's take out a couple of Juan's bodyguards. If that doesn't bring a halt to this, we'll go after the family with the weapon we have at our disposal, thanks to Savannah."

No one protested. His suggestion clearly resonated with his siblings, and soon Angelo also agreed. That part settled, the execution became the topic of discussion. The plan formed quickly. Dino and Judson would head for Atlanta to stake out Amber Johansen's "business" until the Cabreras came around. When that happened, the Carbones would exact revenge.

Angelo's tone was somber when he said, "Before we strike, I want all of you not actively engaged to take up residence here at my house. I'd also prefer that we wait until Benton is well enough to be moved here."

Family members knew that Angelo wanted everyone accounted for. While the don had guards stationed in number at the hospital guarding Benton's room, he wouldn't be satisfied until his son was with them at the family compound.

Within forty-eight hours, Benton had improved enough for him to be moved to the family headquarters, where round-the-clock nurses would be employed to care for him.

Finally it was time to act. Dino and Judson prepared to leave for Atlanta. Angelo met them at the door. "Be careful, my sons. And report to me every morning and evening with an update."

When they agreed, Savannah slipped up behind the don. Dino led her to a quiet corner. Savannah brushed the back of her hand against his cheek. "You'll be careful?"

He smiled. "I will. I promise. I'll see you soon." He pressed his lips to hers before leaving her to follow his brother to their car.

For three days the brothers had little to report. Then, on the fourth morning, Dino told his father that he and Judson had murdered Juan Cabrera's eldest son, Alejandro, and his two bodyguards the night before. They had seen them first at Amber's then followed them to a bar in downtown Atlanta. "When they came out of the bar, we hit them with the spray. It was virtually instantaneous. They were down and out in a flash. We waited a minute or so, then threw them in the trunk of the car and took them to a creek outside town where we dumped the bodies."

Savannah, who was listening on the speaker phone, turned a wide-eyed gaze to the don. He covered her hand with his. "Did you attempt to hide them?"

"Hell, no! We want them to be found. Just not outside the bar. We want this to be headline news, so we don't want the Cabreras to quietly clean up the mess. When it becomes a story, they'll get the message loud and clear that we are not to be messed with."

When Angelo reported to the rest of the family at breakfast what Dino had told him and Savannah, his tone was one of sadness.

Vonell cocked her head. "Why do you sound upset, Dad?"

"I feel badly for Juan. Children are very special gifts from God. When you lose one, it is like losing your life. I knew that the minute I heard Benton had been shot."

He walked to the window, pulled the drapes open and looked out, his hands clasped behind his back. When he turned, he wore the saddest look Savannah had ever seen him display.

"This is a tragic moment. Juan cannot forgive this act. His action will be swift and devastating. In his place, I would do the same."

Savannah's throat tightened. "Now what?"

"You all must go to Dewey Wills." Angelo pointed to his children. "You take your mother and Savannah. Watch over them. Your bodyguards will go with you. Dino will join you there tonight. My personal bodyguards and I will stay. We will be ready for the Cabreras when they arrive."

Chandler and Elliott immediately protested. Elliott leaned forward, both palms pressed to the table. "Father, we are staying, too. We will face trouble as a family."

"No, Elliott, listen to me. This I must face. You and your brothers need to protect your mother, sister, and Savannah. Please, no argument."

Realizing their father had spoken and would not be moved, the two brothers looked crestfallen, but remained quiet.

"As you say, Father." Benton rolled into the room in his wheelchair.

Angelo embraced his eldest child. "My son, how are you feeling?"

"Much better. Treatment here agrees with me."

"Well, I'm afraid it's over. I must now send you to Dewey Wills with your mother and siblings. I shall wait here for the Cabreras. God willing, we will soon be together again."

Two hours later, a five-vehicle caravan was ready for the trip to the Dewey W. Wills Wildlife Management Area in the Catahoula National Wildlife Refuge, the place that had been such a sanctuary for Dino and

Savannah. Farewells were tearful, after which the family members, plus Savannah, got into the cars and the entourage filed out of the drive.

Several hours later, they had made the air boat ride into the swamp and Savannah was reunited with Miranda, although the cook looked a bit mystified, both by her appearance and when everyone called her Savannah.

"It's a long story, Miranda. Tomorrow I'll be up early and will explain everything then, okay?"

Miranda smiled, nodded, and hurried away to help the guests unpack. Soon an unsettling silence had settled over the compound. Almost everyone, tired from the long ride, decided to nap.

Savannah, however, walked to the water's edge with a fishing pole to try her luck. Soon Miranda joined her, and they talked like schoolgirls for more than an hour before Miranda was summoned to begin dinner.

The rest of the day went quickly, and after a dinner of fresh fish and greens, the compound again grew quiet as the guests bedded down for the night. Dino, who had arrived just in time for dinner, and Savannah sat and talked until very late. Sleep, she feared, would not come. Dino was terribly worried about his father. No matter what Savannah said, he could not be consoled. Even when she offered him sex, he turned her down, saying that with his father's life in the balance, he could not begin to think of anything pleasant.

Savannah dozed on the couch off and on. Whenever she opened her eyes, Dino sat there, appearing lost in thought, until the rays of the new sun began to invade the cabin. At last, when eight o'clock came, she gave up on either of them falling into a deep sleep. She sat up and they headed for the kitchen and breakfast.

Although they at least crawled under the covers of her bed that night, Dino continued to be uncommonly restless, and Savannah suspected that he was awake most of the night. The next three nights passed the same way. Even though the family met for meals, talk was at a minimum. No one knew what was happening in New Orleans and everyone was reserved because of it.

38

On the eighth day, when Dino and Savannah walked into the kitchen, the first of the family members at the compound there that morning, they were greeted by Angelo, wearing a broad smile.

He embraced his son and hugged Savannah tightly before holding her out at arms' length.

"My dear, you have saved the Carbone family from great trouble. Your spray worked like a charm. When the Cabreras came to visit, I met them at the gate. The first three people to greet me were swiftly subdued. The battle ended as quickly and quietly as it began. I stood there for an hour, but when no one else showed up, I retired to the house, leaving my bodyguards to keep watch. The next morning, the three bodies were gone, presumably picked up by the Cabrera gang.

"That afternoon I received a call from Juan Cabrera pleading with me to call off the war. I told him that it was his to cancel, reminding him that we had not started it. He agreed with me, but asked that we might again be friends and save our families from further problems. I assured him we would like nothing better, but I also told him that if his words were not sincere, the angel of death would again visit them. He promised me there would be no more problems.

"That was six days ago, and there has been no more trouble. Two nights ago, I called him and asked if the time had come for us to talk and put our differences to rest. We agreed to meet, just the two of us, at our casino in Biloxi. The meeting was everything I had hoped. There is no longer tension in the southland. The Cabreras are again happy with their territory in Georgia and we will be unchallenged in Louisiana. I have come to tell all of you the story and to bring you home." He squeezed her arms gently. "And you, my sweet Savannah, have made this peace come true. Both families owe you much."

"So, the war is over?" asked Savannah.

"It most assuredly is. After your spray left three of the Cabrera musclemen dead, Juan was quick to listen to reason. I told him we never wanted war, but when they seemed determined, we felt there was no choice. A truce was quickly forged. But I waited to come here until I was certain that peace was real."

"Oh, Angelo, that is so very good." Tears slid down Savannah's cheeks. "I prayed this would be the result. I know I must seem a complex personality to you, but I disdain death. The closer I get to it, the farther away I want to be. But if the spray became a peace serum, I'm happy."

"Peace serum. Peace serum. Yes, that it surely was." The don smiled broadly. "I think that not only the Cabreras, but other families as well, knowing we have such a weapon, will be hesitant to take on the Carbones. And if that is the result, I will be very happy. War is not something I enjoy, but I am glad that my sons convinced me not to back away from this one."

That day the swamp was alive with the sounds of celebration. All the family members were happy to hear the news of the truce, and that night Miranda cooked up a feast fit for a king, or at the very least a don.

There was fish, shellfish, and thick filet mignon. In addition to the food, there was a good deal of drinking, much of it consumed following toasts. Savannah was praised over and over again, and it was obvious that she had achieved a new, exalted status within the family.

The next day started late. It was ten o'clock before Miranda served breakfast. The Bloody Marys were coveted, but the eggs went largely untouched. Following the meal, the don urged everyone to pack up their belongings.

"I want us to be home before dark. That means we need to head for the landing in half an hour."

When the announcement was greeted by groans, he shrugged and smiled. "That's okay. Anyone not ready can stay until the next time we have cars going toward New Orleans."

That provided the spark. Members of the group vanished and twenty minutes later the gear was in the boats and the group was headed for the landing. A collection of Lincoln Navigators, black, of course, waited at the landing, and soon the six-vehicle caravan was speeding southward.

When the entourage reached New Orleans, Don Angelo, riding in the front car, radioed the vehicle carrying Dino and Savannah and suggested that she stay at his home for the night, so her house could be thoroughly inspected before she again took up residence there. She quickly agreed.

It was another good night. Dinner was festive, again with numerous toasts to Savannah for her work on the weapon that Angelo credited with allowing them to avoid major heartbreak. She was happy for the adulation, but also weary and tense. One moment's joy could quickly change. It had been a long, long day, and shortly after dessert had been served in the don's study, she excused herself and headed for the room reserved for her.

Dino joined her an hour later. It was a tender night. He was his old, ardent self and she abandoned her earlier decision to keep their relationship familial and enjoyed accommodating his healthy appetite. Truth be told, hers was just as healthy, maybe even more so, and after a strenuous workout, he begged fatigue and they snuggled together in the big bed that was as soft as a hopper of feathers.

"Dino, what shall I ever do if you tire of me? I have grown very fond of your attention."

"Ma cherie, there is no reason to worry. I do not think I could leave you, even if I wanted to. I am a slave to your desires. Never have I been so satisfied. Your hands are like silk and your lips like molten lava. Never would I have guessed that the pleasures of the flesh could be so totally consuming, so wonderful!"

"Mmmm, and I think I still have a number of tricks you haven't experienced."

"Then there is no way I could leave." He kissed her neck, teasing her with his hands.

"Now, now. You keep that up and we'll never get any sleep."

"And that will be fine with me." In spite of his words, his steady breathing shortly turned to gentle snores. Savannah knew playtime was over for the night.

She snuggled into him, folded the pillow close, and let her thoughts wander in a manner she rarely did. I wonder how my niece Julie is doing.

The trust fund of great magnitude would aid her and her son, and Savannah hoped the house she had sold her, or given her, really, was of great comfort and creating no problems for her.

Were Julie and Peggy Russell still fast friends? And what about Detective Allan Rouse? She frowned. *That was a nasty trick I played on him.* At the time, they'd been attempting to return her to Wisconsin to be charged in fourteen deaths, and she'd just been glad that she could continue to enjoy her freedom. Even now, although she felt a bit bad about it, she couldn't fully regret her actions. She loved Dino, and she was glad that life had offered her the chance to meet him. *And what about Kelly Hammermeister, Julie's colleague and roommate in Chicago? Didn't she marry one of those cops? I wonder how she's doing.*

Not once since she had escaped from Al, Charlie Berzinski, and Rick Olson had she given in to temptation. Several times her fingers had hovered above the keyboard of her computer as she thought about Googling Julie, Dr. Olson's wife Peggy, or any of the men pursuing her. She couldn't afford to take the chance. The technological revolution was unfurling faster than people could assimilate, and she wasn't about to let anything as simple as an errant keystroke direct the law to her whereabouts.

And so she was content to play a guessing game during pensive moments like tonight. She hoped that Julie's son Brody was doing well. He would be in college now. *Did he go to school in Illinois or somewhere else?*

Soon her thoughts grew slower and fainter as sleep overcame her and cast her into a pleasant, dreamless coma.

39

At 9:30 the next morning, the first Tuesday in April, the phone on Al's desk rang. He was busily working on several reports, and had to shuffle papers to find the phone. Having his desk messy was anathema to him; he hated messy. Disorganized messes made him feel inadequate, gave him nervous fits.

And so his voice reflected his frustration as he dug the receiver from the pile. "Rouse, here," he answered grumpily when he got the receiver to his ear.

"Hey, buddy, it's Rusty. We just picked up some news down here that I thought you might be interested in. We think the Carbones may have had a battle with their associates from Atlanta. We hear there may have been fatalities."

Al's eyes widened. "Really? What else do you know?"

"Not much. One of our snitches picked up the report from someone on the fringe of the Carbone organization. He told our guy that the Cabreras were upset because the Carbones had begun to change their image to something more law-abiding. Apparently the Cabreras decided they should take over New Orleans. Even went so far as to kill a couple of Angelo's security team and shoot one of his sons. The way we hear it, the whole thing was on the edge of open warfare until the Cabreras made a move one night two weeks ago and lost three guys to a mysterious weapon used by the Carbones."

"Wow." Al slid to the front of his chair. "That's amazing. How sound is the snitch?"

"I don't know him, but the guys who run him say he's always on target."

"What about the mysterious weapon? Do you know any more about that?"

Rusty Cunningham didn't respond for a full thirty seconds. Al caught the sound of rustling paper in the background before the detective spoke again. "Sorry. Just reviewing some notes from the night group that runs our snitch pool. The notes say the weapon was invisible, silent, and odorless. When the Cabrera team approached Don Angelo's house, three of the men hit the ground dead before anyone knew what was happening. The others fled, then returned later to pick up the bodies and get out of town."

Al drummed his fingers on the desk. "Sure as hell sounds like some kind of poison, doesn't it?"

"That's what we think, too. Which is why I called you. I know enough about the gal you're chasing to know that she puts together powerful knockout drops, right?"

"Absolutely. She has a strong chemistry background and, as far as we know, has used poison on all her victims. She's good enough to know what to use and what amount of it will kill and what won't. I can testify to that, since she escaped from me by injecting me with a drug that knocked me out on the spot and allowed her to get in the wind. That's going on four years ago, but we haven't given up finding her."

"I don't have anything more solid than that for you now. But you're right, it does seem kind of funny that this new relative comes to town and the next thing we know, we have three guys on the ground for the count. Victims of some unknown weapon."

"Seems too coincidental, doesn't it?"

"Absolutely. There were no shots fired. Apparently both sides were loaded for bear, but there were no shots. The men just went down and stayed there. But that's all we know. These guys clean up any messes before we find them."

Al pursed his lips. "Have you talked to Aaron in New Orleans?"

"My next call. Tried you first."

"Would it serve any purpose for me to come down there, do you think?"

"Tell you what, let me talk to Wingate. If there's anything more solid than what I've got, or if we think of something for you to do, one of us will call you."

"Call today if you can."

"If there's anything, you'll get a call. And you're welcome down here anytime. You know that. But there likely isn't going to be anything to find. The only reason for you to consider a trip is that we aren't going to spend any time looking into things when there's no evidence. If you were here, you'd be able to concentrate on trying to find out if the killing agent is from the woman you're looking for."

"Yeah, no reason to travel yet. But maybe your talk with Aaron will change that."

"We'll see."

"All right. In the meantime, I'm gonna talk to the chief. I'll also get a hold of Charlie. You remember him, right? The big guy, the eater? If you and Aaron think there's any point to it, we'd love to come down and sniff around."

"Got it. I'll be in touch. If you do end up coming, just let me know when and who'll be with you. And bring your summer clothes, it's been hotter'n hell. Temps in the nineties almost every day. And when it doesn't rain, the humidity's over a hundred."

A few more pleasantries and the conversation ended. Al typed the notes from the conversation, saved them, then tidied up his desk. After printing his notes, he headed for the chief's office. When he got there, Whigg was just finishing his morning news conference, so Al stood quietly outside the door, waiting for the conversation to end.

When the reporters left the office, the chief gestured for him to come in. "What's up, Al? Nothing too terrible, I hope."

"No, not troublesome, but interesting." Al handed his notes to the chief.

Whigg studied them, returned them to Al, and leaned back in his chair. Folding his hands across his belt, he said, "Let me guess, you want to make another trip?"

"Well, ummm, it does seem as if ..."

"Al, we can't go funding travel whenever something interesting comes up. The last couple of trips brought interesting results, but nothing solid in terms of the whereabouts of the killer. I just don't think I—"

Al held up a hand. "Chief, I wasn't going to ask you to fund another trip. What I was going to ask you for is time off so I can take a vacation to New Orleans. I think a couple of weeks away will be good for me. I hope JoAnne will go, too."

"So you want to take a vacation in the south." The chief picked up a mug from his desk and took a swig of coffee before setting it back down with a thud. "I sure as hell can't fault your willingness to go out of your way to try and find some new evidence. But, Al, you have to get over this thing. The old girl is gone. Hell, maybe she's dead. We have plenty of work right here, right?"

"I can't, Chief. I know she's out there, likely moving in on more victims. I can't rest until I know she's behind bars."

The chief blew out a breath. "I know this thing is gnawing at you. Tell you what I'm gonna do. I'm gonna approve your request for vacation, but I'm gonna put the request in my desk drawer. When you're back, we'll talk about whether it stays buried or goes on to payroll. Fair enough?"

"Very fair. I know this thing has me tied in knots, but I feel as though I have to somehow correct the wrong I committed when we were bringing her back here."

"Al, dammit, you didn't commit any wrong. Anyone in your position would have had the same result. And you're the only one who blames yourself for her escape. She's a foxy old witch, that's for sure. Either she thinks damn well on the spur of the moment or she was planning way ahead of us."

"She's crafty, that's for sure. But I still have trouble sleeping. I just have to track her down. It's the only way I'll get some peace of mind. I really need to get this done."

"Al, you're the best damn detective I have. Hell, you're the best detective I've ever had. You don't need to apologize to anyone for this one thing. So if you decide to go down there on your own time, I won't stop you. But if this is another dead end, let's end it, okay?"

"Not sure that I'll be able to. But I am going to try something different this time. I'm going to treat it like a vacation, JoAnne and all. Maybe that will change my luck."

"And what about Charlie and Rick? Do you expect they're gonna take vacations, too?"

"That's up to them, but I'd like them to go along. And Kelly and Peggy, too. In fact, if I could have my way, I'd take Julie Sonoma, too, Genevieve's niece."

"Yes, I know who Julie is, Al. And I suppose you know there are rumors floating around about how close the two of you are. Now that's none of my business, and it will stay that way unless it affects your work. I hope you won't let it."

Al hung his head, paced a bit, hands behind his back, then faced the chief. "Brent, I've never told you anything but the truth, and I'm not going to change that now. Yes, we're close. Too close. It cuts me up. JoAnne is wonderful, a great wife, doting friend, terrific household manager, and wonderful lover. But Julie is … well, Julie is something extraordinary. She's beautiful, kind, loving, patient …. Frankly, I can't face losing either of them."

His posture slouched more, his head dipped. "I don't know what to do about this. I've tried to treat my job with the same respect I always have. I've tried to keep my personal life and work life separate, but this thing is killing me."

The chief shrugged. "Al, there will be no judgment from me. Your work hasn't suffered a bit. Maybe I'd like a magic wand so I could rid you of this guilt complex you're nursing, but there's never been any question about your effectiveness. I hope you know that."

"But I do feel guilty, like I'm cheating work and JoAnne. I can't get over being such an idiot. It's driving me nuts."

"Al, telling you to get over it isn't going to make a difference. But you need to know that you are the best when it comes to detective work. Now as to this Sonoma woman, you're an adult. I'm not going to give you any advice. She must be incredible, because I know that JoAnne is an angel."

"She is. They both are. That's the problem."

"Well, I can't help you with that one. Although I will confess to being a bit envious. If ever there was a case of being interested in a man's rejects, this is it. I don't know how you do it, Al, but you're a chick magnet, do you know that?"

In spite of his angst, Al burst out laughing. "Chick magnet? You gotta be kidding. This old guy is just trying to hang in there against the kids these days. Everyone is so damn smart, so creative, and so damn young, too."

"Ah, isn't it true." The chief clasped his hands behind his head. "But you know what, Al? Those young pups have one helluva lot to learn, and we're just the people to teach them. The one thing they haven't got is seasoning. And we have that in abundance."

Al laughed again. "But I'm not sure if I'm vanilla or chili pepper."

The chief chuckled. "We're a terrific blend of both, Al. That's what makes us so special. Wish I could help you with the personal situation, but short of taking one of the women off your hands, there isn't much I can offer. And I don't think Martha would like that."

"Chief, you're the best. And your wife's an angel, too. I wouldn't do anything to offend Martha. But every time I come in here, no matter the news, I feel better when I leave."

"Wonderful. I guess that's a big part of my job, so if I help you a little, I'm happy. Sometimes I think the degree in criminal justice was useless. I think psychology would have been better."

"Even without a degree, you're pretty good at it. Thanks, Chief. I'll get that vacation request in here in a minute."

"I'll be here."

As Al walked back to his office he shoved both hands in his pockets, nearly bumping into furniture as he walked, unseeing, the path he had trod many times before. Was he right to think about a vacation to New Orleans? Or was it just another wild goose chase...and an expensive one, at that?

40

The first thing Al did when he got back to his office was call Charlie. Without telling his friend the reason, he asked if he could lunch with him at the La Crosse Club. His buddy was quick to accept. Then he called Dr. Rick Olson. Rick too was open and happy to accept.

When they met, Charlie was practically beside himself. "Can't wait to order. Rick, they have the best damn French dip in the world here, the absolute best."

Rick opened his mouth to respond, but Charlie had already gone on to talking about the walnut burger. "That's the best in the world, too. Whad'm I gonna do? Too damn many choices. Goddamnit, Rick, the apple pie is world class, too. Crap, more choices than I should have to make."

"Charlie, you're choosing lunch, for god's sake. This isn't about the preacher that's gonna preside at your funeral. Wait, on second thought, the way you eat, it could be. The way you eat, each bite could be your last. If I were you, I'd order both of 'em, and apple pie, too. After all, Al has to pay—he's the member here. Then Al and I will sit and listen to your arteries close as you indulge."

"That's right. Al's treat. Having both is a great idea, Doc."

"Not on your life." Al jumped in before things could get out of hand. "You're a big boy, Charlie, and quite capable of ordering what you want for lunch. But one item will be plenty for you."

"Ah, c'mon, Al. I'll pass on the walnut burger, but you gotta let me have some pie. I gotta have the apple pie. Please don't make me pass up the pie."

"No problem. Just pay for the pie yourself. How about that?"

Charlie looked like a hound dog stopped two-feet from dinner by a tight chain. Then he brightened. "Well, hell, I can't pay for the pie, Al. I ain't a member. You gotta be a member to pay for anything, right? I think you're buyin' the pie, buddy." A smile lit his face as the three sat down to dine and Charlie ordered both the French dip and apple pie. "With some ice cream, too, if you don't mind, ma'am," he said to the server, who was typing his order into her iPad. "Two scoops, okay?"

Al and Rick laughed. Charlie sat back in his chair, a smug look on his face.

"Well, I suspect Al didn't invite us here just to watch you eat, Charlie." Rick unfolded his burgundy cloth napkin and laid it across his lap. "Want to tell us what's up to call for lunch at a ritzy place like this?"

Al fiddled with his silverware. "I think we all need a vacation. And I'm inviting you two and Peggy and Kelly to join me for a week or two in New Orleans."

Charlie's eyebrows shot up. "New Orleans? You're kiddin', right? It's gotta be hotter'n hell down there now. Why would we want to go there? We oughta go up north fishin', don't ya think, Rick?"

"I suspect there is something beyond a trip down south for food and fun, Charlie. What's up, Al?"

For the next twenty minutes, until their food arrived, Al talked about the mafia war in the South and how he thought it might have been solved and by whom. "That secret killing weapon that Rusty told me about had to have come from Genevieve. It just had to. I think if the six of us go down there and poke around, we'll stir something up. Aaron told me that Savannah's—that's the new relative—mother will have a horse running in the Kentucky Derby this year. If we drive, maybe we could time it to stop in Louisville on the way down and check out the race. Do you think you could get ready that fast?"

Charlie grinned. "That'd be great! I love the damn horses. Never seen a race, though. It would be fun. And, what the hell, if it's Genevieve we're out to catch, is Julie goin', too? She knows her best; they're blood."

"How the hell would I pull that off? Do you really think I can waltz in on JoAnne tonight and say, 'Honey, I'm gonna go on vacation with Rick, Charlie, Peggy, Kelly, and Julie. Not sure how long I'll be gone, but maybe up to two weeks. See you when I get back'." Al smacked Charlie on the arm. "You schmuck!" No need to mention that he'd had the same thought, and had even expressed it to the chief.

"Well, I jus' thought she'd be better'n the rest of us at knowin' things, bein' how it's her aunt and all. Just a thought. Relax, okay?"

Rick patted him on the back. "Don't feel too bad, pal. I was going to suggest the same thing. You just beat me to it."

"Well, ya don't have to be so goddamn touchy, Al. I was just tryin' to be helpful."

"I'm sorry for snapping, Charlie. I'd love to have her go, too. There's just no way to make it happen."

Charlie leaned back to allow the server to set his plate in front of him. When she had served everyone and gone, he picked up his fork. "I've never had a go-away vacation. The old slob, bless 'er departure, never wanted to go anywhere."

"Peggy and I haven't been away since our honeymoon. It would be fun, especially with the four of you." Rick took a bite of salad and chased it down with a sip of water. "Of course, if we had a purpose that would be even better. I'd also love to see the Derby, but how the hell are we going to manage that? Tickets have probably been sold out for a year or more and they cost thousands."

Al bit his lip. "Good point. But we're cops. That's gotta be good for something. Maybe the chief can swing a deal to get us in if he talks to the organizers and tells them we're working an investigation. Or Aaron Wingate might be able to help us out; he seems to have a lot of clout. I'll check with both of them."

The excitement of the Derby and the hunt fired up all three of them, and pretty soon ideas were hitting the table in abundance. Before lunch ended, all three agreed the trip was a great idea and suddenly they were planning the details. Since none had been on a real vacation for a long time, and with the Derby in mind, Rick suggested they consider renting a motor home and driving. Al liked the idea; Charlie wasn't so sure.

"I lack some in the manners department." His confession made the others laugh, given that it wasn't exactly a revelation. More of a massive understatement. "Would JoAnne and Peggy be offended by my farts, do you s'pose?"

"Charlie, your farts are legendary. Trust me, Peggy has heard all about them. I'll bet JoAnne has, too."

"She's heard the real thing." Al's comment was punctuated first with a chuckle, then a laugh. "But maybe you could promise to fart outside whenever possible."

"Well, ummm, I s'pose I could do that. But I have a lot of gas, a lot. When we're drivin' I couldn't hold it for a long time."

Al swallowed the last of his sandwich. "You'll just have to do the best you can, buddy."

The server appeared with the bill and Al tugged his wallet out of his pocket and handed her a credit card. When she'd given it back, smiling at the large tip he always felt obliged to leave when someone had been forced to serve Charlie a meal, he pulled on his jacket. "So you and I will look into what it would cost to rent a motor home, Rick, and we'll all put in for vacation time and work out the details with our wives, okay?"

Rick and Charlie nodded and the three of them headed back out into the warm spring day.

Once back at the office, Al searched all of the motor home rentals in the La Crosse area. He found nothing that interested him. Then he remembered that his neighbor, Jack Jacobson, had purchased a beautiful new motor home when he retired a year before. Jack had just gotten the vehicle when he suffered a debilitating stroke. As far as Al knew, the motor home had never been used.

Al got home about four-thirty. Jack sat on a lawn chair on his small front porch. Al walked over and settled himself on the top step. The two men talked for a while. Then Al asked him about the motor home.

"Wanna buy it?"

Al cocked his head. Was he serious? "I don't think I can afford it, Jack, but I wondered if you'd consider renting it for a couple of weeks. Some friends and I are thinking of taking a road trip."

"Well, it's a cinch I won't be using it. I keep hoping that won't be the case, but I can't see my doc clearing me for any trips, and even if he did, he wouldn't want me wrestling around a 35c Windsport, that's for sure."

"Is it really thirty-five feet?"

"Sure is; sleeps eight comfortably and ten if you don't mind being cozy. You think you can drive a beast like that?"

"What sort of license do you need? Anything special?" Al was ticking off the possibilities in his head as he talked.

"Nah, just a driver's license. But it's a helluva lot different than driving a car, that's for sure."

"I have a commercial license. Got it when I was a kid and I keep renewing it. Don't know why, but I do. Used to drive my dad's eighteen-wheeler. We had one on the farm to haul grain. He got it when I was a junior in high school, and we all learned how to drive it."

"Well, if you drove an eighteen-wheeler, that'll sure as hell help. It's not necessary, but it will help. It's not that the thing is hard to drive, it's just bulky. The big thing is taking care when you turn a corner or into a driveway or parking space. It's bulky, that's all."

"Would you consider renting yours to me for a couple of weeks? We're hoping to drive to New Orleans."

"Damn, planned to go there myself. Not sure that'll happen now. Damn body just turned on me."

Jack gazed off into the air, thinking, Al presumed, about all the things he'd thought he would do when he retired. Al let him think for a few minutes then gently jogged his friend with one word. "Rental?"

"Oh, hell, forgot you were there. Use the motor home? Hell yes, whenever you want. Just take the damn thing. It looks as if all I'll be doing with it is selling it. If you want it, I can make you a helluva deal."

"If it were a few years down the road and I was ready for retirement I'd be talking to you about that, but it's still a ways off. So how much to rent it for two weeks?"

"Tell you what, you pay the insurance. That's not cheap, but it's probably cheaper than you could rent a Windsport Class A for. Insurance is expensive, that's all I know."

"I'm sure it will be reasonable, if we all split it. You've got yourself a deal, Jack."

"Oh, yes, you'll have to clean it up, too. It's been sitting in the storage shed since I got it."

"No problem. Let me talk to the others about it and I'll let you know."

"Wish I was up to taking 'er out; she's a beauty."

Al grinned. "You sound like you're talking about your wife."

"Hell, she's better'n Mabel. I don't have to shout to get her to hear me. All she needs is a nudge on the accelerator or the brake. And she never talks back, either. She's a helluva lot newer model, too."

"Jack, you know damn well that you couldn't get along without Mabel. How long have you guys been married?"

"Fifty-six years and countin'. Some days I'd like a different model, but we're pretty used to each other by now. Guess I'll have to keep the old girl. 'Course, she might like a newer model, too."

Al glanced at the front door. "You better be careful; if Mabel hears you there will be hell to pay."

"Guess so. But we're both fairly tolerant. Hell, when you've been together more than fifty years, you get to know a person pretty damn well."

"I guess you would. I'll get back to you tomorrow, okay, Jack?"

"Yea, sure, whenever you get around to it. I ain't goin' nowhere."

Al strode into the house and tossed his jacket over a chair. JoAnne walked into the living room. "What were you talking to Jack about? Looked interesting."

"I was asking about using his motor home. Rick and Charlie and I talked about the six of us going to New Orleans for a couple of weeks. How does that sound to you?"

JoAnne planted both hands on her hips. "Don't try to slide one past me. We're taking a couples' vacation so you three guys can look for Genevieve, aren't we?"

His cheeks warmed. Like his neighbor said, after years of marriage, you got to know each other pretty well. "Yes, but New Orleans is a great town. You haven't been there, so I think it will be fun. Don't you?"

"It would be fun. We haven't been away for a long time; how long has it been? Twenty years?"

"It couldn't be that long, could it?" Al thought it over. "You know, I think you're pretty close to right. The last few times we've gone away it's been to conferences. I think the last time we were gone overnight was when the kids were fifteen or sixteen. That's a lot of years ago. We went to the Dells, remember?"

"How could I forget? It was a disaster. The kids were just getting to the attitude stage. Charleen was going into junior high school. She was a brat. And Tanya wasn't much better."

Al shook his head. "Let's forget that; it's over. The kids have their own families now. There's nothing holding us back, is there?"

"Nothing. I'm in. But if we're going to search for Genevieve, what about Julie? Shouldn't she be going, too?"

Al blinked. His jaw worked, but no sound came out.

"Oh, for god's sake, Allan Rouse, how naïve do you think I am? Do you think I don't know that you and Julie have a relationship? I hate her and I like her. I hate her because I love you and I don't like the fact that you spend time with her—time doing things, I suspect, that you shouldn't. I like her because I know she's a good woman, the kind of woman in need of a helping hand. And Al Rouse could never pass up a damsel in distress. This one just got out of control on you, didn't it?"

Al drove his fingers through his hair. "Why haven't you said anything before now?

JoAnne swiped at a tear that had started down her cheek. Her lower lip trembled. "Because I didn't want to drive you into her arms. Would I like it to end? Of course. But I haven't said anything because I wasn't sure of the choice you would make. I love you, Allan Rouse, and I want to keep you as my husband. I can't tell you how often I've cried about this; how often I wanted to just hit you with it. I thought of walking out; I even began to pack one day. But I couldn't do it. I love you too much."

JoAnne slumped into a chair, buried her head in her hands, and sobbed, her shoulders shaking.

Al's chest ached. He sat there dumbfounded for a long while then looked at his wife of almost thirty-five years. "JoAnne, I feel so guilty. And the thought that you knew tears me up. I never wanted to hurt you, not in any way. But Julie … well, she became a good friend. There were things about her I liked. At first it was just friendship. Then, you're right, it got out of hand. I didn't know how to stop it." Al rubbed his face with both hands. "No, no, that's not right. Of course I knew how to stop it, I just couldn't bring myself to. She's a good woman. At first I helped her with some things she didn't know how to do then things just escalated. JoAnne, I am so, so sorry." His throat was so tight he could barely get out the words.

JoAnne came to him and held him close. "Al, you big goof. You wear your guilt on your sleeve. I know how much you love Julie and I know that you love me, too. Or at least I think you do. Otherwise you'd be gone. At first, I was so angry at both of you, especially her. But when I met her, well, there was no way. She's too kind, too gracious, just plain nice."

"JoAnne, I feel terrible. I never meant …"

"Al, quiet. It is what it is. I haven't said anything because I didn't think I could change it, and the thought of losing you just about killed me. So I decided to try and make peace with it. As long as Genevieve Wangen is at large, you are going to have contact with Julie. I know that. And so I try to cope with it, hoping you will always come home."

Al hung his head. "JoAnne, you have been a wonderful wife. You're my best friend. You will always be both of those. I want you to know that. No one could ever take your place. I just got into something I didn't seem able to stop. And I still don't know how."

JoAnne hugged him tightly, rubbing his back. "No need to say anything more. I know that. Now, how about we talk about this vacation?"

And so they did, late into the night. When they finally went to bed, Al snuggled JoAnne close and made tender love to her. After they were satisfied, JoAnne reached up and kissed him. "Al, you have been a wonderful husband and father. I know you love me. Part of me wants you to feel guilty, and I want this thing to stop, not because I feel threatened, but because you need to do it for you—and for Julie. And you need to do it for us."

In spite of her almost incomprehensible understanding, guilt robbed Al of the ability to sleep and he lay awake, staring at the ceiling, thinking about the situation he had gotten himself into and what to do about it. As he twisted and turned, the clock crept past 4:00 a.m. Finally he slept, but the alarm clock ended that an hour later and he was instantly wide awake, as always.

41

Al's talk with JoAnne was crippling. He had to share with someone. He settled on Charlie. Before leaving the house, he called his friend and suggested breakfast at Ma's.

"I can be there in twenty. What's up?"

"I've got lots to tell you, things I need help with."

The date made, Al went back upstairs and kissed JoAnne, who rolled over and told him she loved him and wished him a good day. "Last night was awful in many ways, I know, Al. But in some it was wonderful, too. We've needed to have this talk for a long time. And the end of the night was so tender. I need you and I need to be with you. Please don't ever take that away from me."

"I'm going to try and be a better husband, JoAnne. I really am. Honest." He gave her another kiss and headed for the door.

Charlie was waiting for him. His friend was sitting in a booth, a cup of coffee cooling at his right hand when Al approached the table.

"I'm goddamned glad you're here, Rouse, I'm hungry enough to eat the ass off a skunk."

"Now that's hungry. But then you're always just about that hungry, aren't you?"

Charlie started to fire back then appeared to think better of it. "You know, I guess I am. But this morning I really need a big breakfast. Kelly went shopping with Peggy; they're meeting Julie in Madison and staying overnight tonight, so I need to get fortified for a long day without home cookin'. Know what I mean?"

"I do. I'm glad you told me, because I need to talk to Julie one of these days."

"What about?"

"Well, last night I broached the topic of a motor home vacation to JoAnne and she loved it. When I told her where we proposed to go and why, she was even more in favor. Then came the bombshell."

"Bombshell?" Charlie's bushy eyebrows drew together.

"JoAnne looked at me and said, 'Well, Al, if we're going to look for Genevieve, shouldn't Julie be going along?' I didn't know what to say. I just sat there. Then she said, 'C'mon, Al, do you think I'm an idiot? I know you've got a thing with Julie'."

Charlie's mouth, empty, thankfully, dropped open. "You gotta be shittin' me. Really? She said that?"

"She did. I couldn't believe it either. I felt absolutely terrible, as though the bottom had dropped out of my world. When I finally got up enough courage to respond, she told me she is well aware of the relationship and is envious of the time I spend with Julie. She said she hadn't said anything for fear of breaking up our marriage. Can you believe it?"

"Shit. If I did that, Kelly'd have me laid out on the cutting board and little Willie Wonka'd be in the hot chocolate … the boiling hot chocolate."

"She told me she's known for a while that Julie and I had a special relationship. It has bothered her terribly, but she has tried to reconcile herself to it because I always came home."

"Well, she's right about several things. One, much as I kid, I don't think people should run around on their spouses. I haven't said anything to you because I could see how much you cared for both of them, but I've also seen how much it's been tearing you in two, so I think it's a good thing that you are finally facing it. And, two, Julie should be going along. She has the best chance of identifying Genevieve, that's for sure."

"And we'll have room. But I still wonder how we'll make that work."

The two men sat there, staring at each other, until Ma yelled at them from the kitchen. "I need to know what you want, right now. Can't be takin' up seatin' just to talk."

Al might have laughed if he didn't have so many thoughts whirling through his mind. He ordered his breakfast before turning back to his friend. "Other than the bombshell, I also wanted to tell you that my neighbor, Jack Jacobson, has a thirty-five-foot motor home. Jack bought it just after he retired a year ago, and about a week later he had a stroke, a big one. Left him pretty much disabled. He's paralyzed on one side and can't drive, so the RV just sits in storage. Anyway, when I got home last night he was on his porch and we sat and talked for a while. He's offered it to me for the trip if I pay the insurance before we take off. It's a damn generous offer, that's for sure, but I have to check on the premium. Jack gave me the name of his insurance guy."

Charlie started to speak, but snapped his mouth shut when Ma came by with four plates in her hand, one for Al and three for Charlie.

Al shook his head. "How the hell can you eat so much and not look like a blimp?"

"Genes, Al, genes. I got great genes from both ma and pa. They were slim and trim right up to the time they died."

"Well, you're not slim and trim, that's for sure. But you're not fat, either. It's amazing."

By now Charlie was at work on his multiple-plate breakfast, and food was disappearing at an amazing rate.

"Damn, that's terrific," mumbled Charlie, his mouth full of eggs. "We should also take a car or two, don't you think? We'll need something to drive in New Orleans, won't we?"

"You got some egg on your shirt." Al pointed to Charlie's chest. "And, yes, we will, but I think if we take one car, it will be enough. We can always rent another down there if we find we need one. We probably will, but I think that would be the cheapest way to do it, don't you? I checked rentals last night and we can pick one up for about $300 for the two weeks."

"That'd be a steal. We could let the girls drive the car one day, the guys the next. We can alternate motor home drivers, too, to break up the grind. How long will it take us to drive from La Crosse to New Orleans, do you think?"

"I checked that out. It's about 1,200 miles. It's all freeway, so we ought to be able to average fifty miles an hour. That would mean twenty-four hours of driving."

"How far is Louisville?"

"Not quite halfway, but almost. We could, say, leave on a Thursday and drive to Louisville, see the Derby and check out the crowd, then head for New Orleans on Sunday. We could be there by Monday. With the motor home, each of us could sleep some, so we would arrive rested and ready to go."

"Sounds like a plan."

"We need to get on this. The Derby is May 7, just a month away."

When they were ready to leave, Al held the door for Charlie. The wind was raw. Al pointed the key fob at his car and pressed the start button. "I asked the chief about Derby passes. He's going to make a call. If that fails, I'll call Aaron Wingate in New Orleans to see what he can do," said Al. "I'll also call Rick, bring him up to speed on developments, and ask him to check on motor home insurance."

"How about I work on a meal plan and have Kelly check it when she gets back," offered Charlie. "I can also search for places along the way to park the motor home."

Al's eyebrow rose. "I don't know about that. Letting you decide how much food to bring is a little like asking Danica Patrick to set our pace."

Charlie snorted. "I'll keep it reasonable, don't worry. Damn, this is exciting."

"It is, make your calls today. Let's meet here again tomorrow to go over the details. You can pay this time."

"Fine with me, Al, I'm no cheapskate. You can even tell Rick to join us."

The one task that had Al worried was talking to Julie about coming along on the trip. He needed to invite her soon, obviously, but what was the right way to do it? And what on earth would she say when she found out that JoAnne was aware of their affair?

42

By the end of the day, Al was satisfied that things were coming together, but the thought of talking to Julie had been gnawing at him all afternoon. With the exception of that, most things were falling into place.

Chief Whigg took care of the Derby issue without Al having to go to his New Orleans friend. The chief called someone he knew and by midafternoon had seven passes for the Derby. There were no seats attached, but they would have the run of the place and could get into almost any area by showing their passes. When Al called Aaron Wingate in New Orleans, Aaron suggested they park the motor home behind the Second Police District headquarters at 4317 Magazine St. He said there was plenty of room behind the precinct station, and both men's and women's locker rooms inside for showering. Electrical hookups and water were also available.

Rick found out motor home insurance would cost between $1,000 and $4,000 for the year, something they had agreed to purchase for Jack. In his email, he said he had a better idea. He and Peggy had been thinking of buying a motor home. If Jack wanted to sell, they'd look at the rig, make a decision, and if they liked it, they'd buy it and cover the insurance bill. Rick also said that he and Peggy would take their Lincoln Navigator on the trip as a second vehicle.

Charlie promised he would have a tentative meal plan by the next morning. Al didn't doubt it, but he hoped that Kelly would work some realism into the process. Since she was away on a shopping trip, Al suggested Charlie take a couple of days to develop the plan.

When Al walked into the house that evening, he had only one task on his mind: getting hold of Julie, something he had put off all day.

After he had hung up his coat and walked into the kitchen, JoAnne hugged him and suggested he pour them drinks so they could sit down for a while. "Stroganoff for dinner. Do you want it with noodles or rice?"

"I love rice. Do you mind?"

"Not at all, especially if you pour me a glass of Chardonnay."

"Is there a bottle open?"

"You'll have to open one, Al, but I imagine you'll be going into the pantry for brandy. You are going to have an old-fashioned, right?"

"Of course. Oranges and cherries in the fridge?"

"Absolutely."

A short time later, he returned with a glass of white wine for her and a large old-fashioned for himself. He slumped into the chair, but before he could relax, she said, "I talked to Julie today."

His mouth went dry. "You what?"

"I talked to Julie. I knew that she, Kelly, and Peggy were shopping. What a nice lady she is. She was a little taken aback when I told her I had surprised you last night, but she quickly got over it and we had a great visit. I think she feels awfully guilty, and I guess, like you, she should, but I tried to set her at ease. I think she'll go with us. She's going to need you to convince her, but you can do it. She's never been to New Orleans and she loves horses, so it will be a great trip for her."

Al blinked several times. When the silence grew deafening, JoAnne smiled at him. "Well, Al, think about it. If I had left it to you, she might never have been asked. I know how you are about things that concern you. You like to put them off. And sometimes you put them off too long."

"You're right; absolutely right. I was having a real problem getting up enough courage to call. And I was embarrassed, too."

"Well, now she knows, so call her up. If you're worried, call her now. I'll be on the line, too. I think she knows the relationship with you has ended. You'd better be fine with that, too, because it's time."

"You're absolutely right. It never should have started, and I will never forgive myself for hurting you. Isn't this trip going to be a little awkward, though?"

"It probably will be, to a certain extent. You've earned that. The punishment the trip might offer is deserved. You know that, she knows that. So buck up and call her."

"All right."

"Now, Al; you need to do it now."

"Okay, I'll do it."

He dialed slowly, not sure what he would say. His chest tightened when Julie answered. "Hello?"

"Hi, it's Al. And before you say anything, I want you to know that JoAnne is also on the line."

After a pause, Julie drew in a breath. "I thought you might call, I just didn't know when. I talked to JoAnne today, and tonight I feel like a heathen—totally unclean and desperately in need of forgiveness. I am so sorry, Al. I'm sorry for hurting JoAnne, and I'm sorry she found out about us. I thought we would end it before that happened. But then I began to love you more and more and I just couldn't let go."

Al could hear Julie sniffling.

"I feel terrible. I never meant to come between you and JoAnne."

Al's stomach churned. How was it possible he could have hurt both the women he loved so much? "Julie, what we did was wrong, very wrong, even though at the time it seemed so good. And we became close friends. Thanks to JoAnne, we don't have to change that. We just have to work very hard to make sure everyone knows that's all it is, friendship. I think so much of you; I hope you will understand that friendship is the limit of what it can be. I love Brody, so I don't want that to change." His voice broke and he stopped and cleared his throat.

The silence lasted for what seemed hours, but was in reality a couple of minutes. Then a soft voice said, "But I love you so much, Al. I don't know if I can be just a friend."

He sucked in his breath. "Yes, together we can become just that. And I believe we can do it in such a way that it is believable, too. Because if we believe it, others will too."

Again, the silence was deafening, but she finally replied. "If you say so. But, Al, there's no way I can go on this trip. I thought I could, but the more I think about it, I just don't know if I can do it. Can you understand that?"

"I do understand, but if you and I are going to be friends, I need you to do this for me. You must go because it would show me that you are serious about helping me erase two major problems from my memory: our infidelity and Genevieve. I have to find her, Julie. I can probably do it with the help of Charlie and Rick, but it would be so much better, so much easier, if you helped, too. Will you do that for me?"

When Julie spoke again, her voice sounded strained, as though she was barely holding herself together. "I don't know. I already felt badly enough about helping you to chase down my aunt, but now … I just don't know."

Al took another deep breath and rubbed his hand across his flat-top. "Julie, listen. I know it's hard to think clearly right now, so why don't you let me think for us. If we are really serious about trying to make all this better, both of us should go. We should apologize to JoAnne and our friends and we should—through our actions—assure everyone that we are serious about putting this behind us, about becoming just good friends. I think it would be cathartic."

"I'll think about it, Al; really, I will. But I don't see how I can put us through the horror of having to see this thing in the faces of those who know. How can I ever look JoAnne in the eyes again?"

"I think she's truly serious about forgiving us, that she's willing to give us both a second chance. I think we need to do this for both of our sakes, so we can move forward from here."

The wait was excruciating. Al stared at the family picture above the mantel, the memory of a simpler time squeezing his heart like a fist.

Finally Julie drew in a shuddering breath. He could picture her, the way she would draw herself up and push back her shoulders whenever she had to face something hard. The thought sent fresh waves of pain through him. "All right, I'll come."

The line went dead.

Al quietly set the phone in its cradle, sat on the couch, and buried his head in his hands.

JoAnne padded down the stairs and over to him. Wrapping her arms around him, she rested her head on his shoulder. "Thank you for doing that, Al. Now, as hard as it will be, we can start over. With each other's help, we'll get through this, the two of us."

After a long silence, he looked up at her. "I know we will."

She kissed his ear, then told him, "Dinner is going to be burned, I'm afraid. We should eat."

She took his hand as they walked to the kitchen. He took a seat while she busied herself at the stove. He stared, unseeing, at the table. *How could I have created such a mess?*

43

The next two weeks passed quickly. Al tried to focus on the details of the trip, but all he could think about was the possibility of finding Genevieve Wangen. JoAnne, Peggy, Kelly, and Julie made lists of items they would need to bring. Al, Charlie, and Rick went over the details of how they would travel, what shifts for driving would be used, and how they would go about trying to determine if Savannah Harlowe was, in fact, Genevieve Wangen.

Finally the day of departure arrived. April 30 dawned sunny and warm in the coulee region of Wisconsin. The group met in the Gundersen Lutheran parking lot in Onalaska, just north of La Crosse. Al drove the motor home, which Peggy and Rick had purchased two weeks earlier. Charlie and Kelly rode with him. Rick was driving his Lincoln Navigator and Peggy was with him. JoAnne decided she would ride with Rick and Peggy for the first leg.

The group planned to stop for a stretch at the rest stop near Janesville. JoAnne had packed a picnic lunch and Julie was going to eat at home before meeting the group at the intersection of I-90 and North Arlington Heights Road near her home. They expected to make that connection sometime between 1:00 and 2:00 p.m., then travel straight through Chicago before catching I-65 south once beyond the Chicago area. They would overnight in the neighborhood of West LaFayette, Indiana, which should allow them an easy drive to Louisville on Friday morning. They had reservations at a motor home park near Churchill Downs and would spend Friday afternoon and most of Saturday at the race track. If all went according to plan, they would leave Louisville early Sunday to continue the drive to New Orleans.

In the motor home, the mood as they traveled through southern Wisconsin and northern Illinois was festive, if a little apprehensive. Al and JoAnne had updated everyone on their situation, so they knew Julie was worried about joining them on their trip. They stopped, as scheduled, in Arlington Heights, where they had made plans to rendezvous with Julie.

When they pulled off the interstate to meet Julie, Al wondered if she'd be there. Her blue Honda Accord was parked at the walking trail lot near the exit ramp. Julie was there, leaning against her vehicle, looking uncertain, and clasping and unclasping her hands in front of her as everyone got out of the vehicles and approached her.

Julie, her face red, kept her eyes glued on JoAnne as she walked over to her. For a moment, neither of them spoke. Then JoAnne reached out and hugged Julie.

Al's stomach twisted into a painful knot as he watched the two of them together.

When she let her go, JoAnne met Julie's gaze. "I'm looking forward to our ride. We'll have a real chance to talk." Julie nodded and the two of them climbed into the Navigator while everyone else piled into the motor home for the first leg to Gary, Indiana.

At Gary, the group stopped for gas and bathroom breaks. The crisis seemed to have passed. For now, at least. Julie seemed back to her old self and both she and JoAnne were talkative as they milled around the station lot, waiting for their turn in the bathroom.

When the group headed down I-65 toward their overnight stop in West Lafayette, Indiana, Rick took over driving the motor home because he was anxious to test out the rig. Al joined JoAnne in Rick's Navigator and Charlie and Kelly climbed into the back seat behind them.

They arrived at Wolfe's Leisure Time Campground at 4:45 p.m. Rick backed the rig into their spot and Al parked the Navigator alongside it. As soon as everyone had clambered out of their vehicles, Julie gestured for them to come over. A circle formed around her and she cleared her throat. "I know you're all aware that JoAnne knows about what happened between Al and me, and that it is now over. I want to apologize to all of you for putting you in the middle of what was going on. I never meant for it to get to this point. I was selfish; I know that. I hope you will all help me make amends for what I have done."

Al lifted a hand. "Please remember that two of us were involved. It wasn't just Julie's fault. I was every bit as responsible—maybe more. I'm going to do everything I can to make it up to JoAnne—and to Julie. I have hurt them both and I feel like such a heel. I need your help, too."

Charlie lifted his massive shoulders. "I'm definitely not perfect, as Kelly can tell you, so I'm not going to judge anyone. I'm sure we all agree that we're here to support all three of you, whatever you need."

Kelly, Rick, and Peggy nodded.

JoAnne blinked back tears. "Thank you everyone. Now, I suggest we head to the public washrooms to clean up and then find a good restaurant. I'm hungry."

Charlie clapped his hands. "Fabulous idea. I'm dying for southern barbecue."

Rick laughed. "Charlie, this is the Midwest. Purdue is in the Big Ten, for God's sake."

"Goddamn, Rick, we're south of La Crosse, aren't we? Besides, Rutgers is in the Big 10, too." Charlie leaned against the side of the trailer. He was a sight to behold, in his red-and-white-checkered shirt and blue and green polka-dotted shorts. Kelly had clearly not had anything to do with dressing him.

"Charlie, Charlie, Rutgers is in New Jersey. That's sure as hell not the South."

Charlie looked crestfallen. Kelly came to his rescue. "I've heard that New Brunswick, New Jersey, is famous for its barbecue."

Charlie straightened up. "That's true. I've heard that too."

"Okay. Point made," Rick conceded.

Al, until now morose, suppressed a grin. With so many of them sharing a small space and long hours together on the road, he was determined not to antagonize Charlie. That didn't mean he couldn't enjoy it when others did, though.

South Street Smokehouse was great. Everyone was astounded at the food that Charlie packed away. He tried every dish on the buffet and every sauce, too.

As the meal ended, Charlie mopped his face, which was mottled with barbecue sauce and other bits of food, then excused himself and left the restaurant.

Kelly just smiled and shook her head. "He loves to eat. Somehow there's not an ounce of fat on that man's body, but after a big meal it's a lot like living next to a refinery. I suspect he's outside getting rid of some gas."

Al smiled. "We need to put him at ease. We pick on him all the time, and he's damn good about taking it. I'd suggest one of us guys let one rip the next time we need to. That should allow him to relax a bit."

Rick looked perplexed.

Al cocked his head. "Don't doctors fart?"

Kelly rolled her eyes. "I'm not sure about that plan, anyway. It gets pretty wicked around our house sometimes. I think we should stick with the outside idea for the sake of everyone's health and comfort."

"Okay, but let's not pick on him so much, okay? He's a really great guy. He's smart and effective, too. Sometimes we pick on him so much that it bothers me."

Rick's eyebrows rose. "Is this the Al that I know and respect? Aren't you the guy who ribs him more than the rest of us put together?"

Charlie rejoined the group before anyone could respond, and they all returned to the campground. As they settled into the motor home, they drew for beds. With Julie a given for the quarter-berth above the driver's seat, Charlie and Kelly drew the master suite in the rear, Al and JoAnne landed the bunk beds, and Peggy and Rick ended up with the queen-sized fold-out sofa in the kitchen area.

Al climbed into the bed and wrapped one arm around his wife. Although there would likely be bumps in the road ahead, he and Julie had faced their first big hurdles, ending their relationship and asking JoAnne and their friends to forgive them. Maybe now they could all put what had happened behind them and move forward with their quest to track down Genevieve Wangen.

44

Al was up early the next morning, working to wake everyone. He then made coffee, got out cinnamon rolls, and organized the breakdown of the motor home. Everyone was ready to roll by seven-thirty. The excitement in the group was palpable. Julie, Kelly, Rick, Charlie, and Peggy all squeezed into the Navigator, and JoAnne accompanied Al, who drove the big rig.

As Al pressed down on the accelerator, JoAnne leaned over and kissed him on the cheek. "You seem better this morning. A little weight gone?"

"I was so worried, JoAnne. Yesterday was among the worst days of my life. But you know, it was a better day than I expected. I still feel like a heel, but I am relieved. So yes, I feel better."

The morning went smoothly, and although traffic picked up considerably as they entered the Louisville area, and became especially dense when they reached the south side of the city, where Churchill Downs was located, they made good time. Al had grown increasingly comfortable driving the motor home, and now quite enjoyed maneuvering the big vehicle in and out of traffic. When the twin spires of Churchill Downs came into view, JoAnne cheered, and the drivers of both vehicles tooted their horns in celebration. Miraculously, given the density of the traffic, as Al drove into the campground and stopped to register, the Navigator was right behind him.

Charlie rolled down the window and waved at Al. "This is one sweet vehicle. If Rick ever decides he's sick of it, I'd be happy to take it off his hands." He caressed the side of the Navigator.

Al grinned. When Charlie loved something, everybody knew it.

The line was moving with agonizing slowness. From the passenger seat, Rick leaned closer to Charlie. "You're welcome to it, Charlie. This damn thing drinks gas like an alkie drinks booze."

Charlie winced. "If the Navigator's bad, what about that?" He pointed at the motor home. "You bought it, Rick—another gas hog! How many gallons to the mile are we getting, Al?"

"Actually, I've been pretty happy. We've only filled up once and we averaged almost thirteen miles to the gallon across Wisconsin and Illinois. That's better than I expected."

"Yeah, not bad." Rick shot Charlie a smug look.

The attendant finally walked up to Al's window. "Oh, yes, Detective Rouse, we've been expecting you. We have two spots reserved for you against the fence on the track side. You're right near the gate, so it will be a short walk to the race. Enjoy your stay."

The reservation confirmed, the group successfully found their reserved spots, right at the gate and very spacious. With Rick and Charlie directing, Al backed the motor home up to the fence. That done, they got the other vehicle parked in the remaining space then went inside and maneuvered the two slide-out areas of the big rig into place and spotted up the leveling jacks. Within thirty minutes, everything was shipshape and the group was ready to go to the track for the running of the Oaks.

As they got ready to leave, Al said, "Listen up, JoAnne has a surprise."

"It's Breast Cancer Awareness Day here today," she told them, distributing new dresses for the women and hats for the men. "So these are my gifts to you, a thank you for your love and support."

Charlie nudged Al in the side. "So tell me about this event."

Al had never been before, but he'd always wanted to, and almost always watched it on TV. "Okay. Kentucky Oaks is sponsored by Longines, and is the most lucrative race in America for 'old fillies.' The race is held each year on the day before the Derby, and the three-year-old fillies are racing in a Grade 1 stakes race worth a million dollars. The winning filly will be awarded a garland of lilies, aptly named 'lilies for the fillies'."

Peggy clutched her program tightly, eyes wide as she scanned the crowd. From the corner of his eye, Al caught a glimpse of Julie bouncing on the balls of her feet, appearing equally excited. *Good, maybe she can actually get past the last couple of days and enjoy herself.*

None of them was prepared for the spectacle of Churchill Downs on Derby Week. The crowd was huge, the mood electric, and many of the revelers had obviously been drinking mint juleps or something stronger for a long time. The group pushed and shoved its way to the grandstand, where Chief Whigg had somehow wrangled tickets that got them into the Jockey Club suites area. The table for eight on the sixth floor commanded a great view of the racetrack and many of the seating areas, especially the high-priced sections.

Thanks to Julie's foresight, each of them was wearing pink. The men looked a bit conspicuous in their pink hats, but the women, all of them beautiful, looked spectacular in pink dresses, each a different style and shade.

The color worried Al, who felt they may be too conspicuous and would be noticed by the very people they were looking for before his group could identify them. As they got to the stands, though, his worry eased. Everyone was wearing pink, it seemed.

When they arrived at their table, the fourth race had just been called and the horses were parading to the post. It was a beautiful sight. Al waved a hand through the air. "If anyone wants to place bets, this would be a good time." Charlie, Rick, and JoAnne headed over to the window.

Everyone was upbeat. The people at their table were no exception, and when JoAnne's horse went wire-to-wire for the win, the party gained momentum. Clinking his glass with JoAnne's, Al said, "Just remember, you guys, we're supposed to be on the lookout for Genevieve Wangen. We know she likely had her face altered, so look for walk and mannerisms. Those things won't change."

Although he was on constant alert, he saw no one who either looked like or acted like Genevieve, although there were so many people, it was hard to focus on one without being quickly distracted. No one else spotted her either. They had a good time, nonetheless. Each of the women cashed some tickets, so it was a good day. They ate at the track and when they returned home, Al gestured toward the trailer. "Let's get to bed. If you think today was busy, imagine what tomorrow will bring."

Derby Day dawned brilliant and sunny, and as the group gathered for coffee and pastries outside the motor home, the sun was shining. It was already seventy degrees, and the music and noises of the track made for an upbeat mood. The potential of seeing Genevieve just added to Al's anticipation. She was close; he could feel it.

By noon, everyone had showered and donned their Derby best, including for all the women garishly decorated hats.

American Pharoah was the odds-on favorite, but Honey Harlowe's horse from France, Grand Garçon Doux, or Big Gentle Boy, was getting plenty of attention. Al closed a fist around his program, crumpling it in his hand. His heart pounded. Honey had to be here somewhere. He scanned the crowd. Was Savannah with her? Aaron Wingate had been unable to pinpoint the Carbone seats, but he'd assured Al they would likely be located in the Jockey Club suites, although the group would probably move outside near the track for the Derby.

Aaron had provided Al with pictures of the entire Carbone family, including several of Savannah that he'd clipped from the Times Picayune. The group had been thoroughly briefed and had seen the photos that Aaron had sent, in addition to reviewing the newspaper clippings. Al's skin tingled; he was emotionally charged for the moment when he might see his target. He'd asked everyone, if they spotted a woman who might be Genevieve, to watch for any identifying mannerisms they might remember from when they'd met her. As if sensing his excitement, his companions talked non-stop, and appeared to be watching everything, taking in every detail as they walked. Good. He needed them on high alert.

The seven of them walked through the gate. Al couldn't get over how close they were to the action. They arrived at the grandstand, took the elevator to their floor, and settled into comfortable seats that afforded each of them a commanding view of the track. The temperature was high, and Al was thankful their seats were in air-conditioned comfort.

The first three races passed quickly, excitement mounting as the big race of the day moved closer. Julie was the big winner, collecting on each of the first three races. She looked a little sheepish as she came back with her money. "I just picked them because I liked their names." She fanned her face with her card as she sat back down beside Peggy.

The fourth race came. Julie's string was broken, but Kelly picked up a small win on a "show" bet. As the group was waiting for the fifth race to be called, an excitement invaded the area they were in. A large group entered and settled around two of the tables below them. Angelo and Dino Carbone were instantly recognizable. They were tall and dark with sharp features set in handsome faces. Each was tall and displayed pearly-white teeth when he smiled. Rosalyn, the don's wife, held his arm. Al's breath caught at the sight of the beautiful woman on Dino's arm.

Savannah.

She looked just like her pictures in the paper.

He nodded discreetly in her direction, and everyone in his party swiveled to study her. She radiated beauty and youthfulness. Her face was without wrinkles and her hair had no trace of gray. Al bit his lip. How could this be Genevieve? The woman was about the right height. She was thinner, though, and her legs were spectacular, clearly not the legs of an octogenarian. And her figure? Well, that was straight from the book of Marilyn Monroe. The woman on Dino's arm was breathtakingly gorgeous.

Peggy touched Julie's arm. "Could that be your aunt, Julie? She doesn't look anything like her."

Since all of them but JoAnne knew or had met Genevieve, the stares were numerous. Al turned to Rick. "Doc, could that be Genevieve?"

"I'm no plastic surgeon, but the art—and it is an art—has come a long, long way. That far? Not sure. Maybe."

As the Carbones settled into their places, Al encouraged everyone to watch the woman, but not so closely that they would arouse suspicion with the Carbone crowd.

Charlie's jaw dropped. "Holy balls, those cats are really decked out. Just gimme one of those hats, and I could get that 'vette I've always wanted."

"And probably a Mustang, too, to keep with the theme of the day," muttered Rick, who was staring at the menu. "Are we eating today or just drinking again?"

Al lifted his menu a little higher too. "Yesterday was fun, today is work, so let's pay close attention. Just don't get caught gawking."

But gawking was something everyone in the Jockey Club was doing. No one could take their eyes off the people that had just arrived. Savannah sat nearest the window, opposite Angelo. Dino had claimed the seat at her side. It was obvious that he cared deeply for her. He leaned close and whispered in her ear periodically. It was equally obvious that he seemed to be enjoying the excitement they were causing. Every few minutes he glanced casually around the area, as though assessing who might have noticed them. Each time Al resisted the urge to duck out of sight. No need for that. Dino Carbone wouldn't know him if he bumped into him on the street, and Savannah didn't look around at all, just focused on the track.

As 3:00 p.m. approached, Angelo waved to a waiter, who came over with a young woman bearing a large box. Soon the men were lighting up cigars. The women didn't seem happy about that, and Savannah, Rosalyn, and three other women left the table, presumably to visit the ladies room or to place bets.

Julie rose. "I'm going to place another bet." She lowered her voice and bent slightly so she was close to Al. "I'll try to get a good look at Savannah while I'm out there."

Al nodded. "Be careful. Remember, be casual about it. No staring."

"I'll be careful, promise."

Kelly stood up too and said she'd accompany Julie. "Let's go to the restroom first." They strolled away, two extremely attractive women who looked good in their dresses and matching hats. Like the Carbone women, they too drew plenty of stares from the males in the crowd.

Julie followed Kelly to the restroom. As her friend opened the door to the ladies room, she came face to face with Savannah, who looked her up and down. Julie's throat tightened. Could this beautiful woman really be her aunt? Savannah's gaze came to rest on Julie and she smiled. As Kelly moved aside to allow Savannah and Rosalyn room to exit, Savannah politely said, "Thank you." When she passed Julie, she said, "Have a wonderful day. Remember to bet on Grand Garçon Doux."

Her heart sank. That accent. That voice. This couldn't be the woman they were looking for. "Is he the favorite?" asked Julie softly, eyes down.

"My dear, he is simply the best horse in the race. He's my mama's horse, a Frenchman. All the Americans are betting on American Pharaoh, but they don't know Grand Garçon Doux. This is his first race here."

Julie smiled at the woman who spoke with a heavy French accent. "Thank you for the tip. I will bet on him."

"Please do; he's family, you know," replied Savannah. "You won't be sorry."

With that, Rosalyn and Savannah left the restroom, and Kelly and Julie continued inside. When they came out, Rosalyn and Savannah were nowhere in sight. Julie and Kelly went to the betting window and placed some wagers, then returned to their table.

Julie's hands fluttered as she told the group about their meeting with Savannah and Rosalyn. The two women had returned to their seats down below, so she kept her voice low. "Savannah was friendly. And she made a reference to *family* in a way that seemed strange. But I couldn't peg her as Genevieve. Her voice was a mixture of French-tinged southern drawl, and it seemed real. Sorry, but there was no clue to her being anyone other than Savannah Harlowe."

Kelly nodded. "I don't disagree, but she was fascinated by Julie. There almost seemed a familiarity, as if she expected to bump into us. It was kind of weird, to my mind."

Julie sat back in her seat. Al's face had lit up when she first told them she'd bumped into Savannah, but it had fallen as she confessed she couldn't identify her as Genevieve. As badly as she felt for her aunt, Julie wished she could offer Al proof that the woman she'd just met was the same one he'd been searching for so desperately. The fact that she was still missing ate at Al, Julie knew, and she'd give anything to help him solve the case and find peace.

As the horses paraded to the post for the tenth race of the day, an excited hum of voices filled the air. The horses entered in the Woodford Reserve Turf Classic seemed to sense the importance of the event. They moved in perfect alignment to the gate for the mile and an eighth race that would be run on the grass. When the bell rang, Finnegan's Wake charged to the lead and held it all the way for the win.

Finally it was time for the crown jewel, the Derby. Julie and Peggy walked to the window to place bets for the table. When they'd finished, Julie had placed a twenty-dollar win bet on Grand Garçon Doux, the French stallion who stood at the line, seemingly unconcerned, looking so majestic and stately that many heads in the crowd had turned in his direction.

When they returned to the table, they all stood to sing, "My Old Kentucky Home," and when that ended, Julie glanced toward the Carbones. Savannah waved at her, held up her ticket then pointed to it with her left hand. Julie understood immediately, and held up her ticket, nodding in agreement. Savannah made the classic "okay" sign with her fingers before looking away.

Julie's eyes widened. For a second she couldn't breathe, then she grabbed Al's arm. "Did you see that?"

"Did I see what?"

"That gesture. It's her, it's Genevieve; I'm sure of it."

Al's head jerked. "What? How do you know?"

"It was the way she signaled okay. Almost everyone I know touches their index finger to their thumb." She demonstrated, and everyone at the table mimicked her action.

"You're right, that's how all of us do it." Rick held up his hand to demonstrate.

"Well, Genevieve always made the sign with her middle finger. Remember Peggy, how I used to tease her about flipping me the bird?"

"I sure do, it was one of those little identifying mannerisms Al was talking about. We all have one. Most people wipe their eyes with their index fingers; I do it with my ring finger. Julie's right. I didn't see it, but if Savannah did make the gesture that way, she'd be doing it exactly like Genevieve used to."

Julie's heart pounded. Her eyes met Al's. He had to be as excited as she was. What would he do, go and confront—

The loud pop of the starting gun cut her off. Grand Garçcon Doux, whom the announcer introduced as Big Gentle Boy, broke to the lead while American Pharaoh dropped back near the outside of the pack.

As the horses thundered around the track, the order stayed pretty much the same. When the pack rounded the clubhouse turn, Dortmund broke in front, but a quarter mile later Firing Line challenged the lead. American Pharaoh roared along the outside, staying off Firing Line's flank. Big Gentle Boy was fourth, running easy and free. As they rounded the back stretch, American Pharaoh began to fly, but suddenly it was as if Big

Gentle Boy had shifted into overdrive. He passed Dortmund and moved up on Firing Line and American Pharaoh. As they entered the stretch, it was a two-horse race, American Pharaoh ahead of Big Gentle Boy by a head, but as the finish line neared, Big Gentle Boy turned it up another notch and raced ahead of his competition. Not to be outdone, American Pharaoh also went into overdrive, and the two horses drove to the wire neck-and-neck. It was a photo finish.

Every person in the club was on their feet and the Carbone table was going crazy. Everyone jumped up and down, including Savannah, who pressed a hand to the top of her hat to keep it on.

Julie leapt up and down, too. Then Savannah looked up and made the "okay" sign with her fingers again.

"There! There! Did you see it?" Julie stopped jumping and pressed her fingers to her mouth. "She did it again."

Al followed her gaze. "She made that gesture again? The same way as before?"

"Yes. She touched her thumb and middle finger. Genevieve is the only other person I've ever seen do it that way. I think it's her, even if it doesn't look like her. The height is right, but everything else is different. Are the things that have changed things that could have been altered?"

Al drove his fingers through his hair. "I don't know. Rick?"

The doctor shrugged. "Plastic surgeons can change almost everything about a person's appearance. It would cost a fortune to transform someone that completely, but if she's with the Carbones, money wouldn't be an issue." Rick touched Julie's shoulder. "Do you think it's possible it could be her?"

Julie lifted her hand in the air, palm up. "It's either her or we have a great big coincidence on our hands."

Peggy slid a hand through her arm. "Why don't we take a trip past the Carbone table and see if we can strike up a conversation?"

Julie swallowed. Was she ready to confront the woman who could be her aunt? The woman Al believed to be a serial killer? Did Al really want her to do that? What if she suspected that Julie recognized her? She was with a known mafia family; what would they do to Julie if Savannah realized she was in danger of being discovered? She looked at Al, her eyes pleading. He nodded. *I have to do this.* For Al. Julie squared her shoulders and followed Peggy down a flight of stairs. As they moved toward the area where the tables had been set up, they were stopped by a security guard. "Where do you think you're going?"

"We're going to visit some people we know down there," said Peggy, gesturing toward the Carbones.

"The owners of Big Gentle Boy," affirmed Julie.

"No, you're not. Sorry, but this is the owners' floor. Only people who own horses are allowed in here."

When Peggy appeared ready to argue, Julie tugged on her arm, secretly happy to be spared the meeting. "Come on, Peggy, we need to get back."

"But …" Peggy stuck out her lower lip.

Julie shook her head. "Not now."

Just then, the announcer's voice rang out from the loudspeaker. "American Pharaoh has been declared the winner of the Kentucky Derby in the closest race in history. They're calling it a 'win by a whisker.' Please hold your tickets until additional verification is made."

When Julie reached her seat, she glanced down. The Carbone table was empty. She spun toward Al. "Where'd they go? When did they leave?"

Rick spoke up. "They were on their feet and moving as soon as the two of you headed for the stairs. I'm not sure if the sudden departure was due to you or to something they were told about the race."

"We have to find them. That was Genevieve; I'm sure of it." Julie grabbed Al's hand and pulled on it.

As they gathered their things, the announcer confirmed that the race results had now been certified. American Pharaoh was first, with Big Gentle Boy second in the closest Derby result in history.

When the Wisconsin group reached the paddock area, Big Gentle Boy was already in his holding stall and the only person around was a track helper doling out feed.

Al walked over to the man. "Do you know where this horse's owners are?"

"They were here for a few minutes along with his trainer. One of them told his trainer that they should load the horse up for a trip to Virginia. As soon as they gave him those instructions, they left."

Al kicked at an empty bucket. It bounced across the stable floor and thudded against the wall of a stall.

Julie understood his frustration. They'd come so close. Her aunt had only been a few feet away from them, and somehow she'd slipped through their fingers.

"Al." She touched his elbow.

For a moment he didn't move then he looked down at her and lifted his shoulders. "We'll get 'er in New Orleans."

45

"Let's get the hell out of here," suggested Charlie. "We can hold our gravediggers' convention at the campground. Besides, I think I'm on tap to grill steaks for dinner. Remember, we're heading for New Orleans in the morning."

While Charlie's comment didn't reverse Al's dark mood, it did lift it slightly. Soon the group was on its way to the campground and the promise of grilled ribeyes. Charlie was a great cook, and he was clearly taking special care to make sure this meal was a good one. He marinated the steaks, while Al mixed drinks.

"What's everybody having?" Al held up the cocktail shaker he'd brought. "Margarita or old-fashioned?"

Potatoes went onto the grill to bake, along with cobs of sweet corn that Charlie had picked up at a nearby market "because it looked great."

The meal was as good as it looked, and the addition of a couple of drinks made the mood again reasonably positive. Al shoved back his impatience, determined, for this night at least, not to worry about the whereabouts of Genevieve and how to get her back into custody.

With the group relaxed by the liquor, and with the prospect of a long drive the next day, Al suggested they retire early. "I'm setting the alarm for five, and I want everyone up and rolling. I'd love to get to Birmingham around dinnertime. That will allow time to find a campground and get the motor home set up for the night. If we can do that, we'll have a decent drive to New Orleans on Monday."

Al and Rick were the first ones up the next morning. They roused their colleagues and urged them to get through showers hurriedly so they could get on the road. Charlie was the hardest to wake. He'd had four old-fashioneds the night before and seemed determined to sleep all the way to New Orleans.

"C'mon, big guy, move your butt. We have to get the motor home buttoned up for the trip." Al nudged Charlie with his elbow but it seemed to do no good.

"Awww, Al, just close the door and let me and Kelly sleep, okay? It'd be nice just to sleep in and have a little sugar time this morning."

"If you want that, take a joint shower. I don't have time to dynamite you out of the big bed this morning."

"Oh, all right. Just once on this trip, I hope it's gonna be possible to sleep in. Here I've got this great big bed, a beautiful woman layin' next to me, and you want me to get up and take a shower. That's crap."

"It is what it is, and based on your mood, keep the water on cold. I don't want you moanin' all day about the opportunity you lost."

Shortly before seven, the motor home left Churchill Downs, pointed south on I-65 for the 370-mile drive to Birmingham. Al was behind the wheel of the motor home, hoping to average sixty miles an hour with one stop for fuel, which should put them in a campground in Birmingham by three.

It was actually a little after four before the motor home was set up at M&J RV Park near I-65 in Birmingham. It had been a long day. Tomorrow would be another, and so beyond a trip to the grocery story, no one wanted to do anything but eat and go to bed.

Rick had made the trip to a store and picked up several papers. One of them had a story on the Derby that featured "The Mystery Team." It talked about Big Gentle Boy, his owner and handlers. Apparently after finishing second to American Pharaoh, the big colt had mysteriously left Churchill Downs under the cover of night. When Sunday dawned, his stall was empty and there was no sign of him or his handlers.

There were several photos in the newspapers, one of them featuring the beautiful woman known as Savannah Harlowe.

"This time we're gonna get her." Al's fists clenched as he read over Rick's shoulder. "If that damn woman we saw in Louisville is Genevieve, we're gonna catch her in New Orleans. I can't wait to get there and get my hands on her. She's not gonna escape again, that's for damn sure."

Later, Al spent about an hour on the phone with Aaron Wingate, determining that the Angelo Carbone party had arrived back at Lakefront Airport at 10:30 Saturday night. Another plane, reportedly carrying Big Gentle Boy, followed them in.

Al passed the paper, and Aaron's update, around to everyone as they sat around the picnic table, waiting for the burgers to cook on the barbeque. "This is it, folks. We're gonna get the bitch this time." He winced and glanced at Julie. Maybe should have kept that last part to himself. "Sorry. Didn't mean to be offensive."

Julie clasped her hands together in her lap. "It was offensive, Al. Genevieve was very good to Peggy and me. I know she's done some really bad things, but I just can't stand to poor-mouth her. After all, until we knew the rest of the story, all Peggy and I knew was that she was the kindest woman we'd ever met."

"That's the truth, Julie." Peggy slid an arm around Julie's shoulders. "She was likable, helpful, motherly, and doting. Our kids loved her; heck, you, me, Kelly, all of us loved her. I doubt she's changed much. None of us would like to live out our life in prison, either. It's natural for her to want freedom, isn't it?"

Rick shook his head. "Al's right, you guys. Before we get too generous with our praise, let's remember fourteen families who were deprived of a loved one far too early because of her. I don't think sympathy is the right emotion for the situation. I think we all ought to be like Al—anxious as hell to put her where she belongs."

"You're right, Rick, I know that." Julie swiped away a tear that had started down her cheek. "But she was so nice to us. She was kind to a fault whenever she was around us. And the kids did love her."

Charlie, clearly not inclined to be anything but classic Charlie, slammed a fist on the table. "She's a goddamned cold-blooded killer. She needs to be caught and she needs to be put away. Period."

"All I'm saying, Charlie, is that she has a kind side. That side benefitted us. I don't like it when you guys poor-mouth her."

"Well, Julie, I'm glad she was kind to you, but that's not a good enough reason to allow her to stay out of jail. We're gonna put her away!"

Al and JoAnne served the burgers, but a dark cloud hung over the small party, and as soon as everyone had finished eating, mostly in silence, Al stood up. "How about we get to bed so we can get on the road early?"

Charlie frowned. "Goddamn, Al, you sure know how to spoil a party."

Kelly reached for his hand and inclined her head toward the trailer, waggling her eyebrows.

Charlie jumped to his feet. "Okay, okay, bedtime it is."

By the morning things had changed. It was a determined crew that headed down I-65 about six. Charlie was at the wheel. Kelly, Rick, and Peggy were with him. Al, JoAnne, and Julie were in the Navigator, with Julie driving. Al fidgeted with his seat belt in the back seat, still not quite comfortable in the presence of the two women, although JoAnne and Julie both seemed relaxed and at ease with each other.

The afternoon passed quickly, and they sped into the New Orleans area a little before four-thirty. It took another hour to find Second Police District headquarters at 4317 Magazine Street. The folks there were accommodating, helping the group maneuver the motor home into the lot and make the appropriate hook-ups. Then they showed them around the precinct, noting that the men's and women's locker rooms were available to them.

It was apparent that their friend, Aaron, had done a good job of alerting his colleagues because not one officer asked a question.

When they'd finished with the tour, Charlie got directions to a nearby eatery they could walk to, something everyone favored after a long day on the road.

The meal was good, although Charlie complained it was a bit sparse for his liking. When they got home the deputy spoke for all of them. "Not sure about you, but I'm damned tired. The driving today just seemed to get to me. I'm goin' to bed."

His words were like magic, everyone nodding in agreement and then waiting their turn in the motor home to get ready for bed.

46

Up at dawn, Al set up two lawn chairs next to the motor home. Just as he finished, the door of the motor home opened and Charlie staggered down the stairs, clutching two steaming cups of coffee. He fell onto the lawn chair beside Al and handed him a mug. "What're we gonna do, Al?"

"We can't rush into this, Charlie. We're gonna have to be deliberate, or she'll wind up disappearing again. My big question is, how quickly do we let the Carbones know we are here?"

"Shit, Al, they already know. Especially since they saw us at the race yesterday and know we're on their trail. I'll bet they knew even before we entered the city limits. You know how it is back home. Wouldn't we know by now?"

"I guess you're right. But I'd still like the don to think that we don't have a clue."

"And just how the hell are we gonna do that? Shit, it ain't like police from La Crosse, Wisconsin, show up here every day and set up shop. From here on out we need to act on the assumption they are following our every move. If we don't, they'll catch us with our pants down."

"What's going on?" Rick opened the door of the motor home, stepped down, grabbed a chair and joined them. "You guys are waking the dead out here."

"Well, based on what I hear about this place, there's a goddamn lot of 'em to wake. The last time I was here, there was a weirdo on every corner and a couple in the middle of every block. Witches and spooks, there are plenty of 'em down here, that's for goddamn sure."

Al couldn't bring himself to crack a smile, but Rick laughed. "Charlie, as I was going out the door, the beautiful Kelly asked me to tell you to tone it down. She's trying to sleep. She said you should do whatever the hell you want as long as you don't wake anybody up."

"Well, who the hell's to wake? Four women, that's who. Tell 'em to get their asses out of bed and fix me some breakfast."

Before he even finished, the door opened and Kelly, hair flying wild, and presenting a vivid view with the sun shining against her light nightgown, yelled, "Dammit, Charlie Berzinski, tone it down! We've been up at five o'clock every day. This is supposed to be a vacation and we're trying to sleep in here. You seem to think everyone should be up at the crack of dawn. Why don't you guys go and get something to eat. That would be a great gift!"

As Charlie opened his mouth, the door slammed. So he closed it and sat there.

Even Al was laughing now, and both he and Rick were having trouble doing it quietly.

"I think Kelly has a good idea. Let's slip into the station, take a shower, and then head somewhere for breakfast."

"Great idea. How about that Coulis place? That was goddamn good, especially since the don paid for it."

"Yes, he did, but do you think that's a good idea, Charlie? The first day we're here we go to his breakfast place? Why don't we just call him and tell him we're here and we think Savannah is Genevieve and we'd like to stop by and pick her up?"

"Oh, shit, Al, I forgot. I'm really sorry. But you don't have to be so damn nasty."

"Made my point, didn't I?"

Rick slapped his knees with both hands. "Well, I think Al has a great idea. Let's go out for breakfast. How about we also try to find the place that Savannah bought?"

"Great idea; 28 Audubon Place," said Al. "Let's have a look."

Fifteen minutes later, the three men cruised past Savannah's new house in Rick's Navigator. It was a beautiful morning. The trilling of birds brightened the day as they slowly drove past the sprawling house set well back in the magnolias and half hidden by flowering plants of many varieties across its façade.

"What a house! What a goddamned house! Musta cost a half million bucks, don't you think?"

Al and Rick chuckled. Rick glanced back at Charlie in the rearview mirror. "I don't think you could touch it for a million and a half. We can't see most of it."

As they gawked, then turned around in a nearby schoolyard and headed back for another look, a beautiful middle-aged woman walked down the driveway toward the sidewalk. Al's heart rate went into overdrive.

Charlie gripped the back of his seat. "Tha … that's her. As if she knew we were here and wanted to parade for us."

"I doubt that, Charlie, but you're right, that is Savannah Harlowe. If she is also Genevieve, she's damn good looking for her age. But this woman looks years younger. She's beautiful. I love red hair, and look at the color of hers. It's the richest auburn I've ever seen. The whole person is exquisite."

"That color is something, Al," agreed Charlie. He leaned forward between the two front seats to peer out the front window. "I like mine a little fuller in the hips, but she ain't bad, not bad at all," he said. "I sure as hell wouldn't kick her out of bed for eating crackers."

"Geez, Charlie, can't you get some new lines? That cracker comment went out forty years ago."

"Bullshit, Rick. I'm not all that much older than forty and I heard it just a few days ago."

"Charlie, you're a helluva lot older than forty and Rick's right, that line went out with Custer."

"Who's Custer? What the hell does Custer have to do with this?"

Rick laughed. Al's eyes narrowed as he stared at the woman. *Is that her? Genevieve Wangen?* The woman looked nothing like Genevieve. *Still, if she's had a lot of work—*

He sucked in a quick breath as she turned to face them.

"Now look at what you've done. We've attracted her attention." Charlie ducked his head down.

Savannah Harlowe waved and motioned for them to stop.

"Oh, shit," said Al under his breath. "Now we've blown it."

Rick pulled the Navigator to the curb. Al sat frozen. Maybe when she realized there were three men in the car, she wouldn't come over. The woman didn't hesitate, just kept walking toward them. With a sigh, Al hit the button to lower his window.

As Savannah Harlowe stepped down off the curb, Al studied her from beneath the brim of his ball cap. *It's not her.*

"Pardon me," said Savannah, a heavy French accent punctuating her words. "Is it I who make you laugh?"

Al slouched down a little lower. He couldn't speak. If he did, she would recognize his voice for sure.

Rick leaned forward. "Uh, no ma'am. Our friend here just made a comment that's older than the hills." He jerked his thumb over his shoulder at Charlie.

"What hills? I am not aware of these hills. Where might they be?"

"It's just a joke, ma'am." Al tugged his ball cap down a little lower. If this was the woman he'd been searching for years, he really didn't want her to recognize him.

"You make a joke about me?" Her face turned into a sad grimace. "My dog maybe? He is misbehaving?"

As she spoke, the dog danced at the end of the leash, pawing the car.

"Pierre, you stop that. Is not nice to scratch car. Bad dog. You need to learn manners from cat."

Savannah rested a gloved hand on the window frame and leaned even closer to Al, nearly touching him now. A whiff of expensive perfume drifted on the air between them. "I have ze cat. It is, how you say, very well? But zis dog? He is," she shook her head, "une petit merde." She glanced down at the dog and smiled. "Trying to teach to him the manners, yes." She threw up her hands.

Al didn't know what to do. He wanted to speak but some unseen gremlin seemed to have control of his tongue. The best he could do was nod.

"No problem, ma'am, we were not laughing at you or the dog," said Rick. "We were just talking among ourselves."

"But you were traveling very slowly. And staring. I interest you for some reason, no?"

"Oh, ma'am, you are beautiful. Who wouldn't stare at you? You look great. All over. Oh, Christ, excuse me, that wasn't good." Charlie slumped against the back seat. Lucky for him. If he'd still been leaning forward, Al might have punched him.

"How was it bad? Nice compliment, no?"

"Yes, it was a nice compliment," agreed Al, keeping his face averted from hers and his voice low. He pointed at the mansion. "We were also admiring the house that you came out of. Is it yours?"

"Oh, yes, a wonderful gift from a wonderful friend. He is, how you say it? A big report? No, no, no, a big shot. Yes, that's it, a big shot."

Charlie leaned around so far Al could feel his friend's breath on his neck. "He must be a great friend to buy you that."

Al winced. *Let it go, Charlie. We're being too obvious.* Al shot a sideways glance at Rick. *We need to get out of here.* Rick nodded slightly.

"He is. Very rich. Very big man here. We had great party a week ago."

Rick tapped a hand on the steering wheel. "Well, that's very nice, ma'am. But we need to be getting along. Which way is Tulane University?"

"Tulane?" Charlie whirled toward the doctor. "Why the hell, Rick ..."

Al punched him in the shoulder and Charlie sank back onto his seat.

"Is that way." The woman pointed behind them.

"Okay, thank you, ma'am. You have a nice day."

"You have ze sweet day, too." She stepped back onto the sidewalk as Rick made a U-turn and headed back toward Tulane.

In the back seat, Charlie crossed his arms and let out a loud harrumph. "Why the hell are we going to Tulane? I'm hungry as hell and now you want a campus tour?"

"No, you idiot. Rick was trying to get us away from the woman. He just asked her a question to help make that happen."

Charlie thought about that for a while then looked crestfallen. "Oh, sorry."

"No big deal. Let's look for a place to eat."

Al desperately wanted to turn and look behind them as they drove away, to study the woman another moment for any telltale sign, however slight, that she was the killer he was searching for. One more quick glance would do little but attract her attention again, though. Obviously there was no way to prove who the woman really was by her looks. They'd need a DNA sample or fingerprints for that.

DNA or fingerprints. Hmm. Al glanced at the window frame. No, in spite of the warm weather, she'd been wearing kid gloves, likely to protect her delicate hands from the leash. They'd need a warrant to officially collect samples from her, and he doubted the fact that the woman made an okay gesture with her middle finger instead of the index one would justify that.

If an opportunity presented itself again though, he'd make every attempt to collect that information on his own.

As Rick and Charlie argued, Al hardly heard them. He was busy constructing scenarios that would put the woman close enough for him to get what he needed to prove conclusively that she was not Genevieve.

If even one of them worked out, he wouldn't leave her presence without it.

47

For the next four days, the men spent hours with Aaron and driving around the city, chasing every piece of information they had, hoping to find out more. Each search resulted in a dead end. More and more often, the thought crept through Al's mind that maybe they should just call this off and go home.

"I am so goddamned frustrated that I think I'm going to bust." Charlie paced the motor home as the group arose on Sunday. Their vacation was more than half over and they had little to show for all their efforts to track down the escaped killer. "I just don't think there's any way to break this."

"You're right; it doesn't appear so," agreed Rick.

Al's shoulders slumped as he scrambled eggs in a frying pan on the small stove. "I was sure we'd have something by now." He set the pan down on the stove with a thud and turned to face everyone. "Here's what I think. We need a day off. We need to get away from this. Do something fun. Shift our minds away from the issue."

Charlie lifted the plates down from the cupboard. "Great idea, Al. Let's go to Biloxi!"

Peggy dropped two pieces of bread into the toaster. "Personally, I lost enough money at the horse track; I'm not really interested in more gambling. This vacation has been fun, but there's been no real 'girl' time. If the men want to go gambling, fine, they should do that. But we haven't seen New Orleans yet. I'd rather do that."

JoAnne pulled open the silverware drawer. "And we can have lunch somewhere fun. Wouldn't that be great? We still haven't been to Brennan's."

"Or Antoine's," chimed in Kelly.

"And I wanted to go to Commander's Place. That one is credited with changing the taste of New Orleanians." Peggy made it unanimous; no Biloxi for the women.

"We also need to get to the French Quarter. They say everyone needs to see that." JoAnne set out cutlery at each place. "And Preservation Hall. Let's hear some Dixieland while we're here."

"The visual arts here are also incredible." Julie grabbed the coffee pot and started filling mugs. "How about some museums? I'd love to see the Katrina Museum when we're in the French Quarter."

"Apparently the zoo is exceptional, too," said Kelly. "If it's not too hot, why don't we spend some time there? How long do we have, guys? A week?"

Charlie scowled and she laughed. "Just kidding, Charlie. Just kidding. A day or two will be plenty."

JoAnne turned to Al and lifted both hands, palms up. "Looks like we're going to be too busy to go on a gambling junket."

Charlie frowned. "Junket? Why is Biloxi a junket? We're paying for it, aren't we?"

"We are, Charlie." Al clapped a hand on his friend's shoulder. "But I do think a day off is a good idea. What say we plan to go tomorrow? If we leave now, much of the day is gone before we get there. If we go tomorrow, we can get an early start. The women can sleep as late as they want and then get a cab to wherever they want to go. Whaddaya think?"

"Great idea, Al. Count me in."

"Terrific," agreed Rick.

Al scooped eggs onto plates. "For today, what would you folks say to lunch at Coulis? Maybe the don will be there."

"Great idea." Charlie accepted a plate from Al and grabbed a fork. "I can have some of those buckwheat cakes. They were the greatest. Better'n Ma's cakes, even."

After they had eaten breakfast and tidied up the motor home, they all crowded into the Navigator with Rick at the wheel. Coulis was in the GPS and it wasn't long before all seven of them were piling out of the car for lunch at the restaurant near the don's house.

Lunch was enjoyable. Everyone seemed ready for a little bit of vacation, something they had not had on this trip.

After sumptuous fare, they sat back to enjoy Cajun coffee. From the corner of his eye, Al caught the door opening. He straightened up so quickly he nearly tipped over his glass of water. "Guys," he hissed, and inclined his head toward the door. A beaming Don Angelo Carbone walked toward them.

Al swallowed. The don didn't look at all surprised to see them. Charlie was right; the Carbones knew they were there.

"My, my, look who's here, my friends from Wisconsin and their beautiful companions." Pausing and pointing with his finger, as though counting the number at the table, the don rubbed his chin, the grin even touching the eyes of his handsome face. "You must have known I was coming. One of these lovely ladies has no beau. Che peccato!"

Julie wiped her fingers on a napkin and laid it back across her lap. "It is a shame, Don Angelo. Forse si dovrebbe conoscere qualcuno per me?"

The don's face brightened. "Un milione di uomini, mia cara, vorrebbe spazzare via i vostri piedi. Ma forse farò?"

Without missing a beat, Julie smiled and said, "E 'possibile che potrei essere così fortunato?"

"Vorrei deliziare il nostro animo visualizzare la mia casa adottata sulla argine. But first, dessert for all of you." The don waved an arm expansively over the table.

In spite of several protests that they were stuffed, Don Angelo, in a kindly voice, said to the waitress, "Send Chef Jimmy here, please."

As if he had been listening, a sturdily built man with a pleasant face adorned with a white mustache appeared at the table. He wore a black apron and a black chef's hat.

"Chef Jimmy, these are friends of mine from Wisconsin. They have stuffed themselves, they say, on your cooking. However, I shudder at the thought of them leaving without dessert. Might you be able to fix something light and tasty for them?"

"It shall be here directly." The chef wiped his hands on the apron before bustling back to the kitchen.

In no time at all, seven plates of something that looked like clouds outlined in red and blue appeared at the table. Both the don and the chef beamed as seven plates of dessert quickly disappeared.

"Hmmm, stuffed, I see." As the don spoke, he clapped the chef on the back.

Chef Jimmy bowed slightly before excusing himself and returning to the kitchen. Don Angelo towered over the table. His dark eyes made his handsome face even more distinctive and his accent and curly black hair marked him as Italian.

Leaning down, he took Julie's hand, kissed it, and said, "Ah, mia cara, se fossi più giovane di 30 anni, si avrebbe un problema per le mani questo pomeriggio. Ma, ahimè, un incontro chiama." He inclined his head to the group, took two steps backward, turned and left the restaurant.

Eyes wide, Peggy grabbed Julie's arm. "What did he say?"

"Yes, yes, tell us," urged Kelly.

A sly smile crossed JoAnne's face. "I think the don just hit upon our friend in a manner that suggests he wants to keep us guessing."

Rick tossed his napkin onto his plate. "Whatever he said, I think it's safe to say, Julie, that you made quite an impression. And possibly a new friend."

Julie's cheeks were pink. "He's a charming man, don't you think?"

"He certainly is." Peggy sipped her water and set down her glass. "He's not only charming, he's handsome, too. Very handsome."

Kelly rubbed her hands together. "And he looks very wealthy. Those jeans must have cost a thousand bucks. You can't get that kind of fit at a Levi store."

Al frowned. "He's also capable of great evil. We need to remember that about him."

"Oh, Al," JoAnne smacked him on the arm. "You always have to throw cold water on our fantasies. He's a great looking guy: tall, dark, and handsome, fit as a fiddle and, Kelly's right, that outfit he was wearing must have cost thousands. I suspect, like you do when a good-looking woman walks by, we all wondered—just for a second—what it would be like to have those arms wrapped around us."

Kelly giggled. Julie looked down at the hands clasped in her lap, but Peggy roared in laughter. "Girl, you hit it on the head. He's one fine specimen of a guy. I think the term Italian stallion applies quite well to that man."

Kelly clicked her long, manicured nails against the table. "But what did he say? When people talk in languages the others can't understand, it reminds me of my grandma's place, and that always meant something was up."

Julie unclasped her hands and tugged on her sweater. "When he asked which of us was not taken, I responded. I took a little Italian in college, so I was able to understand him pretty well. He just wanted to know what we are doing in New Orleans. I told him we were on vacation and that I am the odd person out. He was very complimentary. He teased me, saying if he were younger and not married, he would join us and I would have a companion."

"Oh ... my ... god." Kelly pressed a hand to her chest. "If he had said that to me, I probably would have fainted dead away. Either that, or I would have grabbed him and we'd have been out of here."

Charlie's eyebrows rose and she laughed. "Oh, babe, once in a while you need to let us have our fun, too. You'll be the one in bed with me tonight."

"Yeah, but who'll ya be thinking of?"

"I can assure you, sweetheart, if you finally decide to make use of the bedroom, you will have my undivided attention."

"Too much information. Let's get out of here before we have to get a room for Charlie and Kelly." JoAnne rose from the table as she spoke.

Charlie tapped a finger against his chin."Now there's an idea. A little romp to work off a late lunch and get ready for dinner."

"Charles Berzinski, I think it's time to go sightseeing."

For the rest of the day, they drove around New Orleans. The saw the Super Dome, went past Tulane, took an extended look at Savannah's house, and drove over the massive Mississippi bridge. They avoided the French Quarter because the men had already been and the women would spend the next day there. They got home as the sun was slipping toward Texas, decided salads were in order after all the food they'd eaten that day, relaxed a bit, and retired.

Although the motor home was quiet, Al tossed and turned. Finally, not wanting to disturb JoAnne, he got up and crept outside. For a long time he sat in a lawn chair, staring up at the half moon hanging just above the tips of the trees. Had he talked to Genevieve Wangen a few days earlier? Heard her voice? Smelled her perfume? The thought that she could have been so close and there was nothing he could do about nearly drove him mad.

His fists clenched on the arms of the chair. One way or another, before they left New Orleans he was going to prove the woman he'd been hunting down for years and Savannah Harlowe were one and the same. And he was going to do everything in his power to make sure she went to jail and stayed there for a very long time.

48

"Julie."

Julie moaned and rolled over, trying to get away away from the voice threatening to drag her from the amazing dream she'd been having. Brody's Minnesota Vikings NFL team had just won the Superbowl and confetti filled the air. Everyone in the stadium chanted her son's name as he—

"Julie!" The voice was more insistent this time. When a hand grabbed her shoulder and shook her, Julie sighed and opened her eyes.

Kelly's face was inches from hers. "C'mon!" she urged. "We have a whole day without the guys. We need to make use of every bit of it. What would you say to breakfast at Coulis? Maybe the don will be there again."

Julie tossed back the blankets and sat up. "I'm not sure that's a good idea. I flirted with him pretty outrageously yesterday. If we go back, he'll think I'm stalking him."

"Oh, for god's sake." Kelly flapped a hand in the air. "He knew you were teasing. You think he's going to want to grab you and spirit you away?"

Julie blinked. "He probably knows better than that. I'm just hoping I do."

Peggy started laughing. Julie's forehead wrinkled. "Why is that funny?"

"Forgive me, girlfriend, but the notion of you taking up with a mafioso is simply more than my sense of humor can stand. I just don't see you as the type."

"I may not be the type, but that's one real specimen of manhood. I imagine in New Orleans, he can pretty much have whomever he wants.

Why should this lonely Illinois gal deprive herself of a romp with someone who obviously has it all: virility, wealth, good looks, status, everything!"

She pushed hair out of her eyes and grabbed Peggy's hand. "Listen to me. I must be a hussy."

A movement behind Kelly caught Julie's eyes and she lifted her gaze over her friend's shoulder. JoAnne stood in the kitchen area, a frown on her face.

Julie climbed out of bed and walked over to hug her. "Oh, JoAnne, I'm so sorry. I was just teasing. Please don't think badly of me. It's just that once in a while I find it helps to laugh at myself. It's no fun being alone, believe me." She stepped back and clapped a hand over her mouth. "There I go again. I think I'm destined to put my feet—yes, feet—into my mouth."

"I don't think badly of you Julie, but it's also no fun knowing that your spouse had a relationship with someone who is as lovely and nice as you. Although I want to believe both you and Al, I worry that with old age coming, I'm the one who is going to be left alone." Her voice caught.

Julie's stomach twisted. "Oh, JoAnne, don't say that. My comments were unthinking and crass. Al and I know what we did was totally wrong. You are such an amazing person; the last thing either of us wants to do is hurt you. I should have thought before I spoke."

JoAnne patted her arm. "I know you meant no harm, but sometimes I feel vulnerable, even when I don't want to. I'll get over this. Let's just let it slide."

Julie reached for the housecoat she'd tossed at the foot of the bed and tugged it on. "Today may not be the time, but the day is coming when we have to talk about it. I need to convince you that you have nothing to fear from me."

"But how do I know Al isn't going to walk out on me?"

"I know that coming from me it probably doesn't mean much, but one thing I do know about Al is that he would never leave you. Never. He agonized over our affair. I also know that it's over—for good."

Peggy pulled a brush out of her purse and walked over to the mirror on the wall. "Okay, let's get off this kick. We've got all day today without the guys, and I'll be darned if I am going to continue this funeral dirge!"

"I agree," said Kelly. "Let's get on with the day and have some fun. I think Coulis is a great idea. And between us, we'll make sure you don't go off with the don, Julie. What do you say, are you in?"

This is a really bad idea. Julie hesitated before nodding. "I'm in—I guess."

"Great." Peggy pointed to the bathroom. "JoAnne, get in the shower and get cleaned up. Our cab will be here in twenty minutes."

"Twenty minutes? You expect me to get this old chassis cleaned up and ready to go in twenty minutes? You must not see what I see when I look in the mirror."

Kelly circled a finger in front of her. "Just get on with it. I think it's high time the girls had a day off without the guys. Let's see how much trouble we can get into in New Orleans."

True to her word, Peggy had the cab waiting outside the motor home in twenty minutes. Contrary to her word, JoAnne was ready, and she looked terrific. She wore a bright blue sun dress, trimmed in emerald green, and had fastened her hair in a loose bun at her neck.

"You look superb. I'd say we're going to set this town on its ear." Kelly waited for everyone else to go down the steps then locked the door behind them.

In just a few minutes, they were walking into Coulis.

"Well, well, who do we have here?" Don Angelo waved at them from a table in front of the window. He looked dapper in a snappy, lightly checked suit that fit him perfectly. He also wore a vest this morning, and his flowered necktie provided a hint of color. His hat, a checked Country Gentlemen edition, rested on the table next to him.

"My lovely new friends, and without their gentlemen companions. This must truly be my lucky day." He gestured to a table adjacent to his. "Chef Jimmy, come see who we have here."

Soon the four women, the don, and Chef Jimmy were talking like longtime friends. While the chef regaled the group with stories of culinary excellence, the don talked about things the women could see and do on their "day off."

"If I had an ounce of courage, I would say torpoedoes be damned, full-speed ahead and I will show you around. Ah, but then, my dolce signora, she would have my cajones! So, how do you put it, about discretion being the better part of valor?" He tugged a phone out of his shirt pocket. "Here is what I will do, though; you shall have my car and driver at your disposal all day."

Julie's eyes widened. Somehow she didn't think Al would approve of that at all.

Before she could protest though, the don had finished issuing instructions into the cell phone and returned it to his pocket. "It is all set. Bruno knows all the best places. He will give you a wonderful tour."

Breakfast concluded, the women paid their respects to the chef, who insisted the meal was on him. They thanked Don Angelo for his kidness as he held the door to his car open for them. JoAnne and Julie slid onto one seat, with Peggy and Kelly across from them, facing the rear of the car.

Before he closed the door, the don leaned down and looked inside. "This car has everything ladies. If there is anything you need, please ask Bruno and he will get it for you." With another wave, he closed the door and stepped up onto the curb.

Bruno, a swarthy-looking character with long, curly hair, appeared to have walked right off the set of *Pirates of the Caribbean*.

Julie studied him. He was handsome in a weathered sort of way, and when he turned and stretched an arm across the back of the front seat, muscles bulged beneath the sleeves of his black T-shirt. With him around, no one would be bothering them unduly.

"So, my friends, what is it we will do today?"

"We want to see the sights," said Peggy.

"And experience some local color." Kelly crossed her legs and looked out the window.

"And museums." JoAnne pulled the seatbelt across her chest. "We'd like to learn about the history of the area while we're here."

Julie bit her lip. She had to put the plan she'd been working on since seeing Savannah Harlowe at the racetrack into place. *It's now or never.*

Peggy touched her knee. "How about you, Julie? What would you like to see first?"

Julie pressed a hand to her abdomen. "To be honest, breakfast didn't sit well with me. I have a horrible stomachache. Would you be terribly offended if I went back to the motor home to rest?"

Peggy's face twisted into a frown and Kelly's manicured eyebrows drew together. JoAnne opened her bag and rummaged inside. "Julie, we want you with us. What would help, a Tums, maybe? Or a Prilosec?"

Julie grimaced. "No, thank you. The thought of a Tums makes me want to throw up. Seriously, I think if I can just lie down for a while, I'll feel better. Bruno, would you mind dropping me off?" Julie gripped JoAnne's arm. "You can call in a couple of hours and see how I'm doing. Or if I feel better, I'll call you. Please, I just feel terrible right now."

"Well, if you're sure ..." Although she didn't look very happy about it, JoAnne gave Bruno instructions to get to the motor home.

Which is pretty decent of her, all things considered. Julie leaned her head against the back of the seat. *I'm almost sorry I have to deceive her, but if I don't do this now, I'll lose my nerve and not do it all.*

49

As soon as the limo disappeared down the road, Julie changed into jeans and a T-shirt, stabbed at her hair, checked the mirror, and looked to make sure her cell phone was in her bag before she left the motor home. She'd forgotten the address of Savannah's home, but knew it was near the university.

Once in front of the precinct, she hailed a cab and climbed into the back seat. Her heart was pounding. *Am I really doing this?* She pushed back her shoulders, shivered, and tried to compose herself. "Tulane University, please. Actually, I hope to visit a friend who lives on the way, but I don't know the address. I may recognize the house if I see it, though."

As they drove toward the campus, the driver turned onto a gorgeous, tree-lined street. Julie glanced at the sign. *Audubon Place.* She leaned forward and peered out the front window. "That's it. There it is." She pointed to a large brick home sheltered by magnolias and surrounded by flowers.

"One damn pretty place," said the cabbie. "You got ritzy friends, ma'am."

The driver maneuvered the cab to the curb. Julie tipped him handsomely and stepped lightly from the cab. As he pulled away, she turned and nearly tripped in the soft grass on the boulevard. Catching herself, she walked toward the house. The curved drive, constructed of stones set in concrete, was guarded by a sturdily built wrought-iron fence, embedded into two brick collonades topped by ornate light fixtures. As she stopped to admire the house, she noticed a woman working in the gardens inside the fence. Her chest constricted. *Savannah.*

"Pardon me?"

The woman turned and looked before rising and walking slowly to the fence.

"Oui? May I help you?" Her voice was tinged with a French accent.

Julie strained to detect a hint of anything familiar in the voice. Nothing. Had this all been a mistake? If so, it was too late. Savannah stood at the fence, her head tilted to one side as she studied her.

Julie walked over to stand on her side of the fence. She placed two hands on the wrought iron bars to brace herself and smiled. "Savannah Harlowe?"

"Oui. Why do you ask?"

"I think we have met before, you and I."

The woman tilted her head, her fingers gnawing at dirt on her cheek. She looked so puzzled that Julie took a step back from the fence. *This was a terrible idea.* The woman studied Julie intently. Julie drew in a deep breath and the sweet smell of flowers filled her nostrils. She jerked at the sound of buzzing near her ear, and swatted at a bee.

"They are my friends—good for, how you say, pollinating, no?" The woman looked down and brushed some dried mud off her jeans before smiling and reaching through the fence to shake Julie's hand. "If we have met, I surely ... Oh, oui, the Derby. Yes, the Derby. That's where was it was, yes? And you are?"

"My name is Julie, and you're right, we talked in Louisville at the race, but I was thinking about Illinois several years ago."

Savannah drew her arm back through the fence. "Illinois? Illinois. Where is it? I do not know this place."

It's not her. "My mistake." The stomachache she'd feigned earlier was becoming a reality. "I think I'd better just be moving on." *Whatever was I thinking?*

"Oh, my dear, I am, how you say it, brand new to New Orleans. I would love to have someone to visit with. Perhaps you would join me for iced tea. It is very hot. When you are refreshed, I can call you a taxi."

The woman reached into her pocket, removed a device, and soon the gate was moving aside to admit Julie.

As futile as her mission now seemed, Julie forced herself to walk to the end of the fence and onto the beautifully landscaped property. *I'm here;*

might as well see this through. She inclined her head to the partially filled plant tray resting on the drive. "You're a gardener."

"Oui. I am, how you say, in love with the soil. I feel good when my hands are dirty. And it is so good to have bright flowers around the house, don't you think?"

"Oh, yes, and yours are beautiful. I've not seen anything like them before. What are they?"

"I plant Louisiana garden around house. I have in already Red Buckeye, Southern Magnolia, Silverbell Tree, and Louisiana Phlox. Now I plant Louisiana Irises, Hibiscus, and Gardenias. You smell Gardenias? They are sweet."

"I do. Very nice. And what is that?" Julie pointed across the drive.

"Is Simpson's Roseweed." Savannah waved her hand. "And next to it is Blue-Eyed Grass. Pretty, too."

"You have a real knack for this." Julie walked slowly along the drive to enjoy the flowers.

"Gives me things to do. I love to be outside in fresh air."

"Well, you've done a magnificent job," Julie told her as they reached the walkway, curved in imitation of the larger driveway, leading to the house.

"This way," said her hostess, gesturing to the flagstone path. When she reached the corner of the house, Julie caught a glimpse of the shimmering water of a pool in the back yard.

"Please, come with me. I will get us sweet tea ... or would you like something else?"

"No, tea would be great." Whoever she was, the woman had such a pleasant smile that Julie relaxed a bit.

"I want to know more about this Illinois place, and why you think we have met there. Come."

They entered the house through the kitchen. Savannah rang a bell before pausing to wash her hands. In less than a minute, a tall, dark-haired woman entered the kitchen. "We have company," Savannah told her. "Come, meet Julie. Julie, this is Idonna. We live here together. She takes care of me."

The woman laughed, the sound like ice tinkling in a glass. "I am helping Savannah adjust to life in the United States," she explained.

"Idonna, Julie comes to visit from Illinois. Might we have sweet tea, please, and maybe some scones?"

"Of course. It'll take just a minute to get everything ready." Idonna busied herself at the counter as Savannah and Julie sat down at the table in the bay window area. As nice as it would have been to sit outside in the gardens, Julie was grateful to be free from the heat of the day.

"And so, this Illinois, tell me."

While Julie couldn't put her finger on it, there was now something strangely familiar about Savannah. *Is it because I knew her before I saw her in Louisville, or does she just remind me of someone else?* Julie worried it was the latter; the woman in front of her just looked so different from her aunt. I'm sure it isn't her. The thought that she might have gotten Al's hopes up for no reason sent her stomach churning again. As they visited, though, she warmed to Savannah, and to Idonna, who had set a plate of scones and a pitcher of iced tea on the table and joined them. She found herself sharing her story with the two women.

"As I mentioned, I came here because I thought you might be a woman I once knew."

Beneath the thick auburn hair, Savannah's forehead wrinkled slightly, but she didn't speak, just nodded at Julie, encouraging her to continue.

"You see, a few years ago I was befriended by a woman in Chicago, Illinois. Her name was Genevieve Wangen. Some of us—I am traveling with six other people—believed you might have been her. She is my aunt and I thought I would set out on my own today to see what I could find out. But I fear I have bothered you needlessly, and I'm sorry. You are much younger than she is, so I have no idea how I got so confused. I feel badly for wasting your time. I should be going."

"Oh, my dear, it is wonderful to have, how do you put it, female company? It is lonesome for me here. Please don't go just yet."

Julie paused, and when she did, the woman's smile won her over. "I can stay just a little while. After that, though, my friends will worry about me."

"Wonderful." Savannah wrapped long, slender fingers around her glass of tea. "So, my dear, tell me more about this Genevieve. It sounds as though she is important to you."

Although she knew she shouldn't, the warmth of the women—and of the sun pouring through the windows of the bright kitchen—lulled Julie into letting down her guard, and she told them all about her aunt. When she finished and reached for a scone, Savannah leaned back in her seat.

"And so this woman, this Genevieve, she was a friend, but a murderer, too?"

"Yes, she has certainly made some questionable decisions for reasons only she knows, but she did my friends and me a huge favor in making her lovely house available to us on terms we could afford. Then she was arrested, but on her way back to La Crosse, Wisconsin, she escaped. That was more than three years ago, and she is still missing. We thought she might be you, which is why we are here."

"Me?" Savannah giggled. "I hardly know anything about your country, but already you think I am a murderer? How can this be? You hear this, Idonna?"

The other woman, who had gotten up to refill the iced tea pitcher, lounged against the counter. "Well, unless this murderer is French, you are not her."

"I know it's crazy, but when we heard about a woman who had suddenly started appearing everywhere with the Carbone family, we were sure there was a connection. We rented a motor home and drove here earlier this week. We saw you at the Kentucky Derby, and I so wanted to talk to you more then, but you disappeared."

"Ah, yes, the Derby. How disappointing it was. Grand Garçon Doux, my mother's horse, he ran a great race, but that Egyptian horse, my what a specimen."

Julie nodded. "It was a great race, and when it was over, you looked at me; do you remember? You made the 'okay sign.' That's why I wanted to talk to you. The only person I've ever known who makes the sign that way, the way you did it, was my aunt Genevieve."

"Like how?" Savannah held up her hand.

When Julie showed her, Savannah nodded. "Yes, that is how I do it. I have always done it this way. Is funny?"

"No, it's not funny, but I have never seen anyone else do it that way. I was so sure when I saw you do that in Louisville that you must be her. And I feel bad that you aren't, because she was such a good friend to my friend Peggy and me and she helped us out so much with a beautiful house. It is my hope that that I will be able to say thank you to her in person sometime. She is a wonderful lady …"

The comment just hung there. When there was no response, Julie gathered up her plate and glass and walked to the sink. "Well, listen to me. Just babbling on. I have to be going. Savannah, I am very sorry to have bothered you. I was just so sure that you were the woman we've been looking for. It was my hope that I would find Genevieve and be able to fill her in on everything that has happened in my life since I saw her last. She has a nephew, and she would be so proud of him, I think. I would just love to talk to her."

"I wish I am the person for whom you look. Except for the fact that I could never, ever kill anyone," Savannah shuddered, "I would like to be her. Then you would feel better. Am I right?"

"Yes, that's right, but I fear I may never find her, and she will never know about my son and how well he is doing." Julie shook her head. "Please don't mind my mood; I'm just a little disappointed."

"Are you sure you must go?"

"Oh yes." Julie glanced at her watch. Noon already. "My friends are either going to call or stop by the motor home we're staying in. They'll worry about me. I really must be on my way."

Savannah walked her to the front gate. Before stepping out onto the sidewalk, Julie turned back. "I may not have found my aunt, but I had a great visit with you. Thank you so much for listening."

"Julie, I much wish I were the aunt you seek. Alas, it is not me. It sounds as if this Genevieve was a good friend, someone who helped you very much."

"Oh, yes, she did. I hope someday to be able to thank her for all she did for Brody and me."

Savannah slid an arm around her shoulders. "Maybe, cherie, she heard us as we talked. Who knows what magic may occur. I would love to be her, because you are a lovely young lady."

They embraced then Julie went out through the sturdy wrought-iron barrier and hailed a cab. While she waited, she threw one last glance over her shoulder at the now-closed gate. *It doesn't seem as if anyone's getting in there that Savannah doesn't want to see.* Why the tight security?

As she rode in the cab along the quiet, shaded streets of this well-kept, mature area of New Orleans, Julie couldn't explain the feeling that enveloped her. Strange as it seemed, she felt as if she had known Savannah for far more than a couple of hours.

It's just that I wanted her to be Genevieve. That wasn't to be.

Julie had no sooner entered the motor home than her phone rang. It was Peggy, checking to see how she was feeling and if she was well enough to join them for the afternoon.

"Please don't be upset, Peggy, but I just want to sleep. Your call woke me up. If I can sleep for a little longer, hopefully my stomach will settle down and I'll be ready to join you for dinner."

"All right, if you're sure. But we're picking you up at five for dinner. No arguments."

"I hope I'll feel up to joining you."

Julie stripped off her outer clothes and reclined on the bed. Soon she was asleep, but her rest was haunted by dreams of Genevieve and Savannah. Eerily, as she dreamt, the faces of the two women merged and suddenly Savannah was transformed into Genevieve, although she still talked with a heavy French accent.

When Julie awoke, shadows filled the room and she was sweating profusely and felt queasy. *That'll teach me. If I lie to my friends, I may be victimized by falsehoods coming true.*

She arose and threw on a robe. Her stomach lurched. She clearly was not well enough to go out to dinner. All she wanted to do was go back to bed and sleep. And that's exactly what she did. She awoke when Peggy called again, talked to her briefly, and declined joining her friends, then took off her robe, tugged her nightgown over her head, and crawled back under the covers. She was just dozing off when a thought struck her. As hot as she'd been moments before, her skin suddenly went ice cold.

What on earth would Al say if he found out I told Savannah Harlowe all about our quest?

50

Savannah stood at the front window, watching Julie walk down the sidewalk and climb into a cab. Idonna came up to stand beside her and Savannah turned to her, one hand pressed to her chest. "Oh my, that was scary. How did I do?"

"You were wonderful. I don't think she had a clue. I was so proud. All I could think of were those long lessons, rehearsing your French accent over and over. They certainly paid off today."

Idonna took her hand and they did an impromptu jig on the living room carpet, until both came to a halt, laughing and gasping for breath.

"Still, I was terrified." Savannah wiped a hand across her forehead. "It might have been a good test, but I believe I sweated right through my clothes. I think I'll go take a shower and change."

Idonna linked her arm through Savannah's and walked her to the bottom of the stairs. "When you're done, we had better call Angelo. He needs to know about our visitor and how well you did."

"I'll only be a minute." Savannah swiftly ascended the stairs and entered her room. Because she had a maid, she dropped her clothing as she walked to the large shower, which took up most of the marble-tiled room between her bedroom and the dressing room.

Back downstairs, she sat at the kitchen table beside Idonna, who handed her the phone. She dialed Angelo and put the phone on speaker.

"Hello." The voice was sweet and female, and Savannah recognized it immediately. "Miranda, what are you doing there?"

The woman who had cooked for Savannah and Dino during their

stay at the Dewey Wills camp had become a good friend and fishing companion, and Savannah had missed her.

"Miss Savannah, I had hoped to hear your voice one day soon. I work here. When I'm not in the swamp I serve Miss Rosalyn and Don Angelo."

"That's wonderful. It will be good to see you again. Is the don home?"

"Yes, Miss Savannah, but he is taking his afternoon nap. I can wake him if it's very important."

Savannah glanced over at Idonna. Her friend shook her head.

"No, please don't wake him, but could you make sure he knows when he comes down that I'd like him to call me? It's not urgent, but it is important."

"I will, Miss Savannah."

Savannah hit the disconnect button to end the call. "I think I might spend some time in the lab this afternoon. I'll take the phone with me in case the don calls back while I'm out there."

Idonna nodded and carried the scones and iced tea over to the counter.

Savannah walked to the garage next to the carriage house and went inside. The light was dim but sufficient for her to find her way to the cabinet and the button that activated the door to the lab. When the section of wall slid noiselessly aside, she hurried through the opening and carefully closed the door before turning on the lights.

She had plenty of work to do. During the time the group had been away at the Derby a number of orders had come in. Now she sorted them into priority order and began to assemble the chemicals she needed.

She had just pushed the filled fourth order to a separate place on the table and was preparing to start on the fifth when the phone rang. Savannah picked it up and pressed it to her ear.

"Hi, Angelo."

"Savannah. What can I do for you, my dear?"

"I was working on my gardens this morning when a young woman walked up the drive and spoke to me. It was my niece from Chicago."

She moved the phone from her ear as Angelo's voice took on a thunderous tone. He cursed in Italian and then English before he paused for breath. Savannah waited. After a few seconds, he exhaled. "I apologize. I knew she was in town, but I had no idea she would come to your house. She must be much closer to figuring out who you are than we'd thought."

"No, I don't think she is. She gave no indication that she recognized me. Just the opposite in fact. She was very open and told me that she and her friends suspected me of being Genevieve, but that after speaking with me she could see they had been mistaken. We visited for about an hour and a half, and by the end seemed quite convinced—and disappointed—that I was not her aunt."

"You are certain?"

"Yes. But it was so hard. Julie is a dear girl; I love her so much. She told me much more than I'm sure the people with her, especially my good friend Detective Rouse, would have wanted her to, but I was glad as it was all very helpful. Without meaning to, she gave us the upper hand. Whatever happens now, we can be prepared."

He sighed. "I suppose it has all worked out then. You must be very careful though, my dear. Be especially vigilant the next few days, until we know that they have left town. I will send over two extra bodyguards to keep a close eye on the place and anyone who might come by who shouldn't."

"Thank you, Angelo; you are very good to me."

"And you are invaluable to us. We will not allow anything to happen to you. And now I have business to attend to so I must go. You did a marvelous job today; I'm proud of you."

Savannah hung up the phone, grateful she had pleased the don. With him and his guards watching over her, she had nothing to fear. She filled order after order, until she realized she could barely see to measure ingredients and looked up. Outside the one-way glass that had been inserted in the sole window in the room, the sun had nearly set. She pressed the button on the phone to light up the screen. Six o'clock. Time to go in for—

A knock sounded on the door and she jumped. Who could that be? Only a very few people knew about the space she was in. Savannah checked the security camera monitor attached to the wall by the door and her heart leapt. She activated the switch. As the door opened, Dino swept into the room, picked her up, and twirled her around, planting a kiss on her lips as he lowered her to the floor.

"You were wonderful today, I hear. We couldn't have created a better test, Savannah, and you passed with flying colors. Congratulations!"

"Oh, Dino, I was so nervous when she showed up. I almost blew it."

"But you didn't. Idonna thinks you did wonderfully well. I spoke with her on my way through the house."

"Yes, yes, I think so, too, but it was close … very close."

Dino's hands still rested on her hips. A faint, masculine musk wafted from him. "What was it like, seeing her again?"

"In a funny way, it was really good. But I know I need to be careful now. Is that why you came over?"

"It is, but not the only reason. Dad sent me over to pick you up for dinner. He says your work today is worthy of a celebration."

"But Dino …"

"But Dino, nothing, you're coming with me. When Dad gives me an order I do it. So wash your hands and let's go."

"Look at me." Savannah glanced down at the powdery residue coating her jeans and blouse. "I must change clothes."

"Yes, you must." He leaned in and kissed her again, a slow, lingering kiss that weakened her knees. "And put on your fanciest gown. Tonight we dine in style."

51

Julie shoved the cobwebs aside, eventually opening one eye. Sun streamed into the motor home but she didn't feel any better than she had when she went to sleep the night before. So soundly had she slept that she didn't hear her friends come in from their night out. In addition to the queasiness that gripped her, she was badly unsettled. She was certain that there was something she had overlooked in her conversation with Savannah and Idonna, something left unsaid, some clue that remained unexplored. Nonetheless she was awake now and it didn't seem that more sleep was an option. She crept quietly from her comfortable bed and slipped into her robe, taking care not to wake her friends.

She moved noiselessly to the kitchen, filled the coffeepot with fresh water and grounds, then activated the machine, which softly sputtered and gurgled as it began to produce the liquid needed to fully awaken her.

She took a cup and slipped outside to the picnic table. Sitting at the table, chin in her hands, she was lost in thought when a soft touch on her shoulder startled her. "Penny for your thoughts." When she turned she saw Peggy, mug in one hand, her face soft with concern.

"How long ...?"

"I just came out." Peggy slid onto the bench across from her and rested a hand on Julie's arm. "How are you? You know, Julie, I'm troubled by yesterday, because I'm not sure you were sick at all. I think you were just trying to get away from us."

Julie began to protest, then thought better of it, and looked her friend in the eye. "Peggy, you know me so well. Don't be upset with me, but I've felt ever since we began this trip that there is something I have left undone.

Yesterday, I felt the strongest urge to try and get rid of that feeling. It's not a terrible feeling, really, just very unsettling, as if something is within reach but just out of my grasp. Do you know what I mean?"

"Not really. But I do know you haven't been yourself. I haven't given it much thought, just assumed the presence of JoAnne was making you tense."

"It did, at first, but JoAnne has been a dear. When we rode together that day, we had a long talk. She's not happy about the relationship, of course, but she knows that Al loves her and that it's over. She knows Al inside and out. I cringe when I think about the two of us trying to deceive her. I'm sure, on some level, she knew all along."

"And you're both okay with it being over?"

"No, not okay at all. But we are resigned to what is. I love Al; JoAnne knows that. She loves him, too, and has for a lot longer than I have. And now she has what she wants. Al is back and totally hers."

"Why don't you find someone else? Goodness knows, you're young enough, attractive enough, pleasant beyond belief … all traits that would land you a man in a heartbeat."

Julie wrapped her arms tightly around herself, and tucked her feet beneath her. Memories of the short time she and Peggy had been in a relationship flooded back. "You know, Peggy, I was never completely … comfortable with you and me. But our together times always felt so good, so incredible. It was like a fire that wouldn't go out. But when you and Rick got married and left, it was if a chapter of a book had ended. Do you know that I mean?"

Peggy inched forward on the bench. "I think so. It was kind of like that for me, too, in a way. And now you're reading another book, right? And you need to turn the page to find out what happens next?"

Julie studied her friend. "Yes, exactly. There's something there; it's on the next page, I sense it. And I do have to turn the page."

"And that means you need to continue whatever it was you started yesterday, right?"

Julie nodded.

Peggy covered Julie's hand with hers. "So let me help you. Let's just say you're still not feeling well. I'll get the girls out of here for more sightseeing and you go and do whatever it is you have to do. I'm sure I can keep us away all day."

"When will the guys be back?"

"In time for dinner. Rick texted me. Apparently they're winning and having a hard time getting Charlie away from the buffets in Biloxi."

As they giggled quietly, Peggy leaned closer. "But, Julie, the deal is you have to tell me what you're up to and how it goes."

"I will." She turned her hand over and squeezed Peggy's. "Thank you. I really do need today."

The door of the motor home flew open and Kelly emerged, stopping on the step when she saw them. "Hey, Julie, how're you feeling?"

Peggy let go of Julie's hand. "She's still ill. She's got some kind of a bug, I think. I took her temp a few minutes ago and it was just over 100, not distressing, but not right, either. I think another day in bed will do her good."

Kelly tilted her head. "I'm sorry to hear that. So a quiet day for us, then, right?'

"Actually not. How much rest do you think Julie will get if we're here? Sleep would be best for her. So let's go and explore some more—without Bruno this time—and hopefully Julie will feel up to joining us for dinner when the guys get home this evening."

"Sounds like a plan. JoAnne was up when I came out. I'll go and move her along."

"Great idea," said Peggy. "It's warm here in the sun. I'll stay with Julie until you're ready. Then it will just take me a few minutes."

When the door opened again, Peggy leaned close to Julie and lowered her voice. "I'll make sure we don't come back before four."

"Okay. Thank you."

"Good luck."

Julie offered her friend a small smile as Peggy stood up. JoAnne came over and rested a hand on her shoulder. "Will you be okay here alone?"

The thought of deceiving JoAnne—again—sent her stomach roiling, but Julie forced herself to meet JoAnne's eyes. "I'll be fine. A few hours of sleep and I'm sure I'll be good as new."

"All right then. See you this afternoon." JoAnne patted her shoulder and the three women headed for the cab that had pulled up to their site.

Julie thought about the day for several minutes, devising a rough plan, then got up and went into the motor home for a shower. Twenty minutes later she was dressed and had called her own cab for a lift to Savannah Harlowe's house.

When the cab stopped at the Harlowe driveway, Julie again saw her new friend tending to the plants along the driveway, inside the gate. After paying the driver, she turned and saw Savannah waiting for her, the gate now open.

"It's good to see you. I had a feeling you'd be by, so I gave Idonna the day off, thinking we could have a quiet chat."

The two women embraced then Savannah led Julie inside, poured tea for both of them, and brought a plate of cookies to the table, where they sat in the sun-dappled kitchen.

When Savannah had grabbed a cookie, Julie said, "I left here yesterday unsettled. I believe there were things that weren't said that should have been. I just felt that I knew you better than the circumstances suggested. Do you know what I mean?"

"I do, dear; it's so good to see you and have a real chance to talk."

"Why do I feel as if I know you?"

Savannah studied her in silence for a moment.

Julie held her breath. What was it about this woman that drew her so strongly? Would Savannah tell her?

The older woman nodded, as though she'd waged a battle with herself and come to a decision. She tucked a strand of auburn hair behind her ear. When she spoke, the French accent was gone. "Because you do. And I think you know that."

"It sure feels that way. But you don't look like anyone I know."

"Plastic surgery is a wonderful tool, child. And for the most part, I have a new everything, except for my heart and soul, that is."

Julie contemplated her a moment. Could it be? Her heart thudded so hard against her ribs she was sure Savannah must be able to hear it. The older woman touched her middle finger to her thumb and held it up for Julie to see.

Julie drew in a sharp breath. "Genevieve? Is it really you?"

"You know it is, dear. Thanks to my good friends, I look nothing like my former self. I had a full-body array of plastic surgeries. There are no scars, but the same heart beats beneath my skin; I have the same feelings. And it is so very good to see you."

She rose, went to the younger woman, and pulled her to her feet before wrapping her arms around her. The two women embraced for a long time. When Julie's trembling legs refused to hold her up any longer, she let go of her aunt and sat down.

"My goodness, Genevieve, there is nothing left of you that once was. Nothing! You are thirty years younger, from head to toe."

"It's true, I appear totally different. But that is thanks to skilled surgeons and the great gift of money from the Carbones. I feel somewhat free of the past, but I could never be free from you. I managed to keep my secret from you yesterday, but as soon as I saw you today I knew I couldn't do it any longer. I've longed to see you, Julie, and to hear about your life and about Brody, sweet, sweet Brody. He's a man now, isn't he?"

For the next two hours, the women caught up on the years that had passed while they'd been apart. Many tears dropped onto the table and there were smiles and laughter, too. Julie talked about herself, her career, Brody and his successes.

"It is how I knew it would be. There is a measure of greatness about you that is plainly visible to everyone but you. And your son has it, too."

"I don't feel great, although I believe Brody is. But I still have so many questions, Genevieve. Like why did you tell Al and Charlie that you were the killer? Why would you do that for me?"

Her aunt's forehead wrinkled. "Do what? Do you think somehow that I took the rap for you? If you do, you're silly. I did most of those killings, Julie, almost all of them."

"But … but I was the killer. I know I killed those men."

"Child, you're hallucinating, pure and simple. You may have wanted to kill them, but it was I who had the knowledge, the means, and the skills. I got a perverse kick out of watching them disappear in the water."

Julie blinked rapidly. The past seemed shrouded in mist, as though someone had thrown a veil over it. Somehow the details of the killings wouldn't come to her. All she could conjure up in her mind were shadows, no clear images.

Savannah glanced at the clock on the wall. "Oh my dear, it's one-thirty. You must be starving. Idonna left us lunch." She stood and went over to the refrigerator, extracted two large bowls filled with scrumptious-looking shrimp salads, then opened the cupboard and took out a basket of rolls. She set everything on the table and went back for a pitcher of pink lemonade.

"Idonna did all of this?"

"She did. But I asked her to. I had a feeling you would be by."

"I guess you know me well. Because I had no idea when I woke up that I would be here."

"Oh, I think you did."

"I was restless, as if something was missing. It was weird." She rubbed the side of her hand across her forehead. "Now that feeling's gone and I'm just totally confused. My head is so messed up, I can't think straight."

"That's understandable, Julie." The older woman's voice was as soothing as satin. "We've talked about many deep subjects. It's natural to be confused."

"There's still so much I want to ask you, but I need to leave soon. I don't want the others to know that I've been with you. I think that would be harmful—to you."

"It would be. I quite like my new life; I'm having a great time. I never thought I could or would be this happy. I would not like it to end just yet. There are so many things I'd like to do, now that I have the means."

As Julie ate, her aunt shared with her the details of her new life. Time flew by, and before she knew it, it was after three. Julie piled up their dishes and carried them to the sink. "I must go. And this time I can't come back. We'll be leaving New Orleans soon, and I don't want to put you in any danger, so this needs to be the last time I see you." The words caught in her throat but she pushed back her shoulders.

Savannah came over and took her into her arms. "Oh, child, I will always be available for you. I'll give you a cell number that you can call when you need to talk to me. Please, though, for both our sakes, don't use it just to say hello. I can be of much greater use to you if we keep our distance. There are some things you don't know, things that will benefit you and Brody if I'm not in prison. So, please," she stepped back and reached for both of Julie's hands, "please keep my secret."

"You know I will." Julie squeezed her hands and let her go. Savannah pulled open a drawer and drew out a pen and notepad. She wrote down a number, tore the top sheet off the pad, and held it out to Julie.

Julie took it, then picked her bag up off the counter and tucked the paper into a side pocket. "It's comforting to know that you'll be there if I call. Don't worry, I will protect you."

Which means betraying Al. A pang shot through her chest, but at the moment, she couldn't bring herself to care. *Savannah is blood and I have few relatives, let alone any willing to help me.*

They walked together toward the street. Savannah opened the gate as the two women waited for the cab to arrive. When it did, Julie embraced her aunt and slid into the back seat of the cab. She turned to watch Savannah out of the back window until the distance and her tears made seeing her relative impossible.

52

The motor home, when Julie arrived back at the precinct, was dark and lonely, adding to the sense of melancholy that had draped itself over her on the way back from her visit with Savannah. She had just walked out on a true friend—an aunt—and she was despondent over the loss.

She fell onto the bed. Chilly, she grabbed a blanket, pulled it over her and soon was asleep.

At five-thirty, Peggy, Kelly, and JoAnne returned, happy to report they had a great trip and anxious to check on Julie, who assured them she was feeling better. They were bubbling, because they had returned to Coulis for an afternoon snack and bumped into Angelo.

Peggy was excited to relate all the details. "He talked a lot about Savannah and how good it was for him to find her. Apparently Savannah has been a great help to him in his business."

If they only knew. Julie picked at a piece of lint on the sleeve of her blouse. *I have to make sure to guard Savannah's secret, which means the less I mention her, the better.*

No sooner had Julie gotten up, changed into a dress, and fixed her hair, than the men arrived back from their trip to Biloxi. Charlie was filled with stories about the great food he had consumed, Rick was happy that he had done "much better than break even" at the blackjack table, and Al was quiet and reflective.

Al had never recovered from Genevieve's escape in Wisconsin, and Julie felt as if she would not know the real Al until something happened to put the woman back in custody. And that left her dejected, too.

She tried to engage him in conversation, but finally gave up when the look on his face—especially the sadness in his eyes—threatened to break her heart.

The men, more serious than the women had expected to see them, suggested a good dinner that night, and they all headed to Mulate's Cajun Restaurant.

"We have things we want to tell you," Al blurted out as soon as they had all settled around a large, round table in the corner of the restaurant. "We've had lots of time to talk while we've been away and we have an idea we'd like to propose."

"Propose?" JoAnne tilted her head.

Al smiled at her warmly. "We've had a great vacation, right? We've had some time away, and hopefully you've had a chance to do whatever it is that you have wanted to do over the past two days." He ran his hand through his hair.

JoAnne touched Al's knee. "What are you trying to say, Al?"

Al looked at Rick, then Charlie. Both nodded. Propping an elbow on the table, Al took a deep breath. "We want to stay."

"Stay?" Julie's eyes widened. "It's Wednesday. I have to be back at work Monday."

"I know you do, but to be honest, three of us came hoping to solve a mystery. We don't know much more now than we did when we left La Crosse. Thanks to Julie, we do know there is a slight chance at least that Savannah Harlowe could be Genevieve Wangen. Since we're here, we feel we need to at least look into that, see if we can prove it either way, before we leave town."

Julie's fists clenched under the table. "And how do you propose to do that?"

Al studied her a moment, as if he detected something in her voice he couldn't quite identify. Julie forced herself to meet his gaze steadily. *He knows me too well.* Al pursed his lips. "Other than getting her fingerprints, which would be tricky, there's really only one way. If we can grab something that will get us her DNA, we'll soon know exactly who she is."

Kelly unwrapped the napkin from around her silverware. "I understand that, Al, but as Julie said, some of us need to get back to work, And

Charlie ..." she elbowed her husband in the ribs, "... your ex-wife is dropping your kids off on the weekend, remember?"

Charlie grimaced. "Believe me, I know. We're not suggesting we all stay, just Al, Rick, and me. And only for a week or so. But if you want me home, I understand that. I can leave the two of them to it."

In spite of her inner turmoil, Julie almost laughed at the reluctance in his voice. Clearly it would just about kill Charlie to leave his buddies and a big, juicy case to go home to his ex-wife and kids. He must love Kelly an awful lot to even suggest such a thing. Her chest squeezed. Would anyone ever love her that much? Enough to give up everything else for?

JoAnne frowned. "But you all have jobs too. What about that?"

Al set down his glass of water. "We talked to the chief and the sheriff and they understand. They know how important it is that we solve this case. They'll go along with another week."

"And I talked to Adolph at Gundersen, and he'll give me the time, too," said Rick.

"So you talked to your boss before you talked to me." Peggy planted one hand on her hip.

"Yeah, I guess I did. I'm sorry." Rick slid an arm around her shoulder and drew her close.

Peggy blew out a breath. "And you also know a little sugar always gets you your way."

Rick grinned and kissed the top of her head.

"Oh, Al, you big goof," said JoAnne, taking his hand. "Do you think we're oblivious to how much this case eats at you? Do you think we don't want you to get Genevieve? We'd love for us all to go home together, but we're not going to stand in the way of you trying to end this thing. I just pray you get it done."

She rested a hand on Julie's arm as she spoke. Julie was touched. *She knows how torn I am about all this.* Tears pricked her eyes but she blinked them back.

Charlie sat with his head hanging down, his ears red.

"Oh for God's sake, Charlie Berzinski, look at me." Kelly punched his shoulder. When he looked up, she said, "Honey, it would be nice to have you there as I try and take care of your kids, but I think I can do just fine—as long as I have the credit card. And if you want to run around New Orleans looking for a killer, who am I to say no? After all, that is your job."

"Great." Al smacked a hand on the table. "Then it's settled. We knew you'd understand. Eventually." He winked at JoAnne.

Julie watched the two of them together. It still hurt, a lot, but it was right. She repressed a sigh. Part of her wanted to stay and see what happened with her aunt. Whether she'd help Al or protect Genevieve though, she had no idea. Probably best if she left and let whatever was going to happen, happen.

She shot one more glance at Al and JoAnne. Like pretty much everything else in her life, the decision was out of her hands.

53

Before six the next morning, the women were ready to depart. Rick went over the route with Peggy, who was at the wheel. Al lounged against the other side of the Navigator, his arms resting on the roof as he talked to JoAnne, who was in the backseat, and Julie, riding shotgun.

"I have a strong feeling we're close. I can't believe we haven't nailed this down yet, to be honest."

"I know; I'm so sorry it hasn't quite worked out the way you'd wanted it to." Julie clutched her bag to her chest. *Because I haven't been honest about who Savannah really is.*

"What will you do now?"

"We have some ideas." Al pushed himself away from the car as Peggy started the engine. "I think we'll go with a two-pronged approach and see what happens."

What does a two-pronged approach mean? Will they find her?

"Well, good luck. I hope you make progress." Julie's throat was so tight she had to push out the words. Once again, Al studied her, his eyebrows drawn together, but he didn't speak.

As Peggy shifted the SUV into gear and they began to move, Al touched both Julie's and JoAnne's outstretched arms, then Julie, JoAnne, and Kelly waved good-bye, craning to look behind them until the Navigator made the turn onto Magazine Street and the men disappeared.

Julie slumped back against her seat. Whatever happened now, it was out of her hands.

Al straightened the sleeves on his shirt. "That went smoothly." Rick and Charlie nodded in agreement. "How about we get cleaned up, grab a bite to eat, and get on with it?"

"Sounds good." Charlie rubbed both hands together, always excited at the prospect of a meal.

A half hour later, a rental car, a Toyota Camry, had been delivered and the men were ready to launch their plan.

With Rick driving, Al beside him, and Charlie in the backseat pleading for "air conditioning, please," Al began to tick off the steps they had decided on the night before.

"First, we need to either call or stop by and see Aaron, let him know we're hanging around. It's the right thing to do and he may have some good ideas. Besides, we might need his help, or a place to work. After that, we need to get back in touch with the chief and the sheriff."

"Why don't we stop by and see Aaron." Charlie mopped his forehead with a handkerchief. "Maybe he'll have breakfast with us?"

"Good idea." Rick turned at the next lights and headed for Aaron's office.

Half an hour later, the four of them had gathered around a table at a small café near police headquarters. Aaron lifted his cup of coffee in Al's direction. "I'll help any way I can. Although you might be able to poke into places that are off limits to me. The Carbones are pillars of the community here, and a long time ago we agreed that as long as they don't stray too far off the agreed-upon path, we stay clear of them."

"Understood." Al spread jam on a piece of toast. "Other than attempting to get a DNA sample from Savannah Harlowe, any thoughts on other leads we could follow?"

Aaron nodded. "I've been thinking about that. What about contacting the French authorities? You could ask them to look into the claim that Savannah Harlowe was born there, see if that story holds up."

"Excellent idea." Al waved his knife, his heart rate picking up. "I doubt even the Carbones will have the money or the reach to change the records in another country. If there is no such person as Savannah Harlowe, we'll know she's not who she is pretending to be. I'll call the chief when we leave here and ask him if he can get on that."

"Sounds good." Aaron drained the last of his coffee and set down his mug. "And now I need to get back to work. Keep me informed of your progress, okay?" He shook hands with all three men before tossing a ten on the table and disappearing out the door.

"We should head out too, guys." Now that they had a plan, Al was anxious to get going. Charlie and Rick swallowed the last few bites of their breakfast and the three of them paid and left the restaurant. As soon as Rick started driving, Al pulled out his cell phone. "Might as well call the chief right away. His morning news meeting should be over by now."

He dialed and waited for the familiar greeting from his boss.

"Mornin,' Chief. We just had breakfast with Aaron. He suggested we contact the French authorities and ask them to look into Savannah Harlowe's background, see if it checks out. Can you contact them for us? In the meantime, we're gonna move ahead down here to try and get a sample of Savannah's DNA."

The chief promised to call the Madison FBI to see if they would get in touch with the French authorities on their behalf, and Al ended the call. He tucked the phone back into its pouch. "Why don't we drive past Savannah's house and see if an opportunity to interact with her presents itself. One way or another, we have to figure out a way to get our hands on something that will provide us with a sample of her DNA."

54

When they reached Audubon Place, Rick slowed the vehicle a little so they could get a good look at the handsome single-story brick home. Al's heart thudded in his chest. *This is it. The moment I've been waiting for since Genevieve Wangen took off three years ago.*

Without warning, Charlie shoved an arm between the two front seats, nearly taking off Al's ear as he pointed out the front window. "There she is. Goddamn, there she is."

Rick drove on for a few blocks, then turned and eventually reversed direction so he could pass the house again, this time nearer than before. As Charlie had earlier pointed out, Savannah, looking much younger than their quarry, Genevieve, knelt at the edge of the driveway, weeding.

"Goddamn great, right?" offered Charlie. "She's home. Right where we want 'er."

Al stared at the woman. Some of the enthusiasm that had been pushing him to get going with their search dissipated. *There's no way that woman is the same one that poisoned me. Is there?* "Based on what I see," said Al, "that's a far cry from the woman we're lookin' for. She's about thirty years younger than Genevieve. If that's her, some doc did a magical job, that's for sure."

"That's not impossible." Rick took a hand from the steering wheel to tap Al on the shoulder with his fist. "It's not that hard to take quite a few years off. Plastic surgery has come a long way."

"But it's not just her face." Al shook his head. "It's the whole damn package."

"A nip here, a tuck there, a little autogenous material somewhere else."

Rick tapped him again before returning his hand to the wheel. "The results can be stunning. I wouldn't rule it out, especially if she had a good specialist. And you know the Carbones wouldn't take her to anyone but the best."

Charlie rested both hands on the window ledge and peered out, like a dog. "It's that easy? And what the hell is auto-genius material, anyway?"

Rick chuckled. "Charlie, a good plastic surgeon is an artist. The training isn't easy, it's rigorous, another five years after med school. And as for the material, it's pronounced auto-jenus, which is a fancy way of saying taking material from one part of your body and using it in another."

"Wow! What if you went in and they put a leg where an arm should be?"

Al snorted as Rick looked back over the seat at Charlie. "It's not like that at all. They don't move limbs around. Much of what is used is fatty tissue. It's a lot safer than using synthetic material, because if it comes from your own body, it's less likely to cause infections."

Charlie pursed his lips. "Makes sense, I guess. Ya gotta be pretty talented to be a plastic surgeon, right?"

"Absolutely. And it's not all working on faces and boobs, either. There are lots of areas of the body that plastic surgery can help or improve."

They'd driven past the house so Al turned from the window to face his friend. "The central question remains: can it take thirty years off a person?"

"I think it could, Al," said Rick. "A first-class plastic surgeon can do unbelievable things."

Some of the tension left Al's shoulders. "Good. I'd hate to waste money on a wild goose chase."

"We can't know for sure if she's our girl though until we have her DNA, right?" Rick pulled the Camry over to the curb and put it in park. "How do you propose we go about doing that?"

"Well, we can't all go." Al tapped the dashboard. "I think Charlie has the best chance of getting close to her. She'd recognize me in a minute. And we gotta figure out a way to get her to open the gate."

As they talked about how to get Charlie close enough to the woman to grab something to get them what they wanted, a large man came by, whistling as he walked a dog on a leash.

"Look at that, will you?" Rick leaned forward, pushing against Al to get a better look. "That's a Soft-Coated Wheaten Terrier. Never thought I'd see one of those down here."

"Gives me an idea." Al grabbed the door handle and climbed out of the car. As Rick and Charlie watched, he hurried over to the whistler, pulled something out of his pocket and showed it to the man, then shook his hand. The two talked briefly as they walked back to the car, the dog in tow.

"This is Henri Archimbeault and you're right, Rick, it is a Soft-Coated Wheaten Terrier. I showed Henri my badge and asked him if we could borrow the dog for a minute or two and he agreed. Charlie, meet Beauregard."

"It means handsome." Henri leaned over to shake hands with Rick and Charlie.

"Charlie, you walk Beauregard past the Harlowe house. See if you can figure out a way to attract Savannah's attention. Henri will ride with us. We'll wait for you up the block."

"Beauregard, you be good." Henri handed the leash to a surprised-looking Charlie before replacing him in the backseat.

Charlie knelt and petted the dog, talking to him softly. When he straightened, he turned to the occupants of the car and said, "Wish me luck." He guided Beauregard back to the sidewalk. Rick drove past the house and parked just around the next corner, where they could still see what was happening. Al cracked his window open to try and hear what Charlie and Savannah said to each other.

Charlie and Beauregard walked along, looking for all the world as though they belonged to each other and were enjoying this gorgeous day.

The two stopped when the gate to Savannah's house opened and she hurried out and crouched down to pet the dog. As the men in the car watched, Charlie reached out and slapped the woman on the shoulder.

Al's eyes widened as he watched his friend in the visor mirror. What did Charlie go and do that for? If any security guards were watching, they'd be swarming through the gate any moment. He held his breath, but no armed men appeared, although as Savannah straightened up, she did hold up a hand as if to stop someone approaching from deeper inside the property.

"What did you do that—" She cocked her head and smiled. "Do I know you?"

"No ma'am, but you may have seen me at the Derby in Louisville. A group of friends and I sat near your table."

"Oui, I remember … nice ladies. But what are you doing here?"

"At the moment, just taking a friend's dog for a walk, Savannah. It is Savannah, isn't it?"

"Oui, Savannah. And you are?"

"Charlie Berzinski, ma'am."

"Hello, Charlie Berzinski."

"Hello, ma'am. And to complete the answer to your question, I am vacationing here and visiting a friend who pointed out where you lived, so I offered to take his dog for a walk. I wanted to see your house, since everyone at the Derby seemed to be talking about you and your friends. And when you came out, I saw a bee on your shoulder and I didn't want you to get stung."

"Bees are my friends, Charlie, but as long as you only pushed it away, is good."

"Yes, ma'am. Well, my friend and I better get back to walking. You have a good day now."

"And you, too, Sharlee."

Charlie tightened the leash, spoke to Beauregard, and strode casually back to the car.

Once Savannah had disappeared back through her gate, Al frowned. "What was that all about?"

"Gimme a minute to get Beauregard here back to his master and wipe my brow, will you, it's damn hot out here. Then I'll tell you."

Charlie handed the leash to Henri, knelt and petted the dog, straightened and thanked Henri, then tugged a handkerchief from his pocket and swiped it across his forehead. The man and his dog disappeared down the sidewalk and around the next corner as Charlie climbed back into the car.

"Charlie, for god's sake, you nearly knocked her down."

"I had to Al. She had something I wanted."

"Something you wanted?"

"Yes. Rick. Why don't we get going? I can explain as we drive."

Rick shifted into gear and pulled away from the curb. Charlie leaned across the front seat to talk to his companions. "Henri inspired me. When

I went past the house, I was whistling loud enough for Savannah to hear. And she did just what I hoped. Saw Beauregard, opened the gate, and rushed out to pet him."

"And you hit her."

"No, I swatted a bee off her shoulder, or at least that's what I told her."

"Did you see any security guards? I thought they might come running when you attacked her."

Charlie threw him a disgusted look. "I didn't *attack* her; I just brushed her shoulder. And yes, I saw at least four armed guards start toward us, but she waved them off."

Al shook his head. "What was it she had that you wanted?"

"These." Charlie opened his hand to reveal three long, auburn hairs. "You wanted a DNA sample Detective Rouse? Here's your DNA sample."

Al almost hollered for joy. Grinning widely, he glanced over at Rick. "I had no idea Charlie was such a good liar, you?"

Rick shrugged. "Personally, I've always found him a little too honest, if anything,"

"Charlie, I just plain underestimated you," admitted Al. "Once again, you have completely amazed me. I'm not sure what I can do to make it even."

"Well, Al, a few of those bengays would be perfect. And sooner than later."

"Damn right," said Al, "you sure as hell have earned them. Rick, head for Aaron's office and then we'll get Charlie a dozen beignets."

A half hour later, the hairs safely delivered to Aaron, who promised to take them straight to the DNA lab himself, Charlie munched away at his beignets. Rick was about to pull away from the parking lot near the place they had bought the doughnuts when Al's phone chirped. Rick put the car back in park as Al answered.

"Hi, Chief, what's up?"

"Al, I spoke to a friend of mine over at the Madison FBI. They're willing to contact the French authorities on our behalf, but they need you to fill out a report so they have all the information they need. I emailed the report to you."

"That's great, Chief. Charlie and Rick and I will get on that right away and return that to you ASAP."

Al disconnected the call. "Let's head back to the motor home. I'll call Aaron and see if we can get pick up the Wi-Fi from the police station. I can fill out that report on my laptop."

A minute later he had called Aaron and gotten the New Orleans P.D.'s Wi-Fi password and the trio was headed for their home away from home.

As Al got the laptop ready and got on line, he suddenly remembered the article in *The Times Picayune* and looked it up. He included every detail he could find in the paper about Honey and Hiram Harlowe, Rayford Carbone, and Honey's daughter Savannah. Rick and Charlie read the report over his shoulder, suggested a couple of other details he could include, and in less than ten minutes he'd sent the report off to the chief.

Chief Whigg called him a few minutes later to thank him for the work, tell him he thought it was first rate, and say that it was on its way to Madison.

Al sank back against the upholstered bench at the kitchen table. There was nothing more they could do now until the results came back from the French authorities and from the DNA lab.

He sighed and rubbed the side of his hand across his forehead. *Now, once again, we wait.*

55

The chief called at nine the next morning.

The three men were sitting in the kitchen in the motor home, so Al put the phone on speaker and set it in the middle of the table.

"You oughta see this thing." The chief's voice boomed through the phone. "Don't know how they do it, but this express delivery even has a gold seal on it. Imagine you want me to open it up and see what it says."

"Damn right," said Al.

"It's from the General Directorate for External Security of France," said the chief. "Pretty damn official looking."

They heard the tearing of paper. Then the chief said, "Thank God, it's in English." Next came a shrill whistle.

"We got us a live one," said the chief. "Here's what it says: *Honey Harlowe in Bordeaux reported no knowledge of any Savannah Harlowe. The investigators who made the visit to Mrs. Harlowe report she appeared confused when they asked if she had a daughter by the name of Savannah. Mrs. Harlowe stated twice for the record that there is no such person. Mrs. Harlowe and Mr. Harlowe had no children, after marrying later in life. Mrs. Harlowe also stated that she was romantically involved very briefly with a Rayford Carbone, but insists no children were born to them.*"

Al's hands trembled. There it was, no such person. *Why didn't we start with that step first? He mentally kicked himself.*

Charlie let out a whoop.

Al held up a hand. "It's good news, but a little early to celebrate. Let's not go overboard."

"Wait a minute," the chief's voice echoed through the trailer, "there's another sheet of paper here. Let me see what it says. *Transcript of interview with Mrs. Honey Harlowe forwarded by voice mail to phone of Detective Allan Rouse*. Holy crap, let me go take a look at your phone. I'll call you in a sec."

They waited, all three of them staring at the phone, for ten seemingly unending minutes. When Al's phone rang, three sets of hands reached for it. Al got there first.

"What have you got, Chief?"

"Sorry, goddamn phone system," swore the chief. "I had no damn idea about how to get you on the phone at the same time I played the recording. Had to get the damn IT guy. He asked me why I just didn't call you on my cell and play the recording for you. Christ, what a dummy …"

"Chief, it's okay, can we just play the thing?" Al forced calm into his voice, although both hands had tightened into fists on the table.

"Sorry," was the Chief's meek response. "Here we go."

The men listened intently as the investigating officers, who identified themselves as Roberto LeBlanc and Étienne DuBois, began the interview with Honey Harlowe.

Are you aware that reports in the United States say that your daughter, Savannah Harlowe, has purchased a house in New Orleans?

This comes as a complete surprise to me. I have no daughter and I know no one named Savannah Harlowe.

Were you married to Rayford Carbone from Louisiana?

Rayford and I were close, close friends. Romantically involved? Yes. Married? Never.

I know that you raise racehorses here on your farm and also grow grapes, some of which have won awards. Did one of your horses run in the Kentucky Derby?

Oh yes, Grand Garçon Doux, finished second, a photo finish. He is a wonderful horse. He is here now, living his days as a stud—an ideal life for a big, strong boy, some would say.

Do you know Angelo Carbone?

I have met Angelo, yes. But he and Rayford were not friendly, so I never knew him well.

When is the last time you met with or talked to Angelo?

I had a call from him prior to the Derby. He told me he would be there and would cheer for Grand Garçon Doux. It was a short conversation in which I told him I would not be at the race, nor would my health permit me to travel, so it is unlikely I will again visit the States.

Do you have any idea how the stories of a daughter with Rayford Carbone began?

Oh goodness, no, but in France stories such as this are common, are they not? The French, they are great lovers, no? And stories about illicit romance and illegitimate children are common. Who knows, it could have started anywhere.

To sum up, Mrs. Harlowe, you have no knowledge of a woman named Savannah Harlowe and are being truthful in saying she is not your daughter?

You do not believe what I say to you? I suppose that too is very French. But the answer is, the first I have heard of this woman is from you two days ago. As I told you then, no, I do not know her, and I most certainly am not her mother. Those are truthful answers, on the soul of my dead husband. Please believe me.

Will you seek to meet this woman in order to find out more about her and the story of how you came to be listed as her mother?

Sergeant, I am an old lady, frail, not well. I am unbothered by this story, just as I have been unbothered by other untrue stories in the past. As an old lady, a little, how should I say, mystique is perhaps a good thing; it keeps the name alive.

The interview closed with thanks on both sides and with the sergeant declining a glass of Honey's award-winning 2011 Bordeaux.

When the tape expired, the lawmen sat silently for a long moment. Charlie broke the silence. "Goddamn, we got 'er. This time we got 'er!"

56

"Shit." The exclamation came from the Chief.

Al frowned. "What's the matter?"

"Well, Al, up until now this junket was on your dime. But based on what we just heard, I won't have a leg to stand on if I try to make that stick. That's the first problem. The second problem, Charlie, is that I gotta tell Dwight that he has to pay too. Do you two clowns have any idea how tight budgets are these days?"

Al looked at Charlie, who stared back at him. They wouldn't refuse to fund the rest of the investigation, would they? He couldn't afford to keep footing the bill, but they couldn't quit now, not after what they'd just heard.

The chief's laughter filled the small space. "I can see the panic on both your faces from here. Don't worry; I'm just pulling your leg. I am so goddamned proud of you two guys. You too, Rick, but I doubt I have any pull with Adolph. I'll gladly pay the bill—hell, joyfully. And, Charlie, if Dwight gives you any shit, I'll pay for you, too. But don't you dare tell him that. Hear me?"

"I don't suppose, Chief," Rick leaned forward to speak into the phone, "that since you're in a spending mood, you'd also like to pay for the motor home I bought for this trip?"

After a moment of silence, the chief's voice reverberated through the motor home. "No way. I'm proud of you guys, but not that proud."

Just as the Wisconsin trio was thinking about celebrating their good fortune, Charlie's phone rang somewhere in the back of the motor home.

He moved as fast as a big guy in a small space can move, then after a bit of silence, they heard a shout.

"Hey you guys," he called. "Aaron is on the phone. It's her; it's definitely her. Wahoo!"

Charlie brought his phone into the dinette area, plunked it on the table next to Al's and said, "We're all here now, Aaron."

"Hey, guys, good news. The lab sent me their report this morning—I'm gonna owe them something for the quick turnaround, I suppose—and it proves conclusively that the woman we know as Savannah Harlowe is also Genevieve Wangen. It's a 99 percent match. Great work."

"Thanks to Charlie." Al slapped his friend on the back. "And, Aaron, we also got the report back from France and it included an interview with Honey Harlowe. Big surprise, but she knows no one by the name of Savannah Harlowe and she has no daughter. She knows Rayford Carbone, but she says they were never married and never had kids. We can go get her now, right?"

"Damn straight. No one here can ignore the two reports, that's for sure. Why don't you guys come over as fast as you can and we'll put a plan in place to bring her in?"

"We'll be down as quick as we can shower and dress." Charlie hit the button to end the call.

The chief rang off too, saying, "Great work, all of you. Go get 'er, Al. It will be good to have this over."

Truer words were never spoken. Al leapt to his feet, propelled toward the shower by a surge of adrenaline. Today was the day. Genevieve Wangen was in their sights.

By late morning they were downtown and so anxious for action that Charlie didn't even ask about eating. They hustled into Aaron's office and found him, hands behind his head, feet on the desk and beaming.

"Hey," chided Al, "there's work to do, man; we better get busy."

The feet came off the desk, the chair squeaked and rattled as it settled into an upright position, and Aaron joined them at the table.

Al led the session. "We'll need a search warrant and an arrest warrant. Hopefully, we'll find her at her house, but you never know. The Carbones are security experts—it's likely they caught us all on video yesterday when Charlie talked to Savannah. They may also have a mole in the DNA lab who has already tipped her or Carbone off."

"I'd like to think not," said Aaron, "but it's a possibility, so we need to get on it. Maybe we can draft the reports here—I already have the one from the lab—but we'll need to cover that with why and how we got her DNA. Any problem there, you think?"

Al bit the inside of his cheek. "We better consult our chief and officials up north."

As calls were made, reports written and meetings set up, Al finally straightened up from his laptop and asked, "Can I plug this thing into your network to get some copies?"

That task taken care of, Al called Chief Whigg in La Crosse and asked that he be available for a conversation with the New Orleans police superintendent. "Aaron's working on that meeting now. We're hoping to get in by mid-afternoon and make the arrest later today."

"Got it. I'll stay by the phone until the call comes."

When Al ended the conversation, Aaron clapped him on the shoulder. "We can see the superintendent at two. And I have a magistrate lined up that we like to work with. We should have all we need by three or so this afternoon. Then we can sting 'er at dinnertime."

As they waited for the meeting with the superintendent, they talked about human resources.

"She's slippery as an eel." Al loosened his tie and rolled up his shirt sleeves. "We need to have the property surrounded or she's likely to get away. She had escape routes in houses in Georgia and Alabama so there's a good chance she has one in this place too. And when Charlie was talking to her, he saw at least four armed guards. I'd be surprised if there weren't more than that on the property."

Aaron nodded. "I'll call in the SWAT team then. We should have about twenty men there, plus the four of us. Enough?"

"I think so. We have to be careful to keep Rick in the back line since he's not an officer."

"Al, don't forget that as county coroner I am an officer of the law."

"That's right." Al popped his forehead with his palm. "Sorry, Rick."

"Doesn't mean I want to be on the front line, but it does mean I can be there without anyone worrying about me."

"Do you wanna carry?" asked Aaron. "I can take care of a permit."

"I'd be more comfortable with something like a taser. I can stay out of the way but still have something to immobilize a suspect if by chance one comes my way."

"Good idea." Aaron reached for his phone. "We'll get you one of those."

When it was time to meet with the superintendent, Rick gestured to Al's pocket. "Why don't you get Chief Whigg on your cell so he can participate in the meeting?"

Al tugged the phone out of his shirt pocket, his fingers trembling so badly he nearly dropped it. All this procedural stuff drove him crazy. Now that they knew Savannah was really Genevieve, all he wanted to do was drive over there, grab her, and toss her into a cell for the rest of her life.

The superintendent's office was on the third floor of the building. It occupied a spacious corner overlooking the French Quarter and the Mississippi River. The super looked right at home surrounded by rich mahogany wood and expanses of glass. Al gulped as the man stood to greet them. *Must be six foot five and a good 280.* He almost made Charlie look small in comparison.

"Tom Dolfing," he said, smiling and extending his hand. "Must be important if we have visitors from Wisconsin and one of our aces asking for a meeting."

"It is, Tom." Aaron indicated the row of chairs in front of the large wooden desk, and the men all took a seat. "We brought the La Crosse Chief along with us by phone."

"Hi, superintendent," said Whigg through Al's speaker phone. "Chief Brent Whigg in La Crosse. Sure wish I could be there with all of you."

"What's up, Chief Whigg?"

"Please, call me Brent. And Al and Charlie and Rick, with the help of Aaron, have carried the water on this one, so I'll let Al, our chief of detectives, give you the explanation."

Al clasped his hands together to keep them from shaking. "Superintendent Dolfing, four years ago we arrested a person in Illinois who confessed to committing fourteen murders in our community. As we were transporting this woman, Genevieve Wangen, from Chicago to La Crosse, we stopped for lunch and gas and she escaped. I was the arresting officer, so you can imagine how I felt."

Dolfing nodded. "It's happened to the best of us, so I can imagine."

"We thought we had lost her, sir," said Al, "but we picked up her trail again recently when she was reported to be traveling with Angelo Carbone's youngest son. That's what brought us here and in touch with Aaron. At first there was nothing, then one morning I picked up *The Times Picayune* and read about this new relative of Angelo Carbone's, Savannah Harlowe."

"Aha, the Frenchwoman," replied the superintendent. "Is there a link there?"

"Yes sir, there is." Al nodded emphatically. "Given the timing, we suspected she might be our killer."

The superintendent's eyebrows rose. "But she's from France and she's, what, fifty-something? You said your killer was eighty when you arrested her."

"Yes sir, I did. But there was something about her that didn't ring true, so we came to New Orleans to see for ourselves. On the way down here we stopped at Louisville for the Derby."

As the story came out, the superintendent scribbled notes on a pad of paper. "Do you have any proof that this Savannah Harlowe and Genevieve Wangen are the same person?"

"Yes sir." Al leaned forward. "Aaron suggested we ask the French authorities to do a check on Ms. Harlowe's background. They interviewed the woman Savannah claimed was her mother, and the report came in this morning. Honey Harlowe insisted she has no daughter and has never heard of a Savanna Harlowe. According to French records, there is no such person. Then, yesterday we stopped at Ms. Harlowe's house. Charlie spoke with her and was able to grab some strands of hair from her blouse without arousing her suspicions."

"Here's the report on the DNA samples from our lab, Tom." Aaron handed over the set of papers. "The report says there is a 99 percent match between the hairs and the woman sought for the murders in Wisconsin."

"Wow." The superintendent slumped back in his chair, closed his eyes for a moment, apparently deep in thought, then opened his eyes and said,

"You sure know how to scramble a day. The Carbones aren't going to be happy, that's certain."

Al held his breath. How willing were the police down here to look the other way when the Carbones veered outside of the law? They wouldn't stop him from going in to get Genevieve, would they?

The superintendent's next words loosened the tight muscles across Al's neck and shoulders and sent a fresh wave of adrenaline coursing through him.

"So when do we take her down?"

57

With the clock past the dinner hour, the New Orleans SWAT team, Al, Rick, Charlie, and Aaron gathered on the Tulane campus, a couple of blocks from the Harlowe house.

The group that had ridden in Aaron's car approached the SWAT vehicles and the men gathered beside them. Aaron held up his hand for quiet then introduced Al as the leader of the group from Wisconsin and the man who would, with Aaron, captain the evening's effort.

"Al is going to explain tonight's action." Aaron looked out of place next to the men in their camos with blackened faces. Al knew he must look equally like a fish out of water. He straightened to his full height. Regardless, he and Aaron were in charge, and they needed to look like it. "We are here to capture a serial killer who escaped from me—us—several years ago in Wisconsin. She is wanted for killing fourteen young men."

He scanned the faces of the men and women in front of him. As he would expect, none showed any reaction to his announcement. All appeared to be completely focused on his words, though.

"A few weeks ago we obtained a lead that led us to New Orleans and now we have indisputable evidence that the woman we will arrest tonight is our killer."

Aaron stepped forward. "We met with Superintendent Dolfing this afternoon and put together the plan. Who's the SWAT leader?"

"Here, sir." The speaker was a man of average height and weight.

"Your name?" asked Aaron.

"Hodding Carrier, sir."

"All right, Carrier, join me here. The rest of you gather around so you can see." Aaron handed Al a roll of paper. Al unrolled it to reveal a map of the area.

"This is the Harlowe house." Aaron pointed to a lot outlined in red. "We are hoping to take her by surprise, but we aren't going to take any chances. Hodding, you will deploy your people in the alley behind the house here, here, and here. We'll take three to the front to back us up.

"When you are in place, Al, Charlie, Rick, and I, along with the three people you designate, will take up position in front of the house. Al will walk to the front door and ring the bell. When someone comes to the door, we will show the warrants to search the property and arrest Ms. Harlowe.

"Our target is elusive. She escaped in Wisconsin and fled successfully from traps set for her in Georgia and Alabama. That is why we are urging you to be on your toes as the mission begins. It is now eighteen-forty. We go at nineteen hundred hours. Questions?"

Carrier raised his hand. "Sir, are we expecting to take fire?"

Aaron glanced at Al. "We're hoping not." Al rested a hand on the weapon strapped to his chest. "But we're not ruling it out. We've had visual confirmation of four armed guards on the property and there may be more. Be ready to fire, but we encourage you to shoot to wound rather than kill. Is that understood?"

"Yes sir," said Carrier. "Other than the guards, how many people might be in the house?"

"We aren't sure. We're hoping no more than five or six. We know that Ms. Harlowe has a companion, a woman, and two couples who are responsible for the house and grounds who also live on the premises. Any or all of the six of them could be armed. Ms. Harlowe is posing as a relative of Angelo Carbone, which explains the armed guards. We also can't rule out that they may have been tipped off to the fact that we could be coming after this woman."

Carrier again raised his hand. "Sir, you did say Angelo Carbone?"

Aaron nodded curtly. "Yes, he did."

Carrier lowered his hand.

Aaron asked, "Any other questions?"

Carrier offered him a salute. "No, sir. We're ready."

"We will leave here in twelve minutes." Aaron returned the salute before he and Al rejoined Rick and Charlie.

Twelve minutes later, Aaron raised his hand. "Time."

The SWAT officers were already aboard their vehicles and ready to roll. Just before the carriers headed out, Al asked for a check of comm packs. Everything checked, the two carriers left the lot. Five minutes later, they pulled into a tree-sheltered vacant lot half a block from Savannah's house. Aaron's unmarked vehicle, carrying Al, Rick, and Charlie, pulled in right behind.

The carriers were quickly unloaded. Al stopped the three who were going with them. He talked to them for a minute, then the two burly men and a woman, who Carrier had informed them was the best sharpshooter in the group, began their walk. Wingate turned back onto the street and stopped his car just beyond the house.

As they walked, one of the troopers said, "This is probably the ritziest street in town, you know that, right?"

"No, I guess I didn't." Al was not interested in chit-chat.

"Houses here start at five million."

Al held a finger to his lips then pointed out where he wanted the SWAT members. Just ahead and barely visible, he could see Charlie, Aaron, and Rick taking up their posts.

"Everyone ready?" Al's statement was barely audible, but all three SWAT team members nodded. "Okay, here we go."

Al quickly covered the space to the door and pressed the bell.

Seconds later an overhead light came on, the door opened, and an officious-looking woman scowled at him. "Yes?"

"Chief Detective Allan Rouse from the La Crosse, Wisconsin, police department." Al displayed his shield. "I have a warrant here for the arrest of Ms. Savannah Harlowe and an additional warrant for the search of these premises."

The woman jerked, and then in a loud voice said, "You have a warrant to search the house?"

She's warning everyone else. We need to move quickly. Al pulled both warrants from his pocket while the SWAT members covered the driveway along with Aaron, Charlie, and Rick.

"Is Ms. Harlowe here?"

"We have a right to an attorney during the search."

"No, ma'am, that is not your legal right under the laws of the State of Louisiana."

The woman planted both hands on her hips and scowled. "I hope you know who you are bothering here. You are in for an awful lot of trouble, because I plan to call Angelo Carbone."

"You may call anyone you want, but not while we are searching the premises. I will ask you one more time, is Ms. Harlowe home?"

She just stared at him.

After three seconds, Al pushed into the house. "Excuse me, ma'am. This way please." He inclined his head down the hallway.

Behind him, the three Swat team members and Charlie burst through the door and took off in different directions throughout the house.

"Rick, come with me." Al gave the woman beside him two seconds to cooperate. A vein throbbing in her neck, she spun on her heel and stalked down the hall. When they reached the kitchen, Al gestured toward a table in a small, glassed-in alcove. "Take a seat, please. Rick, watch her."

In less than two minutes, two members of the SWAT team had returned, escorting four more people, two men and two women, into the kitchen.

None of them was Savannah.

Aaron called for a SWAT member to guard the occupants. Al shifted into action mode. "Is there a basement in the house?"

The woman who had met him at the door hesitated then pointed to a doorway at the side of the room.

"Charlie and Aaron, look down there. You two," he pointed at the SWAT team members, "check the main floor and the upstairs again, every room, every closet, every possible hiding place. I'll wait here for everyone to report back."

The search took ten minutes but turned up no one. Aaron's phone chirped and he pulled it from the holder on his belt and glanced at the screen. "They've got six guards pinned down and disarmed. No sign of the perpetrator though."

Al frowned. *Were they ever going to get their hands on this woman?*

Aaron typed something into his phone before shoving it back into the holder. "They're loading up the guards. Officers, take these five out to the carrier. We'll take them down to the station on suspicion of aiding and abetting."

Al's eyes met his across the empty kitchen. Aaron shrugged. "We'll get her. I've ordered roadblocks to be set up; she can't get far."

Al nodded. "I'm going to check the property again." He went out the back door, followed by Charlie, Rick, and Aaron. As soon as they stepped outside, two loud reports came from the back of the property and all four dropped to the ground.

A slightly acrid smell drifted across the patio on the night breeze. "Tear gas," shouted Aaron. "They must think they have something."

They scrambled to their feet and approached the garage at the rear of the lot. Smoke roiled from what must have been a hundred places in the building.

"Looks like a water balloon filled with pin holes." Al held up a hand to stop Charlie, who'd been running toward the garage.

The building was surrounded by SWAT officers. As the four approached, the small side door opened and a woman stumbled out, gasping for air.

Heart pounding, Al leapt toward her, grasped her arm, and spun her around. "Savannah Harlowe, also known as Genevieve Wangen, you are under arrest on charges of murder, escaping custody, and being unlawfully at large." He pulled her other arm behind her back and snapped handcuffs around her wrists. Aaron read the woman her rights. The whole time he was talking, the suspect held Al's gaze, her eyes defiant, almost amused. Ten minutes later, Genevieve Wangen was handcuffed and riding between Al and Charlie in the backseat of the unmarked car.

58

When they reached police headquarters, Aaron pulled into a lot behind the building and they moved the suspect inside through a rear entrance and into a conference room.

"Ms. Harlowe," began Aaron, placing a tape recorder in the center of the large table in the room. The suspect sat alone on her side of the table, a blank wall behind her. Across the table, Aaron Wingate sat in the center, flanked by Al and Charlie, with Rick sitting beside Al. Behind them was a mirror that was actually one-way glass. Superintendent Dolfing had told them he'd be watching from the other side. Aaron fiddled with the recorder. "We will be taping this session. Do you understand?"

Just as the woman was about to answer, the door was pushed open and one of the tallest women Al had ever seen entered, demanding, "Don't say a word. Not one word."

Al blinked. The woman, whoever she was, must have stood six foot six. Her features looked as if she could be on Mount Rushmore between Lincoln and Roosevelt. Her jet-black hair was pulled severely into a bun and she wore all black. Blood-red nail polish and lipstick and dark eye shadow finished the look. Sinister and authoritative were words that came to Al's mind. The woman dominated the room as she stood there, hands on her hips, and looked each of the lawmen in the eye.

"Just what is going on here?"

Wingate arose, smiled, and said, "Gentlemen, meet attorney Sarah Broelstrom."

The woman nodded stiffly. The other three men rose. Al extended his hand. The woman ignored it and sat down beside Savannah.

"Are you all right, my dear? Did these men hurt you in any way?"

Savannah didn't speak, just shook her head.

"Okay. Now then, Savannah, dear, have these men read you your rights?" Savannah nodded.

The woman turned to the men across the table. "Which one of you read them?"

"I did." Aaron's answer was strong and clipped.

"All right then, I will assume it was done correctly. Has my client been charged?"

"That will be done tomorrow in district criminal court," replied Aaron. "She has been arrested on a warrant issued by Judge Samuel Aldoin and will be appearing in his court tomorrow morning at ten for a probable cause hearing."

"And may I ask what the charges will be?"

"At the very least, she will be charged under Louisiana's criminal impersonation statutes, but these gentlemen, depending upon her real identity, may seek extradition for more serious crimes committed in Wisconsin."

Sarah Broelstrom wrinkled her nose. "Criminal impersonation? You must be joking. Angelo Carbone assures me that Ms. Harlowe is his recently found cousin. She holds French citizenship."

Al pulled out his phone. He'd recorded the voice mail message on it as the chief played it, and he called that up now. "Ms. Broelstrom, I believe this recording will establish basis for the charge. It won't take but a few minutes."

His gaze settled on Savannah. "Ms. Harlowe, Ms. Broelstrom, this recording was taken two days ago in France, by police there acting on a request from La Crosse authorities. The proper authentications for the interview are in the possession of Judge Aldoin."

He pressed play.

As she listened to the recording, Savannah's eyes initially flashed fire that was extinguished as the interview went on.

When the recording finished, Al returned the phone to his pocket. "So you see, ma'am, it would appear that your client does, indeed, have an identity problem."

Savannah looked Al in the eye, smiled wryly, and said, "Yes, it would appear that way."

"Savannah, be quiet," snapped the attorney. "So she will be held here overnight?"

"She will be taken from here to Orleans Parish Jail," said Wingate, "and held in the women's lockup until she goes before the judge tomorrow."

"That hellhole. I trust you will make special arrangements for her safety."

"She will be safe," said Wingate.

"And I will have access to her there?"

"Of course."

"Then I insist she be moved now."

Al repressed a sigh. They'd been so close to being able to question Genevieve. They had to follow the law rigidly, however. The last thing he wanted was for Genevieve Wangen to get off on a procedural technicality.

59

An hour later, the four police officers, having turned Savannah over to be transported to the Parish jail, gathered in front of police headquarters.

Al looked at Aaron, a deep frown marring his face. "Do you have to deal with that woman often?"

"Very. She is the favorite attorney of those in New Orleans with one foot over the line—or sometimes both feet. She's something, isn't she?"

"Monstrous," offered Charlie. "In size and attitude."

"You don't want to mess with her, that's for sure." Aaron leaned against the brick wall of the building. "Let me bring you up to date on the search of Savannah Harlowe's home."

As they stood there, a gentle breeze stirred the leaves of two giant Magnolia trees across the street. The movement did little to alleviate the thick humidity hanging in the air.

"Two of our best detectives searched 28 Audubon Place. A number of items were seized. Of particular interest were DNA specimens taken from the woman's bathroom, most notably a hair brush. In case there is any question as to the methods by which the initial DNA samples were obtained, we'll run a second set of tests with items taken during a legal search of the home. We should also be able to get some good fingerprints off the brush to compare to the set taken the last time she was arrested. All were sent to the New Orleans lab for prompt processing.

"Also of interest was a state-of-the-art laboratory that appears to have been recently constructed in the coach house. It was extremely well equipped with chemicals and equipment. Dr. Olson, we're hoping you will visit the lab tomorrow. We are particularly interested in finding out if Genevieve Wangen used it to manufacture and compound drugs that could cause unconsciousness and death."

Blood pounded in Al's ears. "If so, that should provide concrete proof that Genevieve had access to the drugs that killed our victims in La Crosse."

"I should think so." Aaron pulled a handkerchief from his pocket and wiped his forehead. "I expect that we will get the first reports on the samples tomorrow. The superintendent told the folks in the lab to drop everything and concentrate on items from the search."

"I guess there's nothing more we can do today then." A trickle of sweat made its way down the back of Al's neck.

"I can't think of anything else until the court appearance tomorrow."

"In that case, I called Chief Whigg earlier to fill him in on everything that has happened, and he ordered the four of us to go to dinner at Brennan's. His specific words were, 'You are to spare no expense, Al.' So whadda ya say?"

Charlie clapped his meaty hands together. "Hooray. I'm hungry enough to eat a horse. Oops, that's a no-no, isn't it?"

"We do like our horses down here, Charlie, but I don't think anyone who heard you would have a problem with what you said."

At that exact moment, a handsome carriage pulled by a well-groomed horse rattled down the brick street. The horse neighed as it passed.

Charlie flushed. "No offence intended, Mr. Horse." He glanced at Al. "What the hell are we waiting for?"

The celebration was somewhat reserved, but the meal was wonderful, the service extraordinary, and all four ate well. After the first round of drinks, Al lifted a hand. "A second round is fine, but that will be it. Court tomorrow."

While Charlie restrained himself on alcohol, when eating he indulged himself in a manner befitting a world-class gourmand. In fact, Al, Rick, and Aaron finished a full forty-five minutes before him.

After Al paid the bill, he staggered out to meet the other three, feigning the weight of the payment. In greeting, Charlie let out a belch, rubbed his stomach, and began to walk toward police headquarters. "Hurry up, you guys, a brisk walk will be good after all we ate."

Rick shook his head. "After all *who* ate?"

Charlie waved a dismissive hand. "Everyone ate high on the hog. A little exercise will do us good." And he was off again, his head swiveling as he passed sights typical for the French Quarter but rarely seen in La Crosse.

"Hey, Aaron, where are those beads they wear down here? You know the kind …"

"I do know the kind. We save those for Mardi Gras, Charlie, so you're either six months early or six months late.

Aaron left them at the station and Al, Rick, and Charlie headed back to the motor home. Although Al could barely keep his eyes open while they were driving, by the time he got into bed, his mind whirled so chaotically he couldn't sleep. For several hours he stared up at the curved white ceiling of the trailer. *What will tomorrow bring? Would the Carbones' high-priced lawyer somehow be able to get Genevieve off or would she finally be brought to justice?*

Exhaling loudly, he turned onto his side and punched his pillow to fluff it up. Whatever happened, it was sure to be interesting.

60

Savannah glanced at her watch and her eyes widened. Nine-thirty already. She sighed loudly. Her cell was a brick six-by-eight box with a concrete floor riddled with cracks and stains that looked like dried blood. The spartan accommodations consisted of a cot hung from the wall with brackets and a chair bolted to the floor with a metal night stand beside it that held a lamp. A toilet and a metal basin, beneath faucets labeled hot and cold, were tucked into the corner.

This isn't how I envisioned spending today. I wonder if the Carbones are worried about me and willing to do something about all this.

As she sat on the chair fretting, her late dinner arrived, although calling it that was more than generous. She would dine that evening on an overcooked piece of beef filled with gristle, two boiled potatoes, a couple of spoonfuls of peas, a small pat of butter, and salt and pepper in paper containers.

Savannah contemplated the meager offering. It was less appealing even than anything from McDonald's. With a sigh, she reached for the fork, hoping she wouldn't have to eat too many more meals there. At least most of the guards she'd encountered had been friendly. *But, oh god, that one large, greasy guy.* She shuddered. *His look frightened me.*

When the guy had brought her dinner, he looked her up and down, almost drooling. *Wonder what he'd think if he knew how old I am?* In spite of her circumstances, a small grin had cracked her face. Her visitor's face lit up.

"Oh, darlin' yer churce. What say we get it on when things quiet down this evenin'?"

She didn't know how to respond, so she didn't.

When he came back to pick up her tray, he again looked her up and down, spending a long moment gazing at her breasts. "Fahn. Vera Fahn. Thar's nothing about ya that ain't churce. Ah'll be making ya moan latah."

As he turned to leave, she shivered at the thought of him touching any part of her. She immediately began a search of her cell for something that might fend him off. Both the lamp and the table it stood on were bolted in place. The bar of soap was hotel size, the wash cloth and towel thin and threadbare. Even the spindle that held the toilet paper roll was locked in place. Her search produced nothing, not a single thing that would be useful if he did come back. As she thought about "Greasy," as she had decided to name him, he returned with a visitor. Vonell Carbone trailed the guard as he brought her to the walkway outside her cell.

"Sorry, ma'am, but we got a full herse her ta-nite. Yer gonna have to talk to her here. I can getcha a char if yer want."

The way he said it cast no doubt about what he really meant; he would not be happy if sent to find a chair. Clearly wanting to get rid of him quickly, Vonell shook her head. "I'm fine to stand, thank you." She turned to embrace Savannah through the bars.

"Oh, my dear, I am so sorry to see you here. If only we had found out sooner."

"It wouldn't have made a difference, Vonell. I don't think if God had intervened it would have made a difference. They came armed with clear evidence that I am not Savannah Harlowe. What's worse, they know exactly who I really am."

Vonell frowned. "We were told you are not Savannah Harlowe, but that's all. So I am totally unaware of your true identity."

Savannah gestured for her to come closer. Vonell stepped to the bars and leaned her head as close to Savannah's as possible. Savannah whispered the truth in her ear. Thankfully her cell was at the end of the block, so no curious ears could overhear.

When she finished, Vonell reached through the bars to grasp her upper arms. "I would have done the same thing. Those damn young creeps who think they can get guys and girls young and then take advantage of them deserve to be snuffed out. I mean that, Savannah. I hate those young guys who always have erections and think they are God's gift to women."

"But the fact is, having escaped once, I think I'm headed back to Wisconsin for a life in prison."

"Don't be so sure. Dad and the boys were huddled with our lawyer when I left to come over here. I'd be surprised if they haven't developed a plan by now. My biggest worry is your having to spend the night here. Will you be okay, do you think?"

"I'm not sure. The guy who brought you down here? I think he has something in mind. I'd rather die than have him touch me."

"I thought that might be the case. They searched me when I came in, but I hid these in the lining of my coat." She dug deeply into a pocket and produced a nail file and a small can of mace.

Savannah couldn't help laughing. Vonell tilted her head. "Something funny?"

"The irony got me. The notion of you bringing me a spray to help me out seems a clear reversal of roles."

Vonell chuckled. "Angelo made me promise to get these two things to you. He's extremely worried about you. I'm not sure what the guys are cooking up, but you have to be alert every moment. Promise?"

"I promise. But you have no idea what might happen?"

"I'm not sure, but they're definitely focused on getting you out."

"That'll be a big order. Especially after the DNA results come back."

"Just be ready for anything."

Vonell stepped back from the bars. "I wish I could have smuggled in some food, but it was tough enough with the file and mace."

"I understand. Thank you." Savannah reached for her hand through the bars. Vonell squeezed her fingers, slipping a few bills into her hand as she did, before letting her go and walking back the way she came.

Given what Vonell had told her, Savannah knew she wouldn't have slept, even if her accommodations had been better. Besides, she wasn't about to let her guard down and allow Greasy to sneak up on her. She did lie back on the bed and close her eyes, careful to keep the nail file by her side and the mace secreted in her hand.

It wasn't likely that Greasy would approach her until other prisoners were asleep, but she was sure that she would not escape with a trouble-free night. Twice, when she was about to drop off, she got up and walked about her cell, keeping her weapons with her at all times.

When the lights went out at 11:30 p.m., she steeled herself.

Just after midnight, soft steps sounded in the walkway. They grew louder, until they stopped outside her cell. Savannah tightened her grip on the can of mace as whispered words reached her. "I hope y'all are ready, because I got a big stick that needs some action."

A key rasped in the lock, followed by a squeak as it turned. The door opened slowly and soon she sensed someone standing over her. The sound of clothes being removed was followed by a creak as he kneeled on her cot.

As his fingers ran up her leg, Savannah raised the nail file and drove it into his hand. The file penetrated deeply and even before he could cry out in pain, she sprayed the mace full in his face. Greasy let out a holler and stumbled off the bed, both hands pressed to his eyes.

The file came free in her hand. Savannah jumped off the bed, shoved him out the door, and pulled it shut. Completely naked, Greasy stumbled around the hallway, still rubbing his eyes. She shuddered at the thought of him upon her as she threw his clothes out through the bars after him. Although she had no means to lock the door, he was too busy moaning to make another attempt to get to her.

Squinting, Greasy bent down, scooped up his clothes, and staggered toward the exit. The door to the cell block slammed behind him with a crash that shook the walls.

Satisfied that he wouldn't be attacking anyone else that night, Savannah, trembling all over, sank back down on her cot, waiting for what she was sure would be a visit from other guards. She didn't have to wait long.

Fewer than ten minutes after Greasy left, the lights in the area came on. Her eyes widened. Large splotches of blood dotted the floor outside her cell.

A female guard walked down the hallway outside the cells. When she reached Savannah's cell, she stopped. "Are you the one he was after?"

"Yes, ma'am."

"Between you and me, honey," said the guard, a stout black lady with a wild African hairdo and a bosom that threatened to break out of her blouse, "you gonna be the subject of cheers aroun' this jail. That ol' boy is one mean sucka! He know better'n to go afta me, but he's done molested lots of women aroun' here—prisoners and jailers. He a bad one, fa sure!" She leaned a hip against the bars. "Is there anything I can get you?"

Savannah crossed her legs. "I am a little hungry."

The guard grimaced. "The stuff we serve here is slop. We got vendin' machines, if ya want chips, nuts, candy, or coke."

Savannah handed her a twenty from the money Vonell had left and told her to keep the change. The woman returned a few minutes later with a small pack of cookies, a Snickers bar, a bag of peanuts, and a plastic bottle of Dr. Pepper.

"Thank you." Savannah set the food on the table beside the bed.

The woman smiled. "No problem, honey. You have a good night now."

When the woman left, Savannah munched on the peanuts and sipped the soda. She dropped the cookies and candy bar into her coat pocket then stretched out on the bed, covered herself with the tattered blanket provided, and slept. Her slumber was interrupted by dreams of Greasy trying to get to her. She awoke with a start to find sunlight filtering into the confined space from one of two small windows set high in the wall.

As she rose from the bed, the female jailer returned. "Better clean yourself up best you can; you're going to court at 9:30 a.m."

The guard turned to go then stopped. "Burleigh, the ol' boy who went afta ya, was in the chief's office shoutin' about bein' attacked by ya last night. He had to get stitches, eight of 'em. The chief's no dummy, though. Tol' him ta take his gripe somewhere else. Said if he was smart, he'd shut up and ferget it."

The woman laughed and smacked the bars. "I'll be back with breakfast soon; just don't expect too much."

She hadn't exaggerated. Breakfast was runny scrambled eggs, an overfried sausage patty, two pieces of dry toast, and coffee, which was heavy with chicory and strong. Nonetheless, wanting to keep her strength up for whatever might lie ahead, Savannah consumed it all, then washed up to get ready for court.

As nine approached, the woman returned. "I ain't s'posed to know this, but the DNA samples are back and they know who you are. Honey, I'm goin' off duty now, but good luck to ya, ya hear? Thanks for taking care of Burleigh. He had it comin' fer sure."

The woman left and Savannah sat down on her bed to wait for whoever was going to come and get her. *Well, I'm going home. And then prison—for the rest of my life. Too bad; I have a great new face and body. That's probably going to make me popular in prison.* She wrapped her arms around herself and shivered.

61

Al awoke to the sway of the motor home and the sound of Charlie's heavy footsteps as he paced the length of it. He groaned and rubbed his eyes with his fingers. What time was it anyway? The blinds were closed so it was hard to tell.

Before he could ask, Charlie stopped beside his bed and tapped his watch. "It's almost eight and I'm hungry, goddammit. I'll be damned if I'm waitin' for you slowpokes! You can meet me in the restaurant, unless it's after nine. Then you can meet me at police headquarters."

His eyes still closed, Al mumbled that he and Rick would meet Charlie for breakfast in a few minutes.

When Al and Rick entered the restaurant twenty minutes later, Charlie was destroying the pile of food in front of him. An empty plate provided evidence that eggs and bacon had already been consumed. Another displayed leftover tidbits of pancakes and ham. Charlie sliced off a piece of waffle and shoved it into his mouth.

"Just one waffle?" Rick slid into the bench beside him and nudged him with his shoulder.

"No three," mumbled Charlie through a mouthful of food. "This is the last one."

After the other two had consumed a light breakfast of toast and coffee, the three of them headed downtown. They parked near police headquarters, walked into the building, and were passed through quickly. Charlie led the way to the detective division and Aaron Wingate's cubicle.

As Charlie folded his arms on top of the makeshift wall, Al slid onto the one chair in front of the desk and asked, "DNA report back?"

"Sure is. She's your girl. No doubt about it. The second round of tests confirm, nice and legal-like, that she is Genevieve Wangen from Arlington Heights, Illinois."

A thrill of pleasure coursed through Al.

"Your D.A. has already been in touch with ours to get extradition started. We're dropping our charges to make sure we get her out of here with you as quick as we can. She's set to make her first appearance in municipal court next door in just a few minutes. She will be asked to waive extradition, but there's no telling what she'll do. She's with her attorney right now."

Al gritted his teeth. As much as he wanted to just go grab Savannah and drag her back to Wisconsin, they needed to follow the law to the letter to avoid her getting off on a technicality.

Sometimes he really hated the law.

Which, for a lawman, was not good.

A guard showed Sarah Broelstrom to Genevieve's cell. She took the chair while Genevieve made herself as comfortable as possible on the hard cot. Not wasting time on small chat, the attorney told Savannah that DNA evidence and fingerprints taken in the search of her home had been analyzed and compared with samples from the ones they had taken last time she had been arrested. "I guess you know what that showed."

"I do. They know I'm really Genevieve Wangen and they want me back in Wisconsin, right?"

Her attorney nodded and Savannah asked, "Is there any point in fighting it?"

"Normally, I would say yes, but I spoke with Angelo this morning and he wants you to waive extradition. He'd like you to ask to be taken to Wisconsin immediately."

Savannah frowned. "Did he say anything else?"

"Only that you should remain alert while being transported to the airport to begin your trip home. At that point, I asked him to stop. If I am to represent you, I didn't want to know any more. I hope you understand."

Savannah's shoulders slumped. "My trip home. Where is home? I was so happy in New Orleans; it felt like home."

Sarah shifted on her chair. Clearly she was not a woman comfortable with sentimentality. "Savannah, I want to go over what will happen in court." She tapped her perfectly manicured red nails on the top of the table as though making sure she had Savannah's full attention. "When the judge asks if you waive extradition, I will answer for you and tell them that you do, and that it is your wish to be moved immediately. Do you understand?"

Savannah nodded and began to gather the few things she had brought with her to the jail, among them the nail file and mace from the tiny table.

"They didn't take those? Better give them to me."

Savannah handed them over and Sarah tucked them into the leather briefcase she'd brought with her.

A tall, thin man with black curly hair came through the doors and walked to Savannah's cell. Keys jangled in his hand as he fitted one into the lock. "They're ready for you in court."

"We'll just be going next door," said Sarah. "The walk will be inside."

The guard took Savannah's arm and gently led her down the hallway to a skyway between the jail and the building that housed municipal court. As they prepared to enter the courtroom, Sarah whispered in her ear to say the judge had been changed. She would now appear before Buford Devareaux. "It'll be a simple process, but you should know that the judge is a very nice man, fair and gentle and, most importantly, very friendly with Angelo."

The muscles that had tightened across Savannah's back as they'd walked to court loosened a little.

When they entered the room, the guard directed them to the area where people scheduled to appear waited, then left after gently shaking her hand and thanking her for "taking care of Burleigh." Savannah smiled at him as she took her seat next to Sarah.

A movement at the entrance caught her eye and Savannah glanced over. Al Rouse, Charlie Berzinski, and Dr. Olson entered the courtroom with a man she didn't know.

They sat through three cases before Savannah's came up.

The bailiff called the case of the state of Louisiana versus Ms. Genevieve Wangen for criminal impersonation. Sarah and Savannah moved to the defense table inside the railing separating the operatives from the audience. The district attorney was already in place and on his feet.

"Your honor, in light of new information, the State of Louisiana wishes to withdraw its charges against the defendant on condition that she agrees to waive extradition to Wisconsin."

The judge looked over his glasses and said sternly, "This is very unusual. What are the circumstances leading to this condition?"

The D.A. introduced Al, Charlie, Rick, and a detective named Aaron Wingate. Aaron, dressed smartly in a dark suit, white shirt and tie, rose to his feet. "Your honor, DNA samples have confirmed the defendant is, in fact, Genevieve Wangen, wanted in Wisconsin for capital murder. While being returned four years ago from Illinois to face charges in La Crosse, she escaped from custody. Her whereabouts were unknown until recently. Two days ago, a DNA sample confirmed her true identity. On the basis of that, a warrant was issued for her arrest. Yesterday she was taken into custody by New Orleans authorities, who then conducted a search of her premises here."

The D.A. explained the circumstances behind the original arrest in Illinois, the escape in Wisconsin, suspicion that Savannah Harlowe might be the person wanted in Wisconsin, and the interview with her alleged mother by French authorities, as well as the findings from the night before.

When he finished and sat down, the judge turned to Sarah and Savannah. "Ms. Broelstroem?"

"Your honor, Ms. Harlowe wishes to return to Wisconsin. She does not desire an extradition hearing."

The judge lifted his gavel, but Sarah held up her hand. "There's more, your honor."

The judge nodded and lowered the gavel.

Sarah cleared her throat. "It is Ms. Harlowe's wish that the trip to Wisconsin be accomplished as quickly as possible. Today, if that can be arranged."

"That's an unusual request, Ms. Broelstrom," said Judge Devareaux. "Are there special circumstances?"

"Yes, your honor. Last night while asleep in her cell, Ms. Harlowe was attacked by a male guard. She managed to fight him off, but for that reason, she wishes to leave New Orleans as quickly as possible."

"I see," replied the judge, a grim look on his face. "Ms. Harlowe, please accept my sincere apologies on behalf of the state of Louisiana." Looking at the D.A., he asked, "Is this guard in custody?"

"No, your honor."

"Why not?"

"He maintains he was simply delivering a towel, wash cloth, and soap to Ms. Harlowe when she attacked him with a nail file. He was stabbed in the hand, a wound that required a number of stitches to close."

The judge scowled and crossed his arms, the loose sleeves of his black robe flapping. "Who was this guard? And if you're about to tell me it was Burleigh Benadott, don't waste your time. If it was him, I want him arrested, charged with attempted assault, and in this courtroom before noon. Is that clear?"

"Yes, your honor. I have nothing further."

"So it was him," said the judge with a snort. "It's always him, always. I want him in here as soon as you can get your hands on him."

Peering down at Savannah, a kindly look on his face, the judge said, "Ms. Harlowe, based on what I just heard, I am going to ignore that either a nail file was smuggled into your cell, or someone missed it when you were searched. In this case, I'm grateful you had it, and even more grateful that you used it. Mr. Benadott should have been prosecuted long ago. Given the situation, I can certainly understand you wanting to leave New Orleans." He uncrossed his arms and glared at the D.A. "Is Wisconsin prepared to take her immediately?"

The D.A. inclined his head toward Al. He pushed to his feet and addressed the judge. "Your honor, I have been authorized to secure a private plane to carry Ms. Wangen, me, and my colleagues back to La Crosse, Wisconsin. It is my understanding that we will be able to leave this afternoon."

"Very well, in that case, I will bind Ms. Harlowe over for extradition to Wisconsin this afternoon. I will have someone take a statement from you before you go regarding Mr. Benadott so that you will not be required to appear in person to give testimony. Mr. Wingate, I trust that you will provide an escort for Ms. Harlowe or Ms. Wangen, whichever is correct, to whatever airport is selected?"

"Yes, your honor."

"Then, Ms. Harlowe, I wish you a safe and uneventful trip." The judge rapped his gavel and the hearing was over.

62

The curly-haired guard waited for them at the courtroom door and accompanied the two women back to the jail. As they reached the door to the cellblock, Sarah Broelstrom stopped.

"Savannah, there is no need for me to go farther. I wish you the very best. If there is anything I can do for you or your attorneys in Wisconsin, please contact me. Here's my card."

Savannah took the card, smiled, then turned back to the guard as he opened the door to the cellblock. As she walked in, she was greeted by cheers.

"News travels fast in here," the guard told her. "They already know what happened in court, and that Burleigh will finally get what's coming to him."

Savannah sat down on the bunk. "Thank you for your kindness."

"No, ma'am, I'm thankin' you. You've rid us of a real problem."

Left alone, Savannah laid back and folded her arms behind her head. *How long will I have to wait for the next chapter in my life? Will it be in Wisconsin?*

After two hours and another despicable lunch, which she only picked at, the guard returned. "Time to go."

She looked around, thankful to be leaving the pit of a cell.

"I know what you're thinkin'; you just wanna be out of here, right?"

As she eased herself from the bunk, she nodded.

He opened the door to her cell and led her to the booking room. A collection of uniforms waited for her, along with Al Rouse, Charlie Berzinski, and Dr. Rick Olson.

"Genevieve Wangen," Al said, stepping forward. "We're taking you back to Wisconsin this afternoon, and you are going to travel in style, a private plane. Now if you'll turn around, I'm going to handcuff you. Once in the vehicle, we'll be shackling you, too. No escaping this time."

"Gentlemen, I wish I could say that it's nice to see you again, but I hadn't planned on making a trip to Wisconsin today. I suppose it's likely that I will again be known as Genevieve, but to tell you the truth, I prefer Savannah."

Charlie snorted. "To be perfectly honest, I really don't give a shit what you prefer; it will be Genevieve from here forward. Understand?"

"Aw, Charlie, where's that nice fella I spoke with a couple of days ago? You were so polite then. Is it true you're married to Kelly Hammermeister now?"

Charlie's thick eyebrows drew together. "Now just where would you have heard that?"

"I have my sources."

He snorted again.

"Let's get going," said Al, looking at the officer in charge. "Anything else we have to take care of here?"

"No, sir." The man waved a hand toward the door. "All the paperwork is done and signed. You're set to go."

Al cuffed Genevieve and took her by one arm. Charlie took the other, while the officers Aaron had sent over moved in front and behind the contingent to escort the prisoner outside where a large black SUV was waiting.

Al and Charlie helped the woman into the vehicle then Charlie took chains, which were attached to the floor in the back seat of the vehicle, and locked the shackles around her ankles. The two men then took up positions on either side of her. Rick joined the uniformed officer in the front seat.

"Are we okay," asked the driver, "with a direct trip to Lakefront?"

"Sure are." Al smacked the top of the seat in front of him. "The quicker, the better."

With a second black Suburban in front and a third behind, the caravan left the lockup and proceeded southeast on Perdido Street. It turned northeast onto I-10, where two additional cars joined the caravan, one on the left and one on the right.

The caravan left the interstate at Downmann Road to travel north toward Lakefront Airport. The additional two cars left them at that point. As the caravan neared the airport on Wales Street, two black Hummers suddenly cut between the lead and trailing cars, effectively boxing them out. A third Hummer came roaring up beside the vehicle carrying the prisoner. The police SUV was forced to the curb.

Al's heart thudded against his ribs as he leaned forward to see what was happening. *Not again. No way she is getting away again.*

His heart sank as he glanced out the front window then whirled around to see out the back. The two vehicles that had been escorting them had been neutralized. Their occupants had been pulled from the SUVs and were now sprawled on their stomachs on the ground, their arms behind their heads. As Al watched, four surly-looking thugs armed with what appeared to be AK-47s surrounded their vehicle, wrenched the driver's side door open, and yanked their driver to the pavement.

One of the assailants leapt into the driver's seat, another pushed his way into the other side of the front seat, crowding Rick to the middle. The second intruder turned and pointed the gun at Al. "We're gonna change routes a bit here. No one'll get hurt if you just stay calm."

The new driver pressed on the gas, maneuvered around the SUVs and Hummers stopped in the street, and headed toward the airport, turning right at Lakeshore Boulevard. Al's hand inched toward the Glock in the holster across his chest. The thug in the passenger seat lifted the AK-47 and pointed it at his face. "Want to rethink that?"

Al moved his hand back. His Glock would lose in a battle with an AK-47 every time, and in an exchange of gunfire in the vehicle, they would all lose. He clenched both fists in his lap and exchanged a look with Charlie. *This is not happening.* The SUV headed east on Hayne Boulevard. The driver maintained the speed limit, likely trying to avoid any unwanted attention. Obviously he had complete confidence in his buddies to keep the occupants of the other two SUVs from radioing for help. Al swallowed. If so, they were on their own.

The vehicle turned back south on Read Boulevard and shortly made a left turn. Reaching a parking lot marked with a sign that proclaimed "Joe Brown Park," the driver cut between two ponds and headed into an area that was marshy and surrounded by trees, deserted and desolate.

Not good. Rick looked back from the front seat and his eyes met Al's. They reflected the same trepidation Al felt.

The vehicle came to a halt and the driver threw a look over his shoulder. "End of the line … for some of us."

The gunman herded Al, Charlie, and Rick out of the car.

"This is as far as the three of you go. On your knees." The man gestured to the ground with his weapon. When they complied, he held out his hand. "Gimme your phones." All three of them pulled a device from their pocket and tossed into his outstretched hand. The man dumped them into the pocket of his jacket and nodded. "Wait five minutes then head back to Read Boulevard. Have yourselves a nice day, and remember, around here we take care of our own. You'd best get back to Wisconsin and stay there. Next time we might not be so nice."

With that, he climbed back into the passenger seat and the vehicle sped off, taking Savannah with it.

Al and Charlie, stunned, looked at each other, saying nothing. Charlie recovered his voice first. "Goddamnit, not again!"

Took the words right out of my mouth. Al clambered slowly to his feet. Blowing out a heavy breath, he drove his fingers through his hair. "Didn't that seem just a little funny? It occurs to me that our driver wasn't as surprised as he should have been."

Charlie stood too, and swiped gravel from his knees. "Now that ya mention it, ya, seems funny to me, too."

"I agree." Rick clambered to his feet and kicked at a clump of dirt. "I was sitting next to him and his foot was on the brake even before the Hummer cut us off."

"Well, nothin' we can do about it from here; let's get back to civilization so we can contact Aaron immediately. Maybe he can throw up roadblocks in time to catch them." Al started toward the road leading out of the park. When they reached Read Boulevard, they stopped.

"Now what?" Charlie threw his massive hands in the air.

Al looked at his friend, shook his head, and said, "Not sure which way to go. If we had a phone, we could call 911, but that's out."

"Why not try and hail someone and get them to call?" Charlie pointed at a vehicle approaching the gates of the park.

The car turned into the parking lot near the entrance and stopped.

The three men jogged over. A young woman got out of the vehicle, dressed to go running, and stepped back when she looked up and saw the three of them.

Charlie held up his shield and smiled. “Ma’am, we’re law officers from Wisconsin and we were just forced out of a vehicle while transporting a prisoner. Could we get you to call 911 for us?”

The woman crossed her arms over her chest and studied the shield.

Come on, come on. They’re getting away. Al snatched the badge he’d clipped to his shirt pocket and held it up too. “It’s true, ma’am. We were in a SUV transporting a prisoner wanted in Wisconsin to the airport when our vehicle and prisoner were hijacked.”

The woman took a deep breath, opened the car door, produced a purse, dug in it, found her phone, and dialed 911.

“I’m at Joe Brown Park,” she said. “I’m with three men. They say they were in a car carrying a prisoner when they were hijacked. Yes. Yes, that’s right, Joe Brown Park.” She paused a moment before nodding. “All right. I’ll tell them.” She lowered the phone and hit a button. “They’re looking for you. The dispatcher said a car would be here momentarily.”

Just as she dropped the phone back into her purse, the wail of a siren filled the air. The sound grew steadily louder then cut off as a police car sped into the parking lot and squealed to a stop.

The man behind the wheel rolled down his window and waved them over. “Officer Carson Boudreau. Glad to find you. Hop in; the others will be waiting at Lakefront.”

Al lifted a hand to the woman. “Thanks for your help.”

She nodded and he headed for the police car. Al hopped into the front seat while Charlie and Rick slid into the back. The officer again engaged the siren and screeched out of the lot, heading for the airport.

When they reached the general aviation terminal, they found Wingate and a group of blue-clad officers waiting for them.

Wingate was pacing, his face streaked with sweat. “You aren’t going to believe this. You got hijacked, but not when you think. You got hijacked at the jail. None of those vehicles were ours. Someone knew way too much and we’re trying to find out who.”

Charlie pounded a fist on the hood of the cruiser. A bright red flush began somewhere under his collar and spread to his forehead. “What the hell? Not yours? Christ, how did that happen? Goddamnit, doesn't anyone around here know how to do police work?"

Al whirled on him. "Charlie! That's enough. Aaron, do you know what happened?"

"We think we were suckered at the prison. Apparently these guys dressed as cops walked in just after noon with authentic papers, authorizing them to take Genevieve and you to the airport. Pretty brazen, huh?"

"Brazen isn't the word for it." Al stalked back and forth in front of the police car. "How the hell could it happen?" He ripped off his suit jacket and slung it over his shoulder.

Aaron's jaw clenched. "There's only one guy who could pull off something like this. Angelo Carbone. That's what I think, but no one's gonna admit it, that much I'd bet on. No one will have the nerve to point at the Carbones. But they're the only ones with balls big enough and pull strong enough to make something like this happen. You can bet your ass that when we find these guys—*if* we find them—we'll never be able to pin this on the Carbones."

Al stared at Aaron, his mouth slightly open. Was Aaron actually saying there was nothing they could do? He smacked a fist against his palm. "Are you telling me that the Carbones have enough pull in New Orleans to obtain papers that looked sufficiently realistic to take a prisoner right out of the prison while the good guys looked on?"

"Yup; that's what I'm saying."

"So what do we do now?" A headache began throbbing behind his temples. *No way we're just gonna stand by and let this happen.*

"You can hang around here for a few days, help us track down every possible lead."

"Will it help?"

Aaron shrugged. "Not sure, but it's the best we can do at this point."

Al studied him. *What aren't you telling me?* "Has anyone gone after them? What about roadblocks? Would they try to get her out of the state? We could check all airports, train stations, bus—"

Aaron shook his head. "Roadblocks won't help. Shortly after you were dumped in the park, a Carbone plane took off from here. No information on who was in it or where it was going. Want to make a bet on who was aboard?"

Al smacked his palm again. It didn't help to release any of the pent-up rage that was choking him and making it hard to breathe. What he really wanted to do was pound someone right in the face. The gunman from their vehicle maybe, or the guards who stood there and watched while Savannah walked out with Carbone's men. Al lifted his head. That was it. Angelo Carbone. He wanted nothing more than to plow his fist into the bright, beaming face of the old man who'd repeatedly welcomed them into Coulis and treated them to one fabulous dish after another, all while plotting to destroy their plans and make them all look like fools.

Aaron clapped a hand on Al's shoulder, yanking him from his reverie. "I'm sorry about all this, Al."

Al blew out a long breath. "Yeah. Me too."

With nothing else to do, the La Crosse contingent returned to the motor home.

His stomach twisting in knots, Al grabbed the phone Aaron had loaned him and got the chief on the phone. He asked him to patch in the sheriff so the five of them could talk about the situation.

"We lost 'er again, Chief." Al moved the phone away from his ear as the chief let loose with a string of expletives.

"How the hell could that happen?" he roared. "Just how the hell could that happen?"

Before Al could answer, the sheriff spoke up. "Are things as corrupt down there as the news media say?" Hooper's tight, controlled voice was almost scarier than the chief's histrionics.

Al pressed the phone to his ear again. "I've been told that's the case, Sheriff. Aaron says it's likely the mob was responsible for hijacking our caravan and stealing the prisoner away." He shoved back a fresh surge of anger. It was time to stop being emotional and start looking at this rationally. "Aaron Wingate, the detective we've been working with, thinks we should stick around awhile longer, that our presence might keep things moving."

"And we'll get on the phone and put some pressure on the PD down there, loud and often." Al didn't doubt the chief's words.

The sheriff agreed. "I'll threaten those guys with everything we have. We'll try and stir up some trouble. You guys do what you can on your end and we'll see what we can do from here, okay?"

When Al disconnected the call, Charlie punched him lightly in the shoulder. "Now what?"

"Well, we're sure as hell not going to sit around here doing nothing. I vote we make Coulis our home away from home for the next few days. Sooner or later Angelo Carbone is likely to show up there. And when he does, the four of us are going to have ourselves a nice, long conversation."

63

Heart pounding, Savannah huddled in the back seat as the Suburban was commandeered. After the men from Wisconsin had been dumped in the park, the vehicle stopped on the other side of the woods where a white Navigator waited.

The driver unlocked Savannah's handcuffs and shackles and opened the back door of the Navigator. Savannah blinked. Chandler and Elliott Carbone sat in the vehicle.

"Sorry for the drama." Elliott fiddled with his hands. "We had to pull a few strings to make sure you weren't returned to Wisconsin. Dino tells us you own another property somewhere. We have a plane waiting to take you there."

Savannah slid onto the seat beside Elliott. *Is this really happening? Could I actually be free?* "It's not your fault. I'm more grateful than I can tell you that you have rescued me. Which airport are we going to?"

"We're taking you to Lakefront, too. But we aren't sending you to Wisconsin, of course. To be honest, we don't know where we're sending you." Elliott's hands relaxed and he managed a small smile. Had he been expecting her to blame them for what she had gone through?

"Okay." Savannah tugged the seatbelt across her chest.

Chandler turned around from the front passenger seat. "We're trusting you have a destination in mind."

Oh, I do. I know exactly where to go. It seemed only seconds until the Navigator pulled into the airport. A sleek, cream-colored jet, trimmed in blue and red, waited for her, its stairs extended.

Chandler and Elliott wished her well. When Savannah entered the plush cabin, Dino strode toward her, hands outstretched. Heat rushed through her.

"Hello, my love." He clasped her fingers and kissed her gently on the cheek. "So sorry for the trauma of the jail stay." With a hand on the small of her back, he directed her to a seat then took the one facing her. He reached under the seat and pulled out her purse and an overnight bag. "I went to your place and grabbed a few things for you that I thought you might need."

Savannah took the bags and set them on the seat beside her. "Thank you. This will get me to where I'm going, at least."

As the jet climbed smoothly into the azure sky, passing through a few wispy clouds as it sought altitude, Dino took her hand in his. "Speaking of which, you once told me you have a hideout waiting. I don't want to know where it is, but I do want to know where you want the plane to take you."

"Give me a few moments." Savannah disengaged her hand. "I need a little time to think."

The next ten minutes passed quickly, but with Dino studying her, his forehead wrinkled, she realized she was going to have to make a decision. "Tell the pilots to take us to Portland, Oregon."

As her heart rate returned to normal, Savannah settled deeper into the comfortable seat. "Oh, what about Julie?"

"I thought you'd never ask." Dino motioned to the flight attendant. "I think we have a small passenger stored aft. Could you bring him forward?"

"Him? I was told its name was Julie. One moment."

Soon she was back carrying Julie in his traveler. Savannah opened the door and the cat sprang into her lap, settled there and began to purr. Savannah stroked his back as she looked at Dino. "Is there anything to eat? The jail food was horrible."

"I think we're fully stocked. What would you like?"

"Eggs?"

"Sure. Over medium?" He remembered her preference. "And ham and toast, too, right?"

"Perfect. Absolutely perfect."

The attendant brought a carafe of coffee, cream, sugar, and cups. "Enjoy. Breakfast will be here soon."

Dino chuckled at the statement as he glanced at his watch. "It's almost 3:00 p.m.—a little late for breakfast, huh?"

"Not if you're hungry. And I am very hungry."

Soon the plate of food was before her and Savannah attacked it.

Dino touched her knee. "I don't suppose I could talk you into dessert?"

She bit her lip as she set down her fork. "The last time I made love was the last time *we* made love. How long ago was that?"

"Has to be months."

"To me it seems like a hundred years."

For the next hour, they chatted pleasantly, the time broken only when the copilot came to them. "Any preference for which Portland airport?"

Savannah tapped a finger on her chin. "How about a private aviation field that is somewhat out of the way?"

The copilot nodded. "There are several we've used in the past. We'll call and make the arrangements."

After the man had gone, Dino slapped his forehead with his hand. "I almost forgot. How much money do you have?"

She opened her purse, dumped the contents on the table, then counted the change, adding it to the ten left from the money Vonell had given her. "Looks like $10.76."

He laughed. "That's not going to get you far. Good thing Dad thinks of everything." He reached into his coat pocket and extracted a fat envelope. She opened it to find a thick stack of hundreds, and an assorted collection of twenties, tens, and fives. "That should get you started. Can you access any of your accounts?"

She nodded. "Most are offshore. I won't have any trouble obtaining whatever I need."

"Good." Dino reached into his shirt pocket and pulled out a small white card. "This is a secure line. You can reach me at this number day or night. Don't hesitate to call if you run into any trouble. Do you want us to get you new identification?"

Savannah shook her head. "That's all right. I won't be able to tell you where I am, so I'll have to take care of it." She had just tucked the envelope into her purse when the pilot announced that they were beginning their descent. "We'll be landing at Aurora State Airport, about twenty miles south of Portland," said the voice over the intercom. "It's operated by the state but it's small and out of the way."

Dino pushed a button. "Aurora sounds perfect." A few minutes later, the plane was parked on the ramp, engines winding down.

The pilot joined them to tell Savannah they had chosen Aurora for its proximity to I-5, which would take her into Portland. "Not knowing exactly where you were going was a bit of hindrance, so we hope we didn't bring you too far out of the way by landing here."

"This is fine." Savannah shook his hand. "Thank you for everything."

When he had gone, she and Dino walked to the door. He stopped at the top of the stairs. "Here's where I leave you, my love. Dad needs me at home and I promised I would come back as soon as you had been safely delivered to the airport of your choice."

Savannah reached for his hand and held it between both of hers. "Thank you Dino, for everything."

He touched her cheek with his free hand. "It has been my pleasure. If we do not meet again, know that I will never forget you." He leaned in and pressed his lips to hers gently.

When he lifted his head, she offered him one last smile before letting him go and turning to make her way down the stairs. She walked into the FBO office to inquire about a ride into Portland. There had to be a shuttle, or bus service, or something like that available. She would have rented a car, but until she had her new identity, she had no ID to use for that. After depositing Julie's carrier on the floor, she headed to the counter, where a young, handsome man was on duty.

The man's eyes widened as she approached. *Hmmm. Maybe there's an easier way for me to get to Portland.* "Can you tell me the best way to get to Portland from here?"

As she talked, she leaned far enough forward that the young man got a liberal view down her blouse. For a long few seconds the man stared at her chest then, as though realizing what he was doing, he shook his head, looked up, and offered her a guilty smile. "Maybe I can help. Where were you planning to go?"

"To a good car dealership in Portland. I need to purchase a vehicle."

"I know a few good ones. What're you lookin' for?"

She told him she wanted something nice, comfortable, rugged, durable—and used. "It must be tough, fast, and good-looking."

"Pretty much limits it to Portland Auto-Plex on Sandy Boulevard. Great cars. Great prices."

"Sounds like the place to go. How do I get there?"

The man cleared his throat and glanced around. "I'm not expecting any flights for a couple of hours, and I'm due a break. Why don't I just drive you there?"

Savannah pursed her lips and ran a finger along his arm. "I wouldn't want you to go to any trouble, just for me." A bright red flush crept up the man's neck. "It's no trouble at all, ma'am. Just give me a minute to lock up and I'll be right out."

Savannah slung her purse and the bag Dino had brought her over her shoulder, and carried Julie outside. The young man came out a minute later and gestured toward a rusted-out Camaro in the parking lot. He took the pet carrier from her and set it in the back seat as Savannah climbed into the front. Half an hour later, they pulled into a car lot.

Savannah pushed open her door and got out of the car. The young man bounded around to her side, took Julie out of the car, and offered her to Savannah. "Are you okay from here?"

"I'll be fine. Thank you so much." Savannah took his hand and squeezed it.

The man ducked his head as he shook her hand briefly. Then he rounded the front of his car, slid behind the wheel, and was gone. Savannah was on her own.

She strode into the dealership, flashed a wad of cash, and an hour later drove onto the street in the best car they had on the lot, a beautiful, glistening-black-with-hints-of-Castelton-green Sentinel.

Savannah settled for a questionable-looking motel on the outskirts of Portland. As she'd suspected, the clerk didn't ask any questions or request ID when she offered cash as payment for the room. He didn't even take his eyes off the TV screen in the corner as he handed her the key, which suited her fine. Once she and Julie had been safely locked inside, she got ready for bed, made sure Julie was comfortable, then crawled under the covers to plan her next move.

Ultimately, she was headed for a hideaway deep in the Flathead

National Forest, just south of Glacier Park in Montana. She had owned the place for years, always, in the back of her mind, thinking that in the future it could serve her well. Now she needed it. For her, it would be an adventure. There would be much to do, but her fingers trembled with excitement as she handed in her keys at the front desk the next morning and began the nine-hour drive to a new life.

64

The SUV drove like a dream. Savannah found a good country station and enjoyed the music and the scenery as she traveled along I-84 at a steady seventy-five miles an hour.

With her windows open, the push of air through the vehicle gave her a great sense of freedom. She cranked the radio up, sang along with Garth Brooks, and for a time, everything was right.

Highway 84 took her just north of Mount Hood and south of Mount St. Helens as she touched the edge of the Mount Hood Wilderness while speeding northeast. It was a beautiful day. She drove through mountains and into the Yakima Valley where she was greeted by a new kind of beauty; fields of green, gold, and red parted for her as she drove.

Savannah drummed her fingers on the steering wheel. *There's no lab at the place. That's an immediate first step, but I have to find someone I can trust, someone who can do the work quietly and not talk about it. Once she did, she would be back in business.*

The sun had slid a little to the west by the time she sped through Spokane and headed for Coeur d'Alene. Except for the occasional stop to grab gas and something to eat, Savannah kept moving, determined to reach her destination by nightfall. There was no direct route to Kalispell. She chose I-90 and headed east. When I-90 turned south, she took Highway 138, a four-lane road that became Highway 28 when she got to Plains, Montana. She then threaded her way north, through the foothills of what she presumed were the Bitterroot Mountains until she bumped into Flathead Lake. She followed the lake north, then turned east onto an unmarked gravel road that after six miles turned to dirt. *Rustic and hidden.*

Just the way I want it. Six bumpy miles later, the road ended in a meadow of tall grass and wild flowers. Across the meadow, a log cabin, bathed in the pink glow of the setting sun, faced a small pond. A garage had been added to the far side of the cabin. She drove slowly through the grass.

Savannah stopped the Sentinel ten yards from the house and put it into park. This is one picturesque place. *If I can handle the loneliness, it'll be ideal.* She climbed out of the vehicle, reached into the back seat to open the carrier, and lifted the cat into her arms. Holding Julie close, Savannah leaned back against the hood and studied the house.

The place needed a lot of work, but she could see it. A lab, built under the garage with one entrance from the house and another that would let her out into the woods at the back of the property, in case she ever needed to escape again. She had money, and time, and determination. What more did she need?

Savannah scratched between Julie's ears, reveling in the soft purring sound the action produced. At the moment, she felt as completely content as that old cat, vibrating peacefully in her arms.

"You know, Julie, I think we are going to be just fine here." Sure, she'd miss Dino, and all the Carbones, and she had no idea when she would see her niece again. If ever. Still, if she had to start her life all over again, this was the place to do it.

"Yep." At the sound of her voice, the cat lifted its head and looked up at her, and Savannah smiled and patted his head. "I think we're going to be just fine."

1

The April sun scratched its way up the back side of Mount Cleveland, in the Bitterroot Chain of western Montana, its promised glow casting the proud peak as an angelic being. At least that's how it appeared from the rustic cabin in the woods inhabited by Genevieve Wangen, now known as Samantha Walters. This Thursday promised to be a busy day for the eighty-three-year-old, who looked not a day over fifty-five. She'd risen before dawn and now was bathing in the still-icy waters of the lake that she fondly referred to as "My Lake."

Of course, no one had seen the body of water since she had moved here, and therefore no one knew of the name she had given it. She hoped that wouldn't change for a while, although she longed for company. While she loved talking to both men and women, it was the company of men she missed most. She had been without male companionship for more than sixteen months, since arriving here from New Orleans two-and-a-half years earlier.

In her wake, she had left a trail of bodies—many more attributed to her than were due—that had resulted in the posting of an old picture of her on post office walls from Bangor, Maine, to San Ysidro, California, and from Baudette, Minnesota, to Brownsville, Texas.

Few were the people in the United States who had not seen a picture of the woman known in various places and at various times as the Wisconsin Whacker, the Black Widow of the Woods, and the Murderess of the Mountains. Few also were the people who, happening along on this cloudless day, would suspect a relationship between that woman and the darkly tanned woman in the lake, softly singing to herself in the early morning light.

In fact, although no one in the Bitterroot Valley knew where she lived, many knew her by sight. She was a person who, in times of financial hardship, reached into her purse and found money for the unfortunate, although anonymously.

People in these parts, if they knew her at all, knew her simply as "Sam." She had appeared on the scene without introduction but, before the first winter was over, had established herself as someone who belonged. And if people in these parts felt you belonged, then damned be those who would seek to take you away. Sam was known by a few business associates from Polson to Finley Point, Bear Dance, Woods Bay, and Bigfork on the east side of Flathead Lake to Kings Point, Elmo, Dayton and Somers on the west. Those same few called her by name, bought her a drink whenever she was in town, and even took her to lunch, yet none knew where she lived. The best anyone would say, if pressed, was, "Somewhere in the hills, I guess."

On this day, she hoped to end her temporary celibacy; the idea of having a man in her bed excited her as she soaked in the lake waters and dreamt about the pleasure of wrapping her legs around a real human being.

She planned to drive some fifty miles, the first twelve on a rutted, private dirt road, to Kalispell, Montana, a community of 22,000 about thirty miles north of Flathead Lake that served as the "capital" of the Flathead Valley. The community was the retail, professional, medical, and governmental center for the more than 140,000 people who inhabited the area.

In previous trips to Kalispell, Sam had cultivated a friendship with Molly O'Leary, general manager of the Golden Lion Hotel. On her last trip, the two women had talked candidly about their likes and dislikes and the things they missed in their adopted Montana homeland.

As one drink became two, and two became a half dozen or more, and Sam decided to rent a room and stay the night, she told Molly that her biggest need was male companionship.

"I'm sure that stuns you. There are some things you never get over, and I have always needed and wanted sex." After taking another sip of her drink, she added, "When I was married, my husband was a great lover. He developed my appetite for assignations and I've never lost it."

Molly tapped a finger against her chin. "I'm not sure why you decided to favor me with this conversation. Perhaps you think you know something. If you do, all I can say is you shouldn't." Glancing around the empty room, she tugged her chair closer to Sam and leaned in. "As a bit of a side business to build my retirement nest egg, I do a little matchmaking. I have always chosen my customers carefully, mostly to make sure they have tightly controlled lips." Her eyes narrowed as she leaned back and studied Sam. "Now I have to wonder, which one of those people has the kind of lips that they say sink ships. I am very bothered by this."

Sam blinked. "Oh, my goodness, Molly, there is no reason for you to be worried. I have talked to no one, absolutely no one. I had no idea that you might be doing a little, how do you say, moonlighting? I was simply commenting about my situation, and I felt I knew you well enough to tell you about the thing I miss most."

Molly contemplated her a few seconds more before her lips broke into a wide smile. Grabbing a cocktail napkin from the table, she wiped sweat beads from her forehead. "Then have I got a deal for you. Come on, let's take the bottle and go to my apartment where no one will overhear us."

She led Sam to a door directly over the check-in desk on the second floor of the Golden Lion. The spacious and comfortable apartment surprised Sam, both for its size and for how tastefully it was decorated. There's more to Molly than a hotel manager. A lot more.

"This is lovely." Sam waved a hand around the room. "If this was mine, I'd love to manage this hotel, no matter the pay. If you did the decorating, I must commend you for a great touch."

"For better or worse, I did it all. I was pleased to get the job and even happier when the owners told me to furnish the apartment to my liking, using their money. I spent it carefully, but this is what emerged. To me, it's home. And, Sam, the best part is they pay me very well for the work I do. I think I may be one of the highest-paid residents of Kalispell—better than almost anyone but the docs."

Sam grinned. "That's impressive."

"Yes, I do very well. And my side business has begun to produce a handsome profit. I'm very careful to recruit quality clientele and match them with people who are talented and committed to pleasing their customers in every way. You wouldn't think that would be an easy thing out here in the middle of nowhere, but the rugged individuals who come here to live seem to be skilled in the bedroom arts. You just never know, do you?"

"I guess not, but I sure would like to have a night with one of your most skilled gentlemen. If you could set me up, I think you'll have earned repeat business from a very needy customer."

"I believe I have just the guy. Not much to look at, maybe, but a real stallion. And equipped like one, too. Sound good?"

"Perfect. What's his name?"

"Pete Pernaska. He came here to join a timbering crew. He did that for a few years, but he'd wander in here now and again looking for women. I fixed him up a couple of times and it wasn't long before the girls started asking for him. I wondered what made him so special, and decided to try him for myself. Wow! That's the only word I have. I offered him a job. He took it, he's busy, and he loves it. He quit his timbering job. If you're not happy, I'll be stunned."

"I'm sure I will be. My life is close to perfect right now, and Mr. Pete Pernaska sounds like he just might be the last piece of the puzzle I've been missing."

From *Death by Payback,* coming Fall 2018